DARK
WINTER

The Jake Mahegan Thrillers
by Anthony J. Tata

Dark Winter

Direct Fire

Besieged

Three Minutes to Midnight

Foreign and Domestic

DARK WINTER

ANTHONY J. TATA

KENSINGTON BOOKS
www.kensingtonbooks.com

KENSINGTON BOOKS are published by

Kensington Publishing Corp.
119 West 40th Street
New York, NY 10018

All Kensington titles, imprints, and distributed lines are available at special quantity discounts for bulk purchases for sales promotion, premiums, fund-raising, educational, or institutional use. Special book excerpts or customized printings can also be created to fit specific needs. For details, write or phone the office of the Kensington Special Sales Manager: Attn. Special Sales Department. Kensington Publishing Corp, 119 West 40th Street, New York, NY 10018. Phone: 1-800-221-2647.

Library of Congress Card Catalogue Number: 2018944162

Kensington and the K logo Reg. U.S. Pat. & TM Off.

ISBN-13: 978-1-4967-1790-0
ISBN-10: 1-4967-1790-2
First Kensington Hardcover Edition: November 2018

eISBN-13: 978-1-4967-1791-7
eISBN-10: 1-4967-1791-0
First Kensington Electronic Edition: November 2018

10 9 8 7 6 5 4 3 2 1

Printed in the United States of America

For my dear mother, Jerri Tata, the world's greatest mom. Her love of reading Louis L'Amour and Zane Grey piqued my interest in writing even as a child.

CHAPTER 1

*J*AKE MAHEGAN KISSED THE SCAR ON CAPTAIN CASSIE BAGWELL'S BACK as the sheer curtains fluttered inward from the southwest sea breeze on Bald Head Island, North Carolina. He ran a hand from her bare shoulder along the taut contours of her back, heard a slight moan escape her lips, and continued running his fingertips along her hip and leg.

"Been a week," she whispered, her head turned toward the open patio sliding door. "No phone calls."

Mahegan concentrated on the task at hand, which was pleasing Cassie. Plus, phones didn't ring when they were turned off. Ignoring her comment, he brought his hand back up and firmly traced the muscles on either side of her spine, starting just below her clipped blond hair near her shoulders. He found a few knots and worked the kinks out. He'd learned that she carried her stress between the scapula bones. He rubbed the lateral muscle of each for a few minutes, feeling her body let go of a little more anxiety.

Every day had been the same. Make love. Rest. Sleep. Eat. Make love some more. Walk on the beach, which was just over the dunes beyond the fluttering curtains. Swim in the Atlantic Ocean. He furrowed his brow as he recalled the worry on Cassie's face yesterday when he had swum a mile out to sea and a mile back. An easy swim for him. Something he had been doing most of his life, especially during his rehab from his combat wound.

He had grinned walking up the beach, spotting her cut body in the flimsy bikini. His smile slowly faded, though, as he noticed the concern etched in her countenance. Fixed gaze, doubting look, full but straight lips, arms crossed.

"Don't do that again, Jake," she warned.

"I just swam, like I always do," he replied.

"You were . . . gone. I couldn't see you—" She stopped, covering her mouth. A full tear slid from her eyes. "I'm sorry."

He had hugged her and pulled her tight, his feet on either side of hers in the sand. She had slowly relented and wrapped her toned arms around his large mass. Mahegan was nearly six and a half feet tall and a former high school heavyweight wrestler. All muscle, no fat, Cassie was five feet ten inches. She rested her head on his chest and shoulder. He felt the tears continue to flow.

He had asked himself, *isn't this what you've always wanted? A good woman to love and to love you?*

At that moment, he realized Cassie was precisely who he wanted. Never considering himself fortunate enough to find his person, she'd suddenly become a fixture in his life.

Now, this morning, he looked from Cassie's bare back to the sun rising over the dunes and said, "I won't."

Cassie turned her head on the pillow slightly and then rolled toward him, pulling him toward her.

"You won't what?" she asked.

She had a dreamy smile on her face as if Mahegan had spent the last hour finding every spot of pain and pleasure on her body, which was exactly what had transpired.

"I won't do that again," Mahegan said.

The smile faded and then grew into something more deep and meaningful. Her eyes opened a bit, green irises radiant as blazing emeralds. A tear fell off her cheek, the first of the day.

"I've been trying to hold back, protect myself from being hurt, but I can't any longer, Jake," she whispered. "Loving you is worth the risk."

Mahegan said nothing. He let his heart receive her love, something that perhaps he had been incapable of doing before. Ever self-reliant, Mahegan had enjoyed the company of other women, for sure, but the mission always seemed to come along and nip any budding relationship before it had a chance to bloom. Still, the others had been different. Maybe it had been fate just clearing the way for Cassie. She was unique. And they'd shared dangerous combat action together, not in the sandbox of Afghanistan, Iraq, or Syria—though they had both served in those locations—but in North Carolina.

"Are you just going to stare at me with your blue eyes and square jaw?" Cassie asked. She ran a hand along the fresh shaved sides of his head. Two days ago, he had gone to the town barber, a former Marine from Camp Lejeune just up the coast, who convinced Mahegan he needed a Ranger high and tight. Ten bucks later, he looked good as new.

"Pretty much," Mahegan said. "View of a lifetime right here."

More tears. Her fist pounded his shoulder.

"Don't you dare do this, Jake Mahegan. Don't make me love you," Cassie said.

Mahegan frowned but understood. They had all been through too much combat, too much loss to ever risk the pain of having this connection and losing it. Dull and muted emotions were more manageable than the highs and lows of plumbing the depths of love. Solitude enhanced decision making. There were no other factors to consider. He could die a hero instead of growing old—as the Croatan saying went—without the worry of hurting someone else. The ultimate selfless sacrifice: don't love, don't hurt, don't feel. Pure execution. In thirty years of life, he had lost his mother, father, and best friend in the worst possible ways. What good was love if it was just going to be snatched away from you?

"Don't give me that puppy dog look, damnit," Cassie said, sobbing.

He kissed her forehead and then her lips. She kissed him back, opening her mouth, pulling him deep.

"Don't *let* me love you, damnit," Cassie said, pulling away briefly and then diving back in for more.

Mahegan let his actions do the talking, taking them both for another physical and emotional ride that ended on the floor, the sheets wrapped around them like a shroud. A rectangle of sunlight spotlighted them. The end table lamp lay askew on the floor and two pillows were scattered around them.

"Oh my God," Cassie said, laying her arms flat on the floor. She looked outside and then back up at Mahegan. "I just hope you can keep up."

Mahegan smiled. He was beginning to wonder, as well. Cassie was relentless in bed. At first, he'd chalked it up to her working out aggression or past issues, but now he believed something different.

She loved him. No question. And she was giving herself to him. Every bit.

The helicopter blades chopped in the distance. Mahegan reared his head like a German Shepherd sentry. His instincts had been muted, lost in the moment. This was what love did.

He rolled off Cassie, placing himself between her and the patio window, protecting what he held dear. Then there was a loud pounding on the front door, like a battering ram.

"My gun," Mahegan said, turning his head.

But he never had time to retrieve it.

CHAPTER 2

*L*UIZ YAMASHITA SMELLED NORTH KOREAN PRESIDENT PARK UN Jun's morning fish breath, thinking *I can't believe I'm this close.*

Jun had just finished his breakfast and now leaned in close to Yamashita, whose only job was to interview the president. Jun was small and seemed less of a caricature in real life than the thousands of pictures and cartoons Yamashita had seen. They sat across from each other on the man's favorite balcony adjacent to his palatial living quarters. Sloped and tiled roofs overlapped above them. The courtyard was well secured with heavyset armed guards at every possible entrance. The security personnel were heavily armed with Uzis and were wearing special glasses that provided situational awareness.

A U.S. based global technology company called Manaslu had provided the glasses. Yamashita knew this because Manaslu had hired him to conduct this interview about Manaslu's new corporate facility being constructed north of Pyongyang as part of an economic development initiative. The glasses were just one of many products the hegemonic tech giant had developed. Word had it that Jun was enamored with Manaslu and its enigmatic leader, Ian Gorham.

Yamashita was a Japanese reporter living in Vancouver, Canada. While he enjoyed the rainy days and the excellent coffee, he was ready for his big break. When a mysterious man named Shayne had reached out to him to conduct the interview, he'd leapt at the opportunity. He had visions of his article appearing in the *Atlantic, Washington Post, New York Times, Huffington Post, Breitbart,* and other highly read news sources. Appearances on CNN and Fox News would follow.

He could see it now: *Luiz Yamashita, the man on the ground in North Korea, forging peace through economic development with Manaslu's enigmatic leader, Ian Gorham.* Gorham was viewed as the young new visionary. Bigger, more badass, and better than Elon Musk, Mark Zuckerberg, Jeff Bezos, and Tim Cook combined.

Shayne had provided him the documents, the questions, the access, the $100,000 advance—one hundred thousand dollars!—an unbelievable amount, and the unrestricted travel budget. Claiming to be a senior official with Manaslu, Shayne looked more like a young hipster than a corporate chief technology officer.

"Mr. Yamashita," Jun began. "A Japanese reporter in North Korea. I am opening North Korea to many new experiences, aren't I?"

"Yes, Supreme Leader. You are forging a new path for North Korea," Yamashita said.

Jun nodded and smiled. "I know you will be asking the questions in a minute, but I want to make sure you get me on the record as thanking Mr. Gorham for allowing North Korean workers and materials to build his Manaslu factory in North Korea."

"Yes, Supreme Leader, I agree that Mister Gorham's generosity is unprecedented. But it is the strength and will of the good people of the Democratic People's Republic of Korea that have built this facility."

Jun nodded and smiled. "I'm glad you understand."

Out of the corner of his eye, Yamashita noticed several guards moving to his two o'clock, a far corner about ten yards away.

"Do not worry about my security detail," Jun said. "They are the best."

"I am not worried about anything in your presence, Supreme Leader," Yamashita said, though the entire security detail had converged to one spot and their faces, all covered in sunglasses, were peering up at the morning sky. The tall ivy-covered walls provided only a small opening of fresh air. The sun peeked through the firs angling off the steep mountain slopes overlooking the presidential redoubt.

Concern creeping into his subconscious, Yamashita hurried with the interview. "What is it you are most excited about, Supreme Leader, when it comes to the opportunities that the deal with Manaslu will provide to the good citizens of the DPRK?"

"I am thankful that UN negotiations have provided for this opportunity," Jun said. "As you know, the legacy of the Eternal President, my grandfather, is Military. The legacy of the Chairman, my father, is Self-Reliance. My legacy will be Economic Development while I continue the legacies of my mentors and family."

"All great legacies, Supreme Leader. Do the people of the DPRK believe that hosting a Manaslu factory will offset the halt in nuclear weapons production you agreed to as part of the Beijing Accords?"

Jun smiled. His lips pulled back against his teeth, making him look like a Gila Monster. His oily black hair was swept back in a youthful swatch. The jowls on his cherubic face were beet red in the cool morning air. "Next question."

Yamashita wondered, *Was he not going to comply with the accords? Of course not. No one expected him to.*

"What excites you about the Manaslu factory?" Yamashita pressed ahead. "You've said you will allow for the distribution of products but not the social media or search aspects of the Manaslu platform."

"We have twenty-five million citizens who need the same products people everywhere need. They get their information from Korean Central Television. This is the only satellite and Internet we need. We are one people."

Avoiding the topic of information and social connectivity, two of the most important and profitable platforms of Manaslu, Yamashita dove into the essence of the production and warehousing of products that Jun had agreed to perform. "What is your vision for Manaslu, an American company, in the DPRK?"

Before Jun could answer a question that truly had no answer—

Yamashita believed Jun's cooperation to be a ruse—he saw a drone hovering high overhead. It was a standard quad copter, though bigger than the ones he'd seen previously. Its four whirring blades held the unmanned system in a perfectly stabilized orbit over their heads.

While it was disrespectful to break eye contact with the Supreme Leader, Yamashita's self-preservation instinct took over.

"Relax, Mister Yamashita. This is my security. We have gone high tech," Jun said. He laughed a feminine, high pitched chortle.

"Then why is there an artillery shell inside the cargo claws?" Yamashita asked.

His question was too late. The shell dropped.

Luiz Yamashita's last thought before dying was that perhaps there was more to Manaslu's overture after all.

The explosion created a fireball that incinerated everything and everyone in the courtyard.

At exactly the same time Luiz Yamashita was watching a bomb drop from a plastic hover copter in North Korea, Janis Kruklis huddled in the bushes only four hundred meters from the mighty Eighty-second Airborne Division's basecamp along the Estonian border with Russia. While Kruklis had been unable to kill any of the famed paratroopers when he was serving as an ISIS mujahedeen, he was glad that someone had recognized his skills as a mortar man. He pushed the 81mm mortar baseplate into the ground, leveled it, and covered it with dirt. Then he inserted the tip of the mortar tube base into the opening on the baseplate, twisting it to secure it in place. Screwing the mortar sight onto the frame of the weapon, he began adjusting the angle and deflection of the weapon based upon the numbers he had received this morning by coded and encrypted e-mail.

He wasn't sure why he was shooting at the Russian army, but if it would result in killing American soldiers, then he was just fine with that.

One of many ISIS fighters to flow into Europe as the quasi-caliphate in Raqqa crumbled, Kruklis had returned to Latvia forlorn. His friends had wondered where he had gone, but he never told anyone, though he imagined if someone were good enough they could monitor the chat rooms he had visited as he had prepped for war in Syria. A former sniper and mortar man with the French Foreign Legion, Kruklis missed the combat and had turned progressively against the West based upon the atrocities he saw his peers commit in the Central African Republic.

Over the past week, he had used a flat bottom boat to transport his forty rounds of 81mm mortar ammunition to his hide location less than a kilometer north of Latvia. He had good cover and concealment and hoped that he could fire all forty rounds, race to his boat, and escape to Latvia before the counterfire became too intense.

In the cool October evening, Kruklis checked his phone one last time, confirmed the elevation and azimuth of his settings, and waited for the prompt, which came almost immediately. Kneeling in the damp ground, he sighed, his breath turning to vapor. He lifted the first bomb, which looked more like a nerf football with fins than a weapon.

He lowered the fins into the tube, released the body of the projectile, and then turned away. The mortar made a loud *thunk!*

Loud enough to hear a mile away, he thought. Knowing that while the round would be in the air almost a minute, Russian and American radars had already detected it. He raced to get as many rounds into the tube as he could, one right after the other.

Thunk! Thunk! Thunk!

He heard the explosions that were some three or four miles away in Russia, thunder reverberating back toward him.

He was over halfway through his pile of ammunition when he heard Humvees along the road leading from the American paratrooper base. Machine-gun fire whipped over his head. They didn't know exactly where he was, couldn't see. They may have had the grid coordinate, but it would take them another minute to find him. That was at least ten more rounds.

He shot all but three mortar rounds before American soldiers surrounded him.

"Cease fire!" one soldier wearing night vision goggles shouted. As Kruklis raised his hands, he heard the familiar whistle of artillery rounds screaming overhead. Russian counter battery fire. He smiled. He would kill some American paratroopers after all.

The heavy artillery tossed him into the air, along with the Americans. It was incessant and unrelenting.

His last thought was that these were big bombs, not the little ones he had been shooting at the Russians. As he lay there dying, he stared at the open eyes of a dead paratrooper and smiled again.

Ian Gorham, the CEO and founder of Manaslu, Inc., the conglomerate that had overtaken Facebook, Amazon, and Google in the social media, retail distribution, and advertising marketplace, sat in the back of his chauffeur driven Tesla S70. He stared at the information being piped to his iPad via Manaslu's microsatellite constellation he called ManaSat.

He had four such satellite constellations in the atmosphere as he prepared for his mission. Gorham viewed himself as a bona-fide genius. A Mensa member at an early age. Trouble understanding and relating to others as a child. His lineage was of average education—rural farmers and manufacturers. He had somehow hit the jackpot in the brains department. A one in a million chance. An odd mutation that combined the best of everything from both lineages—separated wheat from chaff—and distilled into his cerebral cortex.

Algorithms and code were a first language, English a second. Rapidly acquired wealth led to newly interested parties—women, men, transgenders—in his late teens. It was all so confusing.

In his early twenties—a few years ago—he'd read about the Jungian study of deep psychotherapy and realized he needed to unpack his brain so he could understand it better. With his wealth, he'd hired the best deep psychiatrist in the world. Given his exploration of the Deep Web, he'd thought it was fitting that he was going through therapy with an expert of deep psychology.

As the Tesla idled, exhaust plumes rose like fog. The bar was the target. It had a sign that read MOTOWN MIXER. Actually, a cook in the bar was the real target. In a few seconds, Gorham had a complete dossier on the bar and its owner, Roxy Bolivar, who was no longer alive. She had bequeathed the bar to her son, who ran the place. He was gay and had the beginning stages of pancreatic cancer. His medications had just started, but the doctors didn't believe there was much hope.

He had mined this information through the ManaWeb, Manaslu's own private domain within the Deep Web, where algorithms and machine learning matched information and automatically continued to dig and match until a complete profile had been developed . . . within seconds.

During his search, he had profiled everyone associated with the bar. One profile frustrated him. The apparent cook, reported for duty at six pm, had hacked the ManaWeb. This person had penetrated the domain Gorham thought was impossible . . . and improper. It was like penetrating his own psyche without permission.

In response, Gorham had launched a delivery drone with a spy camera to the Internet Protocol address location. It had followed someone wearing a hoodie pulled over the head and face, a chef's white shirt hanging beneath the hoodie, and black pants. The cook went into the back of the Motown Mixer. The drone had attempted to gain facial recognition, but the hacker's hoodie was like a tunnel hiding the face way back in a cave.

On the brink of executing his elaborate plan, Gorham could ill afford a minor issue. The hacker was an issue. Gorham's considerable business experience taught him that minor issues often became major problems. And this hacker was an issue. He began to spin, cycling faster and faster, thinking of possible outcomes, some not so good, others very bad.

With a shaky hand, he looped his Bluetooth earpiece around his right ear and pressed a number from the RECENT selection in his phone.

"Yes, Ian," the voice said. Part melody, part syrup, part Eastern Europe. She always gave him pause.

"Doctor Draganova," Gorham said. "Spin cycle, again."

"Please. As always, I must remind you, it's Belina," she said.

There was noise in the background. Banging, as if she were in a construction zone or kitchen somewhere.

He couldn't call her Belina. She was as beautiful as the name. He stared at the picture on his phone. Long black hair. Light blue eyes. High cheekbones. Full lips constantly pursed. Fashion model collarbones. Long neck. Slim hips.

No, he had to call her Doctor Draganova. He couldn't think of her as an object of desire *and* a therapist. It was counterproductive. "I'm spiraling a bit," he said.

"This is not a regular session, Ian. You pay me well, but we schedule our sessions. I'm almost always available, but right now I have little time."

"It's . . . okay. Just soothe me. I'm about to do something . . . high stress. I know my motives. You've helped me understand them. I know the purpose of my genius. I'm bringing all of that together. We've unpacked my mind, layer by layer. Now I need to bring it back together so I can execute."

Depth psychology focused on understanding the motives behind particular mental conditions in order to better resolve them. Draganova had been focusing Gorham on discovering the catalyst for his actions whether they be conscious, unconscious, or semi-conscious. All the big names in psychology had contributed to this field of study: Jung, Blueler, Freud, and so on.

"It's . . . it's not that simple, Ian."

Was she worried? Ian thought she sounded concerned. Her soothing voice took him back to that place he didn't want to be—viewing her as an object of desire instead of the mechanic of his mind.

More noises in the background. Some shouting. She was busy doing something. It never occurred to him that she may have a personal life. Perhaps she was entertaining guests and preparing a big meal or just in a noisy restaurant with friends . . . which made him a little bit jealous.

"I know," he whispered. "It's been a month since I've seen you."

"We've talked on the phone since. Sixteen times. We've even used ManaChat," she said. Manaslu's equivalent of FaceTime or Skype.

"What are you doing?" He realized his question sounded too familiar, and said, "I mean, what are those noises?"

"Ian, we can talk tomorrow. You know your drills. Please do them. Good-bye."

The silence in his ears was a screwdriver through the brain. Just like a Ferrari needed the world's best mechanic, his mind needed Dr. Draganova. Regardless, no matter how much he tried, he couldn't unpack his drive and desire for her. She had become shorter and shorter with him on their phone sessions. In person—always in a neutral place to which they both had flown at his expense—her clothing had been more and more provocative. Was she teasing him or challenging him to focus? Like Tiger Woods' father rattling change when he was a kid practicing putting. Perhaps that was her technique for getting him to focus on the matter at hand.

But she had helped scramble his mind, unpack it completely to its core. The drive and ambition to create a dominant global tech conglomerate came with personality traits that he needed to understand. Draganova had helped him reach in his mind and more objectively observe his mania, his fears. Obsessed with success and power, Gorham was relentless, but to his credit he wanted to know more about himself. Or was that just more megalomania coming out? He didn't have time to think about all that now.

He was at the moment where he needed to be able to synchronize a global operation. He could do it, of course. It would just be harder. Require more thinking. More individual construction of his mental faculties. Put everything back together himself instead of with her help. And he needed to do it right now.

You know your drills.

He did a few body meditation drills, working his hands into his quadriceps and hamstrings, massaging and pulling. Then he pulled at his face, stretching it in every direction, relieving the tension. Dax Stasovich, his faithful bodyguard, was outside pacing, impatient.

After a few minutes, Gorham felt well enough. He needed to move now. The car with his commandos came rolling around the corner, parking two blocks away. Stasovich looked at him through the car window and shrugged.

It was go time.

Gorham stepped out of the car, tugged the Tigers cap down low over his face, thinking, *get your shit together, Ian.* He was one of the most recognizable men in the world. Bezos, Zuckerberg, Brin, Page, and all the other brilliant entrepreneurs were equally recognizable. In the last two years, though, he had become the hot property. He had to be careful.

He pulled the ball cap bill low over his forehead. Stasovich, a giant of a man, walked in front of him about ten yards. The man's legs pushed out and forward with every step. His bulk swayed. His arms barely moved. The man was nearly seven feet tall. Hard not to notice. That was part of the drill. Like a magic trick. Everyone look at this freak of nature friend, not the normal looking curly haired guy walking behind him.

They entered the bar and Gorham grabbed a booth. There was a slight crowd. He immediately noticed a good-looking short-haired blonde sitting at the bar. Next to her was a big man with a Mohawk haircut. He wasn't as big as Stasovich, but close. What did she see in him?

He looked at his ManaWatch, what he called his equivalent of the Apple Watch. The ManaWatch used the ManaSats and was therefore encrypted. Two messages popped up from Shayne with little green check marks next to them.

Estonia

NoKo

The plan was in motion. He glanced at Stasovich, a bull scraping his hoof looking at a red cape.

Gorham typed a message and hit SEND. "Go."

CHAPTER 3

MAHEGAN STARED IN THE MIRROR, WHICH REFLECTED A MAN IN A baseball cap across the room hunched over his beer in a booth on the far wall near the entrance.

The cap's bill was curved enough so that the man's eyes were hidden. It was a Detroit Tigers baseball cap. The man didn't look like a baseball player, didn't have the build. Wisps of light brown hair curled up onto the blue material. Not that curly brown hair disqualified a man from the major leagues, but Mahegan thought he looked too slight. Maybe he was one of those skinny middle relievers that went a few innings. Or a lanky first basemen. But Mahegan didn't think so. The man looked more like a fan, if that.

But still, that face. He was trying to place it when Cassie elbowed him in the ribs.

"Don't stare," she said.

"I'm looking directly at three bottles of tequila," Mahegan countered.

They were in downtown Detroit because Mahegan's teammate Sean O'Malley had found a nugget of information in the Deep Web indicating an attack would begin in this musty bar. The purpose of the pending raid was unclear, but was supposedly related to something much larger. That was all O'Malley knew. Something big. So, they watched and waited.

It had been O'Malley pounding on their door on Bald Head Island and Patch Owens who had been in the back of the helicopter to pick them up.

Something big had already happened, though. Hours ago, news of the death of the North Korean leader had cycled through the top-secret information circles. Mahegan was surprised that after a few hours the news programs were not covering the story. News of a provocation in Estonia was just leaking out. Apparently the Eighty-second Airborne show of force in Estonia had gotten into an artillery mix up with the Russians. Not good. Something big.

Mahegan and Cassie sat on barstools in the Motown Mixer, a trendy, hipster place intended to look like a seedy bar. The bartender had placed in front of him a tap poured Pabst Blue Ribbon. It was his first beer of the night and he had only taken a sip, which was mostly foam still settling from the pour. It was all for show. Not that he didn't want a beer. He could use one. But he had bigger urges to satisfy than drinking a beer. Stopping a raid. Getting the intelligence. And then moving to the next level of unraveling whatever it was that O'Malley had discovered.

Cool October wind rushed in every time someone opened the front door to Mahegan's eight o'clock. A sticky dark wood bar with a vertical hinged opening at the far end ran the length of the establishment. A dozen different taps shouted the names of popular draft beers, the bartender working the levers like a slot machine. An ancient color television was set to a cable news program in the corner. A reporter was speaking from a windswept field in Europe somewhere. The crawl at the bottom of the program read *Russian artillery causes casualties in Eighty-second Airborne Division deterrent force.*

"At least we had a week," Cassie said.

"Roger. Time to focus," Mahegan replied.

Cassie nodded.

"Paratroopers got hit with artillery," Mahegan said. He showed her his phone, which had practically blown up when he finally turned it on after O'Malley rushed them onto the helicopter this morning.

"Saw that. Any chance it's connected?" Cassie asked.

"Anything is possible." Mahegan scanned the growing crowd,

not sure what they expected to find. "But we've got to have something to connect it to."

Earlier, when the place was nearly empty except an old guy hunched over his whiskey, Mahegan counted exactly ten bar stools, each one stained and sticky from years of beer spills and marginal maintenance. Five booths lined the wall and six tables occupied the floor.

An old time circular battery powered clock showed it was seven o'clock in the evening, which explained why the place was packed with hipsters, prepsters, college students acting twenty-one, and older men trying to pick up younger women.

Two had already tried to hit on Cassie, his "date." She was dressed in hip-hugging blue jeans, a loose, untucked button down shirt, and sharp toed leather cowboy boots. Mahegan was wearing his standard olive cargo pants, tight fitting black pullover, black leather jacket, and Doc Martens boots. With his hair looking something like a Mohawk down the middle, Mahegan, a Croatan Indian from the Outer Banks of North Carolina, was feeling the kinship with his ancestors.

He was also feeling the mission the way someone with a bum knee senses a low-pressure system. "Notice baseball hat guy?"

Cassie didn't look at the throng of people drifting through the bar, but replied, "Roger. You were staring at him. Seems twitchy. Think that's him?"

"Not sure, but he keeps looking at his watch. Pressing it, like he's reading e-mails on an Apple watch. Looks familiar, too. Can't place him, but I'm guessing his Bumble date either stood him up or we're moving any moment now," Mahegan said.

"I've got back door," Cassie replied.

"Gotta be quick."

"Roger that." Cassie scanned the room casually and said, "Use the mirrors above the bar. See shaved head guy in the corner? Like he's watching a tennis match. Us. Then baseball hat guy. Then us again. He's huge. Out of place. Like you."

In the mirror behind the whiskey and tequila bottles Mahegan studied what Cassie mentioned. It was likely the large, bulky man with the shaved head was protection for the guy in the baseball hat, their possible target. Turning back to Baseball Hat, it was impossible to discern his age. From across the room, he looked average in every way.

Was he the target?

The front door slammed open. Cool air rushed in again. A man stood with an assault rifle assessing the throng. The surreal moment hung there suspended in air. The patrons continued their revelry until someone saw the rifle, but even then, the slack-jawed observer could only open her mouth; no words came out.

Mahegan pushed away from the bar, picking a line to the rifleman the way a running back finds the gap in a defensive formation. As he found his own opening, he realized there were two ways into the pub, the front door and the kitchen door in the rear. Mahegan wasn't sure, but by the look on the face of the man with the assault rifle, the potential assailant was studying, looking for a specific person . . . and probably had an accomplice coming in the back way.

That meant Cassie would have a target. As an army intelligence officer and the first female ranger school graduate, she could hold her own.

The man at the front door was wearing all black with what looked like an outer tactical vest. He was short with Asian facial features and black hair cut to a crew. The intel had predicted assault rifles, not suicide bombers, but they couldn't be sure.

The lights went out and all hell broke loose.

As Cassie chose her line to the backdoor, he retrieved his Sig Sauer Tribal, sliding seamlessly through the throng, most of them seeing the look in his eyes, or the pistol, and stepping out of the way. But with the lights out, half the crowd was whooping it up as if the darkness was their newfound friend.

Enough ambient light came from outside to guide Mahegan to the front door. As he approached, the man raised his assault rifle to fire. Mahegan kicked the weapon to the side as the attacker popped off several rounds.

Mahegan shot the man in the leg, snatched the assault rifle, and quickly inspected him for other weapons, yielding a Makarov pistol and Bowie knife. He kicked the man in the head and ran toward the back door where another man had entered through the kitchen. Flashlights crisscrossed like lasers. By now, Mahegan had his night vision goggle on his head. In the green haze of the NVG, this attacker appeared stocky and white, wearing basically the same black uniform. There was a glint of an insignia on the tactical vest.

Cassie used the light of the gas flame to take aim at the man's legs and squeezed off two rounds. The man spun around, the AK-47 spitting 7.62 bullets into the kitchen hood. Smoke poured everywhere, like steam hissing from a pipe. Cassie was on top of the man, knocking him unconscious with a rap of her cowboy boots.

A third man, this one dark skinned, almost Arabic or Persian in appearance, caromed into the kitchen and shot the cook, who was wearing Backbeat Pro earphones, most likely with rock music cranked at full volume. In fairness to the cook, only five seconds had passed since the action at the front door.

Mahegan fired two center mass shots at the black clad intruder and realized he was wearing body armor. Quickly closing the distance, Mahegan leapt over Cassie, who was kneeling and making sure her target was incapacitated and tackled the third intruder. Mahegan carried him to the floor using an inside trip, an old wrestling move he'd learned in high school.

Using the butt of his pistol, he struck the man with his entire force, everything his six and a half foot, two-hundred-and-thirty-pound frame could put into it. The man's head lolled to the side and Mahegan immediately stepped behind him and dragged him through the door into the back parking lot.

Patch Owens, one of Mahegan's closest friends and a former Delta Force teammate drove up in a black SUV with shaded windows. He stopped and was quickly out the door and opening the back hatch where the front-door attacker was lying prostate. Another close friend and former teammate, Sean O'Malley, was leaning over the captive, checking his pulse. With the lights from the vehicles pumping into the kitchen, Mahegan removed and stowed his NVGs in his side pocket. He hustled outside.

"Still alive," O'Malley said.

"Cook's shot in there," Mahegan said. "Got to be the target."

"I'll grab him. What about baseball hat guy?" Cassie said as she darted back into the kitchen after dumping her prey at the rear of the SUV like a cat drops a mouse on the steps.

"No time," Mahegan said to Cassie. Then to Owens and O'Malley, "One more than we expected."

"Let's load, man," Owens said, nervous.

They loaded the other two men, O'Malley standing watch from the back seat. Cassie returned with the cook, a disheveled person wearing a white T-shirt, who was bleeding from his left arm.

"Damn, dude. WTF?" the cook said. The voice pitch was higher than Mahegan anticipated. Forced. Softer, too.

"Do what you need to do, Cassie," Mahegan said. Cassie simultaneously shoved the cook into the SUV and placed a rag filled with chloroform over the cook's nose. She removed a bottle of Betadyne and some gauze from an aid kit in the vehicle, flushed the wound, and wrapped the cook's upper arm tightly. More than a flesh wound, but nothing serious.

"Sean, grab their vehicle," Mahegan directed.

"Already got the keys," O'Malley said. He had rummaged through their captive's gear until he found the keys to a Buick Crossover.

He leapt out and flicked the key fob until lights flashed at the far end of the parking lot. He ran, jumped in, started the car, and pulled up behind Mahegan and team in the black SUV.

What had started as four teammates on a mission to capture two insurgents and an unknown hacker was in progress with four friendlies, three enemies, one wounded civilian, and two vehicles leaving the parking lot. The patrons spilled out of the bar and watched with shocked, curious eyes, perhaps notions of the Las Vegas massacre ringing in their ears.

Mahegan saw the stares and the cell phones to their ears, all calling 911. Some were using their phones to record.

"JackRabbitt okay?" Mahegan asked. The JackRabbitt was a cell phone jammer that was blocking all calls from the immediate vicinity.

"Roger, but something got past it to shut down the grid. Look around. Nothing's on," Owens replied. He had both hands on the steering wheel as he pushed the SUV to ninety miles per hour.

Once Owens had the SUV a mile away, he slowed to just above the speed limit, turned onto the interstate, and raced toward their safe house in Ann Arbor. Everything they passed was completely blacked out.

"This guy stinks," Cassie said. "Smells like onions."

"Suck it up, Ranger," Mahegan said. "Wound okay?"

"More than a scrape. Less than anything serious," she said.

Mahegan nodded. He looked in the rearview mirror and saw O'Malley tracking close behind them. He noticed and gave Mahegan a thumbs up signal. They drove in silence after that, smelling the grease of the unconscious cook and the acrid aftermath of fired weapons.

Reaching the farm, Owens turned onto the dirt road and traveled all the way to the barn. Mahegan jumped out and opened the doors then closed them after Owens pulled the SUV into the brightly lit cavern. O'Malley kept the Buick outside initially.

"Patch, help Sean check the Buick for IEDs," Mahegan directed. Then to Cassie, "Lock the cook in the friendlies cage."

His charges executed their missions and returned in quick order.

"Vehicle's clean. Found a briefcase with some electronics. No explosives. Sean's going to pull it apart. He's pulling the car in now," Owens said. The barn doors opened, O'Malley pulled in, and then the doors closed.

The barn consisted of a high-tech command pod with satellite connections and a ten terabyte Internet drop, providing Mahegan and his team instant access to everything going on in the world and any information they needed. O'Malley, their team's resident tech genius, had been instrumental in building out the barn to a disguised server farm. Owens had used his construction skills to build five prison cells from two by fours, iron rebar, and bricks. Each was completely soundproof if the door was sealed shut. O'Malley had added avatar and music capabilities to the interior of each ten foot by ten foot cell to enhance interrogation of the prisoners they expected to capture. He had outfitted each cell differently. One had a "window" that looked out onto the skyline of Moscow, Russia. Another had the minarets of mosques and the red tiled roofs of Tehran. The third had the drab office buildings of Pyongyang. And two others had Washington, DC and Tel Aviv backgrounds, respectively. The walls of the cells acted in the same fashion as the blue screen for the weather man. O'Malley could make each chamber look like anywhere in the world or even someone's worst nightmare.

Originally an operating base used by the Drug Enforcement Administration to monitor trafficking from Canada, JSOC had assumed control of the property for training purposes, mostly. Because the special mission units' training was so realistic, the facility was basically combat ready.

Mahegan opened the back to the Suburban. The three attackers they had subdued were lined up like freshly caught fish in a livewell.

"Get them to talk," he said to Cassie. "Figure out their nationality."

O'Malley and Owens tugged at the boots of the obviously white, European looking man.

She lightly tapped him on the face. "Water?"

The man nodded, then said, "Da."

"Russian," she said. Not rocket science.

O'Malley and Owens lifted the Russian by his feet and shoulders and hefted him to the Russian cell.

Looking at the man with olive skin and black hair, Cassie said to Mahegan, "Unconscious, but my guess is Iranian."

Mahegan agreed. O'Malley and Owens returned and took the man to the next structure in the barn.

The man that Mahegan had shot and kicked in the head was still alive, but barely.

"Looks Korean. Probably going to die."

"I'll try to patch up that chest wound long enough so we can talk to him," O'Malley said. He and Owens dragged the man to the farthest cell and broke out an aid bag.

The barn was nearly half a football field long and wide. Each of the cells was in a different corner with the fifth, the American cell, along the middle of the far wall from the command center. The barn sat on the back side of 120 acres of heavily wooded timber and farmland purchased several years ago by the U.S. government. Towering hardwoods fronted the property, which eventually gave way to a cleared fifty acres where about twenty cattle grazed. They were live, but props.

Mahegan gathered his team on the floor of the elevated command post and typed into the keyboard. **Secure**.

The response was immediate. **Charlie Mike**. Continue the mission.

There was no immediate need to communicate that they had an extra prisoner. While the intel intercept had come from O'Malley pinging around the Dark Web, they had either rescued the cook or properly detained him, the definition dependent upon what unfolded next. And just like they'd been uncertain of the specific number of attackers, they'd needed the attack to unfold to determine the real target of the raid. The cook had special skills, apparently.

"Okay, team. Now the fun starts," Mahegan said.

He retrieved his Blackhawk knife from its sheath on his riser belt and walked to the cell in which they had placed the cook. Before opening the door to the enclosed room, he nodded at Cassie, who shut the lights in the barn from the command center.

Opening the door, he stepped through the threshold into an anteroom, like an oxygen chamber in a submarine, closed the exterior door, locked it, and then opened the door to the cell. The cook was huddled in the corner of a room that gave the appearance of looking onto the capitol dome in Washington, DC. The hologram effect made it seem as though they were inside an office building, looking through a window onto Grant's statue and the capitol building. O'Malley had done good work. Cars drove by in real time. Pedestrians waited at street corners. An airplane banked to the south, landing at Reagan National.

"You guys FBI?"

Mahegan said nothing. He processed his surroundings and waited, even though he knew that they had no time to spare. The higher pitch in the voice seemed off-key. Forced European accent or perhaps as if the cook was trying to sound more masculine. Blood streaked across the cook's face. The prickly scalp was shiny with sweat. The huddled body, not small, maybe even lanky, but slender. The white apron was splattered with hamburger grease, as were the white T-shirt and black pants. Black Keds high-top canvas sneakers on the feet. Cassie's bandage job expert.

"Come on, man, say something."

Forced vernacular, Mahegan thought. *A woman trying to sound like a man? A man trying to be a woman?* Who knew nowadays?

The cook was shivering, perhaps needing a dose of meds.

"Why were they coming for you?" Mahegan finally asked.

"What? Who?"

"We don't have time for your bullshit. Something major is happening and you know what it is. You found it."

A moment of recognition flashed on the cook's face and in the eyes, recognizing trouble. Mahegan also recognized that this was a woman. She was forcing the octaves of her voice down, like trying to stuff too many clothes in a suitcase. It didn't work. Had the opposite effect. Regardless—man or woman—this person supposedly held the key to murder of the President of North Korea and the Russian attack on U.S. forces in Estonia, at a minimum.

"Look, man. I want a lawyer," the cook said.

"First, quit forcing your voice. I know you're a woman. It doesn't matter. And, no, you really don't. That's not how this works. You tripped over something in the Deep Web and we followed you until we couldn't follow you anymore. I'm done talking with you unless you give me something to work with. I've convinced them that you'll talk. I see it in your face." Mahegan switched his knife to his left hand and then rested his right-hand palm on the gritty grip of his Sig Sauer Tribal pistol.

A long pause ensued. The cook watched the traffic outside, seemed to consider something, and then looked at Mahegan. "How did I get from Detroit to Washington, DC?"

"And here I thought I was asking the questions." Mahegan closed his hand around the pistol grip and inched it slightly from its holster.

"Total combat," the cook said.

Mahegan stopped his motion, stared at the woman, and let the thought sink in. "Go on."

"I call it RINK. Russia, Iran, and North Korea. They're like Japan, Germany, and Italy in World War II. They're attacking asap. Everywhere. Total chaos. Total combat. Computer optimized warfare."

"Why?

"Because they can," the cook said. Eyes averted. Hands shaking like an alcoholic needing a drink.

"Who are you?" Mahegan asked.

"Just a fry cook." The words were quick, tumbling together. Rehearsed but lacking veracity.

Mahegan's hand tightened around the pistol and he removed it from the holster. To the cook, he must have looked menacing. Six and a half feet tall. Native American. Form fitting black stretch shirt. Ranger haircut. Razor sharp knife in one hand and lethal Tribal in the other.

He knelt in front of the cook. "What made you a target?"

Another long pause. Mahegan saw the cook assess him, perhaps seeing everything that Chayton "Jake" Mahegan was meant to be—The Hawk Wolfe. Named by his Croatan Indian father, Mahegan carried the instincts of both predators.

"I know who's running the show."

"Who might that be?"

"This is where we trade," the cook said.

Mahegan leveled a fierce gaze on the woman, who was now kneeling, hands on the walls, feeling the glass partition that O'Malley had built into the cell. Like a room within a room, the glass was six inches from the HD screens upon which the illusion played out.

"The trade is for your life, you understand, right? You tell us what we need, you live. You don't, you don't."

"Where am I?"

"Washington, DC," Mahegan said. "Now, you've wasted a question." He lifted the knife, blade glistening against the backdrop of a Washington, DC night. "Tell me something useful."

The cook's eyes flitted from Mahegan's menacing face to the sharp combat knife to the pistol. Mahegan stepped toward her, worked the knife in his hand, rolled his wrist, working for the best angle. Keeping the cook off balance.

Knife or pistol, which would it be?

"Phase one is conventional. Phase II is nukes."

Mahegan stopped. "When does it start?"

"What do I get for cooperation? Immunity?"

"You want immunity go get a flu shot. Like I said, your life," Mahegan growled. "If what you're saying is true, that is. Now, what's happening?"

"As I said, Computer Optimized Warfare. ComWar. Like those algorithms that figure your buying habits and show in your Facebook feed what you like to get on Amazon. This thing is fine-tuned. Shuts down power grids. Drops cyber bombs. Closes every Wi-Fi hotspot. Electromagnetic pulse. Directed Energy. All combined. Followed by artillery launches. Tanks attack. Infantry rolls through. Computerized blitzkrieg. Then it assesses how effective a particular attack was, makes the necessary algorithmic changes in seconds, updates the programming in all of the weapons and communications systems, and keeps attacking. Does it all in stride. Artificial intelligence and machine learning blitzkrieg. That's ComWar."

"ComWar? When's it start?"

"Dude. It's already started. And there's nothing that can stop it. Well, one thing."

Dude. Mahegan let it slip because he was getting somewhere with the cook. "What's the one thing?"

"Biometric keys. Humans. Russia, Iran, and North Korea each have one person that is the biometric key. It's the lowest tech that supports the highest tech. Brilliant really."

"The keys do what?"

"They unlock the nuclear arsenal. Anything is hackable nowadays. Why would nuclear codes be any different?"

"Where are these people?"

"In their countries, of course."

"Like next to the decision maker?"

"Something like that. Protected. Available until needed."

"Who's behind it?"

"And for that, you have nothing worth trading, my friend. Because you saw they were going to kill me. So, it's either you or them and as scary as you look, I'll take you over what I saw in their Dark Web planning site."

Still, something hung in the back of his mind. *Nothing that can stop it?* That was what people said about actual blitzkrieg when the Germans rolled through Europe during World War II. While he wasn't a computer genius, Mahegan did know that in general, nothing was perfect. Nothing was completely unstoppable. Something may be *hard* to stop, but that didn't make it unstoppable. He thought of an army maxim. *If you can be seen, you can be hit.*

"You're a computer genius. You probably either built this or found it. If you can find it in the Web, you can stop it."

The woman opened her eyes and locked on with Mahegan's flat stare. She had wide oval eyes, brown irises, but those could be contact lenses. She had gone to some length to hide her appearance and her person. Part actress, part computer nerd, she was something more.

"There's only one thing that can stop it. You've got three days or we're all toast. And when you're ready to trade, I'll tell you exactly what's happening."

"The biometric keys?"

"Not saying anything else until we've got a deal."

"What kind of deal?"

"Let me go. I want to live."

"As long as you're with us, you'll live. It's out there that's more dangerous."

"Maybe. Depends on where you are. Stuff is happening fast."

Mahegan nodded. Felt the sense of urgency.

He walked out of the cell and into the barn where he gathered O'Malley, Owens, and Cassie. "If this cook is right, this is World War Three. And we've got seventy-two hours to stop it."

CHAPTER 4

*I*AN GORHAM REMOVED HIS BASEBALL CAP AND SHOOK HIS HEAD. THE assassination of the North Korean leader had gone flawlessly. The artillery duel in Estonia. Perfect. Both setting the stage for the next seventy-two hours. Yet, he was unable to pull off the smallest kidnap action in a Detroit bar. *Ironic?* Perhaps. His skills included grand visions and plans, not necessarily small actions and skirmishes.

Still, he shouted into the car window, "No!"

He expected perfection and therefore was nonplussed that he had successfully engineered the assassination of the leader of North Korea. Failing at capturing or killing someone who had hacked his corporate Dark Web hyper-encrypted room in the Deep Web? That was unacceptable.

He looped a Bluetooth earpiece over his right ear and stuffed the bud into his ear canal. On his smartphone, he pressed Dr. Belina Draganova's number from his RECENT selection again. Her name selection now had the number eighteen in parentheses. Eighteen calls in the last few days. Important business being discussed.

"I'm not available right now. Please leave a brief message," Dr. Draganova's voice mail answered. Her voice was soft and inflected with the tiniest hint of an Eastern European dialect. Soothing overtones mixed with firmness. To Gorham, listening to her voice was like drinking a good wine. The quality resonated long after the words were spoken.

He could listen to Belina's voice forever. Seductive. Reassuring.

But where could she be? He needed her now. He tried a backup number. Another voice mail. Another sigh of relief at hearing her voice, even if recorded. Like a junkie with a quick fix. He needed to talk to her. She had deconstructed him to his core. Unpacked his layers. Unpacked his brain compartment by compartment. Like moving into a new house. Getting the boxes into the correct room. Then opening them. Remembering some of what was in the boxes, but always being surprised by what you would find. Always a surprise. Every room. Maybe even every box.

He knew who he was and what he was meant to become, but needed her. *Wanted her?* No, most important, he needed her to help him navigate the depth psychology therapy they had been undertaking for the last two years.

He shook his head again. Boxes littered on the floor of his mind. Some opened. Some closed. He needed everything organized. Stat. Biggest mission of his life happening over the next seventy-two hours.

He had watched the big man in the bar stop the trial run of Computer Optimized War, or as he called it, *ComWar*. His machine learning, computer optimized, satellite-based method of controlling combat forces integrated the most powerful aspects of the Internet of Things and Artificial Intelligence in an offensive cyber role.

His phone buzzed as the driver of his car made quick turns heading to the Detroit Airport private terminal where his Gulfstream 5 jet waited for him. He had chosen the smaller airplane as opposed to the Boeing 777 he normally used.

"Go ahead," Gorham said.

"Konstantin Khilkov here," the man said.

"Mister President, how are you this evening? I trust we are on secure lines?" Gorham looked at his phone and saw that his corporate encryption was active as he spoke with the president of Russia.

"We are. You are a bastard. You know this, right?"

"I don't know this, actually, sir. My parents are still alive and married. So that's technically not true. What do you mean?"

"You have frozen our nuclear response capability."

"Oh that. Well, yes, I did do that. You can have it back, if you wish."

"If word leaks that we cannot respond against the Americans they will destroy Russia!" Khilkov said.

"Perhaps, but it is unavoidable," Gorham replied. "As we've discussed, meet me in Iran in twenty-four hours and bring your human biometric key. He can walk through the chamber, confirm his identity, and you can nuke whomever you wish."

"This is not possible. The Americans have attacked us from Estonia. I cannot leave the country now."

"It's your choice, Mister President. I have been asking to meet with you for several days. It seems you've got an issue now and you need my help. All I want is you to agree in person on the spoils of war," Gorham said. "Should it occur, of course."

A long moment of silence followed. For a moment, Gorham believed the man had hung up until Khilkov said, "This is very risky. What you are doing is unheard of. It's unacceptable."

"But you'll meet me. You'll bring your man. You'll agree to the terms. Or you lay there naked waiting for the Americans to continue their attack. It may stay conventional or it may go nuclear. And without mutual assured destruction, your country is nothing but a giant bullseye." Gorham took a deep breath, still transitioning in thought from the failure at the bar to his success at checkmating the Russian leadership. "We all must decide what to do with our time and I personally think this would be a worthwhile investment of your time."

He saw his airplane waiting as the car slowed in front of the Signature terminal.

Gorham's chief hacker, Shayne, had penetrated the Russian, Iranian, and North Korean nuclear command and control systems. In Russia, Shayne overrode the launch capability but couldn't gain full access to launch, which was ultimately what Gorham wanted. In Iran and North Korea, Shayne was able to override and take control of the entire system, albeit those nuclear platforms were much smaller and far less capable.

"Why do you need me to bring my biometric key?"

"Because he will walk into the chamber in Iran and unlock your nuclear arsenal. It's that simple. The Russian Cyber Command has effectively locked down our code, and we cannot unlock it without the biometric key. It's a simple security matter. You're stuck and we're stuck."

"You're stuck? You didn't belong in our system in the first place!"

"Come on, Mister President. You're going to sit here and tell me that your cyber soldiers are not hacking China and the United States every day? Please. You're just pissed off because we were able to do it where nobody else could."

"You're damn right I'm pissed off!"

This conversation was making Gorham feel better about the botched pub raid. He was back in his element negotiating with powerful individuals as opposed to watching a tactical mission. But still, it was important for him to see the boots on the ground. It was the experience he wanted that he didn't possess.

He had read Sun Tzu and Clausewitz many times. He understood the theory of warfare and applied it in his business. At the same time, he needed to smell the gunpowder in the air. He wanted to know what it was like in the foxhole, just as he visited his employees all over the world. Dr. Draganova had helped him discover this need to be present and in the moment.

Shaking his head, he boarded the airplane. He was so close to having control of the world's largest nuclear arsenal. If he could lure the Russian president and his biometric key to Yazd, Iran, then he would be back in business.

"I'll see you in Yazd, Mr. President." Gorham clicked off, boarded the airplane, and flew to the Idaho Falls Airport, a few miles from the Manaslu global headquarters.

CHAPTER 5

MAHEGAN WALKED TO THE COMMAND CENTER IN THE MIDDLE OF the barn. "I need three screens, Sean. The Korean DMZ to Seoul; Baghdad to Jordanian border; and the artillery fight along the Estonian and Russian border," he said. "Wide field of view. We don't know exactly what we're looking for, but I think I've got an idea."

As he was spinning the globe to get the shots for each screen, O'Malley said, "Look at that."

Russian tanks were lined up along the Belarus border, well south of Estonia.

"Yeah, give me that. Estonia was a head fake," Mahegan said.

While O'Malley worked the command center optics, Mahegan called General Savage at Fort Bragg, his former Joint Special Operations Command, or JSOC, commander over the last several years. As the phone rang, three eighty-inch flat screens were displaying the Reunification Highway from North Korea into Seoul, capturing most of the South Korean capital; the city of Minsk, with its main highway running east from Moscow toward the west, into Warsaw, Poland and Berlin, Germany; and a high shot of the sprawling city of Baghdad situated between the Tigris and Euphrates Rivers.

"Send it," Savage answered.

"We got them. They were going after a computer hacker who for some reason was working as a fry cook at a pub in Detroit."

"About as good a disguise as any," Savage said.

"She gave us a lot, but not everything." Mahegan recounted his discussion with the cook.

"She?"

"Yeah. Trying to look like a guy, but she's a she."

"Okay. Hiding out. Doesn't bode well. She holding out for a deal?" Savage said.

"Roger. You calling PACOM, EUCOM, and CENTCOM commanders?"

"I never needed guidance before and don't need it now, son," Savage said. "Don't trade but get the information from her." He hung up.

Mahegan turned his attention to the matter at hand. "Nine PM here. Makes it four AM in Europe and five AM in the sandbox."

"And nine AM tomorrow in Korea," Cassie said.

"Something like that."

"What's that?" Cassie asked.

The entire city of Baghdad went black in successive waves, each grid shutting down. To the southeast, near Basra, Iranian tanks and command vehicles massed in the hundreds, then began moving toward Baghdad. On the next screen, the city of Minsk followed suit, the white lights disappearing and leaving behind a black screen. Thousands of Russian tanks, self-propelled artillery, and command satellite vehicles huddled, lined up, and began moving west. And while it was daytime on the Korean Peninsula, there was a discernable difference in the hue of Seoul as its lights hammered shut. North Korean tanks and artillery rumbled along the 38th Parallel—the Demilitarized Zone—like racehorses bucking in the starting gate.

"Power grids? That's been done before," Owens said.

"More than that. Everything." Mahegan looked across the barn at the cell that contained the cook. "We know the woman in there is more than a cook. The question is, who is she?"

"And can she help? This *is* World War Three," O'Malley said, toggling the satellite camera to zoom in on a North Korean field artillery battery just north of the demilitarized zone.

Six North Korean self-propelled artillery pieces fired the first salvos of its 172-millimeter-high explosive round with rocket boosters to propel the rounds into the center of Itaewon, the business district of Seoul, South Korea. Then they began rolling toward the main highway, guns remaining aimed at Seoul. Another volley spit from the tubes. And then another. The tracked artillery pieces looked like giant tanks. They could shoot and move at the same time to avoid the counterfire from South Korean and American artillery.

"Radar picking them up?" Mahegan asked, knowing that the beefed-up defenses in South Korea included Q-36 Firefinder radars that allowed for quick counterfire, the key to the defensive plan in South Korea.

"We're getting no hits from Q-36. The cyber bomb must have gotten them, too," O'Malley said.

"THAAD?" The Terminal High Altitude Aerial Defense system was intended to intercept any North Korean ballistic missiles, including those with nuclear warheads.

"Nothing tested it so far."

"Tanks piling up on the road to Seoul," Cassie said, pointing at the screen. "As far as the eye can see."

"All kinds of targets for our Navy and Air Force pilots," Owens said.

O'Malley slewed the satellite camera over the USS Carl Vinson aircraft carrier off the coast of North Korea. "Jets in the air."

F-35-C's screamed off the deck of the aircraft carrier, leaving vapor trails in their wakes. They paired up in twos and raced toward the targets lined up on the road to Seoul. The radar in the command center showed ten American jets in route to the North Korean attack formation when an equal number of North Korean MiG fighter jets swarmed onto the screen.

"Dog fight," O'Malley said.

Mahegan watched, thinking the American jets should make quick work of the inferior Russian manufactured equipment. O'Malley had panned the camera to follow the two lead American fighter jets. They released air-to-air missiles and, to Mahegan's surprise, watched the missiles smoke harmlessly past the MiGs, which returned fire accurately. The first two American jets exploded when the North Korean missiles impacted.

"What's going on?" Cassie asked. "No way that should be happening."

Watching comrades in arms perish in combat was perhaps a warrior's most challenging task.

"Computer optimized warfare," Mahegan said absently, thinking. "If the RINK alliance has been planning this for a few years, especially when we were disengaged globally, they've had time to infect our weapons systems. Those missiles just flew into outer space instead of knocking the MiGs out of the sky. The Q-36 radars aren't working. This is cyber blitzkrieg. That's how the cook described it. The computer hackers have been distracting us with cyber-attacks on banks, cars, everything else while they've been quietly infecting our weapons systems." Mahegan paused. Was the unthinkable happening? Russians, Iranians, and North Koreans all in alliance to start World War III?

"Remote access Trojans. RATs. They infiltrate one of the big defense contractors and get a guy past the firewall and put a RAT on every missile so that it's one degree off, for example," O'Malley said.

The command post fell silent as the other eight American jets all maneuvered, attempting to close the gap and use their guns as opposed to the malfunctioning missiles. While two were successful in destroying North Korean MiGs, all ten of the American jets were downed.

Mahegan answered the ringing phone. "Roger."

"I know you're watching this. Minsk has just taken a thousand rockets. Russian combined arms teams are on the highway to Minsk now. Looks like the action in Estonia was a feint or fixing action to keep the Eighty-Second Airborne in place. Baghdad is in Iranian hands. Two Iranian tank divisions are pushing through Tikrit toward the borders of Syria and Jordan," Savage said.

"Roger. We're focused on Korea, but tracking all."

"All right. I'll see you guys in a few hours. This thing is going nuclear."

"Literally," Mahegan said.

"That, too," Savage replied and hung up.

"Boss is on the way," Mahegan announced to his team. "We need to talk to the other guys and pull apart that briefcase before he gets here. Not much we can do about this, right now anyway."

He nodded at the screen. The North Korean engineer unit had constructed a series of bridges across the tank ditches beyond the DMZ and on South Korean territory. The Russian made T-72 tanks rolled slowly, infantry walking on either side of them, artillery providing deep fires, and Hind and Hip helicopters leapfrogging into unresponsive villages, disgorging special operations commandos. The sun was up on the Korean Peninsula, shining a bright spotlight on the carnage. North Korean tanks were blowing holes in the sides of buildings as infantrymen followed, clearing the way.

"Oh my, God," Cassie said. "This *is* World War Three."

"Not sure this is all there is to it, but agree that's where we are," Mahegan said.

As they waited for Savage to fly from Fort Bragg to the barn, O'Malley ripped apart the briefcase, finding some interesting circuitry. Cassie interrogated the three prisoners, who claimed to not speak English. They were low-level operatives, she told Mahegan.

"This is an electronic, digital, and directed energy warfare platform. It has state of the art nanotechnology that miniaturizes everything while increasing emission power," O'Malley said. "There are probably more like them in the country. The briefcase is like a reverse JackRabbitt. It throws out a cyber bomb and small electromagnetic pulse to shut down power grids, IP addresses, and Wi-Fi hotspots. It has artificial intelligence and monitors its effectiveness—how many substations it shuts down, number of smart meters turned off, and so on. It learns what it did right and what it did wrong, then self corrects to be more effective the next time. The hospital attack in Miami a few months ago? That was probably a trial run. Every operating room was shut down; every heart monitor turned off. If they hadn't had a generator for critical functions, most of the patients would have died. That kid in Europe that prevented a similar attack? All that means is that they've been probing for a few years. Testing."

"Total combat?" Owens asked.

"It's coming. Trust me," Mahegan said.

A loud chime rang inside barn. The four operatives looked skyward even though the barn loft—filled with high tech radars and weaponry instead of hay—did not afford them an outside view.

"UAV!" O'Malley shouted.

The images on the big screens all flickered from the faraway precursors of combat to a thermal image of each cardinal direction from the barn. Coming from the north was a fixed wing unmanned aerial vehicle about the size of a racing jet. Its bat-wing shape was darting and diving, attempting to appear as much like a live bird of prey as possible. However, it was an air breather with a thermal signature and therefore detectable by O'Malley's radar array.

"Standoff at a half mile, Sean. Where are the guns?"

"Should be up, boss."

"We've got about five seconds to figure this out."

"Shit. They're cyber-bombing us. They severed the slew to cue Wi-Fi link."

"Go to manual," Mahegan ordered.

O'Malley was working his hands across the keyboard. "Manual override," he said.

The big screen showed four Gatlin guns elevate from platforms disguised as mounds of hay.

Patch Owens was in the "gunner's chair" next to O'Malley on the command and control platform. He was holding the joy stick as if he were playing a video game. "Guns active."

The drone bore down on their position, then elevated to gain altitude in what Mahegan presumed was a top attack. When the drone exposed its belly, Owens was quick to fire hundreds of fifty caliber rounds at the angling aircraft. He clipped the wing, causing it to erratically veer from its designated path.

Owens switched to the western set of guns and put the spiraling

UAV in his cross hairs and spat machine-gun rounds until it fell from the sky and exploded in the dense forest surrounding the farm.

"Radar showing any others?" Mahegan asked.

"Not at the moment. Working a fix for the cyber bomb," O'Malley said.

"This place is burned. We've got to move," Mahegan said.

Just then General Savage's voice boomed over the radio. "Saddle up and meet me at the airfield."

Mahegan and team stared at the receiver for a moment.

Then, with no time to investigate the crash site or who might have called in the barn as a target, Mahegan pointed at O'Malley and said, "Give me a quick wide field of view along the road frontage."

O'Malley switched from the drone defense targeting array to their satellite zoom view of the farm property.

"There," Mahegan said.

The white-hot image showed a large man running through the woods, holding a cell phone out, perhaps using it as a light.

"He's headed to that truck on the shoulder about a mile away," Owens said.

"Launch our drone?" Cassie asked.

"Real quick," Mahegan said. "Patch, you do that. Cassie and Sean, grab your go bags and ours."

"Shit. The drone was my idea," Cassie said.

"Go," Mahegan replied. "Patch is in the chair."

"Launching," Owens said.

"Roger. We've got General Savage inbound, so be careful."

Owens launched and remotely maneuvered the midsize Cobra drone onto the asphalt runway adjacent to the barn, revved its engine, and launched it for takeoff. Through the drone's camera, they could see the speck of light that was Savage's inbound XC-17 command and control jet.

"Okay. The runner is on the southwest quadrant. Guns ready?" Mahegan said.

"Roger. Got him," Owens said. The drone slowed as it followed what Mahegan believed to be a spotter or scout that had perhaps somehow followed them from the bar in Detroit.

"There's a firebreak about a hundred yards ahead. Get up there and put it in hover mode with guns ready," Mahegan directed.

"Roger that." Owens maneuvered the drone to a long gap in the trees that the forestry service required landowners to create if their farms were over one hundred acres and more than two-thirds woodland. The purpose was to prevent a single fire from consuming an entire woodland and spreading beyond one landowner's property. The dirt road was maybe twenty yards wide—a long, straight ribbon. The runner would have to cross it to get to his vehicle along the road. They could see the thermal image of the man maneuvering toward the firebreak.

"Here he comes," Mahegan said, staring at the screen.

"Guns active," Owens replied.

The man slowed as he approached the firebreak, perhaps sensing its danger to him. Seeming to catch his breath against a tree, the runner held the phone to his ear.

"Don't let him make that call," Mahegan said.

The drone's machine guns whirred in the audio feedback as the rounds impacted into the tree, the ground, and the runner. The phone flipped into the air, its screen brightly lit on the display. The man went down to one knee, then slid to another. He began to crawl. Like a turtle homing in on its beach, he began sliding across the firebreak toward his car a quarter mile away.

"Put a missile up his ass," Mahegan directed. "See if we can intercept whoever he was talking to."

"Only got two."

"Fire one on him and then one on the truck on the road."

"Any chance this is a stupid kid messing around?" Owens asked.

Mahegan paused. "I don't believe in coincidences like this."

"Roger."

The small rocket smoked from the wing of the UAV and impacted within inches of the crawling man, who went motionless.

Mahegan hoped he was lifeless. "Any guns left?"

"Nothing. Just one missile."

"Okay, hit the truck and let's go."

Owens tilted the drone from hover to airplane mode, flew it to the truck, hovered, and put the last missile on a Ford F150 that exploded into a bright fireball.

"All right. Let's go," Mahegan said.

As Owens was landing the drone, Mahegan walked over and unlocked the Washington, DC prison cell. He placed noise-cancelling headphones on the woman. Then he slipped a sandbag over her head. "Get up."

The cook had been laying in the fetal position, but stood when Mahegan pulled her up by the handcuffs. "Where are we going?" the woman shouted.

Mahegan said nothing.

They walked outside and a quarter mile to the runway where General Savage's experimental C-17 Globemaster was turning to prepare for a quick offload and onload. The ramp dropped and two men dressed in cargo pants, tight-fitting long-sleeve shirts, tactical vests, and modified combat helmets deplaned. Mahegan recognized them as long time operators, Hobart and Van Dreeves. Good men. Faithful to their nation. Always in the fight.

"Hobart. VD. Good to see you. Got three prisoners in there. Cassie worked them. Might be more to get from them. You'll need Korean, Farsi, and Russian interpreters," Mahegan said.

"Roger," Van Dreeves said. "Got the perfect man deplaning now."

Mahegan looked up and saw a civilian walking down the ramp carrying a rucksack. He didn't recognize the person, but he didn't need to.

"We will probably just secure them and keep moving west. This thing's moving pretty fast. Old man has every team assigned somewhere against Korea, Europe, or the sandbox," Hobart said.

"Roger. Sounds about right. See you on the high ground," Mahegan said.

They clasped hand to forearm—the warrior shake—did a shoulder bump, and walked in opposite directions.

"What's going on!?" the cook shouted. "Where are we going?"

Mahegan knew the cook couldn't hear him through the noise-cancelling headphones, but he was feeling the buzz of combat—that adrenaline rush of making a difference. The high of hanging out the door of an airplane before putting paratroopers on target or the energy of vanquishing an enemy in brutal hand-to-hand combat. He'd done it all, but perhaps the stakes had never been higher.

Where were they going? He was certain of only one thing.

"To prevent a dark winter," Mahegan muttered. "Nukes."

CHAPTER 6

A DRIVER PICKED GORHAM UP IN AN ARMORED TESLA AND SOON HE was through the gated entrance to his headquarters. He always went there first, even though his personal residence was fifty miles to the north, straight line distance. He waited as the biometric readers scanned his eyes, checked his facial features, swabbed his cheek for DNA, recorded his handprint, and conducted a bug and bomb sweep of his car. Satisfied, the mechanism triggered the garage door opener.

With his driver pulling into the garage, he slumped forward in the back seat, resting his head on the padded leather. Such careful planning. Would it all be undone? Not if he executed now. He sat upright and gathered himself, running a hand across his face.

His driver's eyes caught his in the mirror and Gorham said, "Don't look at me."

The driver broke eye contact and turned his head away.

Gorham thought through the problem sets—the Russians, the briefcase, and the hacker. The Russians were the key. Seven thousand nuclear weapons. If Khilkov did not show, he could leak to the press that the Russian system was down and that they were defenseless as the brush fire along the Estonian-Russian border simmered.

Then there was the issue of the briefcase. It was a simple device, but if someone knew what he were doing, he would figure out the microdevices that delivered the Internet bomb and embedded electromagnetic pulse to that grid system in Detroit.

Lastly, the hacker. Who was he? How had he been able to penetrate the formidable Manaslu defenses? Gorham had teams of the world's best hackers running offensive and defensive cyber drills every day. It was unthinkable that someone had cracked through their system in the Deep Web and had learned of his idea.

He pushed himself up from the rear seat, knowing that he needed to execute now. He looked in the rearview mirror, saw the crow's feet forming around his eyes. *Since when did I have those?* While he enjoyed the planning and preparation, the magnitude of the situation weighed on him occasionally.

He shook it off, opened the car door, and marched into the headquarters basement.

"You in HQ or the compound?" Shayne said. Microphones lined the walls of the headquarters corridors.

"Compound. See you in a few minutes."

"Okay."

Gorham passed the security tests again to get inside his own building. Big men with barrel chests nodded at him as he walked through the security scanners. He took an elevator down to the portal he had constructed and stepped into his version of Elon Musk's Hyperloop. Of course, Gorham called it the ManaLoop, because it sped at over Mach One. He stepped into the vehicle that looked like a space shuttle without wings. Pressed a button that closed the door. Pressed another button that activated the magnets that levitated the car. Buckled his seat belt. Then pressed another button that rocketed the ManaLoop at nearly 1,000 miles per hour to his compound fifty miles away. He was there in a little over three minutes. A quarter mile a second. One mile every four seconds. Fifteen miles every minute. The transport glided to a halt. The door opened. He walked into the command post he'd had created in the basement.

One of his few friends, Shayne was seated with his back to him, pecking away at the keyboard, ones and zeros flying across the screen.

Even then, Gorham wasn't sure how close he could ever be to

anyone. Like his self-optimizing algorithms, he was constantly trying to evolve, improve and perfect. He wasn't sure anyone could
forever live up to his expectations. Long ago he had given up the
illusion that he would find some peaceful state of satisfaction and
cruise through life. On the contrary, he was obsessively building
his empire until he had literally hit walls in all directions. It was
impossible to be more famous, more powerful, richer, more
liked, or more benevolent. How much fun, sex, love, and de-
bauchery could $100 billion buy someone? He'd been through
those phases as fast as he'd built the company and overtaken the fa-
bled FANG companies: Facebook, Amazon, Netflix, and Google.
The market pundits had changed the acronym to MFANG, appro-
priately placing Manaslu at the front. The joke was that the "M"
was silent, because Manaslu had attacked with stealth. They seemingly came out of nowhere.

So, what next? He walked through another biometric chamber,
which confirmed his gait, handprint, DNA with a sterile Q-tip
swab in the mouth, eye scan, 107-point facial recognition, and
voice recognition.

"Ian Gorham," he said. A series of green checkmarks popped
up next to each of the categories. As he waited for confirmation,
which took a few seconds, he reflected.

His new, fantastic idea struck him one day when he was watching television on one of his liquid plasma wall televisions, eight
feet wide and ten feet high. The news was informing him of another affront to humanity by the American president; another insult to someone's faith; another dig at the media; another rogue
missile strike somewhere. It all began to run together for Gorham,
who believed that in this day of Internet and information, borders
were meaningless. Nation states no longer mattered. The world
was one united people and the only way to unify the global citi-
zenry was to use the forces of nationalism to destroy the very
same ideology. From the security of his walled, gated, and forti-
fied compound, Gorham believed that there was a better way
ahead for the world. And that way was his way—the global way,
the unified way.

But first burn the world to the ground, so that he could rebuild it. Like razing a dilapidated neighborhood and rebuilding in its bulldozed lot. He would construct the global community that he knew could exist . . . must exist if the world was to survive.

As their corporate motto said, they were *Bringing Genius to the World!*

Gorham had at his command the world's largest search, home delivery, and social media conglomerate, which he had named Manaslu after the treacherous Nepalese summit that few dared to climb. More dangerous than Everest and nearly as high, Mount Manaslu was the ultimate challenge in Ian Gorham's mind. Because his wealthy father met his Nepalese mother ascending the Himalayan Mountain, Gorham had proudly named his company Manaslu. The unique L-shaped and jagged snowcapped Manaslu peaks were the company symbol, fashioned in the shape of an *M*. The Manaslu search engine was faster than Google, the social media connections had surpassed Facebook, and the retail endeavor had rapidly overtaken Amazon.

Manaslu's algorithms optimized searches, friendships, and purchases, and now they were optimizing combat. After the presidential elections, Gorham had quickly established his own version of the Defense Advanced Research Project Agency, something he called the MAP Lab, the Manaslu Advanced Project laboratory.

"This is how we beat Facebook, Amazon, and Google," he'd told Shayne, his lead code writer, a twenty-five-year-old seasoned veteran of the hacking world. Like Cher or Bono, Shayne went by a single name.

Gorham walked up to Shayne sitting at the command terminal in the MAP Lab, essentially the basement of his compound. A bank of fluorescent lights shone across the fifty-yard-wide cavern outfitted with the latest high-tech flat screens, touchpads, hologram fields, servers, radios, videoconference cameras, smartphones, and computers. The hologram fields were the chessboards upon which his ComWar would unfold. Gorham and Shayne had developed the capability to build a three-dimensional hologram of each of their target cities. They also had secure, encrypted communications with the command headquarters of each RINK alliance member—Russia, Iran, and North Korea.

"Status?" Gorham asked.

"Well, we've got confirmation on Jun. Dead. Drone came in and grabbed a DNA sample and confirmed it in flight back to the automated launch pad. Sent the confirmation to our Dark Web archive and I got a notification that it is a hundred percent match. Our replica U.S. Air Force Reaper drone took off from the Samjiyon airfield simultaneously and has crashed outside of Pyongyang very close to the presidential palace. News media have been alerted by anonymous sources. The Americans are trying to hide the information in their secure servers, but we're circumventing that with the staged drone crash. In about an hour the world will believe the US assassinated Jun."

"Okay, good. Russia? Iran?"

"Well, one more thing on North Korea. They've found me in the nuke command and control system. We've been playing cat and mouse, but they're pretty good."

"But you're better," Gorham said, anxious.

"I am," Shayne said. He hesitated. "I've been able to remove one nuke from their access. Everything else they've been able to block, and we can't get at it unless we get the biometric key guy."

"Another reason for the meeting in Iran. Get them all there and copy their markers. That way we have redundancy."

"Yes, if ultimately what you want, boss, is to control all the nukes in Russia, Iran, and North Korea then you need all three biometric keys. Three human beings. My abilities as a hacker will help us steal their biometric data, but we'll need Dax to do the dirty work and kidnap them, because nothing happens unless the computer receives their biometric markers as part of the launch sequence."

Shayne had found in the Dark Web a reference to the Russians creating a redundancy to their nuclear program where a living, breathing person would be a part of the chain to lock or unlock the nuclear codes. It was an added security precaution, one Khilkov had mandated that North Korea and Iran replicate to ensure synchronization. In addition to the encrypted cyber codes that all nuclear arsenals required prior to launch, Khilkov required a *biometricishkiy klyuch*—biometric key—to be comprehensively certified before missiles could be launched.

The combination of the encrypted codes and the human biometrics would prevent doppelgangers or mere hackers from simply stealing the codes or impersonating the authorized launch authority. Not only did they need the crypto, but they needed the person. In today's world of hacking, information wasn't safe, no matter how well protected anyone thought it might have been. Having an additional layer of a human in the loop added a low tech, asymmetric precaution to the ever-vulnerable Internet.

"Okay. I just got off the phone with Khilkov. Give me the details of the Estonia operation, please."

"Russia. Total success. The Latvian did his job. The Russians have fired counter battery and the Eighty-second Airborne brigade base is getting chewed up. There's a significant artillery war happening right now. The Russian president has been notified that the United States has killed Jun. Japan knows, also, by the way. Journalist Luiz Yamashita has been identified as being on the scene and that news is being made public also."

"Good call on that one. Sets up our pending Japan action nicely. China doing anything?"

"So far, no. As we predicted, China will protect itself, but can't really get out of its own way to do anything offensively. But Russia, man. The president has put two and two together, so he's ready to launch. Thinks the Americans are starting the war. He's conducting a preemptive attack through Belarus."

Gorham smiled. Of course, that was what he was doing. The Manaslu algorithms had trained the Russian generals over the last year that the best path to western Europe was to ignore the Baltics and plow through the semireceptive Belarus and barrel headfirst into Poland. Germany, Belgium, and France would be in sight from there.

Because, *why not?*

"I've convinced Khilkov to bring the Russian Key. The Iranian

Key we know is housed there. And I planted the seed to have the Russians convince the North Korean Key to come."

"Yes, that works. I'm blocked in Russia and in North Korea. Iran only has a couple of nukes, but it would make sense that we take control of those."

"Agree. So, that's the deal. We meet to discuss post war spoils, sign the agreement, and the countries get control of their nukes, then we steal it back from them."

When Gorham learned that the Russians were allied with the Iranians and North Koreans in preparation for war against the West, he'd had Shayne conduct a deep dive analysis of the techniques of each of the RINK nations.

Khilkov's very concern, that someone could hack and steal the codes thereby taking control of the nuclear arsenal, had already happened. Shayne had breached the firewalls and was gathering the data when Russian Cyber Command operators scrambled and ultimately blocked his efforts, but not before he had disabled the fleet of nukes.

Not good for Russia.

Now, Gorham had the leverage he needed to discuss post war spoils and potentially steal the biometric data. If he could accomplish both of those missions in Iran, the next seventy-two hours would unfold precisely as he planned. "And we fly to Iran tonight. Of course, Iran needs no provocation to attack Iraq or Jordan, so they're on board."

"Okay. North Korea is already attacking South. Iran is ready to blow through Iraq and into Jordan and Israel. Is Russia's ComWar set?"

"They're ready. The ComWar center we built there has impressed the Russians. They are ready to launch. This artillery duel will focus people in the north as they begin to drive through Belarus." Gorham stared at the giant television screen on the wall. He stood in the basement of his operations center alone with Shayne. The room was cavernous, bullpen cubicles for as far as the eye could see. Their elevated command platform had three hundred and sixty degree screen capability.

"What happened at the bar, dude?" Shayne asked.

"That was a cluster," Gorham spat.

"Chill, man. It's all good. Just curious about a raid. *That* was supposed to be simple."

"Nothing simple about a kidnapping. Somebody must have seen something in the ManaWeb."

He and Shayne had developed their own segmented portion of the Deep Web where they did all their coding. Corporations and defense agencies around the world were constantly conducting battle within the Deep Web, stealing secrets, planting remote access Trojans, and fighting for information that could be useful in business or war.

"Man, nobody can see that. The ManaWeb is deeper than the Marianna Trench, dude."

"The cook hacked us. Plus a big Native American guy and a blond female knew something was going down. So that's two different somebodies."

"Get any pictures?"

Gorham punched a button on his phone and the grainy pictures appeared on an eight by ten-foot television screen on his wall. He used his thumb to swipe through the photos until he had a clear shot of the big man and the blonde. "This one's directly before Mini ComWar shut off the lights."

After a few key strokes, Shayne said, "Chayton Mahegan and Cassandra Bagwell. Mahegan is former Delta Force. Been out a few years. Bagwell is technically on active duty but assigned to a special mission unit, whatever that means."

"It means someone has figured something out," Gorham said.

"Not possible for them to know everything."

"They got . . . the cook."

After a pause, Shayne looked away and then at Gorham. "The cook could be different. He was important. Any idea on who that is?"

"You're supposed to be telling me who he is, genius."

Shayne brushed some hair out of his face. "Right."

Distracted, Gorham scratched his chin. "Any word on Nancy? Back to Kiev? Hiding out? Did I scare her away? Given our resources we pretty much ought to be able to track her twenty-four/seven."

"You're forgetting she worked here. So she knows that, too."

Nancy Langevin was Manaslu's chief financial officer. He and Nancy met on a dating app two years ago, fell in love, broke up, and continued working together. Originally from the Ukraine, she was a Harvard Business School graduate. Gorham had never truly moved on, though perhaps she had. A month ago, she'd told him she needed some time to, "think about us." That was how she had phrased it.

He had told her to take the time, but knowing his deadline for this mission, had directed her to be back three days ago. He never intended to involve her in the plan, but he did need to protect her. He loved her. And he couldn't let happen to her what was going to happen to most Americans. Couldn't run that risk. If one in every three Americans was going to die or be wounded within the next three days, he wasn't willing to accept those odds for Nancy.

"No idea. I've called. I've texted. I've e-mailed. I've even turned on the fiber optic cameras you had me place in her home and car. Nothing. No digital footprint anywhere."

"She said she needed time to think. A genius with digits, but hated them just the same. Knowing how they work means knowing how to make them not work . . . mostly."

"So, we need a decision here, boss. I know Nancy's important. Is she worth delaying the entire operation for?"

Gorham paused. "No. Let's do it. With the cook and the briefcase in American hands it's a race against time, isn't it?"

"Doubtful that they can figure out much, if any, of what we've done," Shayne said. "But we're ready."

A beeping noise interrupted their conversation.

"That's got to be Dax," Gorham said.

"Yep. It's his number at least," Shayne replied. He punched the button to answer but the call dropped.

"What happened?" Gorham asked.

"Not sure. I'm calling him back."

"No. That's his one rule. Never call him. He calls us. We don't want to compromise his position."

"Okay. I'll put a narrow sat shot on the geo location."

"Good idea."

After some maneuvering, they were staring at a forest near open grazing land and a large barn. As Shayne zoomed the satellite, the carnage was obvious. Trees were in flames, smoke wafted toward the sky. Dax Stasovich, a large man and former Serbian special operations soldier was lying prone in the middle of a dirt trail that separated two dense forests.

"Dead?" Shayne asked.

"Not possible." Gorham's voice was distant and far away, as if some trigger had been pulled or switch flipped. "He will find his way back."

"Um, he looks dead. Not moving."

Gorham shook his head, thinking *not possible.*

"Here's something. North Korean television just announced that the Americans conducted a surgical strike on the presidential palace, but that Jun survived. They're showing a video of him waving at the crowd."

"You're sure on the match."

"One thousand percent."

"Okay so it's a doppelganger."

"Russia, China, and Iranian governments have expressed outrage. The television is showing the crashed Reaper drone in North Korea."

"Brilliant, yes?"

"Yes," Shayne affirmed.

Gorham had thought the attack through. He had used a quad copter from the ruse of a factory to drop a high explosive round on the president, who they knew took his interviews in his open-air garden. The workers in the factory had built the facsimile Reaper drone expressly so that it could be crashed on the day of the attack. There would be no convincing anyone in the world that the Americans did not use the unmanned system to avert nuclear war by killing Jun.

The other half of the compound was a ComWar center prepared to communicate by satellite and send commands to the North Korean army as if Jun were still alive.

Now was the moment Gorham had been waiting for.

He stood and walked to a small platform in his command center, which afforded him a view of all the holograms, one showing the Korean Peninsula, others showing Tokyo, Baghdad, and a series of cities in northern Europe.

He stepped into a glass walled hallway ten meters long. Taking his usual stride, he walked through the Biometric Key Generator (BKG) Confirmation System that allowed him to activate the ComWar system and override the command and control architectures of the Russian, Iranian, and North Korean Armies. Staring into the eye scanner, the laser quickly flicked left and then right. A green check mark appeared in the heads-up display above his head. A second green check mark appeared once his gait had been analyzed and approved by the system.

He said, "We are bringing genius to the world," waited a few seconds, and a third green check mark appeared, confirming his voice. A mechanical arm reached out and swabbed the inside of his mouth, retracted into the wall, and confirmed his DNA, producing a fourth green checkmark. Once the facial recognition feature was completed, the fifth and final green check mark appeared in the heads-up display.

A computerized female voice said, "Confirmed, Mister Ian Gorham."

He stepped out of the BKG Confirmation System, spread his arms wide, as if he were on the bow of the Titanic, and said, "Execute."

Shayne stared at Gorham, who repeated his command in a high, shrill voice. "Execute!"

Shayne nodded. His fingers skittered across the keyboard. Commands were sent. Satellites bounced signals back and forth. Orders were received. Machines responded. Some humans as well, but mostly machines. And back to the satellites.

They watched the giant television screens on the walls of the ManaLab. Icons moved on the diagram displaying the Korean peninsula. The North Korean military was displayed in red, the U.S. and Allied Forces in blue.

"North Korea moving into Seoul," Shayne said.

He and Gorham turned as the hologram popped to life on the vast floor to their left. Miniature holographic images moved across a map, flowing beyond Shayne and Gorham, who had moved into the middle of the floor. They were standing about where the demilitarized zone crossed the main highway into South Korea.

"Everything working?" Gorham asked.

"There's been some counterfire from the Americans and ROK armies. The RAT must not have affected all of the radars."

Gorham scratched the sparse hairs on his chin and thought for a moment. Mock explosions puffed around their feet in faux fireballs, indicating real time artillery exchanges.

"That's okay," he said, looking at his feet. He was standing next to a holographic North Korean self-propelled artillery battery. "More like a natural thing. Shitty maintenance, but some of them work. Will make them think twice before looking for the digital aspect. How about the jets?" He looked back in the direction of where Pyongyang was on the holographic battlefield, as if looking for the jets.

"The aircraft carrier Carl Vinson got ten airplanes up and then the digital launch mechanism failed."

"How'd they get those up?"

"The algorithm has already fixed it. Shutting down the Truman, Eisenhower, Roosevelt, and the others. That's the point. Not everything will be perfect the first time, but ComWar automatically learns."

"Combo of machine learning and AI," Gorham said, referring to artificial intelligence. "Potent brew."

The holographic display showed the North Korean army advancing along the Reunification Highway, as the North Koreans had dubbed the major traffic artery between Pyongyang and Seoul. Thousands of tanks and artillery pieces were stacked, waiting to cross the bridges emplaced by the North Korean engineers. Tanks and infantrymen were shooting at will as they advanced into the shopping district of Itaewon. The infantry protected Tactical High Energy Laser weapons developed by the Russian/Iranian/North Korean, or RINK, alliance.

While there were limits to Computer Optimized Warfare, they were few. Opposing forces could fire basic weapons such as AK-47s or M4 carbines, but those same troops frequently could not move or communicate. The cyber bomb coupled with a targeted tactical electromagnetic pulse shut down power and anything and everything connected to enemy Internet activity. The Internet of Things, once believed to be a great advantage for US allied forces, was biting their conventional forces in the ass.

"When does North Korea launch the ICBM?" Gorham asked.

Shayne had uncovered the planned launch sequence for another powerful North Korean intercontinental ballistic missile. Having tested dozens over the past several years, North Korea was demonstrating its capability to destroy parts of the United States. In the eyes of the North Korean leadership, mutual assured destruction was the only deterrent to American aggression.

"They have it scheduled for thirty minutes from now. That was before all of this happened though."

"What better time than now?" Gorham asked. "The president is dead. North Korea will believe America did it. The real question is, can you apply the parallel algorithm?"

Shayne had found each of North Korea's nuclear missiles—they had eight constructed and ready to fire—and could mimic the launch sequence of a nonnuclear ICBM, causing the nuclear missile to launch, as well.

"That's heavy duty stuff, boss," Shayne said.

"I'll take that as a yes. So, timing? Thirty minutes?"

"*If* it goes, I'd recommend it goes once we've got Itaewon under control. Remember, I can probably do this one time and I'll be shut down. They know I'm in their system and are chasing me through the wires. These missiles, if I can pull it off, will launch side by side, in tandem. One will overshoot Tokyo, and one will . . . hit Tokyo." He paused, looked at Gorham. "If we do it."

"*When* we do it, Shayne. And all the more reason to fire now. This is when they would strike back. We need to fire one nuclear weapon at Japan so that we can then focus on a breakout to the Pusan area in the south. We need to get to that port before any U.S. or coalition forces can to block offloading of ships and supplies. I'm watching the battlefield here and they look close enough to breaching Seoul. Let's go ahead and launch it," Gorham said.

He applied the same business acumen that had led to the success of his company to his military strategy. Just as he had to outmaneuver Amazon, Facebook, and Google for market share and investors, he had to constantly be thinking in terms of countering the considerable American threat to his vision of a global society. The challenge was part of the enticement. When he had started Manaslu, he'd had to overcome the first mover advantage of those three giants. The struggle had been real, but he had been successful.

Now, with lifetime financial security at such a young age, Gorham didn't want to focus solely on dominance of the social and commercial world; he wanted political power. He had read Von Clausewitz' *On War* and knew that military action was simply politics by another means. Given the state of the world today, Gorham knew that the deep political divisions in the United States and around the globe made the world ripe for a hostile takeover.

"Boss I'm talking to you," Shayne said.

"Yes?"

"You're sure you want to launch the nuke? It's your one freebie," Shayne said.

"Yes. North Korea strikes Japan with a nuke. World's third largest economy. An extension of the United States for all practical purposes. The digital trails we've left for Assange and his lackeys to sniff around show Russia and Iran in full support of the North Korean weapons program *and* the launch. And you've got the follow up congrats e-mails ready for AUTO SEND from Iran and Russia to the acting North Korean president, correct?"

"Yes," Shayne muttered.

"Okay, then. For the third time, execute," Gorham said in an even tone.

Shayne eyed him a second and then said, "You're the boss." His fingers rattled across the keyboard sounding like a thousand beetles on concrete and he hit ENTER.

He panned the ManaSat camera over the Sangnam-Ri underground missile base, the location of many ICBM test flights. Two silos opened. They were maybe one-half mile apart. The openings looked like black dots on the satellite feed. Smoke boiled simultaneously from the two holes. The missiles lifted. For all practical purposes, they looked the same. Pointed tip. White fuselage. Gray rocket boosters. Flame and smoke billowing everywhere.

"Launch," he said.

"Flight time?"

"Thirty-seven minutes."

"THAAD defenses?"

"Should be mitigated. ManaWorm showing activated and effective against American THAAD." Shayne had developed the remote access Trojan, ManaWorm, so that they could plant the virus on unsuspecting defense contractor weapons and equipment a year or two earlier, when Gorham had hatched his plan.

"Shadow missile effective?"

"So far. Looks like one launch. If we're lucky, the Americans will think it's just another ICBM tested and not even try to deploy THAAD."

They stood in the middle of the hologram next to the 3-D image of Japan—businessmen and women walking past them at a busy intersection. Gorham had just ordered a North Korean nuclear strike in downtown Tokyo without consent of the North Korean leadership. It was nearly as simple as when a techie remotely took control of your computer to fix a problem. The cursor moved and magic happened on the screen.

"Still time to abort, if you wish," Shayne said. "I can let the inert missile hit Tokyo. Will still be an act of war."

They watched the ManaSat screen showing the two missiles flying closely together, smoking cleanly into the sky.

"No. We've run models and sims on this scenario a million times," Gorham said.

"Well, a live nuke's still a big deal. A lot different from electrons flowing, man."

"You in or out, Shayne?" Gorham barked. "Don't become a weasel at the last second. The North Koreans have been wanting to do this for a while. We're just facilitators."

Shayne nodded. "You know I'm in. In for a zero, in for a one," he said, referencing the code writing digits.

Exactly thirty-seven minutes of flight later, which took the inert ICBM and the nuclear warhead tipped ICBM over six hundred and seventy miles from the North Korean Launching Ground to the Shibuya shopping district of Tokyo, a five-kiloton nuclear weapon detonated.

"And," Gorham said with dramatic flair, "we have the third nuclear weapon ever dropped in wartime and it is once again on Japanese soil. How ironic."

Shayne remained silent, staring at Gorham's light brown curly locks, boyish face, and deceptively athletic build. A self-proclaimed nerd in high school and college, Gorham had mastered code writing and hacking at the early age of eight, was programming at ten, and began figuring out how to synthesize the algorithms of Google, Amazon, and Facebook in his own, proprietary way. Once complete, he built his company literally out of his apartment, then migrated to an old warehouse that he transformed into a multibillion-dollar business with an economic value worth more than any of his competitors. Stealing business using rapid algorithm integrated learning, something he called RAIL, Gorham assessed industry trends, evaluated what was trending on Twitter, Facebook, Amazon, Snapchat, and Google, and in microseconds, pushed that information in a relevant fashion to his customers. Some sought information, some wanted to purchase the latest trendy products, others wanted to communicate with social circles. Manaslu had it all seamlessly integrated.

It made his platform the best way to optimize combat through constant learning. He didn't need to read the military manuals to know that not everything ever worked perfectly. On the contrary, every action or operation was inherently flawed because humans planned and operated them. He saw it every day with his patented artificial intelligence/machine learning that seamlessly conducted its own evaluations of every action and near simultaneously rewrote the code and updated the newest version of the "app."

"What about Belarus?" Gorham asked, shifting gears.

"ComWar has just initiated lights out in Minsk. Russian tanks lined up on the highway. NATO radar systems disabled. Hospitals, first responders, and emergency management networks being cyber bombed as we speak. Digitized attack messages launched to subordinate commands."

"Okay. Let's move in ten minutes. What else?"

"Understood."

"What is Russia saying about going to war? Why?"

Shayne scanned two of his computer monitors and digested the information quickly. "The Russian president has strongly denounced the assassination of the North Korean leader and says the West has fired on their troops from Estonia. He's saying that the brigade of Eighty-second Airborne troops there have conducted an act of war. That unprovoked, their howitzers fired artillery at the Russian troops along the border. His only recourse is to protect Russia by expanding its buffer zone and fighting back against the West. Have to love these automated counterfire systems."

"Good call on that one," Gorham said.

All it had taken was one mortar tube and a few thousand dollars. Shayne had used a cut-out operative to link up with a former ISIS member from Latvia. The man had gladly accepted the task, fired the rounds onto the Russian troops, and then died. It was, nonetheless, the provocation they were anticipating.

Gorham had also inked a deal with Russia for a Manaslu factory and enterprise that would employ tens of thousands of people in the erstwhile capitalist society. That factory was over eight hundred thousand square feet and included the obligatory ComWar suite in the underground. Once inside Russia's considerable network, Shayne had navigated his way into the inner sanctum of the Kremlin's most classified information. Gorham and Shayne had been surprised at the level of defense that the Russian cyber experts had layered into their system. It had taken several months, and while the Cyber Command had blocked Shayne's efforts to control the nuclear fleet, they were unable to distinguish his presence in the ComWar command center because Manaslu had built that facility. In essence, Shayne was able to issue digital orders to the front line troops if he wanted.

"Middle East?" Gorham walked from the Japan holograph where the nuclear explosion had leveled buildings and started fires in downtown Tokyo, seemingly sucking the oxygen out of the entire country. The destruction was breathtaking. The images swirled around him as if he were walking through the smoldering embers of hell.

He stopped some twenty paces later as he stood on the 3-D LED illuminated map near Baghdad. A hologram popped up when Shayne pressed a button. To his front, Iranian special forces were storming the prime minister's residence during a blackout of the city. Behind him, Iranian tanks and artillery pieces were crossing the border from Iran into Iraq. As they approached each village, ComWar automatically attacked the grid with its DICE system, Directed and Integrated Cyber and Electromagnetic attack. As DICE launched, ComWar's RAIL learning system immediately processed the effectiveness of everything, including human activity. How quickly were the tanks moving? Was the interval between the DICE attack and the arrival of the land forces sufficient? Too long? Too short? How much of the grid was shut down? Left unharmed? Were forces synchronized using air, artillery, infantry, and special forces? What was the predicted culminating point and where would refuel stops need to be made? What actions were necessary to protect logistical replenishment? Launch DICE on enemy airfields to disable control towers and fighter jet navigation systems?

Constant learning. Constant attack. Computer Optimized Warfare.

Beyond Baghdad, Quds Forces pushed into Syria, racing toward the Jordanian border.

"Success in Korea. Artillery is firing relentlessly. Q-36 radars are stymied," Shayne said.

"Belarus is in chaos. Warsaw should be next," Gorham replied.

"Iran is having good success. Al-Maraki, the Iraqi prime minister is dead. They've inserted a Shi'a leader to take charge."

"Okay," Gorham said. "Next targets. North Koreans destroy South Korea and Japan. Russia pushes all the way to Brussels and Mons to capture NATO Headquarters. And Iran destroys Jordan and Israel."

Shayne nodded. On the television screen, the first reports of the nuclear missile strike in Tokyo were scrolling across the crawl as muted anchors were speaking with anxious faces beneath BREAKING NEWS banners.

"The next stage of course is total nuclear warfare. The Tokyo shot was your one blue chip. We need the biometric key for the Russian nukes to attack the U.S. and the biometric key for the Iranian nukes pointed at Israel. Based on my estimates it will take less than seventy-two hours for the United States and its allies to figure out how to remedy the RATs we placed in their weapons and airplanes over the last two years."

In perhaps the most comprehensive and lethal clandestine hacking effort, Manaslu's team of code writers had easily hacked every major defense industry contractor in the western world. Minor algorithmic changes they inputted into the weapons systems' global positioning and target homing systems resulted in major misses for today's highly digitized weaponry. Shayne had done the initial breaches of the defense companies and then turned over the exploitation to a hacker of nearly equal skill. Gorham had named the entire effort Operation Alpine Summit for operational security purposes. The team of hackers believed they were making a video game as Shayne had placed a false environment in the foreground of the digitized environment. They had been mostly successful. RATs sat dormant for up to two years. They had full confidence, but no real idea, whether the plan would work. If it didn't, the U.S. airplanes and cruise missiles would stymie their efforts. But the initial indicators were that the

RATs were able to change at least a digit in the GPS guidance systems, steering the missiles and counterfire artillery off course, leaving U.S. forces defenseless against the lethal and kinetic armament of its adversaries.

Now, with the conventional mission underway and his nuclear provocation in the air, Gorham needed to get to Iran where his Manaslu facility was. Like the others, it had a full command and control center that allowed only those biometrically cleared into the inner sanctum.

He turned and spread his arms, looking out over the empty Manaslu Lab, save Shayne's worried countenance. "Airplane ready? As we say, *we're bringing genius to the world!*"

CHAPTER 7

*T*HE XC-17 GLOBEMASTER CARGO PLANE HAD LANDED AT THE RE-mote airfield near the Michigan farm and picked up Mahegan and his crew, including Cassie, O'Malley, and Owens.

Once airborne again, General Savage joined Mahegan and team in the command and control pod in the belly of the aircraft. They sat huddled in a small containerized high tech center that was secured by multiple fasteners hooked into the D-Rings and metallic ribs of the floor. They faced each other behind small platforms and each had a laptop open, except O'Malley who had three screens he was monitoring. Satellites poked from the aircraft like small shark fins along the fuselage.

"Left the B-team behind at the barn to monitor your captives. Got Hobart and Van Dreeves in there from another team," Savage said.

"They're good men, boss. Not the B team." Mahegan knew Hobart and Van Dreeves from his operator days. They were experienced, professional warfighters. He did, however, wonder what exactly they might do with the prisoners. Neither of the men smiled much, nor did they have a whole lot to say. They were execution oriented to the max.

"Roger. Good men. All of you," Savage said.

Mahegan nodded, curious. It was rare for Savage to provide a compliment and something unpleasant typically followed.

"Sean, keep doing what you're doing, but listen up," Savage said.

O'Malley nodded and continued to click the keyboard.

Savage continued. "We've got a nuke in Tokyo. North Korea steamrolling through the DMZ. Artillery fire is lethal. MiGs flying at will. Same thing in Baghdad. Got a report General Saddiqi, the Quds Force commander, launched a decapitation operation and now Iran is pushing through Syria and leaning on the Jordanian border. Russians have crossed the border in Belarus and Minsk is about to fall. A weird synchronization between power grids, cyber capabilities, directed energy, and these attacks is being reported in all three locations."

"Has to be what Sean found and the cook told us," Mahegan said. "RINK alliance—Russia, Iran, and North Korea. Simultaneous actions."

"Which we know are rarely simultaneous based on our experiences. So how the hell did all this happen without a whiff?"

"Great question, general," O'Malley said over his shoulder.

"I know it's a great question. That's why I asked it."

Given the gravity of the situation, neither Mahegan nor his team commented on the general's crusty remark. Too much to think about.

O'Malley stopped typing and turned around. "Okay, I've still got a long way to go, but the cook has given us some direction here. I've found indicators in the Dark Web that Russia, Iran and North Korea have been working together for two years. They've been trading secrets and technology. They have partnered with someone that I've been unable to locate so far, but I believe it's related to the attack at the pub. This individual or country or whatever it is, has created a form of optimized warfare. They're attacking the Internet of Things, the bandwidth spectrum, frequencies, and electrical grids all simultaneously. Perfect synchronization or close to it, boss."

The plane pushed through the night. The four teammates looked at the general, waiting for him to respond. O'Malley ran a hand through his thinning red hair. Owens scratched at his growing black beard. Cassie's brow was furrowed as she read something on her screen.

"Can you shut it down?" Savage asked.

"Most likely there are ground based command centers in each of these countries that communicate with a single satellite. The satellite is the big computer in the sky. Getting to that though, is impossible, I think. If we can locate the ground based centers we can put a nuke on them or potentially put troops on them if they're shooting our nukes out of the sky," O'Malley offered.

"Okay, I'm breaking you into two teams of two," Savage said.

"No way, boss," Mahegan replied.

"You're not calling the shots just yet, Jake. Listen to me and then tell me what you think," Savage said in his harshest voice.

"Roger," Mahegan replied.

"Two teams of two. Sean and Patch, you guys get Korea. Jake and Cassie, you two get Iran. We're on our way to Wake Island in the Pacific right now. There you'll each board a separate experimental B-2 Bomber. It will fly at forty thousand feet and deliver you close enough so that you can do high altitude opening and steer toward the target. Once you land, your mission is to disable these command centers."

"What about Russia?" Mahegan asked.

"My guys at JSOC are handling that."

"What the hell are we?"

"You're off the books, Jake. The key is that between Sean and Cassie, you've got the capability to take this thing offline from the inside. If our cyber folks can get in, we'll wave you off, but I may need boots on the ground."

"Why can't we stay together and you put SEALs or Delta or Rangers on the others? Seems like a suicide mission. Where are these targets?"

"Like I said. All my deployable combat cyber capability is with you, meaning Sean and Cassie. Regarding the targets, we're not sure. We think we know where the Russian one is and SEAL Team Six is headed that way. But given all the targets we've got, I've got JSOC in a three point stance to go anywhere. I'm prepositioning them around the globe and they will be ready if you need them. The 82nd Airborne is at green ramp right now flowing onto airplanes to get forward deployed. Same with the 101st Airborne and 10th Mountain Divisions. Big Army is moving."

Full mobilization of the U.S. Army's rapid reaction force, the 18th Airborne Corps, was serious business. Mahegan thought of his time in the Eighty-second Airborne and Delta Force and knew that Fort Bragg was a beehive of activity right now. He imagined his team's arc on the airplane. They would be landing on a remote coral reef in the western part of the Pacific Ocean that had just enough hardstand for a runway and a fuel pump. It was curious to Mahegan that Savage was not employing JSOC to its fullest extent against the potential targets at the nexus of the attacks. But then again, with full scale conventional and nuclear war either imminent or happening, the country would be mobilized in a way not since World War II and SEALs, Delta, and Rangers would be needed to attack high value targets such as enemy commanders and political leaders.

O'Malley had gone back to work. Each team member scrolled through current news feeds and read updated Top Secret/Special Category intelligence that was comparted by code words requiring the most sensitive clearances.

After an hour, he stopped and said, "Oh my God."

"What you got, Sean?" Mahegan asked.

"There's a meeting of the RINK leaders at the Iranian command center tomorrow."

"You're sure, Sean?" Savage asked. Skeptical by nature, Savage had been burned before by bad intelligence. He needed no further reminder than the four people who occupied the command and control pod with him. In the not too distant past, Mahegan and Cassie had rescued Savage, Owens, and O'Malley from near death. Syrian terrorists disguised as refugees had penetrated the once secure Zebra communications system and lured each of the operatives, save Mahegan, into a trap.

"We've got North Korea," O'Malley said. "What I've been working on. Saw a confirmation for tomorrow from the North Korean techie reporting to something called ComWar. So I went to ComWar and pushed through as far as I could go. It kept finding me and pushing me out. But while I was in there for a few seconds I saw a response in Cyrillic that I translated as meaning they are attending."

"Meaning Russia and North Korea are in?" Mahegan asked.

"Yes. Yazd, Iran," O'Malley said.

"Yazd. The Kharanaq Mountains. We suspect that Iran's enrichment plant is in Yazd and that's where the Iranians have been making nukes."

"That dumb ass nuke deal with Iran got us here," Savage said, thinking. He rubbed his face and looked at Mahegan. "Jake?"

"You know what I'm going to say," Mahegan said. "Look at those television screens. RINK is on the move. There's a technological thing happening here and there's a ground military thing we need to take care of. The two are probably linked. Sean's the best there is, but we can't count on him beating RINK before Russia launches nukes. Being an American, a nuke in downtown Tokyo is a lot different from a nuke in downtown New York City."

"That's for damn sure," Savage said.

"And if RINK has been able to manipulate the missiles on our airplanes, have they been able to fractionally impact the guidance systems on our nuclear weapons? In that event, mutual assured destruction only applies to us," Mahegan continued, "because our retaliation is meaningless."

Everyone remained silent as Mahegan's words soaked in. He was right. If the RINK alliance had been able to penetrate the defense contractors and military weapons development processes then what would prevent them from boring into the nuclear weapons arsenal and making a minor change that would prevent the opening of a silo, the loading of a submarine tube, the functioning of the missile in flight. With everything digitized today was it unreasonable to believe that someone could hack the system and impact the accuracy or responsiveness of the United States' nuclear arsenal?

It was a chilling thought. The nation's neck would be laid bare against the fangs of the RINK wolves.

Mahegan continued, "So we stay together as a team and jump

into this meeting. Kill or capture who we can. Find out who the mysterious fourth element is. We know who the actors on the ground are, but how do we find the one synchronizing this unless we actually go in?"

Three bells rang loudly in the XC-17.

The loadmaster came running up to the command and control pod and leaned in the open door. "We've got Russian jets approaching!"

CHAPTER 8

GORHAM WATCHED ANOTHER VIDEO. SINCE HE HAD NOT BEEN ABLE to video chat Dr. Draganova at any point in the last few days, he watched videos he had secretly taped using microdrones he called ManaBlades. He had constructed them to conform to their environment. In an office they could be an additional pen in a pen well or a curio on the shelf. In Iran, they looked like desert grasshoppers perched on rocks.

In his meeting place with Draganova, he always deployed a small moth drone to sit on a chandelier or lamp out of her view.

He watched the video on his tablet. The black hair. The pouting lips. The sultry voice. The bare, crossed legs. One stiletto hanging off her heel, dangling by her toes.

"Talk to me, Ian. Unpack that box. Lay it on the floor. Tell me what you see."

"I see myself standing on a miniature globe. Arms spread wide. Providing for the people. My people."

"What makes you think you can provide for everyone? The world?"

"Because I created this company and made it bigger than anything else. Nothing can stop me."

"You don't see yourself as human? Infallible? Mortal?"

"I don't believe in the concept of mortality, Belina."

"So, you can't die? You'll live forever?"

"Quite possibly."

"In this body? Or in some other presence?"

"Can't you see, doctor? I'm everywhere."

He remembered showing her the video of her in her bedroom, masturbating with a vibrator. The slow shower she had taken afterward. Standing on the balcony in a sheer robe, the wind lifting it like a superhero's cape. He returned his attention to the video.

"You watch me? Do you love me, Ian? Is that why?"

"You're not mad?"

She smiled. "You wanted a show, I gave you a show."

"But how did you know?"

She turned and looked at the lamp. "That moth? There's one just like it in my apartment and my office." Dr. Draganova smiled. "Quite the coincidence, huh?"

"I do love you, Belina. I want you," he said.

"Don't you think that's a bit cliché for a man of your stature? Loving his psychiatrist?"

"I have to love someone. It might as well be you," he said, the words ringing hollow.

"Sweeter words a woman has never heard."

"You know what I mean."

"I rarely do, Ian. You're a complex man. Brilliant. Handsome. You can have any woman you want. Why me? Because I'm inside your mind? That intrigues you?"

"Maybe you're right," he muttered.

"If I stood and walked to you. Kissed you. Removed your clothes. Made love to you. Would that make you fall deeper in love with me? Or are you looking for conquest?"

"I would like that," he whispered. "Is that what you want?"

She paused. The video showed her processing.

Gorham remembered the moment. It was a personal question he'd put to her. Initially, he'd thought he had caught her off balance, but upon reevaluation, Gorham believed it was he who had been outmaneuvered. He returned his attention to his tablet.

"Unpack the box. What do you see?"

"Desire, perhaps. Maybe also something—someone—I can't have."

She nodded. "And what is it that you truly want, Ian?

"For everyone to love me, including you."

"And if even I love you, then everyone else must?"

"Yes."

He blushed at her beauty . . . and power over him.

He snapped his tablet shut, stood, and walked the aisle of his up-fitted Boeing Extended Range 777. In addition to the sleeping quarters, he had a smaller version of the hologram battlefield toward the rear of the aircraft. In between that and the comfort zone where he stood was another command center that afforded him total situational awareness of all combat activities.

Shayne pecked away at the computers and provided an update by having each primary battle front on one of four large fifty-five inch monitors. "In North Korea, you can see the DPRK, the North Korean Army, penetrating Seoul. They've taken some casualties, but are about to breakout to the south. Once that happens, the port of Pusan is in sight within twenty-four hours, I would think. ComWar is working. Gets better with every tactical engagement. The refuel trucks are automatically moving up when the tanks hit one quarter full—we originally programmed that at one eighth—but given all the narrow roads it takes longer for the trucks to move through to tanks and other vehicles. The computer optimized it at one quarter so that we don't have as many tanks running out of gas. This will allow them to do a refuel on the move and keep the momentum all the way to Pusan. The jets are providing air cover. The worm we sent into the major defense contractors over the past two years has been everything we hoped for. Remote access Trojans are impacting navigation, guidance, weapons, and flight systems." He pointed at the map where red icons were gathering near bridges that spanned the Han River to the south of Seoul and its vast sprawling suburbs of office towers, apartment buildings, and hotels. Dozens of bridges dotted the map where the half mile wide Han River meandered from the south of Seoul to the west.

To their right, all of this played out on the hologram battlefield. The jet was outfitted with specialized satellite communications systems so much that the entire airplane was like a low orbit satellite. Shark fin antennae protruded from the fuselage in angular fashion, making the aircraft unique with its powerful, standalone capabilities.

They discussed the relative positioning of Iranian Forces pushing through Al Anbar Province into the Syrian Desert and beyond the Jordanian border toward the important crossroads at Mafraq. Tanks, artillery, fuel trucks, and infantry were all moving toward the capitol city of Amman. Beyond Jordan lay Israel, the ultimate target.

The Russian forces were laying siege to Minsk, surrounding the town with tanks, artillery, and infantry forces as bombers and jets pummeled the feeble Belarus military. While the Russian and Belarus militaries had a close relationship, politically the two countries had escalating tensions. The plan for the Russians had been to parlay a joint military exercise into the defeat of the Belarus military. During the war game the military commanders had agreed that the Russian forces would represent themselves, while the Belarus military portray NATO forces defending from Minsk to Poland. Unbeknownst to the Belarus military, the Russian military units were using live ammunition at the onset of the "exercise."

"In addition to inflicting casualties on the Eighty-second Airborne Division brigade combat team, the other good thing here is that the Russians already have troops lined up on the Polish border. Minsk is one thing, more symbolic, but Warsaw will be a whole different ballgame. Once that falls, this won't be like the Crimea issue, as a capture of Minsk might seem to the casual observer. Warsaw was the spark of capitalism in the former Soviet bloc," Gorham said. "That counts."

"So, RAIL is functioning smoothly as it updates ComWar automatically," Shayne said with a hint of pride. He had created the rapid automated integrated learning system that used machine learning, specifically a subfield called transfer learning, that allowed for the simultaneous storing of knowledge learned while solving a specific problem and then applying that learned solution to a similar, but different problem set. What was the perfect call forward time of the autonomous refuel trucks? They had guessed at one eighth tank based upon simulations. But computers rarely emulated the friction of real life, therefore the machine had learned and adjusted automatically. Meanwhile, it was simultaneously updating the call forward times for the fuel trucks supplying every form of vehicle.

"Look at that." Gorham pointed at the fourth flat screen television. He had manipulated the control to zoom in on the firebreak where Stasovich had last been seen.

"Where did he go?"

Gorham smiled at Shayne. "I told you. The guy is unstoppable. "I've already sent him an airplane."

Dax Stasovich ran a bloody hand across his mesh-link wearable technology body armor. The heavy fabric had mostly protected him from the onslaught of weaponry that his nemesis Jake Mahegan had assuredly unleashed upon him. It had also slowed his egress from the farm where he had spied upon Mahegan, Owens, O'Malley, and Bagwell. He had studied them all.

After the machine-gun rounds and rockets had rained down upon him, he had feigned injury, though he *was* injured. Shrapnel had splattered into the back of his neck and hands as he turned his head away from the drone that was wreaking havoc on him. He had laid motionless for fifteen minutes—time he didn't have to spare—out of an abundance of caution. He had used the noise of the cargo plane landing to escape and evade. Unfortunately, Mahegan had been smart enough to destroy his truck, but he had flagged down the next motorist, pulled the unsuspecting man from the driver's seat, snapped his neck, and had made his egress in a prissy Prius that barely allowed for his significant body mass.

He wanted to avenge his humiliation by Mahegan as much as he wanted to satisfy his benefactor, Gorham. As a private military contractor for Copperhead, Inc., Stasovich had taken liberties with enemy prisoners of war—called *detainees* by the bureaucrats—and had been part of a human trafficking chain that ultimately flowed back to the swamps of eastern North Carolina. Mahegan had unwittingly stumbled upon that operation, which had been pulling in some pretty good coin for Stasovich. After Mahegan had blown the cover on Copperhead's smuggling of ghost prisoners to the United States, Stasovich lost his job and everything that was important to him—his women, financial independence, and seventy foot cigarette boat, with which he roared through the intracoastal waterway. It was true that some of the prisoners had escaped from their lair in Dare County to conduct terrorist attacks, but nothing that severe. Just a few hundred Americans killed and injured.

If anything, Stasovich thought, *it was a good reminder to the American public that they shouldn't take their security for granted.*

Additionally, he was beyond curious about everything he had been overhearing between Gorham and Shayne regarding the RINK alliance. After Stasovich had lost his job in North Carolina, he fled the state and holed up in New York City—an easy place to get lost. He met Gorham in a lower east side nightclub where he had been working as security—a bouncer—and Gorham had managed to get into a scuffle with another wormy tech company genius. They were arguing about who was the wealthiest and the verbal lashings had turned physical. Turned out, the other guy had been a collegiate boxer and pummeled Gorham until Stasovich stepped in and landed one punch on the boxer, who dropped like a shot quail.

Stasovich had helped Gorham to his feet and ushered him to a private place where the man could gather his dignity and clean up.

"You saved my life," Gorham said. "What can I do for you?"

"Well, I doubt he would have killed you," Stasovich had replied. "What's that accent?"

Immediately, Stasovich knew that Gorham was thinking something else when he had asked that question. The bouncer had pivoted and responded with an open-ended question. "What are you offering?"

After a moment, Gorham had said, "I like it. The indirect approach. I've read Sun Tzu, Clausewitz, all the others. I might have something for you if you're willing to travel."

"I like traveling," Stasovich had replied.

Gorham had nodded slowly, his curly light brown locks remaining motionless.

"I'm an American citizen, but have some Russian lineage by way of Serbia," Stasovich had added to fully answer Gorham's question.

That conversation had led to Stasovich becoming Gorham's one man personal security detail. He had traveled everywhere with the tycoon, all around the world multiple times. Stasovich had gathered that Gorham was putting into place something big. Combat action on every continent except Antarctica—maybe even there, who knew?

Once Stasovich recovered from the attack by Mahegan, he chatted securely with Gorham, who instructed him to go to Oakland County airfield where an airplane would pick him up to deliver him to an undisclosed location. After securing the vehicle, he pulled into the private jet portion of the airfield and climbed aboard the waiting Gulfstream 5. When he laid back in a leather recliner he noticed two duffle bags in the seat next to him as the pilots shot up from the runway. One duffel had a change of clothes, basic personal hygiene items, and medical supplies such as antiseptic, sutures, and bandages. The other contained all his favorite weapons.

Stasovich stared into the night sky unaware of exactly where he was headed, but certain that his destination included a rendezvous with Mahegan.

CHAPTER 9

"W HAT'S A MIG DOING OFF OUR WING?" SAVAGE ASKED, PEERING into the night through one of the XC-17 porthole windows.

Mahegan said, "Sean?"

"Working it, man. We're over the Pacific nowhere near Russia. I'm inside their operations database and there is an order from yesterday but I can't read it. Just see the date."

"What about the cook? She had an accent," Mahegan said.

"Under no circumstances," Savage barked.

"Boss, we're defenseless up here. Give me a little rope," Mahegan said.

"So you can hang all of us, Jake? No way."

"Look at her. She's tied up with a sandbag on her head."

"You put her on a computer, she can probably tell the rest of the Russian military who we are, where we are, and what we're doing."

"Well, if the MiG puts a missile up our ass it's kind of a moot point, don't you think?"

Savage blinked and looked at the cook's inert form.

Then through the sandbag came a muffled voice. "I can do it. Your guy Sean can watch me. I don't want to die like this," the cook said. When everyone stared at her, she shrugged and said, "The battery died on my headphones. I can hear you just fine."

Mahegan wasted no time. "Patch, untie her. Sean, make room. Let her see what you're seeing. Cassie, keep an eye on the MiG.

I'm thinking we've got maybe a minute before he figures out this is a high value target. He's radioing in the tail number of the aircraft and if their hacking capabilities are as demonstrated, they'll know that he's got a high value target to knock out of the sky."

Owens walked the cook over to O'Malley's computer terminal with the two large monitors reflecting gibberish back at them.

"What's your name?" Mahegan asked.

The cook looked up at Mahegan, who was almost a foot taller. "Spartak," she said.

Mahegan stared at her, nodded, believing it was bullshit, and said, "Okay, Spartak. Figure it out. You've got about a minute."

Her smile showed surpisingly good teeth. Beyond the shaved head and the thin veneer of almost artificially downgraded appearance, she had all the makings of a beautiful woman. Full lips. Wide brown eyes. Small, upturned nose. High cheekbones. Perhaps she was Eastern European.

Only a short while ago, Mahegan had taken on the Bulgarian hackers responsible for the Carbanak hack and the Highway-Hack, as it was being called, that shut down millions of cars while driving on the highways around America.

"Better to strangle someone up close than kill them with a missile," Spartak said under her breath.

Mahegan processed the comment. She was more than a hacker, for sure.

O'Malley stood from his console after blanking the screen and eyed Mahegan. "This is not without risk."

The plane hit a rough patch of air, rattling the command pod as if to emphasize O'Malley's point. Mahegan remained silent and nodded at Spartak and then the seat.

The cook sat down in O'Malley's chair still wearing her grease stained white T-shirt and black pants. Her head was shaved to a stubble and she had the pale features of someone who lived in their mother's basement. Mahegan hoped she could make the computer dance. O'Malley was the best he knew, but there was a legion of capability between O'Malley, who was superb, and someone who bored the Internet with nefarious purposes in mind.

The Internet of Things led to positives such as a refrigerator rec-ognizing the need for more milk and remotely texting the owner to pick some up after his last meeting of the day. But it also height-ened the ease of human trafficking, bank heists, energy grid shut-downs, and now weapons malfunctions.

Spartak's fingers flew across the keyboard in a whir. Her eyes flicked between the two screens. "Two MiG 35-Ds. Two seaters. Four missiles each," she said in clipped sentences.

The tension in her voice was not reassuring to Mahegan, who looked at Savage as if to say, *be quiet. Let her do her job, whatever that may be.*

"They have instructions to make you land in Vladivostok."

"Distance?" Savage asked.

"Let her work," Mahegan said, prompting a glare from the gen-eral. Mahegan nodded. *It's okay, boss.*

Spartak paused and looked over her shoulder at Mahegan. "You were right."

"A minute?" Mahegan asked.

"Precisely."

She turned back to the keyboard as Mahegan put on a headset and switched the internal communications system to the pilots.

"Okay, the two MiGs off our wings have instructions to fire on us in a minute. I'm looking at my watch and fifty seconds from now, I want you to do some pilot shit and slow this beast to stall so that it drops like a stone from the sky."

"You're crazy, Mahegan."

"Stu, thirty seconds we have a missile up our ass."

Mahegan knew both pilots, former air force AC-130 pilots that had been trained on flying this modified version of the XC-17 Globemaster cargo plane. Stu Langley was the pilot in command and had supported Mahegan in Afghanistan and Syria with deadly accurate gunfire on more than one occasion. Brian Sher-rod was his copilot, a quiet professional who loved flying. To get him to say hello was a good conversation.

After a five second pause, Stu said, "I know what I'm going to do."

"Roger. Just do it on my command. Cassie, grab everyone a

crewman's harness and static line with snap hook, please," Mahegan directed.

She darted to the rear of the airplane, secured the harnesses and snap hooks, connecting the two, knowing what Mahegan wanted. She passed them to each teammate, including the cook, who didn't acknowledge it.

Sweat poured from Spartak's glistening scalp. O'Malley watched as he stepped into his harness, perhaps even impressed at her skills. Owens fastened his harness to the interior of the control pod and stared through a Plexiglas window at the 105 mm howitzers that had been up-fitted into the XC-17. Not an AC-130, but the experimental aircraft might one day evolve into an AC-17, perhaps. The cannons could shoot perpendicular to the axis of movement of the aircraft and had limited lateral movement. Mahegan had thought of the guns first, but there wasn't time to reorient them, if it all possible, to the rear of the airplane where the MiGs would certainly take their shots from.

"What you got, Spartak?" Mahegan asked with fifteen seconds remaining. He placed the Velcro flap over his watch face and stared at the cook. Slipping the mesh vest over his large frame, he zipped up the front and snapped the hook into a D-ring on the frame of the command pod.

Like a hummingbird's wings, her fingers were nearly invisible as they clicked the keys. He was certain she was attempting to hack the two jets. How? He had no idea, but that's what he would do if he had the skills. O'Malley looked at him, shaking his head. Mahegan nodded.

Spartak's thumb slapped the space bar with a loud slap. She stood, grabbed her harness, managed to get it over her shoulders, and shouted, "Brace!"

Mahegan pressed his intercom button and said, "Stu, now."

Mahegan felt his stomach lurch into his throat. He had been on his share of wild aviation rides fraught with enemy fire and the accompanying maneuvers necessary to dodge the lead flying at them. But he had never felt an XC-17 in a free fall from the sky. He imagined they were losing a thousand feet per second. He managed to put his hands against the roof of the pod and prevent a head strike that could have left him unconscious. The g forces had the entire team pinned against the roof as if they were in some antigravity ride at the county fair.

The cameras showing the MiGs continued to function. A smoke trail angled toward the camera. Mahegan braced for impact, just as Spartak had warned. Chaff enveloped the airplane and the camera became obscured. Waiting for impact was exactly like the moment before a paratrooper's feet hit the ground at the end of the jump. He knew it was coming, but it would come when it came. There was no rushing it.

Mahegan was surprisingly at peace with his lot in life. Nothing flashed before his eyes. He eyed his teammates as best he could in their awkward positions around the pod. If he was going to die, these were the people he wanted to be with. If death awaited him momentarily, he was doing what he loved doing—serving his country. No sacrifice too small or too great. It all counted. Whether riding in a cargo plane or slitting the throat of an ISIS terrorist, Mahegan had done it all. He had contributed ten lifetimes of combat to his nation in his short life.

A brave man dies once; a coward many times.

Chief Iowa had muttered that phrase once and while not a Croatan like Mahegan, Iowa's sentiment was universal as far as Mahegan was concerned. He thought of his guidepost Croatan adage. *It is better to die a hero than grow old.*

He locked eyes with Cassie, who was secured with a nylon cable and snap link and laying flat against the ninety degree V where the vertical wall met the ceiling of the command pod. She looked comfortable, if that was possible. The g forces were making it impossible for any of them to move other than make minor hand movements. If the missiles did not destroy the XC-17—and them with it—the aircraft was almost certainly in an unrecoverable delta dive, pushing the plane beyond its structural limits.

The aircraft cleared the chaff and the cameras were piping the night sky back at them. Two more missiles smoked toward them. It didn't seem possible that the first two had missed, but perhaps the chaff had tricked them. The two MiGs briefly crossed the lens of the camera.

Again, Mahegan braced for impact by finding that peaceful place in his mind. He found himself wishing that he could reach out and hold Cassie's hand. Mahegan and Cassie's vacation to Bald Head Island now seemed both splendid and stupid. They'd connected. Fallen in love. Made love. Held each other. Scars healed—physical and mental. They'd been wounded in the toughest fight either thought they might face. He wanted to die with those memories of Bald Head Island and Cassie on his mind. Peace. Happiness. For once.

This was what love did.

There, they'd promised to die heroes *and* grow old. In some cultures, Mahegan's thirty-one years would be ancient. There on the tranquil beaches of Bald Head Island, he'd found what had been eluding him—love.

Cassie was tough and nurturing. She had lost her parents, part of the mental healing that had taken place. It wasn't so long ago that Mahegan had lost his father. And he thought briefly of his mother, Samantha, with her blond hair and freckles, teaching him how to surf and swim in the Outer Banks of North Carolina.

Cassie imperceptibly shook her head as the plane began to rattle. But still, the missile had seemingly missed.

"Jake!"

The headset had stayed glued to his ears. He held the coiled wire and transmit button in his hand, which was slammed against the ceiling. He managed to press his thumb against the black button, which seemed a Herculean task. "Roger," he muttered.

"Not much time before we hit the ocean. Four missiles have missed. For some reason they're not using guns."

"Four's all they got. Level this bitch out," Mahegan said through gritted teeth.

"Don't think I can," Stu said.

Mahegan and Stu had shared many a beer where they'd talked about his heritage and Stu's upbringing in Bozeman, Montana. They were more similar than one might have imagined. Both grew up on the frontier. Mahegan in the Atlantic Ocean. Stu on the high plains.

"You can do it, brother." Mahegan's voice was raspy. The plane was shuddering. Rivets started popping.

"You know I'll do my best, brother," Stu said.

Mahegan felt the airplane rattle. Thought he could hear rivets coming apart as the C-17 was in a near delta dive toward the Pacific Ocean.

"Jake!" Stu shouted into the headset again.

The plane was rattling and the centrifugal forces continued to pin him to the ceiling of the command pod, a rectangular insert inside the cavernous airplane.

"Roger," Mahegan muttered. "Anytime now, Stu."

"I can't recover! Need to eject the pod!"

"Come join us then." Mahegan didn't like the thought of the crew biting it while he and the team in the command pod potentially survived.

"I've got to maneuver this so we can drop you," Stu said. "We can't make it back there."

The two operators knew what was being said. Stu was going to sacrifice his life and that of his crew so Mahegan and his team could Charlie Mike—continue the mission.

"Eject?"

"Maybe. If we get you out in time. Our stabilizer is shot. This thing isn't flyable. Only thing I can try to do is lift the nose. I've already dropped the ramp. Trying to get some drag."

"Roger."

The C-17 had not only been equipped with 105 mm cannons, but also with a glass cockpit that allowed for pilot ejection. Given the missions that Savage and his team conducted, the up-fit included safety precautions for the pilots, as well. Mahegan was hopeful that the crew chief outside of the pod had his jump parachute on and would bail when the pod ejected. Two cargo parachutes were secured to the top of the pod and connected to the parachute static lines in the aircraft. If Stu was able to get the C-17 level for drop operations, the pod would slide out and the weight would pull the static lines until they deployed the parachutes from the pack trays atop the pod. A small cotton tie would then snap free from the static line when the parachute and static line were at their maximum length and taut.

The plane shuddered more, but leveled . . . and slowed. Mahegan could feel the adjustments Stu was making. The plane began banking as if spiraling in the air. Without warning, the pod slid from its secure position and they were free-falling through the sky. Mahegan felt the parachutes deploy and slow their descent. With the sudden change in acceleration and speed, the entire team in the pod fell to the floor.

"Stu ejected us," Mahegan said.

"Where the fuck are we?" Savage barked.

"GPS showing us about twenty miles off Attu Island," O'Malley said.

They were all either on their knees or laying prone in the command pod as it floated through the air.

"How soon can we get the backup command aircraft here?" Savage asked.

"It was trailing us by an hour. Let's message it to land at Casco Station while the Coast Guard sends a search and rescue for us." Mahegan was remembering the flight route. The command pod had a beacon on it. "Make sure they send two helicopters. One for Stu and his team."

"Roger. Trying to get our comms to work. All our connections were ripped out, but we have stubby antennae as backup."

The pod worked as designed as O'Malley made contact with the U.S. Coast Guard Station on the most remote island of the Aleutian chain.

"Two HH-65 Dolphins on the way," O'Malley said.

The pod landed with a jarring thud into the water, like hitting concrete.

"Okay, team. Let's get the hatches open and the boats out," Mahegan said.

Though they had never rehearsed the drill, they found the two life rafts and popped the water tight hatches after ensuring they were not inverted. Mahegan helped each member of his team to the top of the rapidly sinking pod. As he pushed on the cook, he said, "Whatever you did, good job."

"You're welcome."

Mahegan noticed her thicker Russian accent. The fear had unmasked her ruse, perhaps.

"And I know you did that to save your own ass, so don't think you're golden," he said.

The cook said nothing as she climbed into the freezing air. Mahegan helped Cassie up the ladder and then followed her. Once on top and assured that he had all of his charges, including General Savage, Mahegan removed a thermite grenade from his tactical vest and tossed it into the container before shutting the hatch. The explosion sounded like a dull thud as half the pod was already underwater. O'Malley had one raft inflated and was boarding Savage and the cook. Owens was inflating the second raft and connected it with a rope to O'Malley's raft. The wind was blowing at least thirty miles an hour. The sea chop was white capping at five to ten feet. Air temperature was below freezing while the water temperature was probably in the high thirties or low forties. They wouldn't last long if the Coast Guard could not find them.

Mahegan helped Cassie into Owens' rubber raft. They all donned life jackets as Mahegan stepped from the sinking pod into the raft. There were paddles, but they were comically useless.

Rough seas filled the boats with water. The sky was black, lit only by the sweeping array of stars in the northern sky. The galaxies reminded Mahegan how vast the ocean was. If the GPS was not working, there was no way anyone would ever find them. The Coast Guard needed to hurry.

After thirty minutes of bailing water using combat helmets and hands, the distant thrum of helicopter blades rode in on the howling wind. Mahegan retrieved the flare gun from the emergency kit, inserted a flare, and fired it skyward. The burning yellow and white arc cut through the black night like the single band of a rainbow. As the blade sounds grew louder, he fired another.

The Coast Guard HH-65 with its unique Fenestron-ducted rear fan blades was soon hovering above them. The rescue swimmer

dropped into the water and began helping each member of Mahegan's team onto the seat and winch that pulled them into the
helicopter.

As soon as they were all wrapped in blankets, Mahegan looked
across the floor of the helicopter at Cassie and nodded. Then he
stared at Savage, who was sitting next to him.

"Is our backup there yet, Jake?" Savage asked. "Check on Stu,
also."

"I'm checking," Mahegan said.

Tugging on the leg of the crew chief, Mahegan managed to get
a headset and confirmed with the pilots that a JSOC command
and control aircraft was twenty minutes from landing.

"No time to waste. We land, we transfer, we take off. We've got
to get to Iran," Savage said.

"I'm with you, boss."

The helicopter spun to a landing near the taxiing backup XC-17,
which lowered its ramp. Mahegan pointed at the aircraft. "There's
our ride. Let's go."

Holding her M4 carbine and rucksack, Cassie smirked at Jake
as she jumped from the helicopter. "That was a hell of a ride we
just had."

"I think it only gets more interesting from here, Cassie."

Cassie nodded as they jogged to the yawning ramp of the C-17,
engines whining. They had named the drop zones near the sus-
pected meeting locations of the RINK leaders. The intel feed indicated that four airplanes had landed within a relatively short
period of time closest to drop zone Romeo near the village of
Yazd, Iran.

Once seated in a replica of the command and control pod they
had just ridden into the Pacific Ocean, Mahegan put on his headset and watched his team take their seats. Savage across from him;
Cassie to Savage's left; Owens to Mahegan's right; and O'Malley
at the far end where he had two monitors and the ability to access
the most remote regions of the Deep Web. Spartak, the cook, was
still handcuffed and seated next to O'Malley, intently studying
the screen full of ones and zeroes.

"Did Stu, Sherrod, and the loadmaster make it?" Mahegan asked the pilot.

"Chopper has three beacons. Don't know yet. Word is they got out, but that could be all bullshit rumor, Jake." The pilot was Rod Miller, another former Task Force member who had flown every special operations rotary and fixed wing aircraft in the inventory. He was as close to Stu and Sherrod as he was with anyone, but he hid the emotion in his voice that Mahegan knew was there.

"Roger that. Let me know when you get word, Rod," Mahegan said. "Flight time?"

"Roger. About ten hours provided we don't have any more incidents."

"Ten hours? This thing will be over in ten hours."

"Sorry, Jake. This baby only goes so fast. I can push her to 500 knots, but that's it unless you want me to rip some rivets off."

"No thanks. Been there, done that," Mahegan said.

Miller chuckled. "Yeah, well we've got escort leapfrogging with us. Word is that the North Korean Army is all the way into Seoul. None of our shit is hitting them. Crypto bombs followed by directed energy followed by electromagnetic pulse."

O'Malley was waving a hand at Mahegan. "Hey, boss?"

"Thanks, Rod." Then to O'Malley, "What you got, Sean?"

"Two things. You see here"—O'Malley pointed at a flat screen monitor above his dual computer monitors—"an orbital image of the earth rotating slowly against a black background." He zoomed in and used his finger to circle the Korean Peninsula, the Middle East, and the northern tier of Europe that included Belarus, Poland, Germany, and Belgium. Just above the earth in each of those locations were groupings of icons that resembled tiny satellites. "Somehow, we've got three sets of stealth microsatellites. I mean DARPA has been working on this for years, but I don't think they ever got there."

"What's their function?" Mahegan asked.

The entire team was huddled around O'Malley's computer station. Mahegan felt a hand rest on his shoulder. Cassie leaned into him, ostensibly to make room for the others crowding around.

Just another comrade joining the huddle. But her touch felt good and sent his mind reeling once again.

They were back on Bald Head Island. He and Cassie were laying naked in bed, her head on his forever wounded left deltoid. A piece of his best friend's Humvee had branded a lazy Z scar in his left arm just below his ranger tab tattoo. Who knew? Maybe a part of Sergeant Colgate was on that hot metal as well. He didn't mind the pain, because it was a constant reminder to do better every day.

As she rested her hand on his chest, Cassie asked him, "Jake, what's your love language?"

He had no idea what a love language was and by extension what his might be. "Thought I kind of just demonstrated that."

Cassie smiled. "Yeah, well, it was a great demo, but you know even though I'm ranger-qualified and army and all that good stuff, I'm still a woman underneath all of that."

"Yeah, the demo made that very clear."

She bit his arm playfully. "Be quiet. Physical touch, words of affirmation, acts of service, quality time, or gifts. Which one speaks to you most in love?"

"I like all that stuff. Except the affirmation thing. I know when I've done well and when I've failed. I've done both and I don't need some bullshit trying to pump me up if I jacked something up."

Cassie laughed. "So we know it's not words of affirmation, such as great job! Which of those is most important, Jake, to you?" She touched his pectoral muscle above his heart as if to point at his soul.

"I always want time," Mahegan said after a long pause. "Because it's the one thing that you can never get back. It's always moving forward."

"So it's quality time. I'll tell you up front. Mine is physical touch."

"Well, the demo had lots of that—some pretty quality time if you ask me."

With her hand resting on that same shoulder, he knew she was communicating to him her need for that touch even through uniforms and in the back of a yawing C-17 aircraft with five others standing around.

"They are controlling the attacks," Spartak said, standing next to O'Malley and pointing at the screen where the circles high-lighted the icons. "A high altitude airplane or rocket deploys these in a pod. The pod opens and the satellites, no bigger than soccer balls, pop open and begin doing their thing."

"Which is what?" Mahegan asked, looking at the woman, un-sure of her ethnicity or nationality. Could he trust anything she said? She had saved them from certain death, but perhaps pri-marily had saved her own ass.

"Cyber-bombs, machine learning, automated resupply, you name it," Spartak said.

"Nukes?" General Savage asked.

"It can launch nukes, yes. The algorithm cycles through a mil-lion codes a second until they break the encryption and can launch. The Internet of Things has made everything easier and everything more vulnerable."

"So the nuke that hit Tokyo?" Mahegan asked.

Spartak paused. "That seemed a bit early, don't you think?"

"Who the hell are you?" Savage growled.

"I already told you. I am Spartak. World's best hacker. I live in the Deep Web. I can disarm Russian MiGs that want to shoot us down. That's all you need to know. Everything else flows from that."

"That's why they wanted you?" Mahegan asked. "The raid at the bar?"

"I was at the bar simply to hide. Off the grid as you say. Some-one posted a Snapchat with me in the background. The enemy you face is so good that they were able to find my facial image on self-erasing snapchat and geo-locate me within hours."

"That's when we got the bump in intel," O'Malley said.

Never one for subtlety, Savage asked, "Are you working for the RINK?"

Spartak looked away, seemed to study the far corner of the command pod. "Enough questions for now. I am with you. I work with you. I am a survivor. These satellites are the real problem."

"Who's controlling the satellites?" Mahegan asked. "What you're saying is that this isn't three separate actions, but one coordinated simultaneous attack."

"I never met the controller. Always very careful. But you are right. One big attack. All at once. That was the plan I saw," Spartak said.

"You saw the plan?" Cassie asked, incredulous.

"You look at a computer screen in the Deep Web and you see ones and zeroes. Gibberish. I see a plan. I see instructions on what code to write and for what purposes."

Mahegan listened, knew Spartak was an intelligence gem, and was glad they had captured her. They locked eyes and she blew him an air kiss that wasn't lost on Cassie.

"What's the second thing you have, Sean?" Mahegan asked.

O'Malley zoomed in on a portion of Iran and switched to the weather effects aspect of their software.

"Shamal headed toward the meeting location. No way you can jump into that," O'Malley said. A shamal was a giant sandstorm that looked like something out of a science fiction movie, an orange wall of sand picked up by winds moving at about forty miles per hour.

Cassie looked at Mahegan, no doubt remembering when they had cliff jumped using flying squirrel suits, as Mahegan had called them.

"That's good news and bad news," Mahegan said. "Makes the jump a little crazy, but buys us some time because their airplanes can't fly through that. The engines will gum up. But we can probably time it so that we come in behind it."

"So we time it to go in on the back side before the planes take off," Savage said.

"Right. What kind of intel do we have about who's on the ground?" Mahegan asked, knowing it was he and Cassie that were going in, not Savage.

Intelligence was Cassie's expertise. She pivoted away from Mahegan and faced the group, then turned toward the computers. "Sean, can you zoom in on the airfield?"

As O'Malley maneuvered the images of the Russian, Iranian, and North Korean leaders, Cassie spoke. "Well, it's either doppelgangers or the real deal. All three of the RINK political leaders. Ostensibly the decision makers. There's a fourth individual. We know this because four up-armored luxury jets landed on that runway."

"So let me ask a stupid question," Savage said. "Why don't we just drop a smart bomb down the pipe of wherever this meeting is taking place?"

O'Malley had four images on the screen. They were expanded satellite shots of four different airplanes, all sanitized with no country markings or tail numbers. Cassie played the video and showed each one landing, pulling into a hangar, and moments later a hardened black Mercedes Benz leaving the hangar and driving across the airfield about two miles to the evident compound in the side of a mountain. Only three cars had made the transit so far.

"There is no pipe," Spartak said, answering the general's question. "And the satellites will cyber bomb any aircraft that get close enough to drop a bomb. Just how I attacked the two MiGs, they can attack your bombers and fighters. Same with cruise missiles. The microsatellites are monitoring naval activities. Once a cruise missile is launched, if RINK hasn't already put a RAT in the guidance system, they will. And the satellites enable rapid machine learning."

"Rat?" Savage asked. "Like the Trojans?"

"Yes. Remote Access Trojan. RINK has been planning this war for at least two years. They've had time to infiltrate defense industry weapons makers and plant passive RATs in every system. They are programmed to sit there until the weapon is launched or until the microsatellite system activates it."

Mahegan studied Spartak. He tried to catch her eyes, but she looked away. She was withholding something.

"What? This is the way? They have something that can stop this?"

Spartak looked at Mahegan and nodded.

"There is a person for each country. They can stop everything. Or they can make everything happen. It is more than a simple flash drive, though. You must capture the person. Biometrics, voice recognition, fingerprints, and so on are required to access the system."

"You know this how?" Mahegan asked.

"I know. That's all that matters."

"And what do you mean when you say, 'make everything happen?'"

"Global nuclear war with the United States destroyed."

"Buy why?" Savage interjected.

"Why not?" Spartak shrugged, her lean shoulders angling up toward her neck.

Mahegan took control. "Who is the person?"

"I'm not sure about that. I imagine it is the man in charge and so have operated on that assumption."

Mahegan sighed, frustrated, but continued to question her.

"But why? Why are you operating on any assumptions? Why are you even here?"

"Because I'm someone who cares about the world and if I find information to nefarious plans I'll try to stop them. Maybe I wanted to be in that restaurant. Maybe I wanted to see them. Did you ever think of that?"

Mahegan had thought about the possibility that she had been hiding in plain sight, hoping to draw out someone connected to the plot she had discovered. But, to what end? Satisfy her curiosity? Or was she more than a waif of a female hacker hiding behind a shaved head? Her large brown eyes would make her recognizable to anyone with whom she'd ever met for more than a minute. Sans make up, and if you could get past the stubbled scalp, Spartak carried a girl next door appearance, crooked smile and all.

"How much time do we have?" Mahegan asked her.

"Like I said, less than seventy-two hours. That's what the plan I saw indicated."

"If we capture the right guys, how do they shut down whatever is planned?"

"It's a series of voice commands, verified by fingerprint recognition, facial recognition, DNA, and eye scan."

"We need to capture someone, but we don't know who it is?" O'Malley chimed in.

The entire team had circled Spartak as she sat at O'Malley's work station with her back to the computer.

"That's not entirely true. I can tell you that those people are most likely at the meeting in Iran. What I saw was that someone had hacked the RINK nuclear arsenals and the RINK nations had countered that, blocked it, but they never regained full access. They couldn't shoot their missiles."

"Including Russia?" Mahegan asked. The implications for Russia to be without any retaliatory capability were huge. Especially with the Russian army plowing through northern Europe.

"Yes, including Russia. But that meeting," Spartak said, pointing at the monitor. "That is a trade of some sort. Russia will get its capabilities back as will North Korea and Iran."

"What about the fourth guy? Is he some kind of master key? Does he have universal access?"

"I don't know." Again, Spartak looked away.

Mahegan wondered why she was being obtuse about something that seemed obvious. She had deliberately led them to this conclusion.

"Okay," he said. "Sean, can we see through those windows or get any kind of facial recognition on this guy?"

O'Malley leaned over Spartak, used his thumb to manipulate the trackpad on the MacBook, and pulled up a grainy image of a face outlined behind a tinted vehicle window. "I've enhanced this shot as much as possible. The light from the hangar was bright enough to offset the tint. This isn't good enough for facial recognition, and it's the left rear of the vehicle, so possibly not the principal we're looking for. It's a start, though. We get him, maybe we get the real guy, whoever is in the seat next to him."

"Any idea how long they'll be in there?" Mahegan asked.

"What I saw in their plans was that this meeting was to divide up the world after nuclear war. Russia gets Europe. Iran gets the Middle East. North Korea gets Asia, to include China, somehow." Spartak said.

"What happens to North America?" Cassie asked.

"Just a nuclear wasteland for one to five years, but the fourth man will control that hemisphere, according to the plan," Spartak said.

Mahegan said, "You sound skeptical."

"I think the fourth man wants to control the world," Spartak said.

As the airplane cruised along through the thin air at 35,000 feet above ground level, Mahegan thought about options. They could drop a nuke on the meeting place, but the 'RINK plus one' could be a half mile underground with all the command and control necessary to do everything Spartak had said. Mahegan's team could conduct a special operations raid into the middle of Iran. The last time the United States tried that, Jimmy Carter was president and a refuel operation had ended in catastrophe for the fledgling Delta Force and special operations commandos on the mission. Mahegan did the math. It was simply too far for a helicopter raid of any substantial force.

But, he thought, *a small team could jump into the compound, snatch the fourth man, and fly out on a few helicopters.*

"So, nothing's getting through? How the hell are we going to jump?" Cassie asked.

"Offset. By the time we get there and fly our parachutes into the drop zone, the storm should be gone," Mahegan said. "HAHO. High altitude, high opening. Fly in. What's the range of these satellites?"

Spartak frowned, looked uncomfortable either because she didn't know the information or didn't want to share.

"We can figure it out, Jake," Savage said. "Why don't you and Cassie get some rest. You'll be running hard once on the ground. We'll get this little genius to talk if we have to pull her fingernails."

"I've got it figured out, I think," O'Malley said. "Just some simple math when you look at each of the satellite systems and where the forces are on the ground." On the display, he had superimposed perfect circles around each of the geo-stationary satellite systems that hung in geo-synchronous positions above the three attacking armies.

"See here? The Iranians are spread from their border with Iraq to Israel's border with Jordan. They've taken heavy casualties in

Israel and are stopped along the Golan Heights, but in the time we've been flying, the satellites have adjusted westward, to remain center mass over the bulk of the attacking forces. Same here on the Belarus and Polish border. The satellites over the Russians keep moving west. They are moving fast, already to Warsaw. And here on the Korean Peninsula the satellites have readjusted southeast to keep up with the Korean advances."

"Holy shit," Owens said. "World War Three is a fucking computer game."

"No game, son," Savage said.

"So back to my original point," O'Malley said. "It looks like the satellites are focused on the attacking forces and not defense of the meeting site. My math shows that the satellites over the Iranian combat forces barely, if at all, range back to the meeting location."

"So just a little windstorm to worry about?" Mahegan quipped.

"Maybe." O'Malley looked over his shoulder and looked at Mahegan. "I could always be wrong."

"Nah. That never happens."

Owens coughed, "Bullshit," into his hand.

"Okay. Compute a release point and time for the jump. We'll get some rack. And don't let her near any computers. If she can disarm Russian MiGs, she can communicate to the ground."

"Would never do that to you, soldier boy," Spartak said.

Mahegan chinned Cassie his way and they walked out of the command pod. Each went to their separate bunks, nothing more than taut canvas racks used to transport wounded out of combat zones.

"Get some rest, Ranger. Big mission ahead."

Cassie winked at him. "You too, big guy."

Frustrated, Mahgean turned around, leaned againt a stanchion that supported the bunks. The ache in his heart was overpowering his typically one hundered percent operational focus. To recenter himself, Mahegan first checked his weapons. He jacked the charging handle of his trusty Tribal Sig Sauer nine-millimeter pistol. Ran his thumb across the razor edge of his Blackhawk combat knife, and broke down and reassembled his M4 carbine with suppressor and Picatinny rail filled with infrared devices and flashlights.

He stood, saw Cassie was already asleep, and watched as General Savage walked his way.

Savage motioned him away from the bunks.

Mahegan walked toward the general, who then put his hand on the mission leader's shoulder. The general's face looked haggard, full of crags. Years of worry and tough missions were etched into his features. His black and gray buzz looked like cut steel.

His dark eyes bored into Mahegan's. "Intel says Russia goes nuclear in less than three days. We've got to stop this now. Find those four people, but most importantly, find the Russian. They've got the most nukes. Hell, bring me back one person from this meeting and we can break this thing." Savage abruptly turned and walked away.

Mahegan said nothing. He watched the general, processed the information, and then crawled onto the canvas and pulled a lightweight blanket over his body.

Nuclear war with Russia? No, the world? To what end? Why?

The thoughts spiraled through his mind like race cars lapping the track at 200 miles per hour. *If one person was in charge, what would his or her purpose be?* Like a hawk soaring above a field, his mind saw the prey, but it was quickly gone, a rabbit into the bush. The answer was there, though, hiding.

Sleep soon captured him, his mind as dark as the night, the illuminated eyes of the prey winking up at the black firmament. But, no, not prey, not a rabbit. This was a predator. For the first time Mahegan wondered if he was the prey.

The elliptical eyes followed him into his sleep.

CHAPTER 10

*T*HE YOUNG MEDIA MOGUL LOOKED OUT FROM BENEATH HIS CURLY light brown locks, wondering about this move. The cavernous airplane hangar swallowed his jet. A black Mercedes waited for him down below, but Gorham had told the pilots to not yet open the door.

So far everything had gone relatively according to plan. Stepping foot onto Iranian soil to meet with the leaders of the RINK alliance was distinctly different from dwelling and brooding within the safety of his bunkered command and control center with its holograms, monitors, and communications uplinks. He needed Dr. Draganova, though. His confidence needed that final booster shot before entering the lion's den here in Iran.

He opened his tablet and retrieved another video file of a conversation with Dr. Draganova. There she was. The black hair cut just a bit differently, angled over her left shoulder. Dark eyebrows. Full lips. Sensuous mouth. Teeth slightly askew. Tight fitting dress, as if she had a date afterward. They were in a conference room in a private club in Chicago. He eyed the sofa upon which he sat, wishing she had joined him there as opposed to sitting in the adjacent leather chair.

"Do you prefer meeting people in person or the separation that your device gives you?" she asked him.

"I like seeing you in person."

"Just me? Others?"

"For others, I guess I prefer the separation."

"You guess? Unpack the box, Ian. You're a brilliant man. Open that uncertainty and let's look at it. Why are you not sure? You're a master negotiator. You've built this massive company. You employ thousands of people worldwide. You've stared down giants of the tech industry and stolen their market share. You guess?" Her voice. The East European lilt.

"That's true. I've done all that."

"Then what's in that box of uncertainty? Remove it from the shelf and look in it. Tell me what you see in there."

He watched himself sitting on the sofa. His hand stroked the armrest as if he were stroking her . . . or perhaps himself. For him, the meetings were foreplay.

"I see the uncertainty of what I'm about to do. With my business, the path was very clear. Market share. Social media. Retail. Search. Advertising. Do it better and faster."

"What are you about to do?"

"Change the world."

"You've done that. Change it how?"

"Help everyone. Change governments so that they help people instead of oppress them."

"You've helped tens of thousands."

"I want to help billions."

"Like McDonalds? Billions served?"

"Technically its trillions and don't make fun of me, Doctor."

"Now there's a box I'd like to open." Playful, teasing.

Flirting? he wondered.

"I want to empower the world," he said. His voice was a whisper.

"Then you need to come face-to-face with the world."

Serious. Deadpan. Dramatic shift from the previous sentence.

"Face your demons and they will respect you. Turn away from them and they will conquer you."

In Iran he was facing three demons: the RINK leaders.

Shayne had moved forward to the command center in the plane as it sat idle in the dim hangar. The black Mercedes was idling at the base of the portable steps that two Iranian airmen had rolled to the airplane door. Gorham wasn't yet ready to deplane, though.

"Here we are, boss," Shayne said.

"Facing demons," Gorham said.

Shayne nodded. "That, too."

"Three human biometric keys. They walk through the biometric chamber, we get their data, and then we leave."

"I'm ready when you are," Shayne said.

During construction of Iran's Manaslu Facility, Gorham had ensured that each of the twenty-meter-long biometric walkways was wired and connected to the antennae on top of the mountain via cables bored through the rock and earth. In addition to the hundreds of other Manaslu buildings he had constructed globally, he had obtained exceptions to the trade embargoes and UN sanctions with Iran and North Korea by working closely with the previous president, who had granted permission for Manaslu to construct buildings under the Partnership for Peace rubric. When muddled into a grouping of over two hundred international construction permits, the exceptions did not seem like a big deal to the administration policy wonks at the time. In fact, creating jobs, their theory went, would decrease unemployment in nations that sponsored terrorism and therefore provide fledgling terrorists jobs that would dissuade them from conducting terror attacks against the West.

With the nuclear arsenals of the RINK nations locked in the vice grip of Shayne's ManaHack software, they had little option but to bring their human biometric keys to Iran to unlock their capabilities if for no other reason than the defense assurances that mutual assured destruction provided.

Interestingly, each country—Russia, Iran, and North Korea—

had expressed interest in allying with Manaslu when he had approached them two years prior. He'd demonstrated via a link in the Dark Web his capability to cyber-attack the guidance systems of conventional and nuclear weapons. Of course, the capabilities were agnostic. He could disable RINK systems or he could disable U.S. systems and those of their allies. Bolstering the RINK alliance was more advantageous to his own political purposes, but he'd been prepared to pivot either way, as any good businessman would be.

Shayne must have noticed Gorham's pensive stare.

"ManaBlades are showing us no changes," Shayne said.

Gorham nodded.

Last year, Gorham and Shayne had deployed a series of micro-drones—the same type he had secreted into Dr. Draganova's office and home—from a low earth orbiting satellite. The container pod was the size of a suitcase with the protective tiles of the space shuttle. It had bored its way through the atmosphere under GPS guidance to a location not far from where Gorham's airplane had barreled through the mountain passes before circling for landing. There, the pod had opened, releasing one hundred solar powered ManaBlades—miniature drones—that then flew soundlessly using micro jet propulsion. The micro battery packs on the drones carried enough charge for four hours of continuous operations as they flew, recorded, and streamed video back to the satellite from which they had been launched. Once the battery hit a fifteen-minute power warning, the drones found the highest altitude and least obstructed perch, pinged their location, and waited for further instructions while the sun recharged their batteries.

Now, Gorham and Shayne studied the video feeds of the drones as they live-streamed to Shayne's iPad. The insect-sized drones had easily penetrated throughout the maze of tunnels, caves, and buildings in Yazd. After all, Manaslu had designed much of the complex.

"Good job on the ManaBlades," Gorham said.

Gorham slipped a Canali silk sport coat over his gray T-shirt. His trim fit blue jeans fell atop handmade burgundy chukkas. The casual attire was his version of "outback."

Shayne was dressed in L.L.Bean hiking boots, khakis, and a new safari vest over his black T-shirt. He tugged at the price tag and snapped the plastic retainer.

"We've got forty-seven of the original hundred ManaBlades left. They can listen and they can jam, providing us real time intelligence."

"And what are we hearing? It might be nice to know whether our hosts are planning to kidnap us or feed us lamb. When I visited the construction site, they fed me lamb. Now, who knows?"

After construction of the Partnership for Peace facility in Iran, a location selected by the government in Tehran, UN inspectors had given the building a green light and an international certification that the operation would put more Iranians to work.

From Iran's point of view, Gorham knew they would be able to turn the enterprise into a spy network, not unlike he had done globally by collecting hundreds of millions of e-mail addresses, videos, pictures, and thousands of other data points that each human willfully shared on a daily basis.

Shayne pulled up his iPad and pressed a few icons until he had intelligence feeds from the remaining microdrones they had dropped months ago. On his screen, sound bars bounced up and down, indicating speech was being intercepted. Gorham had directed two drones to accompany each vehicle picking up passengers from arriving airplanes. The drones attached themselves onto the vehicles looking like pilot fish on a shark.

Only smaller, more like a grasshopper, Gorham thought. He remembered his childhood days growing up in rural Pennsylvania. Rows of corn and soybeans. Fields of grass that would become hay to feed the milk cows. The grasshoppers and locusts. He had modeled the micro ManaBlades after the insects he had studied as a child. Their functionality fascinated him. They could fly, hop, communicate, and camouflage themselves to blend into their environment. They worked in Dr. Draganova's office and they seemed to be working here in Iran.

Shayne's screen showed that the forty-seven ManaBlades were deployed on fourteen vehicles and in seven rooms throughout the compound, all in preparation for his and Gorham's arrival.

"The Russian delegation is here," Shayne said. "Their conversations are mostly bitching about having to come to Iran instead of the other way around. They're also confused as to why there's no vodka. Sounds like Khilkov has his dog with him. So that's a good sign it's him and not an imposter."

"The wolfhound?"

"A Borzoi, as they call it. The dog of the Czars. Looks more like a greyhound with fur." Shayne had a picture of Khilkov's Russian wolfhound. She was a tall, slender breed that indeed had an angular face, as if sculpted for racing. White and tan hair covered the animal's body.

"Why would he bring a dog? Aren't they eaten here?" Gorham asked.

"You're thinking of Korea."

"Speaking of which?"

"North Korea? They landed two hours ago. Their replacement president is here, evidently."

"Most likely a doppelganger," Gorham said.

"They're being very deferential to him, if so." Shayne pinched the screen and tapped an icon. "Facial recognition shows 92 percent chance it is either Son Yung with some facial disfiguration to make it not look like him or someone else made to look like him."

Son Yung was the new leader of North Korea. A former army general, Yung was a devout follower of the previous president and reportedly bellicose in his intentions toward America and the West.

"Remind me to fire the CEO of that facial recognition software company we bought. That's bullshit. We should know one way or the other. There is no margin for error here, Shayne. We're about to step foot into enemy territory, which makes us traitors to the United States. Imperfection is unacceptable."

"Noted," Shayne said, used to Gorham's rants.

"The only thing making any of this worthwhile is our globalist agenda, the prize at the end. Our path is the only way to get there. Farmers must burn the previous crop to grow a new one. And we shall burn the world to reshape it in the only sustainable way forward."

The young, muscled flight attendant who was also a security guard opened the door, his pistol holster flashing from beneath his sport coat. Gorham had recruited his security guards from around the world. He paid each of the twenty men a half million dollars a year. The training he put them through rivaled any special operations, SEAL, or Ranger training course. His main stipulation was that none of the applicants could have any prior service in the United States military. He didn't trust the system and wanted no infiltrators. He had purchased a thousand acres of land near his Idaho compound, developed his own curriculum and training courses, and personally trained his first batch of five recruits.

The central theme to his training was that force could only be used in a few instances. First and foremost, to protect him, the CEO and President of the company. After all, without him, there was no Manaslu. And without Manaslu, there would be no social media empire and no newspaper network to overtly, subtly, or otherwise influence and shape opinion.

His company had spanned the boundaries of nation-states, bringing people together in a way that nation-states were unable, coalescing opinions and visions that a shared economy could become a shared universe, providing for the greater good of all mankind. Just as the British drawn Durand Line separating Afghanistan and Pakistan was irrelevant—harmful even—the boundaries of nation-states today were meaningless. Other than the collection of taxes and provision of services, government's primary purpose was to disaggregate the nation-state to protect itself. Chiefly, James Madison's "Violence of Factions," muted and channeled separatist fervor. Everything was so polarized now that, though, that violence was erupting and spilling over, pushing against the institutional breakwaters that kept rebellion at bay. Gorham's goal was to harness that energy, propel it forward, trample the institutions of nation states, and blend the chaos into a new vision—*his* vision—of a global unified people. In Gorham's view, the factions could become one entity. Laws could be derived from the evolving norms hashed out on social media. Just like the reaction to the dentist who killed the lion in Africa created a new social norm—don't kill lions—Gorham believed that his legions of Internet analysts could rapidly discern public opinion, create a new norm—a law—and regurgitate it instantly on the vast social media and print newspaper enterprise. The result, according to Gorham's extensive collection of personal information, was a diverse world more driven to an understanding of the need for peace.

Less conflict, more agreement. Squeeze out the extremes and move everyone in one direction toward a unified vision—Gorham's vision—of a world without borders. A global enterprise serving all people. Already his company was in the top ten gross domestic products of all *countries* in the world. Manaslu was on path to becoming the third largest revenue generator of all countries and companies in the world. His vision was within reach.

This war would burn the world to the ground so he could reshape it and cause the leading economies to spend untold and unprecedented treasure on defense. Having moved most of his company's stock and assets to cash and precious metals, hedging against the markets that were already crashing, he was fully prepared for the next phase.

The hangar air was stale, musty. Gorham stepped carefully down the movable walkway until he was on concrete. A Persian man with a trimmed black beard stood next to the open back door of a hardened black Mercedes Benz. Gorham looked left and right, saw the ManaBlades looking like indistinguishable black grasshoppers on the front and rear fenders.

Shayne was still looking at his iPad, reading the intel feeds. "All good, boss."

Gorham walked around the back of the car, opened the other back door, and sat in the rear left seat.

"No, sir. Your seat is here," the Persian said from the right rear door as he held it open. His voice was heavily accented. He wore a blank olive uniform. The black pistol on his hip was stuffed in a worn tan leather holster.

"I'm good," Gorham said, sitting in the back left.

The driver protested again by walking around the rear of the car. He opened the left rear door and showed his palm to Gorham, which he swept away, as if to say, *this way.*

"Let's go," Gorham snapped. "We have a meeting."

The man looked across the room briefly and then locked eyes with Gorham.

"Do we have a problem?" Gorham asked.

"No. No problem." The driver shut the right rear door, then closed Gorham's door politely and then stepped into the driver's seat. He put the vehicle in gear and drove through a small opening in the hangar wall.

Shayne was sitting in the front right passenger seat. As they had approached the car, one of the ManaBlades had determined an anomaly beneath the right rear seat of the vehicle. It appeared to be a syringe situated just beneath the padding, needle pointed upward. The imaging capability on the ManaBlades showed no other anomalies in the other seats.

Shayne typed on secure ManaChat. **Not sure what that says about my expendability.**

Gorham responded. **Knock me out. Torture you for the crypto. They think you're the engineer. They get their nukes back.**

Shayne was an excellent engineer, but Gorham had created his empire mostly by writing his own code, developing his own algorithms, and having the prescience to be ahead of the next wave before it came crashing down.

The vehicle moved into the sunlight, which was dimmed by the shaded windows. From the valley floor, the mountains appeared taller, overbearing. Shayne continued to stare at the iPad, which was monitoring potential threats in dozens of locations. The ManaBlades sent miniaturized digital packets either to the Mana-Sat or directly to Shayne's iPad, depending upon which was sending the more dominant signal. A large part of Gorham's plan depended upon continuous situational awareness. Just as in business, he couldn't wait days or even hours to make decisions; he needed intel immediately and made split-second decisions that had helped him surpass Facebook, Amazon, and Google as the largest capitalized technology company in the world. He knew, though, that it was a tenuous position, potentially lost at any moment of the day, week, or month. Tough sledding twenty-four/seven.

The car picked up speed as it rocked across the bumpy concrete. Gorham texted Shayne. **Going to tunnel #7**

Roger

For ease of communication, they had numbered all the caves and buildings in preparation for this mission. Just as Gorham had wanted to be on location when the commando team raided the bar, he needed to present himself as the world leader he intended to be. While he preferred remote video teleconferencing, his reading of Sun Tzu and Clausewitz had convinced him that there was no replacement for *boots on the ground*, as he liked to say.

Two Hind helicopters joined them above. These were Soviet era gunships, not unlike the American Apache AH-64, but far less lethal. The rotor noise drowned them in the relentless *whup-whup* of the blades. The wink of sniper scopes flared from hide sites in the ridges above them as they sped from the hangar.

Are we protected or prey? Gorham wondered.

The syringe in the seat was a pretty good indicator that the twenty-four hours in Iran would not be without incident. Gorham believed in his own safety for two reasons. First, he had the ability to manipulate the RINK alliance weapon systems, as he had demonstrated less than twenty-four hours ago. Hacking into the North Korean nuclear system, he'd been able to launch and refine the accuracy of one of its few nuclear weapons. He could have just as easily put that nuke on Pyongyang, Tehran, or Moscow, and he had made that clear to the RINK leadership. Secondly, he held the key to victory over the West, and in particular, the Americans. Everyone understood that destruction of the American threat was the path to victory. Gorham was not naïve enough to believe that once victory was achieved each of the RINK nations would be properly satiated and simply hand him the keys to the globe. No, he would deal with them when that time came. He had a plan.

As Gorham predicted it might, the Mercedes drove over a mile across the airfield and along a taxiway and then on to a well-worn two track dirt road that led to entrance number seven. As they approached the mouth of the cave, a concrete blast door slid open and the driver pulled into the cavern. The car maneuvered through a narrow passageway and pulled into a large opening, the size of a warehouse. Fluorescent lights shone from the fabricated ceiling.

The car stopped next to a cylindrical tube big enough to hold at least two people. It was connected to a fifty-yard-long Plexiglas, perhaps bullet proof, walkway that led to the center of the room. The ManaBlades had scoped out this meeting area in Yazd, Iran. Designed as a telecommunications facility for Manaslu employees, the cavernous arena looked more like a sports arena. From above, the drones had shown a large *X* of walkways—the biometric chambers—with a cylinder at the start of each leg. In the middle was a protected space where the principal and one assistant could sit and discuss important matters with the other leaders.

Carrying his iPad, Shayne stepped out of the vehicle first. The driver opened the door for Gorham, who nodded at the Persian. The man did not seem pleased, as if their first party trick was a failure.

Gorham and Shayne stepped into the glass enclosed foyer to the biometric walkway. A metal door to their front prevented their entry for the moment. The walkway would measure their gaits as part of a series of identity confirmation steps, including retina, voice, handprint, facial recognition, and DNA. The hydraulic door behind them hissed shut.

After a few seconds, the door to the walkway slid open. Small cameras winked at them with red operating lights as they strode forward. Gorham's chukkas echoed like gunshots, and behind him Shayne's new boots squeaked on the buffed runway. Gorham led the way to the biometric scanning station at the base of the walkway in the middle of the arena.

There were three other walkways, all at 90 degree angles to one another. Russia would come in from the left, North Korea from the center, and Iran from the right. Like four different fighters approaching the boxing ring in a coliseum. This facility—built in part by Manaslu—was nearly as big as a coliseum. The negotiating platform was about the size of a boxing ring.

Gorham glanced over his shoulder at Shayne's iPad, which showed that two ManaBlades had flown to the central meeting place, taking up inconspicuous residence on the back of the Russian and Iranian negotiating platforms.

Stopping in front of the biometric scanning station, Gorham let the retina scanner buzz across his eyes. A mechanical arm reached out and swabbed his cheek with a Q-Tip. He placed his hand on the reader and a red light swept back and forth. He stared into the black glass, behind which were his patented algorithms for facial recognition, the best in the world. Then he said, "Ian Gorham."

Green check marks appeared. Voice. Handprint. Eyes. Gait. DNA. Facial.

A mechanical female voice said, "Ian Gorham. Approved. Enter."

He stepped through the portal into the seating area as Shayne went through the exact same process.

"Shayne. Approved. Enter."

As they approached their seating area, both Gorham and Shayne remained silent. They had rehearsed this visit. They knew there was a possibility that all the RINK members could conspire to turn on them, but there was no incentive to do so. Not without the completion of the transfer of the biometric keys to unlock the nuclear arsenal control. Yet, Gorham didn't discount the fact that each leader was unpredictable.

For the moment, he remained standing. Opposite them, the new North Korean leader, General Yung, strode into the biometric walkway from his waiting area, went through the same biometric confirmation process and then stepped aside for the North Korean Nuclear biometric key.

"NoKo NBiC," Gorham whispered to Shayne, nodding. NBiC

was the acronym that Gorham had developed for the three nuclear biometric keys.

"Yes."

Yung was an older general who had learned from Kim Jong Il to enjoy the company of young, blond women from Scandinavia. He had them imported on a regular basis. Gorham could track the social media accounts of these women after their return to Sweden. Several had committed suicide. Some apparently never made it back. General Yung walked through the biometric scanner, confirming it was him.

The North Korean biometric key, a young woman with black hair and steel-gray eyes strode to the platform. Gorham was impressed. He had not expected a woman. He wasn't sure why, but figured the trusted aide for the North Koreans would be a man. But if the general enjoyed the company of young women, then perhaps it stood to reason that he would choose a North Korean woman to always be by his side, as the biometric keys were sure to do. She was beautiful, wearing a black dress suit with a white silk blouse. Pearls hung around her neck, the largest just below her throat between her prominent collar bones. She gave off the air of a no-nonsense business woman.

Gorham thought he detected a bulge in her carry bag—a small backpack—perhaps a gun. As she stood in the biometric chamber, the analytics were relayed to Shayne's laptop. Gorham was distracted, though, transfixed by the beauty of the woman, yet wanting to look at Shayne's iPad. The eye scan. The mouth swab. The handprint. Her lips moved as she said something in Korean.

"Translated that means, To the victor go the spoils," Shayne whispered. "Kal."

"Kal? That's her name?"

"That's what she said."

Gorham stared at the woman then looked at Shayne's iPad. An image of the woman was displayed in a sort of suspended, revolving 3-D. A green check appeared next to the legs, having already confirmed her gait. Then next to the mouth, confirming the voice. Then next to the hand. Then next to the body with the letters DNA. Because Shayne's algorithm searched the entire database of known North Korean operatives, which he had stolen from the North Korean government, the name *Kal* displayed on the screen.

"Kal?" Gorham whispered to Shayne.

"Means knife in Korean. She's a DPRK special operations commando. Don't let the good looks fool you."

Gorham had an itch for Asian women and Kal couldn't be as tough as she purported to be if she was this beautiful. "Yeah, okay."

"Says here her father saved her from a fire that killed her brother and mother nearly ten years ago. Father was given the Medal of Honor by Kim Jung Il. He's a hero of sorts in the northern part of North Korea. Samjiyon."

"Samjiyon? Near our facility there?" Gorham asked.

"Only Samjiyon in North Korea. So, yes."

The general sat down and stared at Gorham from his seat fifteen feet away. Between them on the floor were server racks and voice receivers that would simultaneously translate the conversation into four languages and display the spoken word on the monitors, like watching a movie with four subtitles, three of which you didn't need.

The general wore an olive military uniform with red epaulets. Kal sat to Yung's left and crossed her bare legs slowly.

Perhaps just for Gorham's show?

He licked his lips and stared at Kal, who returned his gaze with a sly grin. Come hither? An image of Draganova flickered in his mind. *Was this all for his ego?*

"Focus, boss. She's bad news."

"What's on the itinerary after this?"

"Not her," Shayne said. "She was recruited by DPRK special ops after her father was incapacitated while rescuing her."

"How incapacitated?" Gorham asked.

"Wheelchair. In a home in Samjiyon. She lives in Pyongyang, but visits him monthly. Quickly promoted not only because of her skill and intellect, but also because of her father's status. That's her connection. He made her rise possible. Though Top Secret, being the nuclear key is one of the most powerful positions in the country."

As Gorham sat, first checking the cushion, he looked to his left and saw the Russian president striding through his biometric walkway. Gorham thought of the bare-chested photos Konstantin Khilkov posted on his very own Manabook page, the new Facebook. The Russian leader was dressed in a dark business suit, white shirt with no tie. Khilkov held a leash in his hand. At the end of the leash was his prized Russian Wolfhound. It was a beautiful white and rust colored animal with the features of a greyhound, but long fur that had helped the animals adapt to the harsh Russian climate. To Khilkov's left was a large man who had the build of a heavyweight boxer. His muscles pushed at the seams of a dark blue suit that was tight across the chest and shoulders.

"He brought his dog?" Gorham spat.

"Told you. Takes her everywhere," Shayne said. "He also brought a gorilla."

The president, his Russian wolfhound, and the Russian biometric key, Sergi Borlof, walked along the corridor, each being scanned and swabbed, each receiving green check marks. The wolfhound snapped at Borlof and barked, evoking deep belly laughter from Khilkov.

The computerized voice said, "Konstantin Khilkov. Sergi Borlof. Serena. Approved. Enter."

Emerging from the chamber and sitting in their seats to Gorham's left, the president nodded at Gorham. His wolfhound sat on its haunches, erect, alert, protective.

After the green check marks appeared, Shayne whispered to Gorham, "Sergi Borlof. Bodyguard to Khilkov. Run of the mill secret service kind of guy. Fought in the Ukraine. His family is close to the president."

"I brought my best friend," Khilkov said, pointing at the wolfhound. "As you just heard the computer say. Serena."

After a brief pause for interpretation, the North Korean general laughed and said in Korean, "I think you are the only one with a true friend in here."

Khilkov seemed to enjoy the banter and followed with, "Yes, Serena. Beautiful name for a beautiful animal. However, I must admit, you have a beautiful specimen next to you."

Kal flicked her hardened eyes to Khilkov.

Evidently he had not received his diversity training, Gorham thought. This was a stupid conversation. Kal was a beautiful woman, not a *specimen.*

"You have refined tastes, Mister President," Yung said.

Kal's lips clenched. Her eyes caught Gorham's. He was looking at her with his best sympathetic look. She gave him a wry smile that he interpreted to say, *Thank you.*

The last to walk into the arena were the Iranians. They entered the arena from Gorham's right. Walking through the glassed-in portal, they looked like an odd pair. The President of Iran, Rahmad Saedi, was short—maybe 5'6"—wearing a black suit with a white shirt and no tie. His closely shaved beard matched the suit in color. Walking next to him was a man rivaling the size of the Russian dog handler and biometric key. The Iranian biometric key looked like a boxer, bent nose, scarred face, shaved head with black stubble merging with the beard that covered his chin. He was pushing seven feet tall and 300 pounds. Saedi went through the scanner, followed by the hulking Iranian Key.

After the check marks appeared on Shayne's iPad, Shayne whispered to Gorham, "Alexander Persi. Olympic boxer and heavyweight wrestler. Earned a bronze in Rio for Greco-Roman wrestling. Something of a hero here."

Gorham thought for a moment that Persi and Borlof might make for a good wrestling match if the discussions got boring.

"Get all three?" Gorham said.

"Every bit. I'm uploading all the biometric markers to the ManaSat array right now." After about fifteen seconds, Shayne said, "And it's ours."

"Okay. When the principals start talking, be ready to make a big deal about giving them back their nuclear access."

Shayne nodded.

To his left were the Russian president, Serena the wolfhound seated upright on her haunches, and the security guard, Borlof. Across from him about twenty feet away were the North Korean general and his biometric key, Kal. To his right were the Iranian president and Persi, the Iranian biometric key. Each of their seats were like theater balcony seats but shielded by ballistic glass. When they spoke, the servers in the center of the floor automatically translated the spoken word and displayed the meaning in English, Russian, Farsi, and Korean for all to see.

Transparency, as Gorham had planned it.

The host began speaking.

"Welcome gentlemen . . . and ladies. While Mr. Gorham called us all here, I am your host." Saedi nodded at the North Korean woman. "At Mr. Gorham's request, we have used facial, gait, eye, handprint, DNA, and speech recognition to confirm that each of you is who you say you are. And we each have brought our biometric keys for our classified strategic programs, which have been confirmed. I'm anticipating release of our strategic capabilities back to the respective nation-states. It seems that Mr. Gorham drives a hard bargain, but perhaps a necessary one, nonetheless."

Saedi was Harvard undergraduate and law educated. He spoke in precise, clipped tones.

Gorham took that as his cue. "We are prepared to unblock the nuclear arsenals of your nations under one condition."

"There was only one condition," Khilkov interrupted. "That we bring our biometric keys to confirm that each of us has the necessary precautions in place. Anything else is unacceptable."

"I only ask that like any collective security alliance, we agree when strategic launches will take place," Gorham said.

"As you did with North Korea?" Khilkov scoffed. "Please."

"It will be important that we act with one unified voice."

"Again, did we all agree on sending a nuclear weapon into Tokyo? No. We all have economic interests there that have been wiped out."

"The economic interests of each nation are irrelevant to the larger interest at hand," Gorham said.

"Our economic interests are all that matters," Khilkov continued.

"Please, please," General Yung interrupted. "We are the ones who are under international scrutiny now. Whether we launched the nuclear weapon or not, we are to blame. The path forward is a united path, not a divided one. North Korea has led the way. We all must join together now. Our communications, our trade, our technology transfers implicate all of us. Even you, Mr. Gorham. You are as complicit as all of us."

"Thank you, General. Yes, I understand and agree. Though *complicit* is not a word I would necessarily use. We are reshaping the world. Unifying it under common purpose, which is a socialist agenda that should resonate well with each of your philosophies. The only thing left to do is to determine how we rule after North Korea unifies the Korean Peninsula. Iran unifies the Middle East under Shi'a rule and law. And Russia strikes the final blow against the West. The governing doctrine must be one of helping the unfortunate, not enriching the wealthy."

The men mumbled amongst their biometric keys.

They also served as advisors, Gorham presumed.

"Go on," Khilkov said.

"I don't want any land beyond the United States. I want the United States to be burned to the ground so that I can rebuild it in the image I seek. Not unlike what you are doing with Europe, Mr. President." Gorham turned to the North Korean leader who was listening to Kal.

He waited for her to finish, then spoke to General Yung. "And just as you will have South Korea and Japan under your control, I will remove all U.S. troops—those that are still alive—from the western Pacific. Guam, Korea, and Japan. It's all yours. We have no business being there. The farthest west we will be is Hawaii. It's a state and we will keep it that way. You want the Philippines, Australia, whatever else? It's yours. China is a different story. They're neither with us nor against us. Waiting it out to see what happens.

I don't imagine you can do much there." He let the concept of China being too big to get out of their own way to sink in.

Gorham didn't view China as prepared to interject militarily other than to protect their own borders and economic way of life. His calculation had been to rely upon the RINK alliance as an agile way of resolving the conflict in seventy-two hours. Lightning speed. China was slow, lethargic. Like an unwieldy fat man unable to get out of his own way.

Gorham turned to his right. The Iranians. They were watching the monitor in the center. When he noticed Gorham staring at him, President Saedi nodded.

Gorham said, "You have the entire Middle East. The new Persian empire is all yours. It's your call on what to do with Israel and the northern tier of Africa. I've said all along that we can facilitate the attacks so that they are successful."

Turning back to Khilkov, Gorham said, "Just as we have enabled your attack against Belarus and Poland and countries beyond, we could enable their defenses against you. Our nanosatellites are staying in synchronous orbit above each of your countries' attack axes so that our code writers can drop cyber-bombs everywhere your troops go, helping them bypass defenses, making NATO weapons systems inoperable, and easing the way for your soldiers to attack. A few years ago, you got bogged down in the Ukraine, but you seem to be making excellent progress into Poland. You think that's a coincidence?"

Cheeks reddened from Gorham's pointed words, Khilkov looked down and said, "We could do this alone, but choose to strategically align with you for the reasons you state."

Gorham chuckled. "Sure. Okay." Then, with a firm voice, he added, "We can create a revolution in your country tomorrow, Mister President. Manaslu has billions of users interested in your policies. Not only can we render your weapons ineffective, we can create an uprising in your country that will chase you to your Georgian Black Sea retreat, if you make it that far." He looked at each of the three RINK leaders. Left. Center. Right. "Likewise for each of your countries. To the point, the reason for the in-person meeting other than to unlock your nuclear arsenals is that we must trust one another."

"Trust?" Khilkov said. "You and your hackers have left us naked with no nuclear capability to respond if we are attacked. You come here talking about trust?"

"I do, Mr. President. We've caught your hackers attempting to penetrate Manaslu and U.S. government institutions over two thousand times this month alone. You've hacked into the North Korean and Iranian systems. Care to share more? Want to discuss trust?"

Gorham nodded at General Yung and President Saedi, who seemed surprised at Gorham's insights about Russian cyber warfare. Russia had army units that executed the Kremlin's cyber goals. Essentially, there were basements full of teenagers who preferred fighting the war from the comfort of a windowless cube as opposed to the urban warfare of Ukraine or, now, northern Europe.

Khilkov's unblinking eyes looked at Gorham, who guessed Khilkov was assessing how best to kill him and Shayne.

Hopefully, Gorham thought, *our precautions will be effective.*

"I think we will continue. It's clear that none of us trusts the other. The only way to communicate what is about to happen is to look each other in the eyes. Sure, we can start a war, as we have, through remote communications and planning. But the spoils of war have a way of making people greedy. I want to clearly lay out the end game in person and have agreement. To the extent that each of you wishes to retain power and, perhaps, to live, then I suggest we roll up our sleeves and get to work." Gorham gave the interpreters a minute to translate for their principals even though it was plain to see on the robotized monitor to their collective front.

"I already know the success each of your militaries is achieving, so it is pointless in reviewing that. There is only one thing we need to discuss before we outline the end state." He paused again and looked back at the Russian president. "A hacker, perhaps from one of your countries, slipped away from our raid. He was in a bar in Detroit. Three of our best sleeper cell members attacked the bar and were repelled by a cell run by the U.S. Military's Joint Special Operations Command. We have facial recognition of two members. One is Cassandra Bagwell, army captain. She's a military intelligence officer and we must assume she had a heads-up. That somehow our Deep Web communications were breached."

"Maybe you're not as good as you say." Khilkov's face was expressionless other than what seemed to be a permanent large frown, like a clown's painted downturned lips.

Gorham ignored the comment and continued. "The defector, Mr. President, we believe is from your country. This person risks the entire operation."

"Perhaps the defector worked for you?" Khilkov replied. "And believing someone is Russian is quite different from actually knowing this person is Russian."

"The skills we see are Russian techniques. Hacking skills, trained in your country. Cyrillic letters here and there, as if by mistake," Gorham said.

"If so, he is a simple hacker. Perhaps a good one. One would have to wonder what he saw in your operation that made him run."

"Yes. That is good question," Yung said.

"I think he saw the end state and got scared. Wanted no part in it," Gorham said. "We have to assume that he is in American control. Americans captured this hacker before we could. Thankfully, the backlash from Guantanamo Bay and the torture in Iraq means there will be no torture of our defector."

"Torture or not, if he is Russian, he will never give up Russia. As for the rest, I cannot speak. I don't know what he learned from the others."

"We shall see," Gorham said. "I have a plan in action to find and capture him. If we do not capture him, he will be in hiding or on the run, unable to do us harm. However, Mister President, if you have contact with him, we would like to know."

Khilkov's permanent frown lifted into a sneer. "Given your capabilities, I would assume you will know if he contacts us or not."

The Russian president was correct. Manaslu's capabilities were immense, all encompassing. But Gorham didn't flinch. Shayne showed him something on the iPad. Gorham read and nodded.

"We have information this cook goes by the name, Spartak. That is Russian, no?"

"Spartak?" Khilkov laughed. "So this hacker is a football player? Hockey?"

Gorham furrowed his brow, thought through what Spartak might mean, and of course it was derived from Spartan, a gladiator-slave. He recalled there were Russian soccer and ice hockey teams that used the Spartan as a mascot. He felt foolish, but recovered. "Just passing along the information."

"If anything, the hacker going by Spartak tells me he is not Russian."

"Well, the digital forensics Shayne has done reveal a careless mistake by this hacker."

"You are wasting my time, Gorham," Khilkov said.

"Ultimately, we believe he is your responsibility. If I am mistaken, my apologies," Gorham said. "But I don't think so. Regardless, I wanted each of you to know that we have a potential loose cannon out there and while we are still in control of everything, there seems to be some indication that we've had a minor breach. Another reason why we needed to discuss the end state in person, as opposed to over the Deep Web."

"If I may," Khilkov said. He was looking at his bulky biometric key, Borlof, who was holding a tablet device not unlike Shayne's iPad. "We just lost two of our best MiG 35 fighter pilots over the Pacific Ocean. They were shadowing an American cargo plane flying over the Aleutian Islands, given orders to shoot it down, and somehow our two MiGs disappeared from radar."

"That's got to be them," Gorham said as much to himself as to the others.

"Given this and your loose cannon," Khilkov said. "You should give us back our nuclear capabilities. We should accelerate our time line for attack."

Gorham agreed. He lifted his head, turned to Shayne and said, "Give them control of their nuclear arsenals."

Shayne entered a series of codes and three green check marks appeared on his tablet. Gorham looked up and at the three leaders who were all checking with their biometric keys. The Keys were carrying small handheld smartphone-like devices. Borlof, Kal, and Persi all showed the device to their respective leaders and nodded.

"Do you confirm access?" Gorham asked.

Each of them affirmed by verbally saying, "Yes."

"Now the only way for you to to shut down your system is for your biometric key to be confirmed by a Manaslu Chamber and then for some hacker, like the rogue defector, to block you. As we've demonstrated, cyber security on nuclear command and control systems is weak. So, be careful. And though we no longer have control, we do seek cooperation."

"We shall discuss this cooperation," the Russian president said.

"Keep your Keys close to your side and you'll be fine. Lose them and who knows what may happen?" Gorham posited. He looked at the beautiful Kal as he spoke. She smiled and nodded, as if to say, *well done.*

A pistol shot rang out.

To Gorham's left he saw the Russian biometric key dead, slumped against the bulletproof glass that afforded him no protection from his boss, the president. Khilkov held a pistol in his hand. Gorham wasn't an expert in handguns so he didn't know what kind, but it was effective, apparently. Serena the wolfhound walked around the dead man, shook once as if she was shaking off water, and then perched again to her master's side.

"As you said, we have access now. There's no need to keep him around. He's only a liability. I didn't feel like keeping tabs on him." Khilkov chuckled.

Gorham looked at Kal, who stared at the army general next to her. He was moving swiftly to do the same thing. His pistol was up, but Kal was too quick. She jabbed the general in the throat with her fist and then snapped the general's forearm over her knee. She grabbed the pistol, opened the door, and bolted up the glassed-in walkway.

Two North Korean guards took aim at her from the top of the arena balcony. Gorham knew that each of the presidents had security details. She dashed through the walkway, glass shattering behind her.

To his right, Gorham saw the Iranian president holding a pistol and firing at point blank into Persi's chest. Six bullets impacted the big man's body, but didn't faze him.

Must have been wearing body armor.

Persi reached up and took the president's empty pistol and oddly, just stared at him. Gorham was stunned. He had thought through several calculations, but it hadn't occurred to him that the countries would consider themselves immune from hacking again. Who was to say that between now and launch Manaslu or some other entity wouldn't hack their nuclear systems.

To Gorham, these people were to be protected at all costs. Had the Russian president caused a chain reaction? But, regardless, he had the Keys' biometric information, which was the ultimate motive.

"Stop!" Gorham shouted. But Kal was already in the tunnel. In the wind. The North Korean security detail split up, one after her and one to the general to check on his status. The standoff between the Iranian president and Persi continued. Persi wasn't doing anything but holding the president by the shoulder, keeping him at bay. The security guards at the top of the stairwell were conflicted and accordingly did nothing. Persi was one of them. The big man was obviously being respectful of the president, while also protecting himself.

"Looks like we've got a shitstorm on our hands, Gorham," Khilkov said.

"Not my problem." Actually, it *was* his problem. Gorham needed all the nuclear weapons to hit their targets. The conventional war was really a sideshow for Gorham.

"Could be," Khilkov said.

"Killing your Key was your call, naturally. Should something happen again to your system, though, you're screwed."

"Shall I kill you, also, Mr. Gorham? Simply to prevent you from stealing my nuclear arsenal again?"

That was the crux of the argument for Gorham. Every nation had weapons, resources, people, and so on. These were the world's possessions, not arbitrary nation-states. Nationalism was a disease and the only cure was to destroy it through his chosen course of action. He needed Russia to launch the first strike against the U.S.

"Not necessary. But for your information, Mr. President, the American nuclear arsenal is as defenseless as yours was a few seconds ago. It will remain so for about the next forty-eight hours."

"We shall use that time wisely," Khilkov said. The Russian president looked at Borlof's dead body, stood, and began walking up the ramp through the portal.

An alarm sounded, like an air horn blowing at full blast. The Iranian President broke away from Persi's grip and turned toward Gorham and Khilkov, shouting, "Everyone stay inside. Shamal approaching. Winds exceeding seventy-five miles per hour."

CHAPTER 11

*G*ORHAM SELF-MEDICATED BY RUBBING HIS ROPEY MUSCLES WITH
impatience. He needed Draganova. He was a junkie without a fix.
With each day he couldn't speak to the doctor, the more he lost
control of his mind.

What the fuck? What the fuck? What the fuck? That's all he could
think. Murder and mayhem. Isolated in Iran in the middle of a
mountain.

They had waited seven hours in the "luxury" accommodations
of the Iranians, which included a gang latrine and bunk beds with
stained mattresses and ratty sheets. He sat in the metal chair staring at Shayne, who was busy trying to make his iPad connect to
the ManaSat constellation.

"I think the ManaSat pod is moving too far west from here,
boss."

"Got to be a signal somewhere. Can we reach a Bap-Bird?"

Bap-Birds were satellites named after billionaire hedge fund
manager Hector Baeppler, an Argentinian expat, who lived in
Portland, Oregon. He had provided Gorham seed money for his
company when the prospects of overtaking the first mover advan-
tages of Facebook, Amazon, and Google were slim and none. But
with Baeppler's financial assistance, Gorham had been able to
overcome the primary obstacle—money—and retain the services
of many of the best code writers and engineers in the world.

All of that came with a price, of course. Baeppler was a Manaslu
board member and a 49% shareholder. He had significant influ-

ence over Manaslu, at least if he chose to exercise it. So far, he had remained distant from the business operations. But he did frequently conduct mentoring sessions with Gorham. They discussed politics, equality, human rights, and progressive values of ripping away the artificial borders of nations and creating a global enterprise where the poor and uneducated received direct assistance from the wealthy, privileged classes of every country. Baeppler's Utopian notion was an equilibrium of wealth, where everyone migrated to the middle. Gorham knew that Baeppler donated millions every year to families and was proud of his mentor.

And right now, he was thankful that Baeppler had a geo-stationary satellite orbiting above Iran.

"Got it," Shayne said. "Storm passes in about an hour. Should be able to fly out after that."

"Call the pilots and tell them to get ready."

"Okay." Shayne stood from the creaky metal bed. They were deep inside the mountain in one of the tunnels the ManaBlades had been unable to access.

"Any intel on this chamber we're in?" Gorham asked.

"I've got two ManaBlades out right now. They're sniffing. They see Kal hiding in one of the vehicle cubbies. My signal's okay. It's pushing through the Iranian antennae on the top of the mountain that feeds into their command center. So, it's wearing out the battery pulling off the conductive metal in the tunnel. But we're definitely connected to Bap-Bird One."

"At least we've got eyes," Gorham said. "Okay. Let's grab Kal on the way out. Put her in our car. Hook into the cameras and let's make sure we're not being detained. Seven-hour storm? You're shitting me, right? How did we miss this?"

"These shamals just come out of nowhere."

"Nothing comes out of nowhere. Don't forget that," Gorham said.

There was a disturbance in the hallway and Shayne pinched and pushed at the iPad screen until he had a full view.

Gorham smiled. "Told you."

Dax Stasovich was barreling down the dimly lit hallway, an AK-47 in one hand, a bloody knife in the other.

CHAPTER 12

MAHEGAN AND CASSIE STOOD IN THE OPEN BOMB BAY OF A STEALTH B-2 Spirit Stealth Bomber. The XC-17 had landed at Kandahar Air Base in Afghanistan and they had quickly cross loaded to the waiting B-2.

The ground slid by unseen to the naked eye 35,000 feet beneath them. The black expanse appeared to be without relief, yet Mahegan knew the terrain into which they would be parachuting had 15,000 feet of differentiation from mountain peaks to river valleys.

The jump light was flickering red until it switched to green. The loadmaster leaned forward, his black face shield making him look like a storm trooper. He turned toward Mahegan as he pointed at the bay and said, "Go!"

Mahegan waddled forward as Cassie followed. He leapt into the black void and felt the wind rushing all around him. He spun onto his back, using his arms to stabilize his flight and watched as Cassie fell from the bomb bay and angled toward him. Both were wearing GPS trackers in case they were separated in the air or on the ground. Using oxygen tanks and masks, they could survive the thin air seven miles into the troposphere.

Once Mahegan had Cassie beside him, he extended his right arm and pointed at her. "Now," he said through their wireless communication headphones.

Cassie pulled her rip cord and her military parachute opened with a snap. Once Mahegan could see she was stable, he pulled his rip cord and gained full canopy.

The night was eerily quiet at 30,000 feet above ground level. The whine of the B-2 jets vanished and left in their wake the calm silence interrupted only by the fluttering of ripstop nylon. Mahegan steered toward Cassie and they dipped their canopies to gather as much of the prevailing east wind as possible. They had dropped from inside Iran.

The B-2 had been necessary to get them close enough to the target using the stealth technology while also using the standoff necessary to avoid the microsatellite field they had detected. They needed to fly nearly thirty miles through the night sky, sail between two peaks of a mountain—like a football through goal posts—and then circle down into the valley where the Iranian compound was located. By their calculations the shamal was ending within the next thirty minutes. The weather phenomenon that originated in the mountainous regions of Turkey and Northeastern Iraq often reached into the high plains of Iran. If the winds did not diminish, Mahegan and Cassie would be in for a rough landing.

They communicated very little as they were dropping at roughly forty feet per second and flying at twenty-six miles per hour. From 35,000 feet they planned on about fifteen minutes in the air, which made their stand off for the drop at about seven miles from the target. It was close and right on the margins of the satellite coverage that they could discern. There had been no issues on the inbound flight and drop so far. Egress was a different matter.

Their purpose was to kill or capture the four leaders and / or their biometric keys who were meeting in the underground tunnel four up-armored Mercedes had entered, as reported by American satellite analysts. Four airplanes. Four up-armored Mercedes. Maybe not the heads of state, but something like that. Anyone captured would be an intelligence trove.

During the rapid exchange from XC-17 to XB-2 Bomber, Mahegan and his team had received an intelligence update from the general in charge of troops in Afghanistan. The U.S. military was overrun in South Korea, harkening back to the days of Task Force Smith, which preceded the Korean War. The North Korean Army was steamrolling toward Pusan, also a replay of the war nearly seventy years ago. The improved infrastructure—roads and airports, primarily—accelerated the North Korean advance from its predecessor that led to two years of intense combat on the peninsula.

Mahegan wondered how long it would take to restore order this time?

The Russian army had flowed like water into Poland and was churning through Berlin swallowing that beleaguered city. The Iranian forces were laying siege to Amman, Jordan while their special operations troops had infiltrated the Golan Heights and were preparing the attack lanes for Iranian main battle tanks.

Seventy-two hours, Mahegan thought. His guess was that this thing would be over in three days and his team was already about to put a close to the first day. Whatever the end game was, it was being decided at this meeting.

Savage was deploying Delta Force and SEAL teams to shore up Allied and U.S. positions in the three major attack regions. Given that and the time-sensitive nature of this mission, he had decided to send Mahegan and Cassie on the high risk mission of gathering intelligence and possibly capturing one of the attendees.

Task Force 160th helicopters and the pilots known as Night Stalkers were idling along the Iranian border at the firebase near Farah, Afghanistan, 375 miles away. Once Mahegan was on the ground, his first report would trigger the launch of the task force, which consisted of three MH-60 Blackhawks that carried a slimmed down Ranger Regiment platoon of one rifle squad, one heavy weapons squad, the platoon leader, platoon sergeant, radio operator, and two medics. Two Apache attack helicopters were escorting the three MH-60s. Each of the aircraft were up-fitted with four external store fuel tanks that provided a max range of 450 miles. The extra weight mitigated some of the armament they could carry at the altitudes at which they would be flying. Because the Apaches were the enhanced AH-64D Longbow model, the sensor package and target standoff capabilities were especially crucial. Instead of sixteen Hellfire missiles, each Apache was carrying just four, plus two air-to-air missiles. All good for any potential fight at the pickup zone.

Just after Mahegan and Cassie had released from the B-2 Bomber, an MC-130 was to take off from Farah airfield and fly about 175 miles, land on the Lut Desert floor, roll out wet wing refuel hoses and serve as a temporary gas station for the exfiltration force. Despite the external store fuel tanks, the helicopters would need to top off each way if they were to make it into the objective area and then back safely to Farah with the precious cargo of friendly forces and any captives.

The mission was priced to perfection in a known imperfect world. Mahegan knew there was a likelihood that the exfiltration may not succeed and he would ultimately have to improvise. He had asked Savage to send Owens in with them, but Savage said he needed a backup team, consisting of Owens and O'Malley, who were team leads for Mahegan when they were all active duty serving under General Savage's leadership.

And so it was Mahegan and Cassie with the mission to capture one of the four leaders or keys that would then lead to actionable intelligence. The two person team concept made sense from a low signature perspective, coupled with the fact that a platoon of heavily armed U.S. Army Rangers were inbound an hour after their arrival.

"Hanging in there?" Mahegan asked Cassie.

As the wind whistled and nylon fluttered, Cassie answered, "I'm here, Jake. A little nervous, but here." Cassie's muffled voice crackled as the radio transmitted into Mahegan's earpiece. The oxygen mask made Cassie sound as if she were speaking into a tin can.

"What's there to worry about?" Mahegan replied. "We've got good canopy overhead and we're descending nicely through twenty thousand feet. We'll be able to remove these oxygen masks in a minute, but we should keep them on so that we're 100 percent oxygenated when we land. Then we remove our gear and stash it in our kit bags. We'll move together to the mouth of the tunnel along the ridge we studied."

"I love it when you're so romantic, Jake. Talking dirty and every-thing," Cassie said.

Mahegan smirked, glad to hear a bit of pluck in her voice. He struggled to find that balance between personal and professional. He thought his voice might be calming to her and so it was worth a shot. She knew everything he was telling her, but from his place of leadership and out of love, Mahegan wanted her prepared for the mission. She was essential to the mission . . . and she was es-sential to him.

As the first female Ranger School graduate, Cassie had lived up to the high expectations of her leaders and subordinates. Mahe-gan had concerns, though, given the recent tragic deaths of her parents at the hands of ISIS. Was she moving out too soon on a mission of this import? He had studied every war in American his-tory. He knew that these types of operations and the machina-tions of spies and double agents usually won the day. It was always one or two people around which the entire war raged. Like the spies in World War II such as German journalist Richard Sorge, who'd handed Stalin Germany's playbook, or British double agent Dusko Popov, who'd handed FBI director Herbert Hoover the Japanese plan to attack Pearl Harbor, would Mahegan and Cassie discover that nugget of information that would give deci-sion makers the opportunity to stop the world from imploding due to nuclear war?

"Whatcha thinking about?" Cassie asked, her voice more confi-dent this time.

"We're passing through ten thousand feet," he said. "The moun-tains in this area get up to about seven thousand. Remember, there may be some backwash from that shamal. We jumped when it was still active in the target area. It's moving south, so be ready to steer north. You're going to want to climb above that thing if it isn't gone."

"Roger," she said.

"Five thousand," he called out. They entered a chute between two mountains not wider than a football field. Rugged mountain peaks poked into the misty clouds through which they had descended. "I'm seeing some lights. We may be okay on the shamal. Might still be windy."

"Roger," Cassie said.

As they descended through the early evening, Mahegan flipped his night vision goggle from its secured position atop his modified combat helmet that looked more like a camouflaged skateboard helmet. Through the green shaded world Mahegan was able to identify key markers, confirming they had followed the way points in the GPS sufficiently to land at their one kilometer offset landing zone. This was not his first jump with Cassie. They had used flying suits to penetrate the Syrian basecamp near Asheville, North Carolina.

"Prepare to land," Mahegan said. "I've got a pretty strong gust coming from the north, probably the back side of the shamal." He waited a few seconds and then said, "Okay, pivot north now."

"Roger."

They followed a narrow passageway through rugged terrain that seemed to be rising too rapidly.

"Got a tailwind through this pass somehow," Mahegan said through gritted teeth.

Cassie fumbled with her toggles, the square parachute catching the gust and thrusting her forward almost at a ninety-degree angle.

"Toggle back, Cassie," Mahegan directed. He wanted to avoid extensive radio conversations this low to the ground given the Iranians' sophisticated intercept capabilities.

"Trying." She shot like a rocket through the pass, but managed to get control and stabilize her descent somewhat.

Mahegan struggled with the swirling winds and they both landed hard in a rocky area that had about a twenty-five degree slope to it. Mahegan's helmet struck a boulder, which essentially stopped his parachute landing fall. Cassie landed about fifty meters to his right front.

He was instantly in motion, retrieving his M4 carbine and putting his weapon into operation. He unlatched his parachute harness and slipped it into a kit bag, which he promptly stuck under a rock pile. He shouldered his rucksack filled with IV bags, water, 5.56 and 9 millimeter ammunition for his rifle and pistol, frag and stun grenades, and radio equipment for communicating with Savage and the Rangers who should be launching from their refuel site about now, provided all of that went smoothly. Jumping from a B-2 bomber at 35,000 feet was far less risky than landing an MC-130 on a dirt road, whipping out some fuel hoses and refueling four MH-60 Blackhawk cargo and two conventional AH-64 Apache attack helicopters. B-2 bombers were flying protective air cover overhead with F-35 attack aircraft prepared for air-to-air combat or air to ground.

To Mahegan's knowledge, everything was going according to plan. He powered up his satellite radio as he jogged across the ankle-twisting rocks to Cassie's location. He heard her muttering a string of expletives fit for any soldier.

"My foot is wedged between two boulders, Jake," she said. Her parachute was still inflated and catching wind, pulling her taut.

"Release one of your canopy assemblies before you get hurt worse," he said.

She reached up and flipped the metallic cover over the canopy release and then popped the wire cable to allow one set of risers to fly free, thereby making it nearly impossible for the parachute to inflate. He lifted her and pulled her back to where her leg, foot, and ankle were properly aligned with her body.

"Broken?" he asked.

"Doesn't feel like it. Just hurt. I've got an ace bandage if I need one," she said through gritted teeth.

"Okay, let's get moving then. Weapon into operation. Stow your parachute. Grab your ruck. Let's move." He was sensing that itchy feeling of time slipping away.

"I know what to do, Jake." Her voice seemed full of frustration at her situation, not anger at Mahegan.

"Roger. Then do it. Need to move." He clasped his hand to her forearm and pulled her up as she stumbled out of the rock pile.

Her grimace told him all he needed to know about Cassie's ankle. Sprained or broken. Not good.

She shouldered her rucksack and lifted her rifle. "I'm good."

"Roger. Moving."

They continued to communicate over the small headset radio. While the signature was small, it was there. Yet Mahegan believed the risk greater to lose communications with Cassie, a relative neophyte on clandestine missions, than that of detection at the hands of the Iranians.

He led them around the steep incline, shale crumbling beneath their boots. Through the night vision monocle he saw the trail that would lead to a perch above the tunnel complex where the armored cars had driven. To their right was the wall of the mountain, upright and powerful. He also noticed the glint of a small insect—like a grasshopper—sitting on a crease in the rock formation. The terrain seemed too barren for insects, but he hadn't studied the wildlife of the area. He registered the anomaly and kept moving.

Falling away to their left—east—was a valley with a concrete airfield that ran through the middle like a dash or hash mark. The runway was long, maybe two miles. The valley was bigger to the naked eye than it appeared from studying satellite images.

Mahegan used a land navigation technique known as "hand-railing" around the terrain. It was impossible to get from point A to point B in a straight line, so he followed the natural contours of the ground as it rose, dipped, and curved. Finally, they were near the lip of a cave above the mouth of the tunnel. The outcropping was fifty meters to their front. He saw another insect resting on the rocks. It was maybe three inches long, the standard size of a grasshopper or locust. Perhaps they were indigenous to the region.

Two men were chatting softly with one another. Mahegan understood some Urdu and Pashtu, but was not fully conversant in the sister language of Farsi, the native tongue of Iran. While he had taken on some Iranian terrorists of late, he could only make out a few words that the wind carried to him.

". . . the shamal was heavy . . ."

". . . ready for them to leave . . ."

Mahegan touched Cassie's shoulder lightly, looked her in the eyes using his night vision goggles, and leaned forward to whisper, "Watch my back."

Cassie nodded and lifted her M4 carbine slightly, an indicator she understood.

He stepped forward quietly. The guards were not facing him, but his approach route was an unsteady path of slippery and noisy shale. He thought about the satellites and drones that might be watching him and wondered who could see him better in the dark, the drone operators or the unaware guards? There was little cover to be found on that narrow approach along the mountainside. To his right was a wall of rock that protruded upward maybe 10,000 feet. To his left was a precipitous drop of at least 100 feet that would injure, if not kill, him.

His movement was no different from that of an animal following a minor but well-worn trail to water. His boot slipped, though. Shale crunched and then crumbled seconds later down the mountain. He tried to push his massive frame into the wall of the mountain where he remained motionless, hiding behind the slightest of ridges, though given the size of his frame the effort was futile. If the guards moved toward him, he would have no problem killing them with his pistol, though he preferred to remain stealthy, move in for the close kill and continue the mission.

One of the guards said, "What . . . ?"

"Some rocks . . ."

Mahegan caught pieces of the conversation, then suddenly both stopped talking. When he heard the two whispers emit from Cassie's silenced M4 carbine, he ran toward the guards. One slumped backward and slid down the mountain wall, then fell onto the path. The other, however, spun and turned toward them, like a running back taking a hit but continuing to move forward.

The guard lifted his rifle. Mahegan reached down in one fluid movement and clasped his Blackhawk knife from his ankle sheath, flipped the blade open, and then dove toward the man. The knife came arcing down into the guard's neck as Mahegan tackled him to the ground. He looked into the eyes of the defender and dug the knife a bit deeper. As he covered the man's mouth, blood trickled between Mahegan's fingers. He looked up and saw the alcove from which the two men had been guarding the entrance. There were other guard towers and locations, he was certain.

As Cassie limped toward him, he felt the neck of the first man and confirmed he was dead. Mahegan stripped each guard of weapons and communications devices after he dragged both men into the alcove. There were two metal folding chairs canted toward one another. The alcove was a natural fifteen feet deep cut into the wall of the mountain, narrowing as the opening tapered to solid rock. He adjusted his night vision goggles and turned toward Cassie, who was lying in the prone, providing cover across the valley.

They had no idea what type of radars were scanning in the valley and it was possible that hyper spectral audible radars had registered Cassie's silenced shots. He would discuss with her later, but he didn't think the shot was worth the risk.

Never one to waste time on what might have been, he said, "Good shot."

He inspected the rear of the small cave and found nothing but empty water bottles and dead cigarette butts. *Nothing ever happened here,* Mahegan thought.

Bored guards and cigarettes lead to complacency.

"Anything?" he asked, lying next to Cassie.

"Just some dudes scurrying around the hangar about a mile away," Cassie said.

Though they were side by side, they still spoke in their internal radio communications system to keep their voice at a whisper.

Mahegan felt the ground beneath him churn and immediately knew that the tunnel door was beginning to open. One of the handheld radios he had removed from the guards chirped to life.

"All okay?" a voice asked in Farsi.

Mahegan knew the Farsi word for *clear* and used that term.

There was a hesitation in the caller's voice before the voice came back with a sentence he couldn't answer. "*Mishe tekrar konid?*"

It sounded like another question. Mahegan repeated his first comment. "Clear."

Through the handset, he could hear another voice booming loudly in English. "I don't have time for this bullshit! Let's go!"

While he couldn't recognize the voice through the radio, he was glad someone was there to urge the lower set of guards in the target tunnel along.

As he focused on the noise below, he felt a soft breeze switch direction. It was subtle, but it was there. He also smelled human sweat beyond his or Cassie's. He knew both of those smells and this new odor wasn't part of either of their DNA. Without looking, he rose and began to charge across Cassie's back.

But he was too late.

Dax Stasovich leapt from the opposite side of the alcove from which the two intruders had come.

About thirty minutes prior, he had lumbered into Tunnel 7 to find his employer, Gorham. Prior to that, he had conducted a high altitude low opening jump from the Gulfstream airplane and had landed near the runway during the tail end of the shamal. His landing wasn't pretty, but he had survived.

Minutes after finding Gorham, Shayne's iPad had beeped, indicating what appeared to be one or two flying objects that had penetrated the radio wave shield provided by the connectivity of towers atop the four highest mountains. While the miniature ManaSat constellations had continued to move westward with the advancing Persian force, the four antennae on the surrounding mountaintops provided some type of early warning. The plan all along was to never rely on the Iranians.

Gorham had repositioned two small ManaBlade drones to locate and track the potential intruders. Once spotted, Stasovich would do the rest.

He now had a knife to the smaller soldier's throat. He carried a Gurkha Kukri knife, its large curved blade ready to chop or cut, whichever function he needed. He sensed the smaller soldier was a woman. He could feel the softness of her breasts beneath his powerful forearm that clasped her to his chest. He had scooped her up in one motion, catching the two invaders defenseless. Of course, he had perfect intelligence because the ManaBlade grasshopper drones streamed into his ManaGlass, which doubled as intelligence feed and ballistic eye protection.

The small soldier was tugging at his arm, which was doing no good at all. His grip was like steel, her hands scratching at metal. The big soldier, slightly larger than Stasovich, stood five feet from him, calmly staring at him. He held a knife in one hand and a pistol in the other. Stasovich assumed they spoke English and were probably Americans. The same ones who were tracking Gorham in the bar less than twenty-four hours ago.

"You move, this one dies immediately. Simple," Stasovich said in thickly accented English. His Slavic tones made him sound all the more menacing.

Stasovich felt a stinging sensation in his right leg. The clawing hand at his arm was a ruse. The girl had stabbed him. The big soldier closed the distance and put a knife in the arm holding his Kukri. The small soldier spun away as she used surprising power to push his wounded arm away. Quickly, he was in a hammerlock with the larger solider behind him and the female lifting a pistol to his chest.

"You shoot me, you kill your partner. Bullet will go right through me. Let's deal," the attacker said.

Mahegan cranked his powerful forearm like a vise against the man's neck. He watched Cassie as he wrestled the man to the ground using his foot placed against the back left heel of his opponent in a back trip wrestling move. Once on the ground, Mahegan removed his Tribal and swatted the man in the head twice until he went limp on the ground. He dragged him into the cave and used flex cuffs to bind the man's wrists. He knew they had only thirty minutes to capture the target and move to the landing zone.

"Where the hell did he come from?" Cassie asked.

"They know we're here," Mahegan said. "Monitor comms with the Rangers. They should be inbound in thirty minutes or less. If nothing else, we take this guy."

"Roger, but what the hell?"

Mahegan walked about ten meters up the trail, flipped his night vision goggles down, and saw the anomaly. Black and three inches long, looking like a grasshopper. He quickly snatched it off the mountain wall. It fit in the palm of his hand. As he squeezed tight, the device buzzed, as a captured fly might, trying to escape. "A hundred bucks this is a surveillance drone and that there are more than one."

Cassie stared at his hand and then into Mahegan's face. "You're probably right." She flipped her goggles down and began scanning the mountain wall above them. "There!" She ran after a second device, but it flew away before she could grasp it.

"We've got to move," Mahegan said.

"They're watching everything we do."

"We have to deal with it. Maybe we just need him. He seemed . . . different from the first two. Balkan accent. He doesn't belong here. He's an anomaly. Could be a good find."

"No. We're supposed to capture at least one of the leaders or keys. Not their help. No way this is one of them."

"But you're hurt, Cassie."

"Jake, don't go teddy bear on me. I can hang." Cassie was an intelligence officer and she wanted the top prize, not a third-tier capture that most likely wouldn't talk in the first place.

But he pressed ahead. "A bird in the hand, Cassie."

"We can do this, Jake. We wait for the Rangers. That will overwhelm their intel systems and these little insect drones. Then when they're moving, we move and get one."

"Ambitious," he said.

The large garage door rattled open beneath them. Armed men came streaming from the mouth of the cave, AK-47s at the ready. The enemy soldiers were wearing metal helmets that made them look like new recruits. Each had black body armor that covered their torsos. Through the green shaded world of night vision goggles, Mahegan registered two dozen men, half running north with the other half going south. Assuredly they were sealing the only two routes of escape.

"No choice. Let's grab the big guy and go to the landing zone. It'll be close."

"Roger," Cassie said. "I can cover from here."

"Bullshit. We're going to the LZ now. They have eyes everywhere. We'll be lucky to make it out alive." Mahegan entered the mouth of the cave and lifted the unconscious man onto his shoulders. He emerged and said, "Go. Now."

Cassie led the way to the landing zone, which was basically the same area where they had landed. She walked with a noticeable limp, obviously eating pain. Holding her M4 at eye level, she pulled the trigger twice. Ahead, two enemy soldiers dropped. How they had gotten there, Mahegan had no idea. He was still watching the squads of twelve run in each direction below them. Perhaps there were twelve more somewhere.

"Good shot. Keep moving."

Cassie stepped over the dead bodies and almost fell.

The weight of the big man was heavy across Mahegan's broad shoulders. The distinctive chop of Blackhawk rotor blades was a welcome distraction from the chaos swarming around him. "Hawks coming from ten o'clock," he said into the microphone.

"Roger," Cassie replied.

They reached the area where they had landed, which was a small valley a quarter mile from the tunnel complex they had intended to ambush. Mahegan went through several calculations in his mind. This was a combat mission. They had a captive, but he had no idea if the individual was a worthy prize or just another big dude. Was it like capturing Bin Laden's driver, which would be a treasure trove? Or was it like capturing some random infantryman sent to protect Bin Laden at Tora Bora, which would be next to worthless?

Cassie was right. They needed at least one of the biometric keys that Spartak had mentioned.

Coming in was a platoon of Rangers he could employ in a counterattack. Thirty Rangers against the enemy he had seen so far would make for quick work, though he never underestimated his enemy. He considered the intelligence advantage that the

RINK alliance had in this part of Iran. The sophistication surprised even Mahegan. He churned through options.

Get on the helicopter with the prisoner or fight and overrun the position?

He didn't come all this way to go back empty-handed.

"Tribal six this is Ranger six." The voice was scratchy, as if playing on an old vinyl record.

He heard the Ranger commander's voice, convinced that it was him, but used the authentication word regardless. "Ranger six, this is Tribal six. Florida, over."

"Yellow River."

"Roger."

The Yellow River was the menacing body of water that all Ranger students had to navigate during the final phase of Ranger School. It was the established authentication. Having been burned before when his unit's previous communications system—Zebra—was compromised by Syrian hackers, Mahegan remained cautious. General Savage had had O'Malley set up a new system—X-Ray— with so much encryption an Abrams tank couldn't blast through the firewall.

With two points of confirmation—the Ranger commander's voice and the proper authentication—Mahegan radioed back. "Fuel status for time on target?"

After a slight delay, the commander replied, "Fifteen minutes max. Tight."

"Dismount and set up support force on ridge to LZ twelve o'clock. We've got one EPW. Need another. Assault force rallies around me and I'll lead."

Another delay. The commander was most likely conflicted that a civilian was giving him orders. Mahegan didn't care. He had a mission to complete.

"Roger. You've got fifteen minutes."

"And we've got about twenty-four bogies coming our way. I'll give you the standard recognition signal."

The signal was two blips of his infrared light from his night vision goggle. The sound of the helicopters grew louder. They were flying blackout, but the mix of Apache gunship rotor blades and Blackhawk blades made for a symphony to Mahegan's ears.

"Here," Mahegan said to Cassie. He dumped the man on the ground, removed another set of flex cuffs from his outer tactical vest, and zip tied the prisoner's legs. "You're going to stay with the support team. I'm going in to get your principal." He wanted a major player as bad as Cassie did. The Balkan soldier was a good find, but not the prize they sought.

"Roger that," Cassie said through clenched teeth.

"When we get on the helicopter have the medic tape that ankle."

Cassie was already scraping out her support by fire position. "Better get down."

The unmistakable sound of machine-gun fire zipped past him like angry hornets. The cacophony of helicopter blades and weapons fire suddenly filled the valley in digital surround sound, echoes reverberating like ricochets with nowhere to go.

"They're coming up out of that pass to our two o'clock," Cassie said. "Single file like ducks in a row."

"Apaches working on them also." Mahegan flashed his infrared light at the helicopters that he could plainly see through his night vision goggles. The lead helicopter returned the two-blip code and Mahegan had his third point of confirmation that these were friendly forces. Cassie changed magazines and continued to fire. The Apache gunships lifted high and found cover from which to fire rockets and 30mm chain guns. The valley was a light show, rockets and machine-gun rounds whizzing in both directions, nothing seeming to hit their intended targets.

The Blackhawks disgorged the Rangers, who dashed toward Mahegan from a hundred yards away. They covered the rocky expanse quickly as he knelt and vectored them toward him by flashing his infrared light again.

The commander came running toward him and Mahegan began barking orders. "Support by fire here next to Captain Bagwell. There's the prisoner. Make sure he gets on the helicopters. There's twelve enemy coming from that direction." He pointed to the south. "Assault team with me. We're going down the same way they're coming up. Follow me."

The men quickly adjusted as Mahegan leapt over the rock Cassie was using for cover and ran north toward the trail the enemy was using to access the valley floor. In one hand, he held his Tribal pistol and in the other was his Blackhawk knife. He was expecting close combat. Each of the U.S. soldiers wore infrared patches on their left sleeve so the pilots and friendly forces could determine friend from foe.

As he approached the mouth of the opening, there were at least ten bodies dead from either Cassie's weapon or the helicopters.

"Cease fire. Assault team approaching. Watch the south," Mahegan said to Cassie and the support team. He ran as fast as he could knowing that every second was precious. As he rounded the bend, he found two enemy soldiers cowering with their backs to the wall of the defile they had been climbing. He shot them point blank in the face and raked his knife across their necks in stride. Further down, he saw a small group of soldiers huddling. Continuing to move, Mahegan grabbed the Ranger assault team leader by the body armor and said, "Long rifles, now."

He slowed, but didn't stop. The Ranger leader led his men forward and they continued to move as they used automatic fire to fell the group of enemy from nearly fifty yards away.

As they approached, Mahegan said, "Kill any soldiers. Capture the civilians." He rounded the bend in the lead again and saw the expansive door to the tunnel open. A black Mercedes Benz was exiting the mouth at about 100 mph. Its taillights were soon a distant speck. This was what they wanted. Just one of the people deserving of an up-armored Mercedes Benz.

"That's our target! Anything that looks like that."

"Roger."

The defenses were thin and disorganized. The rifle fire above them from the support by fire position indicated that the southern moving group of twelve had entered the ambush set up by Cassie and the Ranger support by fire team. A few unarmed men were scurrying around the mouth of the cave. Mahegan flipped up his night vision goggles as they approached the opening, which was spilling light onto the valley floor. In the light he could see vehicle tracks, but it was impossible to tell if any had left since Mahegan and team had arrived.

"If you see any vehicle, disable it. We want one prisoner from the back seat and we're out of here," Mahegan said.

The Ranger commander was breathing heavily as they leaned against the wall of the mountain. "Roger." He issued instructions to his eight-man team. They broke into two teams of four. One would be support by fire and one would enter the tunnel with Mahegan.

"Stay here with the support. I'll take assault in," Mahegan said.

"You got it."

A second black Mercedes slowed as it drove through a dip in the opening to the tunnel exit.

"Now," Mahegan said.

The small arms fire into the armored Mercedes was relentless, including 40mm grenades fired from the under-rail grenade launcher on the M4. Tires flattened and windows shattered. The Rangers were less surgical than Mahegan had hoped, but the net effect was the vehicle stopped, which was the desired end state.

"See what you got in there," Mahegan said. "There's another car coming."

Mahegan led the newly formed assault team into the manmade tunnel, the white light nearly blinding him. The next car was only twenty yards away and barreling toward them. Mahegan let the Rangers work their magic. Random gunfire echoed from deep in the tunnel. The 40mm grenades worked on the windshield of the car and one Ranger fired a light anti-tank rocket deep into the bowels of the tunnel to suppress whatever fire they were receiving.

A fourth vehicle roared from a darkened alcove and sped past them, running into a hail of machine-gun fire from the Rangers. A 40mm grenade blew out the door of the car, causing it to spin on flattened tires. Still, the driver kept powering through the Ranger ambush. Something was thrown from the car during the spin. Mahegan saw a flash of white then turned his attention to the vehicle they had stopped.

No more black Mercedes were in the tunnel, which meant two had escaped, including the one with the blown-out door. The Rangers closed quickly on the disabled vehicle in the tunnel and used a crowbar to open the rear doors. They snatched two civilians from the rear, finding both dead. Mahegan ran around the vehicle and knelt next to the man who had been riding in the right rear seat. Black hair. Asian facial features. He looked exactly like the new leader of North Korea. The general. Mahegan had no idea if this man was a doppelganger, but hoped he was the real thing. He checked the man's pockets and found identification, which he inspected and pocketed.

"Less than five minutes." The pilot's voice reminded Mahegan they needed to get back up the mountain.

"Bingo on lead vehicle," the Ranger leader said.

"Roger. We're coming out. No joy." Noone useful found alive. He plunged the Blackhawk knife into the North Korea general's heart and retrieved it quickly, wiping the blood on his pant leg. The general was the only occupant of the back seat of that car. No biometric key, unless it was him.

"Fuck," a Ranger sergeant said, watching Mahegan.

"DNA sample," Mahegan said. "Now let's go."

Mahegan led the assault team out of the mouth and stopped when he saw a large dog lying on the dusty exit of the tunnel. The animal had been ejected from the Mercedes the Rangers had ambushed but failed to stop.

"Hang on," Mahegan said.

"We've got to go!" the commander shouted.

Mahegan felt the animal's neck and got a weak pulse. Her breathing was labored, but thankfully present. He always had an easy presence around animals, loved them. Had pets all of his life and admired animals in the wild. He touched the wound on the dog's hip. She yelped. "Okay, I'm bringing her with us."

"We do not have time for a fucking dog, Mahegan," the commander shouted.

Mahegan cradled the animal in his arms, linked up with the

rest of the formation, and then began running at full speed to the trail that led up to the valley floor. The Rangers trampled along behind him under the weight of their body armor and helmets. They dragged a flex cuffed prisoner on a field expedient poncho litter. Easier than carrying him. Negotiating the defile was more challenging, but they made it up. The dog was still alive, judging by the weak heartbeat.

"Coming up," Mahegan said. "Check fire." He flashed his infrared light twice. Friendly fire shifted away and lessened to the occasional rifle shot. The sound of the helicopter blades resonated loudly in the valley. As they filed into the high mountain valley, Mahegan directed, "Support by fire team collapse on helicopter."

Normally he would have had them wait, but he knew he was already over the time limit. He figured the pilot had safe sided the fifteen minutes by ten minutes and they were about five minutes over time. Through his night vision goggles he saw the support by fire team pick up and move toward the helicopters. One of the Rangers was helping Cassie. She was limping badly and falling behind. Mahegan urged her forward in his mind, but kept silent on the radio. He knew she was tough and would make it.

The Rangers carrying the big man who had attacked Mahegan and Cassie stumbled and fell. Mahegan was torn between running the 100 yards in their direction or heading to the helicopter. The crew chiefs were outside of the Blackhawks pumping their fists in the universal *haul ass!* hand and arm signal.

The Rangers carrying the prisoner were back up, but something didn't seem right to him. They had cut the flexcuff Mahegan had placed around the big man's ankles, presumably so he could walk. Was he too heavy to carry?

Cassie and her helper were making progress. Everybody was closing on the helicopters about the same time. The support by fire team ran and shuffled to the rear Blackhawk while Mahegan led the assault team to the lead aircraft. He ducked beneath the whipping blades, put the dog in the middle of the helicopter's cargo bay, and counted the Rangers onto the helicopter. On his chopper, he had everyone they came with plus one dog and an American looking hipster. Thick brown hair fell across the man's forehead. He wore a satchel, like a man purse, over a thin button down shirt and stylish jeans. Had to be worth something.

The crew chief was yelling at him to get in the aircraft. "Have to go now, sir!"

Mahegan watched from fifty yards away as Cassie's helper laid his rifle in the cargo bay of the second Blackhawk at the same time the two Rangers carrying the prisoner began to maneuver him toward the helicopter. Cassie sat on the lip of the cargo bay, her legs dangling over the edge. Knowing her, she would fly like that the entire way back.

"Get in the helicopter, Cassie," Mahegan whispered, not realizing he was broadcasting on the radio to her.

"Trying," she said.

His helicopter began to gently lift off. The crew chief jumped in and manned his M240-B machine gun on the starboard side of the Blackhawk.

The two Rangers handling the prisoner had placed the prisoner on the edge of the cargo bay next to Cassie as they maneuvered around him. Somehow, he had worked his hands free of the binds. There was a struggle. The prisoner jumped from the trail aircraft as it lifted high into the sky. He pulled Cassie with him to the ground, tumbling maybe thirty feet. Soon both helicopters were over one hundred feet above ground level and nosing over.

"We are priced to perfection on the return trip, my friend," the Night Stalker special operations pilot said to Mahegan, as if to accent the disconnect that the lead aircraft pilots were unaware of the brewing problem with the trail.

"Problem with the trail!" Mahegan said. "We've got a soldier on the ground!"

Cassie and the prisoner were on the valley floor as her helicopter followed Mahegan's in trail. The Apache helicopters closed in on the formation and unloaded hellfire missiles on two approaching Shahed 285 attack helicopters. Similar to the U.S. military's Kiowa

Warrior, the 285 was based on the same Bell 206 JetRanger design. It carried 70 mm rockets and a light machine gun.

Surprisingly, the air-to-air Hellfire missiles found their targets, creating two bright explosions that lit the valley floor like two lightning strikes. Not every weapon system was infected. The blossoming explosions shone on tanks rolling across the valley floor in front of the tunnel entrance.

Mahegan was losing his mind. "Man down! We have a soldier on the ground!"

Tank rounds blew past the helicopters.

"Turn around now! That's an order!"

More Iranian troops came spilling over the ridge near the alcove where Mahegan had killed the two guards. They had surface-to-air missiles. The helicopter began to bank under the direction of Mahegan's orders.

Muzzle flashes lit up the night as the Iranian infantry fired from the south and the tanks fired from the east. The helicopters were caught in a blazing cross fire. The only egress was to the north, through the mountain pass.

"This is an airfield! They have gas here. We defend here!" Mahegan shouted into the headset.

"We're taking fire. Trying," the pilot said.

Mahegan knew the code and ethos of each member of this task force was to leave no soldier behind. They would do everything humanly possible to retrieve Cassie.

Her voice scratched over the radio waves.

"Jake, it's okay. Go."

He could hear the wariness in her voice and the physical struggle ongoing. She was fighting, but the man was strong. She had beat him once. Could she do it again? Watching the struggle was like a grate across his heart. A soldier down. The woman he loved in jeopardy.

"No, we're coming back in," Mahegan said.

Cassie was squared off with the big man. They were circling. Did she have a pistol or knife?

"They have missiles, Jake. I see maybe fifty soldiers. It's too dangerous."

One of the Rangers on Mahegan's helicopter doubled over, his hand grasping his neck. Bullets pinged inside the cargo bay, sparking as they richocheted.

"We're taking heavy fire!" the pilot said. "Moving to protected location!"

"Winchester on ammo," came a voice over the radio. The Apache attack helicopters were out of rockets and machine-gun rounds.

Mahegan figured they didn't bring a full load because they had to carry the wing store fuel tanks. It was a trade-off. Distance over firepower. In their defense, it was an extraction mission, not an assault. He had changed the mission.

"We gotta get out of here!" Mahegan's pilot echoed. "Co-pilot shot!"

The nose of the Blackhawk tilted over and sped away to the north with the others in trail. Enemy fire chased them the entire way out of the valley.

"Cassie! Cassie!" Mahegan repeated into the radio headset. He continued to talk into his small boom microphone. "Cassie! Cassie!" He wrestled against the hands clutching him, holding him in the rapidly ascending aircraft. He tried to jump, but the loadmaster had placed a snap hook on the back of his outer tactical vest. He dangled outside of the helicopter, reaching back in an attempt to unhook the snap hook. He ripped at his outer tactical vest, trying to unsnap it. Bright green and orange tracers burned past them like a macabre light show.

"Soldier down! Soldier down!" Mahegan repeated.

The futility of his words grew more profound with every chop of the rotor blades that pulled them away from danger—and Cassie—and toward the designated refuel point in the middle of the desert in Iran.

As he struggled with his tactical vest, hands were pulling him inside the helicopter.

Soon, the valley where they had fought was gone from his view, replaced only by the emptiness of the black void through which they flew and the hollow pang of failure he felt in his soul.

CHAPTER 13

GORHAM AND KAL RAN UP THE STEPS TO HIS JET, DAX STASOVICH behind them carrying the unconscious American soldier over his shoulders. Behind Stasovich, the Iranian Olympian thundered along.

Like Noah's Ark, Gorham thought. The ambush had been devastating, but he had two of the biometric keys with him boarding his plane.

Kal had traveled with Gorham at his urging. When the attack occurred, lights were flashing like strobes. They met in the outer ring of the conference tunnel, security busy rushing to the entrance, concerned for their principals. The North Korean general ran scared, got in the wrong Mercedes, and apparently didn't make it. Gorham had clasped Kal's hand and pulled her into the lead car. Persi followed. Glad to have the North Korean and Iranian Biometric Keys with him, Shayne was somewhere behind, apparently captured.

"Go! Go! Go!" Gorham shouted to the pilots, who had the 777 rolling along the dark runway before anyone had found their seats. He sat in the forward cabin leather reclining chair while Kal sat on the bench seat next to him. Stasovich and Persi lumbered into the next section of the cabin, Stasovich dumping the captured female soldier on the floor. He placed her rucksack on a leather seat, tied her legs and hands with some rope, and then sat next to the rucksack as he pawed through the contents.

Gorham noticed Kal and Persi taking it all in, most likely wondering if they were going to escape whatever attack had come. They locked eyes briefly as Gorham looked over his shoulder as Stasovich retrieved grenades, ammunition, water, IV bags, and other combat supplies from the soldier's bag.

"Careful," Gorham said.

Stasovich lifted his head and met Gorham's gaze with the dead-eyed look of an assassin.

"Careful," Gorham reiterated, as if repeating a command to a dog. *Sit.* Aware enough to understand that every man had the drive for wealth and the need to feed their own beasts, he considered his predicament.

Stasovich was a mercenary and a deadly killer. That he was also a maniacal savage was at times unnerving to Gorham. However, the half-million-dollar annual salary he paid the thug afforded the man a life of luxury. His work to this point—protecting Gorham as he traveled the world ostensibly meeting with clients as he grew his social media/retail/search engine empire—had been child's play. Having overtaken Facebook, Amazon, and Google with the Manaslu platform Gorham was constantly fending off lawsuits much in the same fashion those companies had done as they had competed against like entities, all vying for the lead. He had determined that the only way to win was to beat them all. It was like a game of high-low poker where he had to have the winning hand in both directions.

And then there was the matter of Shayne being captured or more likely dead. He truly relied upon Shayne's skills. Thankfully, everything was already in motion. Perhaps he could survive without him? Doubtful.

Two additional elements, Kal and Persi, had been added to the calculus. He had no idea who the woman was other than someone the North Korean government had entrusted to be their biometric key to unleash their fledgling nuclear arsenal. As for Persi, he looked like he could be useful muscle to help the severely wounded Stasovich.

"She's alive, but her ankle is broken," Stasovich said.

"Set it, fix it, do what you have to do," Gorham directed. "I want her healthy."

He used his phone to snap a picture of her and then a few seconds later ManaRec—Manaslu's facial recognition software—confirmed her identification as Captain Cassandra "Cassie" Bagwell. He scrolled through dozens of articles about how she was the first female graduate of the U.S. Army Ranger School and how her parents had been killed by Syrian terrorists in the Blue Ridge Mountains of North Carolina. Her father had been a four-star general and the chairman of the Joint Chiefs of Staff when he was killed. Newspaper articles had been written about the testy relationship she had with her father. He had not wanted her in the army, much less attending Ranger School.

"Interesting," Gorham muttered to himself. "Same woman from the bar. They've been following us." He picked up the phone wired to the cockpit. "We're going to Amman, Jordan."

After some back and forth with the pilots, the plane banked and headed west.

Stasovich sat across from Gorham as Kal remained silent and watched. Persi sat in the very back of the airplane, perhaps wondering what would happen to him for abandoning his boss.

"Why Amman?" Kal asked. Her first words since joining him.

Gorham studied her. Beautiful. Smart. Deceptive. Seductive. Lethal. All those adjectives came to mind as he looked into her almond-shaped eyes. Her black hair was cut in an angular bob just above her collar. She carried a small backpack that most likely had a variety of weapons. He was doubtful she wasted space on makeup.

"You speak English?" Gorham asked.

"Very well," she replied.

"Can I trust you?"

"Do you have a choice?" she replied.

"I do, actually. I can have my man kill you or at least incapacitate you."

"Doubtful. He's wounded badly. We are on the same airplane and the same team. We want victory just as you do. Why not share information, Mr. Gorham? Isn't that what Manaslu is all about? You call it *publicy*—a word you invented—where others argue for *privacy*. Tell me. Why Amman?"

Gorham paused again.

"Okay. First, publicy for everyone else, not Manaslu. Our secrets are ours. Next, with my operations officer, Shayne, in the hands of the Americans, I want to get lost under the satellites for a while. I need to think. They've got his satchel and iPad. They can probably track me. While I've activated the code to wipe it clean, nothing ever gets wiped clean. Perhaps our own fault, maybe even our own undoing, but to monetize information, we made a conscious decision to never completely erase anything. We have nearly a billion users of ManaMail and we archive everything. A politician's e-mail to a lover from five years ago? He may have erased it. She may have erased it. But we've still got it. If he becomes prominent, we can resurrect it and use it discreetly against him to win votes as we take another step toward stripping the public of their privacy or leak it to the press if he doesn't agree with our position. Either way, we win. So, Shayne's iPad is dangerous to us if they find the right people to work it, which is questionable. Because that risk exists, I want to spend the next twenty-four hours close to the front lines, which I've always wanted to do anyway."

Kal said nothing, but nodded, thinking.

The 777-jet roared through the sky as Gorham switched on his ManaMap system. Without Shayne by his side to keep him informed, Gorham would have to provide his own situational awareness.

"Here's a thought," Kal said, nodding at the woman on the floor. "You trade her for your Shayne. You offer up the intelligence officer for Shayne."

"What's your interest?" Gorham asked.

"I've listened to everything you said. I know your plan. Where you're going. What your needs are." She paused and looked at Stasovich. "What your vulnerabilities are."

"I can kill her now," Stasovich said.

With an invisible flick of a wrist, Kal spun a throwing star at Stasovich. It landed and stuck in the wood paneling above his head and to the left of Persi, who continued to stare, unflinching, his only worry being his fate for having left the president's side.

"That was an intentional miss," she said. "You can't kill me. I mean that in both senses of the word. You cannot, because I will kill you first. And secondly, you cannot because you need me alive."

"Why? The North Korean nuclear arsenal is free to launch wherever."

"*Ne vse v nem kazhetsya*, Mr. Gorham."

Nothing is as it seems, Mr. Gorham.

Stasovich spun his head from the throwing star to the Korean. "She speaks Russian." Being of Serbian descent, he was partially fluent in basic Russian and Ukrainian. "Nothing is as it seems."

"You work for the Russians?" Gorham asked.

"I never said that," Kal replied.

The plane gained altitude and Gorham thought for a moment.

"Back to the woman," Kal said, chinning at Captain Bagwell laying in the aisle. "Is it worth it to us to make the trade? Will the Americans even make that trade?"

Gorham turned his iPad and pinched the screen, then spread it using his thumb and forefinger. He punched the screen twice with his index finger and then repeated the process of pinching and spreading. "This picture, tells me she is." He showed Kal and Stasovich the iPad screen.

Jake Mahegan and Cassie Bagwell were holding hands as they sat on the ferry from Southport, North Carolina to Bald Head Island.

"We've got Cassie Bagwell, and judging from the size of the operative with her, that's her lover." Gorham pointed at the screen.

"I saw that guy in the bar. You're correct," Stasovich said.

"He was in the bar?"

"Yes. He's the one who led the counterattack. Why it wasn't a successful mission to snatch the cook."

Gorham scratched his head and cracked his neck by leaning it in each direction. A habit he'd been meaning to stop, it reflected nervousness. To burn off that energy, he began digging through social media Web sites, then the proprietary facial recognition software until he got a random hit from the Department of Homeland Security black/white/gray list.

"Shit. He was listed as gray, possibly detain."

"His government doesn't trust him, but they let him do this mission?" Kal said.

Gorham grimaced. "Yeah. America can be fucked up like that. Chayton "Jake" Mahegan. Age, thirty-one. Almost six and a half feet tall. Two hundred and thirty pounds."

"Yes. That's him. I saw him twice. In the bar and when I fought him hand-to-hand. And in a different life in North Carolina."

"Seems he got the best of you," Gorham said. He looked at Stasovich, who looked away.

Kal looked at Gorham and said, "Your man survived, though. Don't be so hard on him."

"That's right. I'm here. In their haste, the soldiers did not check my sleeve." Stasovich extended his right forearm and rolled back his black shirt sleeve. A SOG Trident tactical knife with built in seatbelt cutter was resting in its sheath open toward his hand. "They were rushed, thankfully."

"Yes, thankfully," Gorham said.

"So. The girl for Shayne. Where should we make the trade?" Stasovich asked. It was a rhetorical question. Stasovich was just the muscle. But he was also a tactician and a survivor. The fact that he was on the airplane with Gorham was testament to his tactical savvy.

Gorham and Kal exchanged glances.

Stasovich continued, "You don't have Shayne, and you don't have the cook. Shayne was your thinker. You think of me as just a strong guy." He leaned forward so that his face was inches from Gorham's. "I'm here. I outsmarted them. You're here. You outsmarted them by leaving in the first vehicle. We both have good instincts. You treat me like just muscle? I could snap your neck right now, but I won't. You know why? Because I'm loyal."

"And you'd have to deal with me," Kal said. "I'm not so easy." Her voice was level. The tones were smooth and easy.

Gorham's eyes widened. He could smell Stasovich's stale breath. It occurred to him that Stasovich *could* snap his neck right here, right now. Gorham wasn't a small man by any measure. Over six feet tall with an athlete's build, he could hold his own, but he doubted he was a better fighter than Stasovich. Having Kal in the forward cabin suddenly brought him comfort. Whose side was Persi on? he wondered. Or was Persi in shock, suffering from post-traumatic stress?

"I know that we will get out of this alive. I also know that you have a nuclear attack planned on the United States that is supposed to start in the next forty-eight hours or so. I would be foolish to kill you because you are going somewhere safe and I will be with you," Stasovich said.

"That's right. So, let's stop this talk about killing. And back the fuck away from me, Dax."

Stasovich smiled. His teeth were yellow and uneven, some overlapping. "So where do you trade the girl? You have less than forty-eight hours to do so because the cook is still a problem."

Disarming the Americans was key to the plan. It was those weapons upon which mutual assured destruction rested. Like two sheets of metal leaning against each other in perfect balance, the United States and Russia pushed against one another, but neither fell because each had thousands of nuclear weapons ready to respond to any attack. While Gorham was confident that the submarine and B-1 bomber based weapons had been sufficiently disabled, the cook posed a threat to his overall plan. On the second day of ComWar in North Asia, Southwest Asia, and Northern Europe, burning swaths of land were smoldering in the RINK alliance wake.

All of that was important to Gorham's plan. The proxies of America were being destroyed, the primary purpose of the attacks. Japan and Europe, rebuilt by the Marshall Plan following World War II, would be rebuilt by Gorham. Under Gorham's guidance, the world would migrate toward a borderless Utopia as opposed to a series of over 200 nationalistic states focused on their own well-being. Just like the mega corporation he had built with talent from all over the world, Gorham would use those same principals of diversity and equality to reshape the world. His social media empire would unite in common cause, either confirming everyone's beliefs or influencing them to believe what he sought.

He turned and looked at the fifty-five-inch HD screen to his front. One of the ManaBlade insect drones had entered one of the U.S. helicopters and used its magnetic properties to adhere to the fuselage of the airplane. It showed the helicopters landing somewhere with lots of dust in the air.

"Or maybe," Gorham said. Perhaps he could create a crash that might kill Shayne—no way he would hold up under the pressure of waterboarding or other American tactics for extracting information—and if they couldn't make the exchange in forty-eight hours, a better trade was the woman for the cook, though he doubted Captain Bagwell was worth that to the Americans. By now they had to know what they had with the cook, an unrivaled hacker who could penetrate any database or architecture in the world. An army ranger or a hacker? Easy decision to Gorham. The hacker would take primacy. The ranger was less important.

He watched the screen as two helicopters ferried up to what looked like a hose behind an airplane, apparently took on fuel, and then repositioned somewhere else.

One of the mechanisms he had built into the ManaBlade devices was that the Niobium encasements contained a small quantity of high explosive urea nitrate the size of a blasting cap, or to the layman, a slender cigarette. Originally, it was intended to destroy the high tech, proprietary device to keep it from becoming useful to unwanted parties. The ManaBlade not only piped back live streaming video, but it automatically calculated the dimensions of the aircraft to which it was affixed. Using grid style engineering graphics, the monitor showed a Blackhawk helicopter with fifteen personnel aboard.

Gorham had a thought. While the ManaBlade was not situated

to provide facial recognition of the individuals, there were two transport helicopters in the formation and he figured he had a 50% chance of killing Shayne.

Decent odds, especially if he could get a chain reaction out of it. He could potentially destroy everything in that location in one stroke.

As a Blackhawk shifted and moved toward the fuel hose, Gorham adjusted the ManaBlade camera—the eyes of the insect—to get the best possible view of the gas line. Because of the swirling dust, there was no way to determine where the other helicopters were located. A soldier ran beyond the camera eye and stood next to the helicopter. While the drone transmitted no sound, he could only imagine the chaos and noise associated with the refueling operation.

With the power of the downdraft created by the helicopter rotor blades, he did not want to move the ManaBlade. Instead he trained the lens as far to the rear of the cargo bay as possible. Soldiers were all looking toward the back of the aircraft, tired eyes peeking from beneath helmets, alert and anxious. He turned the lens toward the hose, which bulged from flat to swollen. The aircraft was refueling.

"I see what you're doing. Killing your Shayne. Big decision. If you're lucky enough to get the right helicopter," Kal said.

"He'll never hold up under pressure." Gorham pressed some buttons on the MacBook monitoring and controlling the ManaBlade, typed in the control number of the device, and clicked DETONATE.

As he began to click the confirmation dialogue box, the soldiers in the helicopter began scrambling, mouths open in silent screams.

Mahegan ran from his helicopter, which had refueled already and was over one hundred yards to the north of the MC-130 Combat Talon wetwing refuel airplane. Normally a paratrooper dropping workhorse, the MC-130 was versatile with advanced avionics and the ability to carry fuel bladders in the cargo bay that could pump JP-8 jet fuel into the aircraft. The two Apache gunships had refueled first and continued providing protective cover for the refueling of the two personnel aircraft.

He shouted at the refuel operator, "Last one! Roll this up when you're done and get back to Farah!" He briefly considerd turning around all four helicopters but he decided that regrouping and planning was better than heading piecemeal into an unknown situation. Plus, the MC-130 could maybe pull off one wetwing refuel in the middle of the Iranian desert but the odds were against two successful missions.

As he jogged beneath the whirring blades of the helicopter, he saw the tired faces of the Rangers. They had saved him, but lost Cassie.

Mahegan always found on the ground leadership to be the most effective, like Patton at the crossroads. It was early morning, men were tired, the mission was stressful, all of which were important.

However, he had been unable to reach Kandahar Air Base via the Blackhawk communications and knew that the MC-130 would have a better chance with higher frequency equipment. Mahegan continued through the airplane, beyond the fuel bladder, and up into the cockpit, all the while, something from the helicopter registering in his mind.

It was just a glimpse, but it was there. Something significant he needed to remember now as opposed to later. The need to let General Savage know about Cassie overrode that instinct for the moment. The co-pilot handed him a microphone and said, "Make it quick. We're rolling in under sixty seconds."

"Roger." Then into the microphone: "Jackknife Six, this is Tribal Six."

Savage's response was immediate. "Status."

"Mission accomplished, but one friendly captured."

Savage heard the subtle tone in Mahegan's voice. "Charlie Bravo?" *Cassie Bagwell.*

"Roger. At the pick-up zone."

Savage, usually quick to reply, paused. "Roger. Just get everyone else back safely. Will meet you at RP. Out."

RP. *Rally point.*

The helicopters would be lifting off momentarily for a one hundred and fifty mile race to Farah Airfield, the westernmost U.S. forward operating base in Afghanistan. The U.S. military built a two mile runway there, mostly for logistical purposes, but also in the event of a war with Iran. An intermediate staging base from Afghanistan would be necessary.

The grasshopper! Mahegan remembered seeing it attached to the frame of the helicopter that had just ferried into position for refueling. He ran from the cockpit, down the ramp, followed the hose through the swirling fog of sand and dirt and found the hose operator holding the six inch diameter hose that was pushing gas into the helicopter. "Shut it down!" Mahegan ordered.

The man looked at him through thick dusty wind goggles propped beneath his helmet. He had an olive kerchief around his nose and mouth and was mouthing something to Mahegan. The words were drowned out by the kerchief and the rotor wash.

"Shut it down! There's a bomb!"

Mahegan wasn't sure there was a bomb, but he assumed the functionality could include that scenario. He turned to the troops in the helicopter. "Out! Out! Now! Now!"

The men began piling out of the open cargo bay doors. Because the mission had called for more troops than a Blackhawk can carry using seats, the bays were simply open spaces and the Rangers exited quickly. Mahegan climbed into the helicopter, eyeing the small device, watching it glow, something he hadn't seen it do when it was in the objective area.

He grabbed the crew chief in the starboard seat and said, "Tell the pilots there is a bomb on board. Shut down the engines and get out, now!"

To emphasize his point, Mahegan squeezed past the radio console and tapped the pilots on the shoulders and used the universal thumb hook over his shoulder to say *Bomb. Get out!*

He watched the pilots' heads nod up and down. He felt the deceleration of the rotors above him and watched the pilots quickly exit through their doors. He dragged the loadmaster away from his machine gun, shoved him outside, turned and lifted the wounded dog, and dove to the ground.

The refuel operator shut down the gas flow and detached the nozzle from the aircraft fuel port. He was running with the hose toward the aircraft when a bright spark erupted from the frame of the port side of the helicopter where the device had secured itself. Mahegan handed the dog to the loadmaster and then leapt onto the hose as he retrieved his knife and sliced through the rough material, aviation gas showering him. He then stuffed the severed end leading back to the bladder into the sand and placed his body atop as much of the hose as possible.

The detonation was small by any measure, though not without consequence. The red light must have been a countdown light of sorts. Mahegan watched as the refuel operator ran toward the MC-130, carrying the cumbersome hose nozzle in the crook of his forearms, as if he might carry a baby. The nozzle was leaking a steady stream of gas, a product of the inflated hose having been shut off at the outlet and not the source, the fuel bladder inside the aircraft.

The spark from the explosion sent fragments of the aircraft frame whizzing through the air, some stinging him in the back. The refuel operator seemed to get the message and was running away from the helicopter and the MC-130, toward the gaggle of Rangers who had dropped about fifty meters away. A piece of shrapnel sparked on the metal nozzle, wet with aviation gas, which caught fire. The fire spread quickly onto the operator who looked like a Hollywood stuntman running through the desert. And while he wore flame retardant clothing, the fire appeared to be consuming him until a group of Rangers ran toward the man and jumped on him, smothering him.

After a few seconds the fire was out. Mahegan felt the stinging sensations in his back, but seemed to have prevented the major catastrophe that he was sure the enemy hoped to achieve—to kill everyone in the refuel area. He rolled in the dirt to prevent the hot fragments from igniting any of the jet fuel that had sprayed on his clothing.

The loadmaster was wheeling the hose into the aircraft and pumping his arm up and down, the universal symbol for *Haul ass!*

The helicopter buckled, its blades still spinning at a rapid, but reduced rate from full idle. The port side caved and the frame of the helicopter began to collapse on itself, the blades inching closer to the ground.

Mahegan shouted, "MC-130 now!"

The Rangers from the disintegrating helicopter bolted up the ramp into the refuel airplane. Mahegan lifted the dog from the confused crewchief, ran into the MC-130, and grabbed one of the Rangers. "Got everybody?"

Another Ranger came up to Mahegan and shouted, "Counting the last two in now!" Up the ramp came two Rangers carrying the charred refuel operator.

Mahegan turned to the loadmaster and shouted, "Lift the ramp now!"

As the hydraulic arms pulled up the ramp, the MC-130 began rolling. It turned hard right and then began to bounce across washboard terrain at take-off speed. Once airborne, Mahegan looked down at the dog, as if he'd forgotten she was in his arms. He laid her in a litter and strapped her securely for the flight. He went to the cockpit, eyeing the Rangers as he said, "Good job, men." In the cockpit he borrowed the radio handset again and talked to the pilot of the last helicopter.

"Head to RP now," Mahegan said.

"Already OTW," the Blackhawk pilot said. "Saw the cluster unfolding and repositioned away with the gunships. Everyone okay?"

"Maybe."

Through the narrowing gap in the cargo ramp, Mahegan watched the helicopter blades bite into the ground, disintegrating into small chunks of shrapnel, and then ping off the MC-130 fuselage like ninja stars.

CHAPTER 14

*F*ROM HIS LEATHER SEAT, GORHAM WATCHED THE CHAOS AT THE RE-fuel point, the latitude and longitude of which he passed rapidly to Iranian special intelligence.

"Get a bomber over them. Do something!" he shouted as his ManaBlade exploded but did not achieve the desired effect.

The big man had blocked the shrapnel with his own body. How stupid was that man to risk his life that way?

It was a simple tactical maneuver that did not pay off. That was okay. Gorham had fired a nuclear device from North Korea into the heart of Tokyo. What was one minor setback? Not a setback at all, he figured.

"Relax," Stasovich said. "They'll be lucky to make it back alive. And they will come for the girl."

"I don't know," Gorham replied. His plane was making its descent into Amman, Jordan where they would be met by the Iranian commander. The commander would then usher him to the command post for an update on how the ManaSats were working in concert with the equipment Manaslu had helped develop over several years.

"They will come," Kal said evenly.

They landed on a dimly lit runway, dawn still a distant echo to the east. As they deplaned, Gorham noticed black SUVs move silently into position. Soldiers dressed in black uniforms secured his passage from the airplane to the vehicle.

"Welcome, Mister," said General Solhami, the commander of all forces on the Arabian Peninsula, which was basically the entire Iranian military. He was a tall, broad man with olive skin, a trim mustache and beard, and a scar that ran across his nose and left cheek. It was almost certainly from a downward slash of a knife.

Gorham must have stared at it too long, because Solhami said, "Combat. This is what you want to see, right?" The general touched the scar on his cheek and smiled.

Combat *was* what Gorham wanted to see—real soldiers in action on his behalf, as if he were the commander in chief of these men. Soon, he would be. His global empire would include Iran and every other country.

"Thank you, General. I know you have a fight happening. We are here to make sure that all is functioning smoothly with ComWar and RAIL," Gorham said.

"I see you have another guest," Solhami said when he saw Kal walking down the airplane steps.

She turned and looked at him, smiling. "Hello, General. We meet again."

Who *was* she, Gorham wondered?

"It is very good to see you, as well. I'm glad you are still alive after the last incident."

"Did you ever seriously doubt? Plus, they're not getting rid of me, yet. I've got Mr. Gorham to take care of for the time being," Kal said. "We have a world to conquer."

Gorham watched the interchange and began to suspect that she was a shadow in plain sight.

Solhami turned back to Gorham. "Okay. We do this my way."

As he ushered Gorham and Kal into the armored car, Gorham noticed the disapproving look on Solhami's face when he saw Stasovich hustling Captain Cassie Bagwell out of the airplane.

"You have an American prisoner?"

"That's right. We captured her prior to coming here."

A loud explosion rocked the ground beneath Gorham's feet. Several more followed in succession. His throat clenched and he wondered if he really wanted to taste combat. Bright fireballs erupted in the distance, painting an orange glow on the horizon.

"The Israelis are firing artillery, but this is good. We can find them and kill them using your radars," Solhami said. "Thanks to the virus your engineers placed in the missiles and artillery systems, their fire is mostly ineffective. Our advance has been rapid, as you can see. The Israelis are firing missiles over Amman, and the missiles are landing short, in the city. It appears as if we are allies, Iran and Israel, attacking Amman in a classic pincer movement. Of course the missiles are intended for us, but your hackers have done good work."

Everything was mostly working as it should. The remote access Trojans that Manaslu had pushed into the defense industries of all American allies had infected many of the weapons systems so that they were inaccurate. In this instance, the Israeli rocket systems were bombing Amman, an unintended but certainly acceptable consequence.

Persi stepped from the airplane.

Solhami stopped and stared. "Where is the president, Alexander?"

They had a personal relationship. Persi was most likely a special forces soldier. Gorham chided himself for not using his time to create dossiers on Kal and Persi. Everything was harder without Shayne.

"He was killed, General. I came to the front lines to inform you."

"Your job was to protect him," Solhami's scolded. "Without our president, who will negotiate the spoils of victory?" He retrieved his pistol and aimed it at Persi.

"Do as you must, General. I accept my failure."

"Do you want to describe the conditions? Are there mitigating circumstances?"

"The conditions are irrelevant. The president is dead at the hands of American Army Rangers. I deserve whatever punishment you decide."

"Rangers?" Solhami looked at Captain Bagwell laying inert on the tarmac. He turned the pistol toward her.

"No," Gorham said. "She's a trade for the bigger picture. I can tell you that Persi did everything possible to protect your president and it is important that he stay alive. He is the biometric key for Iran. If someone hacks Iran's nuclear arsenal again, you need Persi to open it back up. He must live."

Solhami stared at Persi, then at Gorham. "I know this, but the question is, why do you know this? Kal? You're the only one I trust here."

"He lives, General."

"Very well. But he stays here in a protected spot. Have your big man there keep watch over him," Solhami said, pointing at Stasovich.

They rode in the Suburban until they stopped in front of a Russian helicopter with blades spinning. Stasovich, Persi, and Bagwell were in the trail car.

"Tell me, Mister. Do you want your prisoner with us at the front lines? Or would you prefer my interrogators . . . question her." Solhami smiled.

Gorham considered the question. The sneer on Solhami's face told him that there would be more liberty taking than questioning of the captain. He was unconcerned about that, but she was his leverage to get the cook and possibly Shayne back into his custody. He considered that there was a fifty-fifty chance he would get her back alive if he left her with the Persians. Maybe less than that. On the other hand, she may cough up something useful besides blood. Solhami's men were most likely experts at interrogation and he needed to know where Spartak was. Did he need the Iranians to help him?

"The prisoner stays here. Stasovich will keep guard on her and your man, Persi. Plus, she needs medical attention. I don't need your men to question her. We won't be long," Gorham replied. The risk was too great for him to lose control of the woman.

"As you wish. You are missing a good opportunity," Solhami said.

As are your men, Gorham wanted to say.

They stepped out of the armored car, more explosions lighting up the Amman skyline like the flicker of a movie stage sunset. Fear rattled through Gorham, but he was determined to confront this deficiency in his character so that he could speak of combat with authority.

"She needs medical attention," Kal said. "That should be the first priority. I'll travel with you, Gorham."

Preferring to have Kal with him, he nodded in agreement. Stasovich, Persi, and the woman were led away in the armored car after Solhami spoke in Farsi to the driver. Then, they ducked as they boarded the helicopter. It lifted off quickly. Solhami sat facing Gorham, handed him a headset, which he placed over his ears.

As they rose above the Amman skyline, the world looked as if it was on fire. Rocket launchers were firing pods of lethal munitions into the Jordanian Army's front lines. Counterfire was inaccurate or nonexistent. They flew over tanks racing at ten to twenty miles per hour as their main gun bores slewed and laid accurate fire on Jordanian targets. Bright orange and green tracers lit the black sky like a rock concert light show. The lights were arcing in both directions, meaning that the Jordanian army machine guns were fully functional, as Gorham had expected them to be. There was little that could be done to the low-tech weapons such as rifles and machine guns, rendering the infantryman perhaps more relevant in this conflict than some might have thought.

The only thing that slowed the advance was the incessant machine-gun fire and random mortar and artillery fire, much of which was rendered inaccurate by the ManaSats targeting the mortar ballistic computers the Jordanians had purchased from American defense contractors. By targeting the small handheld devices and scrambling the data the operators had entered, the ManaSats were rendering the Jordanian defenses nearly ineffective.

But not completely.

One bunker was barricaded inside an office building four stories high. Three machine guns appeared to be focusing on the lead tank of the Persian formation. A rocket smoked from the fifth floor and struck the first tank, causing its turret to lift off the chassis and spin on the ground like a top. The secondary explosion seemed to Gorham to be a miniature nuclear explosion within the tank. It was impossible that anyone might survive that attack.

The advancing Zulfiqar Main Battle Tanks immediately spread

from a single file to ten abreast, guns spitting flame and high explosive rounds at the machine-gun bunkers in the building. As the machine-gun fire lessened, the Iranian built Zulfiqar tanks formed in single-file again and led the advance into the city.

"If that tank two hundred meters ahead can be hit, that would mean we can as well, right?" Gorham asked Solhami.

"Of course. That is the nature of combat. Everyone can die. It is the great equalizer."

The helicopter pilot flew cautiously behind the advancing armor unit. Two Hind attack helicopters flanked them, occasionally slinging rockets into the barricaded city streets.

"This is combat," Solhami said. "Your technology has made it easier, but we still have men dying. Kal knows the taste of death, right?"

She nodded. Gorham looked at her wearing the headset. She was a natural. Her face was calm and unworried. Eyes set and mission focused. He looked out of the wind screen and watched the tank burn as they flew low above the flaming debris. Charred bodies were oddly frozen in place, the flames lighting their tortured death masks of bare teeth grimacing with the pain death delivered. The skeletal remains charred inside the tank hull chased away any romantic notions Gorham might have had regarding combat.

Solhami had been watching him. "Do not let beauty deceive you."

Gorham was unclear if he was referencing the fireworks arcing through the skies or Kal.

Solhami continued as if in a stream of consciousness. "Many more will die. Perhaps we will kill more than Stalin and Hitler combined. All because of your algorithm." He chuckled. Maybe even more of a scoff.

Gorham had never thought in those terms. He considered Hitler and Stalin monsters, killing tens of millions of innocent civilians to achieve their selfish goals. No. He wasn't a maniac like those men. He was leading the world toward the Utopian goal of no borders and world peace with shared resources and equality for all. Instead of a more perfect union, he was creating a more perfect universe. "No."

"You are just like them, Mister."

The helicopter dove toward the ground as the pilot called out commands in Persian, translated by the fast thinking Solhami. "Missile. Ten O'clock!"

Cassie Bagwell pulled away from the man she knew was Dax Stasovich.

While lying on the floor of the Boeing 777 her mind had found consciousness like a diver breaking the surface of the ocean on her last breath. Disoriented and confused, she'd replayed what memories she could. The jump. The twisted ankle in the rocks. The fight with the man who turned out to be her captor. Jake rushing into the fray to accomplish the mission, almost at her urging. Their successful return. The Blackhawk helicopters landing. The Rangers escorting her. The big man cutting through his restraints and pulling her off the helicopter at the last second. The firefight. Then her memory was blank until she awoke on the airplane.

She'd logged names and countries. *RINK alliance. Dax Staso-vich. The cook. Kal. General Solhami. Amman, Jordan. Combat for the first time. Manaslu. ComWar. RAIL.* Other terms that meant little to nothing to her.

She was an intelligence analyst and officer as well as an Army Ranger. Her creed was to always continue the Ranger mission. She had no doubt that Jake had done everything he could to not leave her behind and she was okay with whatever decisions he made resulting in her being held captive. Most likely, the helicopters were taking off and under fire and there was no option to come back and get her. Otherwise, they wouldn't have the fuel to make it to the refuel location. She knew the mission and knew that it was priced to perfection. She had pushed Jake and, Mahegan being Mahegan, he had executed what he believed to be the best option. As a result, she owned her predicament.

She saw her position as an advantage for the United States since she had all but heard the enemy plan. *Three days. Nuclear warfare. Rapid computerized blitzkrieg by conventional forces. Tear down the world to rebuild it. War as a means to political ends of an extremist*

that wants a world without borders in some misguided drive to unify a
chaotic world at constant battle over limited natural resources.

Was she currently at the nerve center of the operation? An unwitting prisoner, but apparently one that Gorham intended to use
as a bargaining chip for the cook—Spartak?—and possibly someone named Shayne.

As Stasovich pushed her into the brightly lit hospital room, she
saw a doctor in a white smock guarded by two soldiers in olive uniforms holding AK-47s. By her calculation, she had at least a severely sprained, if not broken, ankle. She could barely put any
weight on her left foot. Her vision was blurry and lacerations on
her wrists had mostly stopped bleeding. Stasovich had bound her
arms tightly with a white zip tie that was now covered in dark, dry-
ing blood. Her body ached, but she was alive and her mind was
clear.

She had to escape.

That was the soldier's creed. If ever captured, it was every soldier's obligation to attempt to escape.

She'd listened as the man called Gorham had determined her
identity in a matter of seconds, if that. The resources this enemy
had at its disposal seemed immense. Facial recognition? Fingerprint? Some kind of biometrics, for sure.

"Who is this?" the doctor asked.

"She is American. I capture," Stasovich said. "Fix her wounds
and I'll watch."

The two guards closed around her, but she kept her pleading
gaze focused on the doctor. She needed him to fix her, as Stasovich said. Before the injured ankle she would have been confident in her ability to outrun any of the men in her immediate
vicinity. Now, she was reliant upon her mind and her training,
which would be good enough.

"Please," she muttered to the doctor.

The doctor barked something in Farsi and the guards stopped
walking by her side. The doctor pulled her forward.

"My duty. Then, whatever," the doctor said, waving his hand.

The two guards and Stasovich watched as the doctor dragged a wheelchair to her side and helped her sit. She was glad to be off the injured ankle.

When the doctor went to push the wheelchair, Stasovich blocked him and grabbed the handles. The doctor decided against fighting Stasovich and led the big man pushing her wheelchair and the two soldiers out of the waiting area.

Not good. Cassie needed the doctor alone.

They entered the emergency room littered with dead bodies and beds filled with wounded and dying men. While she knew they had relocated to Amman from where she had been captured, she took pride in the fact that others were fighting and resisting the advancing Persians, as well. If the world was circling the drain, at least she, Jake, and the Rangers were a part of trying to slow it down.

The doctor approached a small room with an open door adjacent to the emergency room. He stepped inside and swept his hand through the tiny space with a patient table in the middle.

"Please. You can see there is no escape. I have to cut away her uniform. She deserves privacy."

Stasovich didn't budge, but he didn't say anything either.

"Out. I am commander here," the doctor said.

Stasovich nodded and stepped back until he joined the soldiers in the emergency room. The doctor closed the windowless door on Stasovich's stern gaze.

Turning toward Cassie, who had propped her butt on the exam table, he said, "What are Americans doing here?"

"I thought you had a duty?" she replied.

"I do, but answer my question."

"A madman has started World War III. Computers are launching nuclear weapons. Russia, Iran, and North Korea are allied and destroying civilization."

"Much as America did in Iraq, Syria, and Afghanistan?"

"Please. The Persians and Arabs were fighting before anyone could pronounce *Merica.*"

The doctor smiled. Cassie deduced he probably had a western education. His English was excellent and judging by his empathy,

the level of which remained to be seen, he had at least been in-
fluenced by the West in some way.

"True. Though we are in Jordan, the cradle of civilization is in
Iran."

"Might be some Iraqis or Tanzanians that take issue with that,"
Cassie quipped.

As the conversation was developing a rhythm, she turned her
head, grimacing in pain, but also scanning for weapons. Two
scalpels sat unguarded two arm lengths away on a stainless steel
tray which sat atop a wood countertop. A reflex hammer was next
to them. Four boxes of gauze. Dozens of bottles of pills, most
likely generic aspirin or something more powerful like Vicodin.

"Are you okay?" the doctor asked.

"Am I okay? Hell no. But let's start with your name. I'm sure I'll
have to file insurance."

He smiled again. "You're quite engaging, Miss . . . ?"

"Yes, Miss. Never married."

"Brilliant. I was asking your name."

"A gentleman would go first."

He nodded. "Jolly well, then."

Brilliant? Jolly well?

"Hamza Sadiqi," the doctor said.

"Sarah Marshall," Cassie said.

Sadiqi smiled. "I saw the movie."

"Different show, Hamza. Now how about *A*—getting me some
pain meds; *B*—wrapping this sprained ankle; and *C*—stitching up
these cuts?"

"I'm sure you're used to bossing your troops around, but as you
can see, I'm in charge here."

"Just prompting you to quit flirting and start doing your job,
Doctor."

Perhaps that was the wrong move. The doctor's face turned
bright red beneath the olive complexion and trimmed beard.

"As you wish, Captain Bagwell."

So, he knew her name? Why then the theatrics? Was he truly a
doctor or was she being interrogated? For a moment, fear ran

through her body as she looked into the once soulful but now flat eyes of the doctor. Was the scalpel a tool of medicine or torture?

Sadiqi walked behind her. She heard the clink of metal, almost assuredly the scalpel. She could smell his musky aroma, a mixture of sweat, cologne, and hand sanitizer. His smock opened and brushed against her back as he leaned into her ear and whispered, "I stand here every day and watch what is happening and in limps a beautiful woman. Do you know how long it has been for me?"

The scalpel blade winked in the bright fluorescent overhead light as he held it to her throat.

Neither a tool of medicine nor torture, she gathered. He wasn't going to treat her and he wasn't interrogating her. He just wanted a piece of ass.

She turned her head so that she was cheek to cheek with him. The feel of his beard bristle made her want to gag. "Do you know how long it has been for me, Doctor? Perhaps we can make a mutually beneficial arrangement?"

Sadiqi's manicured fingers stopped stroking her cheek. His head tilted. "Really?"

"You think I'm getting any?" Cassie asked.

"So many men, though. Your choice, no?"

His breath smelled as if he had just gargled with mouthwash. The scalpel hovered just below her throat. She studied his nails, trimmed and buffed. She deduced he was a soft man. Beatable. Like a running back finding the gap in the line and looking for the best path through the secondary, she started thinking beyond killing the doctor. Where would she go? On entry to the room, she'd noticed no windows, but saw a closet door. Did it lead elsewhere?

"What if the men come in while we are . . . engaged. Then you've lost your prize, because they will all want some. I would prefer to just be with you, Doctor." It was a gamble. She deduced that the doctor's ego was large and the notion of giving herself exclusively to him might entice him to at least consider the closet.

"But the door is locked."

"Did you see the size of that guy? Plus, they have weapons. Is there somewhere we can go? I'll be with you, but I don't want to get raped." The irony of her words was not lost on her. He fully intended to rape her at knife point. She was simply doing the best she could with a bad situation.

As if to emphasize her point, a big fist pounded on the door with three loud thuds.

Cassie raised her eyebrows. "Better get that. But first you might want to do something that makes it look like you've actually tried to help me."

Sadiqi slipped the scalpel into the lower left pocket on his smock. Grabbing some scissors, he cut her pant leg, calling out, "Just a second!" Removing her boot, the doctor peeled away her sock, which she was sure stunk with sweat.

"Still turned on?" she quipped.

The doctor looked up as the door was pounded again. "I can't tell without an X-ray, but based on the swelling, I think it is broken. I can wrap it tight and immobilize it."

She needed to wear her boots so she could escape. Barefoot would not help her, but if he wrapped it thick enough, that might serve the same purpose of a boot. "I want to be able to wear my boot. I don't want to show weakness in front of these men."

The doctor nodded as if he understood.

The fist pounded on the door again with even louder thuds. "Open the door!" Stasovich shouted.

Already Cassie could recognize his voice.

The doctor turned away and pulled open the metal door, blocking the entrance with his body. Cassie used the opportunity to look to her left, an area she had not been able to scan well. Cabinets of medicine, surgical gloves, more gauze, and needles. Judging the distance, her left hand would be about five inches away from the cabinet with the needles. No way for her to quietly secure the weapon.

"Please, I am working on the soldier," Sadiqi said. "She has a broken ankle. I must set it and then wrap it. Then I have to stitch some wounds. After that, she is yours."

Stasovich peeked his head around the corner of the door and

confirmed Cassie was still sitting there. She grimaced in mock pain, though the injury and hurt were real.

Seemingly satisfied, Stasovich said, "Ten minutes. That's all."

"Ten minutes. I should be done by then," Sidiqi said.

More like two minutes, Cassie thought.

He locked the door and turned toward Cassie, his brow beading with sweat. Stasovich had unnerved him.

While he was still standing there, Cassie said, "What's in the closet?"

Sidiqi looked at the door to his right. Paused. Thinking. "It's not a closet." He lifted the lanyard around his neck and retrieved a white card that appeared to be a fob. He walked to the door, held the card to a black pad that beeped. The door lock clicked and Sadiqi pulled open the metal door. She couldn't tell, but it appeared to be deeper than a closet.

A passageway?

"Finish wrapping my ankle and we can go into your special room, Doctor. Any dead bodies in there?"

"Yours will be if you try anything." His libido was raging, but not so much that he had lost his sense of self preservation.

"I know the only way to stay alive for now is to let you have your way. So, I'm going along with it."

Sadiqi cocked his head. "A smart woman or a survivor? Or both?"

"Can't be too smart. I'm a prisoner of war with a broken ankle."

Sadiqi looked at the ceiling as if checking for monitoring devices. "You're not a prisoner. You're a guest of the Iranian government. I am simply performing necessary medical procedures to help you heal. Then your escorts will take you to your quarters."

Sadiqi was covering his ass for the Red Cross in case the room was bugged. As an extra precaution, he continued talking as he wrapped Cassie's ankle. He even produced a walker boot, which he secured to her foot and ankle. "I don't have cast material, but this boot should immobilize your foot for you to heal. It will certainly help you walk over here with me."

Cassie pushed her body off the exam table, landing on her

good foot and gingerly placing weight on her left ankle. She grimaced even though it felt much better than before. She felt the tight wrap compress around her ankle as she slipped off it onto her right foot and fell onto Sadiqi, stumbling as she clasped his shoulders with both hands, sliding down some until his strong arms grasped her to keep her from falling.

As he lifted her, Sadiqi dragged her toward the blackness that lay beyond the open door.

The pounding on the main door to the exam room began again. "Open now! Too quiet!" Stasovich's voice thundered in concert with the pounding of his fists. Sadiqi's head turned toward the door.

Cassie's cuffed hands slipped into the smock pocket, fumbled with the scalpel, and grabbed it backwards, but that was okay. She pressed up on her injured foot, standing straight up, pushing against Sadiqi with her shoulder to give her enough room to lift her arms.

The main door slammed open. Standing in the well of the side door with Sadiqi, Cassie stabbed the scalpel into Sadiqi's jugular and raked it back and forth until she saw a fountain of blood squirting perpendicular to his neck. In a swift flip of her wrist, she used the bloody scalpel to cut the lanyard with the card fob and then pushed Sadiqi toward Stasovich, who was firing his pistol into Sadiqi's body. If the cut carotid artery didn't kill him, Stasovich surely just did.

She pulled the door shut, but Stasovich's hand reached in and began pulling it back open. The giant Serb was much stronger, her only option being to release the door handle and use the scalpel to lacerate his fingers.

Stasovich howled and lost his grip on the door, which Cassie promptly shut. The lock clicked into place. She hobbled into the darkness as AK-47 rounds punched into the metal wall behind her.

CHAPTER 15

*T*HE MC-130 REFUEL AIRCRAFT FULL OF U.S. ARMY RANGERS AND Mahegan bounced onto the Farah, Afghanistan airfield.

When the ramp lowered, Mahegan instructed one of the Rangers to carry the dog to the headquarters and dashed to General Savage's waiting Humvee. "They've got Cassie."

"Roger that. You told me. We've got eyes on that compound. Got a company of Rangers on standby as QRF if we get a bead. A Boeing 777 took off and headed west. We tracked it to Amman, Jordan. It's possible she's on that. Maybe, maybe not. Once we get a sliver of intel, we're going in. The remaining Blackhawk and two Apaches are fourteen minutes out. Hauling ass. When they get here, I need you to get that prisoner into interrogation. We're a little lean, so we need to work him."

"Roger that," Mahegan growled. He would lead the QRF, quick reaction force, when they had a location on Cassie. His mind reeled. *Leave no soldier behind.* He should have jumped from the helicopter. He tried. They had been ascending rapidly through 100 feet as he saw the big man jump off the trail Blackhawk with Cassie as his prisoner. Maybe he'd be dead now. He was acting on pure instinct. Save Cassie. The woman he loved.

And this was what love did.

Mahegan retrieved his knife, found a rag in the back of the Humvee, wiped the blood off the blade. He handed the rag and the identification from the dead Korean leader to Savage. "You might want to have this checked out. Could be the new North Korean president—that general. Or could be someone who looks like him."

Savage looked at the rag and the identification. "This could be big."

"Maybe. Probably a doppelgänger."

"You kill him?"

"No. Just extracting a DNA sample," Mahegan said. "But he's dead."

Savage nodded.

The Humvee made a couple of sharp turns into the headquarters complex, which was a series of stacked shipping containers and trailers packed into a U-shape. The giant satellite antenna in the back was the giveaway that the surrounding buildings were significant.

"That container over there is where you'll interrogate whoever we've got," Savage said. "We need ten minutes in the command center to update you on the global meltdown that's happening. Fucking chaos."

Chaos was about right. Combat was chaos. The mission Mahegan had just completed was a perfect example. The plan went about 50% according to plan. Then all hell broke loose, which was about the norm in Mahegan's experience. He cycled through several thoughts, always coming back to Cassie. *Should he have jumped? Could he have jumped and lived?* Doubtful. But he wouldn't know now. First it was Sergeant Colgate a few years ago and now a fresh, deep wound with Cassie. He kept trying to find the right spot for the thought in his mind. He needed to compartmentalize because he had to execute and be at optimum performance if he was going to get her back.

The Humvee stopped and Mahegan followed Savage up some wooden steps into a series of trailers. He took a deep breath and blew it out, as if he was conducting a bench press. He loved Cassie as a partner and as a soldier. The pain was deep and sharp, slicing through scar tissue and protective walls he had built over the years. He had let her in through his brick wall defenses two days ago on Bald Head Island. She had navigated the maze to his heart, scaled the inverted walls, and secured the flag that no other woman had been able to. She was in his heart and he felt the pain as sharply as if they had been lovers for years. He yearned for her in a way that he had never experienced. His anguish must have been evident on his face.

"You okay, Jake?" Savage asked.

"We gotta get Cassie back. That's all there is to it. Leave no soldier behind." He turned away, pinched his eyes, then turned back toward Savage.

Savage nodded, looked away. "I know it's more than that, Jake. We will. And we're going to stop World War Three, also. I need you to get in there and interrogate. This thing caught us so flat-footed that I'm only now getting teams into place."

Mahegan steadied himself by placing a hand on a gray desk inside the command post. The trailers were connected along the long sides to create a sufficient work space for the staff. Instead of a double-wide, it was more like a quadruple-wide. In the middle of the space was a circular elevated platform that had large sixty-inch monitors hanging from the ceiling. The place smelled of sweat and burning toner. Printers were spitting out pages of classified documents trying to keep up with the pace of world events.

They sat in the middle of the circular command center and Savage pointed at the left most monitor as Owens and O'Malley were ushering the freshly captured prisoner to the container.

"That's the Korean Peninsula and Japan. The North Korean Army is about halfway down the road to Pusan. We've jumped in two brigades of the Eighty-second Airborne behind their lines to cut off their logistics with another brigade joining the team in Estonia. Two C-17 airplanes were shot out of the sky. Two hundred paratroopers dead, just like that"—Savage snapped his fingers—"not to mention the air crews."

"Computerized assisted warfare. Digits, EMP, and directed energy combined with lethal conventional weapons," Mahegan said, gaining his composure. Electromagnetic pulse was nothing new, but the combination of digital bombs, lasers, and EMP were proving to be unanticipated and lethal.

"Tokyo took a North Korean nuke at about ground zero. No estimates as to casualties yet, but I think it's safe to say that it's not good. Over one hundred thousand dead, I'm assuming. Big bomb."

Mahegan shook his head. *How did this happen?*

"The next screen is Iran, where you just were, but given the limited resistance, the Persians have made it all the way to Amman. Forty-five miles from Amman to Jerusalem. And it's pretty much smooth sailing. The Israeli Defense Forces are shooting rockets and the prime minister is considering nukes over Amman into the advancing Persians or even into Iran to cut the lines of operation. This is a shit show of the highest magnitude. Not sure how effective any of that is, because the Iranian Army can just go through the West Bank and blow through the security fences. There's no question Israel is the goal, though they've not asked for our help yet. I'm wondering if they somehow can shoot straight when we can't. We've got a Marine regiment just offshore and ready to go. We may send them anyway."

Mahegan said nothing. He was still half with Cassie and half with Savage.

"Pay attention, Jake."

"I'm here, General."

Savage switched screens and pointed at Europe. "Here's a classic triple envelopment from the Russian Army. Ten tank divisions coming through the Baltics. Estonia, Latvia, Lithuania, and Kaliningrad are already split in half like firewood. Infantry and paratroopers have secured key cities along the major routes in Belarus with considerable help from the Russian resistance there. Another ten divisions have blown through the mountain passes and will converge on Warsaw about the same time the northern axis will. In the south here, through the Ukraine, another ten divisions are churning along like nobody can stop them, which no one apparently can. They'll follow the southern route and hit the Fulda Gap in Germany, bypassing all the mountains in the Czech Republic."

"I get Iran's objective of destroying Israel. They've been wanting that for decades. I understand North Korea wants to annex

South Korea and the peninsula. That's been their goal since the end of the Korean War. But what is Russia's purpose in Europe?"

"Raw economic need and greed. Russia's economy is imploding. Oil hasn't bounced back and with clean energy and all that bullshit, may never bounce back. So, this is what war is always about. Power and money."

Mahegan nodded. He processed what he was hearing, then said, "Like I said before. If the conventional systems have been hacked, what makes us think that Israel's nukes will go where they're intended to go?"

Savage paused, scratched the bristle on his head. "Damnit, Jake. Why is everything so fucking hard? That's as off topic as it gets, but an important question."

"Just saying, General. Our jets can't shoot a missile. Our radars provide counterfire on the wrong grid coordinates. This is a digital and electronic reverse blitzkrieg. By rendering our weapons inaccurate, the enemy is killing us quicker than a knife fight in a phone booth and we don't have a knife. I mean, think about it, General. You can barely drive faster than these major military movements that have happened in the last twenty-four hours. Baghdad to Amman? Russian border to Warsaw? Pyongyang to Pusan? The bigger implication is that we lose mutual assured destruction."

The chatter in the small operations room stopped. Mahegan and Savage had been talking in measured tones. Mahegan had crystalized the essence of what the quickened combat was all about.

Removing the security of mutual assured destruction from the United States was the end game. Without the capability to counterattack against the RINK nuclear arsenals, the United States was vulnerable. Three against one. No ability to strike back anywhere.

"Let's go talk to our prisoners," Savage said.

Mahegan followed him out of the command center. The sun was rising over the mountains to their backs. His ears were ringing from the explosions and lack of sleep but he could still hear the morning bleat of goats in the distance. Roosters crowed. The air was dry and thin, acrid from the burn pit. Two guards dressed in army camouflage and full combat kit stood at port arms out-side of the container.

"Where's Spartak?" Mahegan asked.

"She's next. Another container."

"Okay. We'll work this guy, but I think she's the key to every-thing."

"Maybe," Savage said.

They walked into the container once the guards opened the squeaking metal doors.

Inside, the container was cool, maybe even cold. The high desert air had chilled some, but the metal walls seemed to amplify the temperature outside from one extreme to the next. Then Ma-hegan noticed a small air conditioner blowing on the prisoner, who was handcuffed to a folding metal chair. The man had shaggy brown hair and a boyish face, partially covered by a tan rag tight across his eyes and secured at the back of his head with a knot. Maybe mid-twenties? He was bare chested and shivering, ei-ther from the cold or the shock of being a captive.

Owens stood before him holding a water bottle as he said, "Who is your boss?"

The prisoner kept shaking his head. "Man, I can't say."

O'Malley was at a small table just inside the entrance of the container that doubled as a prison cell. He looked up, leaned into Mahegan and whispered, "Sorry about Cassie. We'll get her back. In the meantime, this guy's iPad is a treasure trove of infor-mation. I had it all, was sorting through it, downloading it onto our hard drive and then it all just disappeared. Over the air wipe. These guys are sophisticated."

At the other end of the container, the prisoner was shouting. "The best!" He sounded delirious. "We are the fucking best, man."

"Who is *we*?" Owens asked. His voice remained calm, steady, un-flinching.

Mahegan walked across the metal floor, the sound of his boots like the staccato of gunshots. He tapped Owens on the shoulder as if to tap into the ring.

"My friend was being polite," Mahegan said to the prisoner.

"I'm not like that. Your boss, whoever he is, has one of my soldiers. One of your men, a big guy, kidnapped my soldier—"

"Fucking A, man. Dax got himself a prisoner. Maybe we can do an exchange!"

Mahegan looked at Owens in question and mouthed the word *drugged.* Owens shook his head. *No drugs.* Mahegan wrote *Search Dax* on a piece of paper and handed it to Owens, who walked to the mouth of the container and knelt next to O'Malley.

"Eye for an eye, baby!" the prisoner shouted.

"Yes. We trade," Mahegan said.

"I knew it! Yeah baby. Trade my ass. Just like the NFL."

"Yes. Just like the NFL. A player must know his worth. What is your value . . . Shayne?"

O'Malley handed a piece of paper to Mahegan that gave him a summary of Shayne's background, which was nearly zero. Legally changed his name to Shayne—like Cher or Bono, just one name—and had erased his entire identity from the Internet somehow.

"How the fuck do you know my name?"

"Thanks for confirming," Mahegan said. "We've got your iPad. Seems we know quite a bit."

"Yeah, right. That thing is useless as a Frisbee right now. If I don't enter a code every thirty minutes it zeros out. Either that or HQ did it."

"High tech," Mahegan said, leaning back, letting the prisoner talk. The man's mouth was covered in dry, white spit. Two days of whiskers were sprouting on his dirty face.

"You don't even know it, man. We're the best. Better than everyone. The very top, dude."

"We'd like to get you back to your team and of course get our teammate back. Who shall we call?" Mahegan said.

The man rocked in his chair, muttering. "Arms hurt, man." He shook his head, uncertain what to do in this circumstance. Clearly an untrained civilian, but impressive hacker. Perhaps Shayne was thinking more clearly than anticipated if he could be a belligerent smart ass while being questioned in an ice-cold container on the Afghanistan-Iran border.

The man stopped shaking and suddenly smiled. "Call the cook. That fucking cook. We should have captured him."

So, it was them? Mahegan thought. It all came down to the initial skirmish over Spartak, the Russian girl one container over. But Shayne didn't know who Spartak was. *The cook. Him.*

"How do we do that?" Mahegan asked.

Owens walked up to him with a piece of paper. Mahegan looked at it and nodded.

"You guys have him, man. We *know* that. That's how good we are. We're inside your head, not the other way around."

"I understand you guys are good, Shayne. We've established that. I just want to get you back to where you belong. What were you doing in Iran? Should we just take you back there?"

Shayne didn't seem too enthused about those prospects. He shook his head and said, "Nobody's there, man. You guys fucked all that up. I told Gor—I told him we shouldn't go there, but no, he wanted to be a fucking hero. A frontline commander."

Mahegan picked up on Shayne's near slip, and ran with it. "Sounds like Gor, is that what you said? This Gor is your commander?"

"Forget I said anything, man. This discussion is over. Over! You hear me?"

Mahegan changed the inflection of his voice to a saddened, deeper tone as if resigned to a course of action he did not prefer. "Yes. We can progress to the next level if you wish. You are underestimating how greatly I adhere to our creed to leave no soldier behind. Do you enjoy pain, Shayne? Is that your thing? Because I'm out of time. We've got forty-eight hours, maximum, until the world is in a nuclear holocaust. You've started World War Three. Can you help us end it? Or do I have to hurt you? Are you that loyal to Gor?"

The octave switch impacted Shayne, but he remained silent as he shook his head and perhaps started to cry. Mahegan looked at the piece of paper Owens had handed him. He nodded at Owens, who slid behind the prisoner, a foot behind him.

"Now you know how brutal Dax Stasovich is, correct?" Owens asked.

"Yes. He's one of our best assets. Like the fucking terminator, man."

Owens leaned into Shayne's ear and whispered loud enough for Mahegan to hear. "The man talking to you killed your Dax Stasovich."

"I don't believe it," Shayne said.

O'Malley and Owens had followed the action on live streaming video from the powerful special operations dedicated satellite. When Mahegan and Cassie fought the large man, O'Malley had zoomed in and was able to screenshot a reasonable picture of the man they believed to be Dax Stasovich. He looked dead, both Mahegan and Cassie leaning over him, but his face was clearly visible.

"Lower his blindfold," Mahegan directed.

Owens slid the blindfold down and stuck the picture in front of Shayne's eyes.

"Focus for a second on Stasovich. Notice he's dead. Two operatives killed him. Specifically, I killed him," Mahegan said, wishing it were true. "If I could kill Stasovich, what do you think I can do to you? I want you to think about that for a few seconds before we move to the next level of questioning, which is three dimensional."

Shayne was silent as he stared at the grainy photo. There was no doubt that was Dax Stasovich in the picture. There was doubt, obviously, whether he was dead or alive, but importantly, he *looked* dead. "Three dimensional?"

"Right now, we're talking and looking. Next phase will involve physical contact. You don't want that. And we're out of time. If you prove you're worthless, then that's the worst case for you. It gets physical."

"I make seven figures. Not worthless," Shayne said.

"Who pays you seven figures? He's either a dumbass or doesn't care about money."

"My boss is bringing genius to the wor—" Shayne stopped abruptly. He'd made a mistake.

Mahegan locked onto the statement. *Bringing genius to the world.* Where had he heard that before? Somewhere. Television maybe, though he didn't watch much television unless it was news and even then, not much. A commercial in an airport? "Go ahead. Complete the sentence."

Mahegan lost his patience and stepped around the table. He recalled the time he'd killed Commander Hoxha, the handcuffed bomb maker that had used Siri voice command to detonate an IED under his best friend's Humvee in Afghanistan. Hoxha had tried to escape in the confusion. Mahegan had tried to stop him with a butt stroke of his M4 carbine to the man's chest. Hoxha had ducked—maybe Mahegan was a little elevated in his aim— and Mahegan's powerful force had ripped into Hoxha's temple and killed him instantly. Knowing Sergeant Wesley Colgate was most likely burning alive in the car had set a flywheel loose in Mahegan's mind and he had been filled with primal fury.

Today, Cassie was in danger, held captive in Iran, maybe Jordan. He had no time to waste. The flywheel was loose again, spinning wildly with cables flapping everywhere. He'd failed Colgate. He refused to fail Cassie.

"You can't do this!" Shayne shouted.

"Guys, step outside for a moment," Mahegan said. He towered over the diminutive techie as he flipped open the knife blade and pressed it against Shayne's left eyelid. "Where you just were in Iran they have a custom to cut out the eyes of prisoners so that even if they escape they are lost."

"This is not allowed. I'm an American!" Shayne shouted. He was sobbing. Tears streaked down his face. The flat part of the knife was pushing the lid closed. His other eye darted, looking for help.

"Bringing genius to the world. You're with Manaslu?" Mahegan had heard the slogan.

"Move the knife and I'll talk."

"No. You talk. I move the knife."

Shayne digested that he wasn't in charge and said, "Okay. Yes. Manaslu is my company. But it's bigger than Manaslu."

Owens and O'Malley had simulated leaving the container by opening and closing the door, but they had remained inside and immediately got to work.

"Ian Gorham, age twenty-nine. He's one of the top five wealthiest people in the world. Politically active. Not a fan of the current administration. Billionaire Hector Baeppler is said to be his mentor. Baeppler is like Soros. Funds a bunch of leftist groups like Antifa and pays for opposition research on candidates that don't meet his agenda. Lives in a compound outside of Portland, Oregon. Has a series of satellites that could be powering the low orbit microsatellites we've picked up," Shayne said.

"All these guys live in compounds," Mahegan said. "So, we started out thinking we needed an antidote to destroy the remote access Trojans that are making us miss all of our targets and now we're realizing that it's a global conspiracy?" Mahegan asked, the knife pressuring the eyelid perhaps more than he wanted.

"Mother fu—" Shayne yelped. A trickle of blood seeped from the eye.

"Confirm or deny," Mahegan said to Shayne.

After a long pause and more pressure from the knife, Shayne said, "Yes. Ian Gorham is in charge. But Baeppler has a role, too. Not sure what it is."

"What's your role?"

"I'm his go-to guy. Officially I'm the chief technology officer. I go everywhere with him," Shayne said.

"Hear that?" Mahegan said to his teammates. "Ian Gorham, owner and founder of Manaslu, was in Yazd, which means he's got Cassie." With knife still in place, Mahegan said to Shayne, "Okay, those black grasshoppers that followed us and almost killed us all. You know that your boss was trying to kill you, right?"

"He would never do that!"

"He would and he did. If he had his way, we'd all be burning carcasses on the desert floor, including you. Especially you." Mahegan removed the knife and wiped it on Shayne's black shirt. A red tear of betrayal continued to trickle down his left cheek. "When we get Gorham, where does he have to be to call off the strike?"

"He'll claw his eyes out so you can't make him do it," Shayne said.

"Where?" Mahegan pressured. The knife again. Another red tear slid down Shayne's face.

"Idaho. Our headquarters."

"Manaslu headquarters in Idaho? It's that simple?"

"Nothing simple about it, my man. It's in the basement of our compound in Idaho. Enough food in there to last five years. The plan was to be back tomorrow before all hell breaks loose."

"Okay. How do you contact Gorham?" Mahegan asked. "How do you stop the nukes? How do you defeat the Trojans on all of our weapons systems? Answer those three questions and you'll live."

"Gorham. My iPad. But it's zeroed out. Wiped clean, I'm sure."

"You're a hacker. A programmer. Don't bullshit me."

A long pause. Though Mahegan's knife was no longer pressed against Shayne's face, it was a harrowing threat hovering close by in his clenched fist.

Shayne swallowed, figured his time had come. "Yes. There is a way. You have to get into each ground control station. The satellites pipe down to mobile command centers that move along with the armies. Somewhere in the middle of the column you'll find satellite dishes and command vehicles."

"Can't we put a missile on these things?"

"You could, but everything is backed up in the satellites. We call them ManaSats." Shayne hesitated. "It will take a few hours to configure another ground station. You've got to get the satellites."

"But?" Mahegan prodded.

"You can erase everything with the biometrics in the mobile command posts. There is one individual each president has selected whose biometrics can shut down the ComWar automated attack. They control the nukes, also. Otherwise, everything keeps plowing ahead. It's like the automated trading in the stock market. Before they put in the circuit breakers to halt trading when it's going up or down too fast, the markets would crash a million points, you know? The algorithms we put in the ManaSats and ComWar modulate the attack so that it maintains momentum. Never too fast; never too slow."

Mahegan thought of his special operations maxim, *slow is smooth; smooth is fast.* ComWar apparently figured out the same thing.

"Does anyone have override? Any person able to shut down all three?"

Shayne smirked. "You need all three people. You've got to have all three. But I'm telling you man. The Russian president shot his dude. Bang. Right in the fucking head. Like, just, bang." Shayne shivered. "Like, blood all over the chamber, man."

"What chamber?" Mahegan zeroed in on Shayne's emotional stream of consciousness.

"The biometric chamber. I'm telling you. There's one in each of the RINKs, dude."

"RINKs?"

"Russia, Iran, North Korea. The RINKs."

"So, one facility in each country?"

"Two different things. The command posts and satellites control the conventional weapons. The facilities we built are hardened and have the biometric chambers to identify the biometric keys. Each one is a human. The North Korean is a chick. The Iranian is like Thor or the Hulk. And like I said, the Russian is dead."

"So, there's no shutting down the Russian nukes?"

"I had them shut down. We just turned them back on. That's what Iran was all about."

Shayne was singing like a bird. Was he telling the truth? To Mahegan, his words had gained veracity with time. His fear had propelled him to a safe place, like an overboard sailor clinging to a life raft. He could breathe, though he had a knife in his eye.

Mahegan nodded. Shayne would live for now. He pulled the knife away with care. The eyelid was slit, barely. He walked out of the container and into the one where they were holding Spartak. As he was walking, he was thinking about the concept of prisoner's dilemma. Two prisoners, perhaps complicit in the same crime. Who would defect first? The concept was based on rational actors acting in self-interest.

But if they were true believers, Mahegan thought—*believers in Ian Gorham and all that he had to preach—their reactions may be skewed.*

Shayne was certainly more concerned about Gorham than he was nuclear war. Growing up in the Snapchat and YouTube world tended to mesh virtual and reality. Once you saw the reality, though, Mahegan knew it was impossible to forget the searing images of brutal ground combat. He was a boots-on-the-ground soldier trying to squeeze an Internet code-writing pinhead. Two ships passing in the night.

As he closed the container door behind him and approached Spartak, he had a different thought. "Who are you?" he asked with a growl.

"Nobody." She had used a wash bucket to take a field bath. Her buzzed scalp glistened beneath maybe a week of prickly stubble. She wore cargo pants and a black Under Armour shirt someone had given her primarily so the greasy, smelly cook's clothes could be burned. In addition to her more professional appearance, Spartak smelled clean. The entire room smelled like soap.

It all clicked in his mind as he transposed the image of her face in his mind onto the pictures that O'Malley had shown him. "I've got forty-eight hours to stop a nuclear holocaust," Mahegan said. "I had my computer team do some research and it seems that the chief financial officer for Manaslu went missing a month ago. We managed to find some pictures that hadn't been completely erased, but nice try. You went dark better than most people could. Your name is Nancy Langevin. You've been on the run for a month. Didn't want to leave the country but didn't want to stay at Manaslu. You knew there was a plan, but were unsure what to do. They found you penetrating their system and tracked you to the bar where we saved you."

She looked away then leveled her brown eyes on him. "You didn't save me. And nice work. Better than ninety-nine percent of the people could do."

"You're the genesis code, correct, Langevin?"

She paused. "I can shut down all three systems, yes. You do quick work. But call me Spartak, because Manaslu can most likely hear you right now. They have no idea who Spartak is."

"Okay, fair enough. You know Tokyo has already been decimated."

Spartak nodded. "I didn't know, but I figured. It was part of the plan."

"It occurs to me that Nancy Langevin could be a legend, a fake identity. Which is it? Nancy Langevin or Spartak? Are you a Russian mole inside Manaslu?"

"Not a Russian mole. Nancy Langevin is my real name, but as I said, call me Spartak. That's my hacker ID even though I'm American. Russian lineage, sure, but not a spy. I was working a legitimate job for that moron, Gorham. He thinks he could destroy the country and then rebuild it in a socialist image. If I were a good Russian, I would like to see nothing better. However, I'm American. And as a businesswoman, I of course believe it will all be a huge disaster."

"We're getting somewhere. How do we get you into each of the ground servers to shut down the relay from the satellites?"

"It's quite simple. We infiltrate each one in three different hostile countries in the next forty-eight hours or we go to Manaslu headquarters in Idaho and do it all from there."

"Idaho?" Shayne had mentioned Idaho. Two intersecting points. They were getting somewhere.

"Yes. Gorham was insistent on having override capability on everything. He's a control freak. He has built a very successful business, but that has come at a cost because he must do practically everything himself. And when someone is doing everything themselves, they forget stuff, or miss things."

"He missed you adding yourself as a backup biometric override of the ComWar and nuclear systems?"

"Bingo," Spartak/Langevin said, pointing a finger at him. "Well, half bingo. Remember, you've got to have boots on the ground or very accurate targeting of the command posts to neutralize ComWar. ComWar is conventional. The biometric keys are relevant only to the nuclear arsenals. Gorham kept those two fire-walled."

Shayne had mentioned that the Keys also could shut down the satellites that were controlling the ComWar conventional attacks. There was inconsistency in their stories. *Who was telling the truth?*

"The biometrics can't shut off the satellites?"

"No. Only a hacker can do that."

Mahegan nodded and continued. "And you were holed up in Detroit, getting lost in the city until they left so that you could suddenly reappear and tell Manaslu security, 'hey, guys, I'm back. Just going to catch up on some e-mails?' "

"Something like that."

"And now the problem is—"

"That I'm here in this container and time is wasting."

Mahegan shook his head. "That Gorham has put a lockdown on the facility, scanning and looking for you. If you get within a mile of that place, a camera will pick you up and you'll have his thugs on you in five seconds."

"Please. His thugs are pussies."

"Stasovich seems pretty tough," Mahegan said.

"I can bring Stasovich to his knees. I either combat him or use a honey trap. Either works."

Mahegan looked at Spartak/Langevin and could imagine that an attractive woman such as herself would be able to lure a Neanderthal like Stasovich into an ersatz tryst with her to gain her own advantage over him.

"What happens when we bomb the ComWar mobile command posts?"

"The ManaSats take over. We launched those a full year ago. We update their software every week. Those satellites are the most current thing on the market today. Max storage, min power, and ultra-high-speed processing. The AI and Machine Learning functions perform almost seamlessly. There's a delay in the refresh rate of about an hour just because they're in outer space, which is why we use it as a backup instead of the primary."

"We?"

"They."

"You said 'we.'"

"I meant *they*. Don't get technical on me. You're getting info. That's what you want, right?"

"So, *we* knock those out of the sky. Then what?" Mahegan continued.

"You stop the conventional ComWar capability. There is rumored to be some backup in the tunnel complexes in Russia, Iran, and North Korea, but they are rudimentary. I'm doubtful *they* can push out to the extended forces deployed halfway across a continent or peninsula. Half a billion dollars in Manaslu money is in each facility. Was disguised as nonprofit money to help the indigent. We know that each country hid some of the money, but ultimately, we had the facilities built, blending in with the natural terrain. It was a twofer for Manaslu. First, Gorham got access to the leaders of each country and began business negotiations. Won a few contracts for cyber security and to implement Manaslu social media, online shopping, and targeted advertising. Everyone has heard of Amazon, Facebook, and Google. Manaslu is all three of these in one engine. Those leaders saw dollar signs, or whatever their currency is. What they didn't realize is that with Gorham and Shayne inside their wires, everything was possible for Manaslu and nothing was really going to happen for those countries," Spartak/Langevin said.

"So the biometric key people don't control the conventional stuff? Just the nukes?"

"Well, I'm not sure. I know they control the nukes. If you want to shut down the Russian nukes, for example, you need the Russian biometric key."

"What if he's dead?"

"If he's dead and his body is more than two degrees in either direction from normal, then you're screwed. And if the U.S. doesn't get its system online—I saw in the Deep Web that Gorham took it offline, FYI—then the U.S. is wide open vulnerable."

"Yes, I know. We've got that figured out. But no way to back up the Russian Key?"

"Why? Is he dead?"

"Just answer the question," Mahegan demanded.

"I assume Gorham can do it all. Conventional and nukes."

"Okay. So, Gorham gets in and can manipulate the systems to respond to his commands? He issues orders to the field commanders? He has the launch codes for nukes? The whole thing?"

Spartak/Langevin nodded. "I'm sure of the nukes. The meeting in Iran was for him to steal those codes. Every country has hand-print, voice, eye, gait, DNA, and facial recognition—everything you can think of—and we built the facility in Iran to steal every piece of biometric data, collect it, assimilate it, replicate it, and then be packaged in metadata that can be used to trigger their nuclear devices. That's just the offensive capability.

"For two years Gorham and Shayne have been putting RATs in every major defense contractor's weapon system as well as the nuclear arsenal. Boomers, GPS guided bombs, and the ICBMs. All infected. The sweet spot is that it will take them and the U.S. forty-eight to seventy-two hours to figure out what the hell has happened, find a way to defend against it, develop that defense, and then deploy it effectively. Meanwhile, you can damn well be assured that Shayne will be swatting that shit down as fast as developers can make it happen."

Mahegan said nothing.

"What?" Spartak/Langevin asked.

"Who is next after Shayne? Can Gorham write code?"

"Yes, but he's not in Shayne's league. Nobody's in Shayne's league. Wait," she said. "Did you capture Shayne?"

Mahegan said nothing.

"You've got Shayne, don't you?"

"Hypothetically, if we had Shayne, what purpose could he serve for us?"

"Hypothetically? You've got Shayne!"

Mahegan stared at Spartak/Langevin, whose eyes were round and wide.

She ran her hands across the buzzed scalp, muttered something unintelligible to herself, then looked back at Mahegan. "If you have

Shayne, well. Shayne is the brains behind this entire thing. Sure, Gorham had the vision, but it was Shayne who worked his way into every defense contractor and national security system for these countries. Two years of work. Every day. He was the one who created platforms better than Amazon, Facebook, and Google and combined them as one synthesized entity. That's how Manaslu has gotten so much traction. Why do you need the others when you've got one platform? They've got dating sites, everything. If you truly have Shayne . . ."

Spartak/Langevin paused, looked away at the corrugated metal ribs of the shipping container.

"Yes?" Mahegan asked.

"Then you've got the world."

Cassie had been in tougher situations before. At least that was what she kept telling herself.

The fate of her escape still undecided, she hobbled through the labyrinth until she came upon a rectangular gate with metal bars. Her eyes had adjusted to the darkness, making visible the night sky beyond the rebar. Footfalls chased after her deep in the tunnel through which she had raced. She figured she was maybe thirty seconds ahead of being shot in the back in some nameless medical facility in . . . Jordan? She wasn't even sure of her general location, only that the man Stasovich had been talking to— Gorham?—had mentioned Amman.

The staccato sound of machinegun fire echoed through the night. Green and orange tracers painted Day-Glow lines across the black firmament. The tunnel was dank and smelled of decay. Perhaps this was the way the medical personnel ferried their corpses. Distant explosions were powerful enough to shake the earth beneath her feet.

Pushing on the gate, she was greeted with unwelcome resistance. The footfalls grew louder behind her. She inserted the scalpel into the lock that looked like it might take an old fashioned skeleton key. Twisting and turning the scalpel, Cassie muttered, "Come on, you mother," under her breath. She was inches from escaping with useful intelligence that could possibly prevent a global meltdown. In her gut, she believed that this man, Gorham, was the mastermind.

Air pushed toward her, a harbinger. Men were shouting and racing along the corridor from behind her, probably being careful to avoid an ambush, but nonetheless moving quickly.

Click.

The scalpel had done its job. She turned and saw Stasovich barreling toward her, pistol at the ready. Something told her he wanted a personal kill, not a pistol shot. Cassie pushed the gate open, spun past it, then slammed it shut into Stasovich's face. Stunned, the man stared at her through the iron bars, a leering prisoner eager to escape. The malicious smirk gave way to a howl of pain as she raked the scalpel across his forehead, left eye, and cheek.

The big man reached out and clasped her wrist, nearly crushing the bones. She quickly used her left hand to grasp the tumbling scalpel, nicked her hand, righted the blade, and stabbed it into Stasovich's hand, causing him to release his grip. She reached through the bars and snatched his pistol from his bleeding clutch, a Glock 19.

She fired at Stasovich, who had ducked and was reaching for her injured ankle. She wasted two rounds on his arm, but managed to evade his vice grip, allowing her to flee around the corner, chased by automatic gunfire.

She hobbled away into the darkness, moved around a corner, still clasping the scalpel and Stasovich's Glock. The big Serb's body at the base of the inward opening gate gave her a few seconds of time. Moving along a dark alley in the complete opposite direction of what she figured her escape route had been, Cassie got maybe one hundred meters before the first rifle shot snapped past her head. She continued to move toward a glow beyond the high stucco walls to her left and right.

Reaching the end of the alley, she slipped around the corner to her right. Looking over her shoulder to her left, she bumped into a man, who immediately cupped his hand over her mouth, knocked the weapons out of her hands with keen precision, took her down to one knee, and slipped a pair of flex-cuffs over her wrists. Another man tied a blindfold over her eyes and a gag through her mouth.

She sensed the presence of more men beyond her.

A harsh voice whispered, *"Alan!"*

Cassie knew it meant, "Now!" in Arabic.

But her captors were Persian. Iranians. Why would they be speaking Arabic?

A deafening explosion rang her eardrums and she felt the men scamper away from her, save one man, who kept his knee in her back and she presumed the metal pressed against her head was a pistol. Gunfire erupted behind her, automatic weapons fire echoing along the alley through which she had just run. Others must have stayed behind. It seemed she had stumbled upon a team conducting a mission.

Sounds of gunfire erupted deep inside the building adjacent to the medical facility. After a minute, she heard the men scrambling back in her direction.

"Adhhab! Adhhab!" Go! Go!

"Alsajin?"

"Ahdur! Alan!"

She guessed that the men had briefly discussed her fate as two arms lifted her and practically dragged her for a minute or two. Amidst the confusion, she lost her bearings. The men's hands were strong, their voices forceful. The light chop of helicopter blades sang in the distance. The pace quickened until they were beneath the hot downward draft of the rotors. They tossed her into a helicopter and then strapped her to the floor. She felt the men board the aircraft, which was lifting away before anyone was settled but her.

The helicopter flew quickly, darting and banking as if evading enemy fire. She had been on dozens of training flights such as these, and only a few times in combat. Twice it felt like the helicopter was going to fall out of the sky. After about thirty minutes they slowed and landed, rolling to a stop. The men were quick, reversing the process, unloading the aircraft. They had something, or someone else, that they were carrying.

She heard soft commands of "Lift," and "Careful," and "Heavy," in Arabic.

The helicopter flew away.

The whispers became shouts. The silence rang in her ears.

For the second time in one night, Cassie was dragged into a room and left alone, the haunting clank of a bolt sealing her fate.

CHAPTER 16

"*D*AMN DRONES ARE EVERYWHERE," SOLHAMI BARKED AS HIS ANTI-aircraft gunners spat 30mm lead at the bat winged planes. As far as Gorham could tell, the drones were not armed. Perhaps they were information collectors and not weaponized? Through the haze of the nighttime battlefield, a drone no larger than a coffee table tumbled from the sky, breaking into pieces less than fifty meters away.

Rotor blades chopped the air behind them as a helicopter landed to their rear. A young man in an olive drab uniform dashed off the Russian Hip helicopter, famous for spraying hydraulic fluid everywhere while in flight.

Approaching the general, the young man stopped and saluted. Everything Gorham had read was to never salute in combat. Apparently Solhami agreed with this maxim, because he retrieved his pistol and aimed it at the courier, who was holding an envelope.

"Drop the salute," Solhami directed.

The soldier did and began to hand Solhami the envelope.

"No. Open it and read it to me."

The courier gave Solhami a puzzled look, but complied. He carefully opened the envelope and retrieved a white piece of paper. "The American woman has escaped. Location unknown."

At that point, Solhami pulled the trigger and literally shot the messenger in the forehead.

"He should have never read me that message," Solhami said. "Besides, he was useless. Saluting me in a combat zone?"

The young man lay motionless on the street where they were huddled behind a blockade of concrete rubble, burned car hulks, and flaming tires. The apocalyptic scene was everything Gorham imagined combat to be, but he was unprepared for the thunderous boom of Solhami's pistol. Gorham turned and vomited in the street.

"Grow a pair, mister," Solhami spat at him when he turned around, wiping his mouth. "Now you've seen combat. My troops are about to break through the Jordan Valley and into Israel. This will be the toughest fighting of all."

"General, pace yourself. You do not want to endanger Mr. Gorham," Kal said.

"Kal, you've been on a lot of missions. This is bigger than anything you've done though. And why do I give a shit about this guy?"

As if to emphasize his point, a deluge of rockets peppered the ground on either side of them, explosions sending shrapnel in the air, whistling overhead and clattering into the barrier.

"Because he will help all of us maintain the momentum. Iran and North Korea are allies. We need this victory. Destruction of America is within our grasp."

A rocket soared overhead, leaving a smoky vapor trail in its wake. While Gorham was ill, he was also resolute. His plan was still intact. He was on the front lines of a war he had helped initiate without warning to the rest of the world. The Russians were making progress against Western Europe. The Iranians were about to break through Jordan into Israel. The North Koreans were racing toward the Pusan port. All this action had taken place in twenty-four hours. The element of surprise was the key to everything happening and now there was no way to *unring that bell,* as the saying went.

They had achieved surprise. The progress was unbelievable. The American military had been caught completely unprepared. By hiding in the Deep Web, they had been able to do almost all the preparations necessary to conduct this blitzkrieg across two continents.

"Listen to Kal, General. You need me. Kal and I will fly back and get out of your way. I've seen what I need to see. Continue with your great work here and kill the American sponsored Zionists in Israel. In forty-eight hours I hope to see you in Tel Aviv."

"I'll be there in twenty-four hours, Mister. Have a safe trip." To Kal, Solhami said, "You should really stay here with me."

Gorham noticed that the Korean operative held his gaze. Perhaps they were former lovers. Maybe a one-night stand in a lonely city on a random operation. He got the sense that combat might bring together those who enjoyed the thrill. Like Comic-Con for comic book lovers or SHOT Show for gun lovers. All the same to him.

Gorham and Kal walked with the Iranian guards nearly a mile to the rear of the combat before boarding the helicopter. Dusty shale crunched under their boots. The whistles and explosions of combat surrounded them in a surreal 3-D display.

The flight to the airfield medical facility was brief and without incident. As they landed, he saw the Manaslu jet sitting idle on the runway. The stairway was down, though, and the pilots were walking around the aircraft as if doing preflight inspection. He waved over Chaz Wakefield, his longtime corporate pilot.

"Ready to go in an hour," Gorham said.

"Roger. Things getting hairy here, boss. Where to?" Wakefield asked.

"Will let you know after I see what happened to this woman."

"The American? We're walking a tightrope here, boss. I never question your ethics, but we are Americans. Iran, Jordan, everything's on fire. Chatter over the pilot networks is that Russia is in Poland. North Korea in South Korea. We're looking at World War Three. Don't want us getting shot down."

"We won't be shot down. I just need you to fly, Chaz. Let's be ready," Gorham said and walked away. When he turned Kal was standing next to him. She had been listening.

"I have an idea once you can focus. Let's do what you need to do here and then we can talk." She took long strides, keeping pace with him. Their feet crunched on the shale and gravel leading up to the medical facility. Walking past the doctors and the confused staff, he found Doctor Sadiqi dead on the floor of the room in which Captain Bagwell had been held. He saw the open doorway that led to a tunnel. Kal came up behind him.

"She's definitely gone," he said.

"She was here?" Kal asked.

Gorham nodded. He walked out and found the commander in charge of the hospital. "Where is the Iranian Olympian?"

Kal stopped. "You mean the Iranian biometric key?"

"Yes. Remember. We left him here."

The hospital administrator looked confused, disheveled. Gorham saw Stasovich approach through the front doors of the hospital.

"They're both gone. Jordanian special forces, maybe Mossad, too, picked up the Iranian biometric key and the Captain," Stasovich said. He was bleeding profusely from three or four different places on his body. A knife cut across his face had perhaps blinded him in his left eye. His hands were a mangled bloody mess. And his left arm was in a sling that had blossoming stains.

"How did they find Persi, the Iranian biometric key?"

"As you can see, I went after the girl. I had the guards lock Persi in the building next door. Somebody is digging through our stuff. That's all I can think. Most likely Mossad hackers tracking us. We're in a global war. The cyber domain is just as competitive as reality, just less bloody."

It was not good for Iran that their biometric key had been captured. If the Jordanians could get him to the Iranian facility they could shut off the Iranian nuclear capabilities. Of course, Gorham could override everyone now that he had stolen their biometric data from the Iranian facility, but he would have to be at one of the four Biometric Recognition Terminals in Russia, Iran, North Korea, or Idaho to take control of one of the RINK arsenals.

He sighed. He missed Shayne, despite wishing his employee had died in the attack attempted at the refuel site. Stasovich was all brawn, very little brain. But he was there and alive, so that counted for something. He required some element of savvy and intelligence to remain alive. No one was that lucky all the time. The man needed medical attention, though. Gorham wanted one

ally that he could rely upon. Was Kal an ally? He needed to unpack that box. Needed to separate his desire from his execution.
Or was it all okay? He'd read dozens of biographies of military
generals and they all seemed to get laid routinely while in battle.
Maybe that was part of the deal.

There was a package in his brain, an entire floor of packages,
that Dr. Draganova had shown him. They were on the phone, as
usual, and she'd walked him through his desires.

"Do you want just women, Ian?"
"I know I want you, Doctor."
"But you always want what you can't have."
"I can always have what I want, so far."
"Have you had me?"
"I hope to."
"Hope is not a method. Where's the confident entrepreneur?"
"I'm here."
"Do you like men, also, Ian?"
"I prefer women, honestly."
"Why? So you can conquer?"
He paused. "Perhaps."
"Women are weaker?"
"Perhaps"
"You want nothing left untouched by Ian Gorham?"
"Perhaps."
"You desire immortality?"
"Perhaps."

Now it all made sense to him. Here was Kal, for whom he felt
the stirrings of desire. Just another conquest? Wise move? He
would find out soon enough, he presumed. Was he just a narcissist needing a fix from a beautiful woman?

Perhaps.

Focusing, he found another doctor in the Iranian military emergency room and said, "Will you do what you can to patch up my
friend here?"

"There are so many. He must wait in line."

Stasovich may have been severely injured, but that didn't prevent him from clutching the doctor's throat with his vice grip.

"I think you'll find sufficient incentive to move Mr. Stasovich to the front of the line. We hold some sway here," Gorham said.

The doctor nodded, his eyes bugging out from Stasovich's grip, which stayed in place until the doctor began backing up and prying at the hulk's arms. "O-okay," he muttered, and led Stasovich to an operating room.

Gorham turned and walked outside, stared across the courtyard where Persi said Captain Bagwell had been snatched. The woman had some pluck. Who were these people that believed they could get in front of his plan? No one was better than he. Not even some Delta Force wannabe and her pals. He stared into the night sky, retrieved his iPad, and listened to the sounds of warfare pop in the distance. A rocket here, machine-gun chatter there. Whistling artillery shells exploded closer than he would have anticipated. He smiled. He was an on-the-front-lines hardened combat veteran.

As his iPad connected with the ManaSats overhead, he felt Kal's presence beside him. She was stealthy, like a ninja. Maybe she was one.

He scrolled through several login protocols. Finally, the iPad geo-located him and then began searching for Captain Bagwell. While in captivity, he had placed a mini-ManaBlade tracking device in the middle of her back using a hypodermic air gun. The device was no bigger than a wood splinter or a grain of rice and it was unlikely she would feel it as he had anesthetized the entire region with an ointment. Even if she did figure it out, Bagwell would not be able to reach it herself. She would need help removing the device, which was located very close to her spine. Good luck.

The iPad chirped. A series of concentric rings spread outward, circling a solid blue dot that bore the label BAGWELL. He zoomed in and saw that she was in a mountainous area near the Dead Sea. He plugged in his earbuds and used his iPad to call General Solhami via the ManaSat array above them.

"Yes, Mister?" the general barked.

"I've located the woman. She is on your path of attack through the Jordan Valley into Israel."

After a pause, Solhami said, "Good work, soldier. While of little value to us, I'm sure we can find a good public use of capturing her."

"I actually need her back," Gorham said. "All the success you are achieving is because we have created defects in the weapons and missiles of the enemy. I can just as easily make them more accurate. So, I need the woman back quickly. I intend to trade her for someone much more valuable that can help your cause even more."

Static filled the airwaves for several moments. The general certainly didn't enjoy being questioned or challenged. "I don't believe you," Solhami said. A chuckle resonated through the speaker on the phone.

"Stand by a second," Gorham said, confident.

"Believe him," Kal said. The microphone on the earbuds picked up her voice.

Solhami frowned. "Kal? But why?"

"Because she knows what I can do," Gorham interrupted.

Like a consigliere, she mediated between the two men. Gorham studied her a moment then returned his attention to his iPad. Her black hair and black jumpsuit contrasted with her translucent white face. Somewhere she had changed from the professional outfit she had worn at the Iranian Biometric Center. She was combat ready, it appeared.

"I still don't believe him. As much as I trust you, Kal. I have no time for this Internet coward," Solhami scoffed.

Gorham pinched and pulled at his iPad until he found a Jordanian artillery unit that was in reserve to the west of Amman. He punched on the icon and typed in *Disable RAT*. He then sent Solhami's location to the commander of the field artillery battery via the Jordanian secure chat command and control system, which Shayne had previously hacked. He typed *Confirmed location of General Solhami, Iranian Special Forces Commander. Fire immediately.*

"What am I standing by for?" Solhami asked.

"A demonstration," Gorham said.

"Just do what he says, General," Kal reiterated.

It took longer than he wanted, probably because of confusion and human intervention, but the icon flashed *Rounds Fired!*

Calculating a thirty second parabolic arc, Gorham said, "General, you have about twenty seconds to find cover. A 155 mm artillery battery just fired a converging sheath of high explosive rounds on your ten digit grid coordinate."

"What?"

"Now about fifteen seconds."

The icon flashed with *Repeating!*

"Oh, and you better stay down. They're repeating."

Scrambling and heavy breathing filled the microphone. Gorham could hear the whistling of the shells through Solhami's phone. He had no idea where the general was finding cover, but the explosions thundered over the phone, which then went dead.

He removed the earbuds and lifted his head. The artillery volleys rumbled to the west, echoing along the desert floor.

After about ten minutes, Solhami called, "You idiot. Turn them off!"

"Problem is, General, I can't. We can get in there, but once I'm out, I can't get back in without considerable effort. I can send a command to cease fire. Would you like for me to do that?"

"Yes!"

"Okay. But first, will you get Captain Bagwell for me in the next few hours?"

"Blackmail me with my own life?" Solhami growled, then paused. "Kind of respect that."

"Twelve hours. This is very urgent." Gorham typed the command, which was sent from the Jordanian Artillery Command Center. *Cease Fire. Target Neutralized.*

"That"—Kal paused—"was interesting." She cozied up to him, slid an arm around his waist, and put her cheek against his. Whispering, she said, "We should go. I know just the place."

He had been prepped by Dr. Draganova for this reaction. He had inquired about combat and the impact of it on men and women. After an initial flurry of questioning as to why he was interested, she'd relented and described that many people found the death and destruction of warfare to be a major aphrodisiac.

The North Korean woman's mouth against his cheek stirred something deep inside him. He knew he had more boxes to unpack in his mind. So much to know and learn. He was mission-focused right now and could he really stand to have a romantic distraction? The doctor had tried to get him to realize that his life was happening all at the same time and that he needed to embrace everything simultaneously, not sequentially.

Another way of saying *live in the moment,* he assumed, but he *was* a complicated man. "Where did you have in mind?"

"Your airplane. Get your goon and let's go." Her lips brushed his ear.

He felt the flicker of a tongue against his lobe. His heart raced. Slid a hand around her back, pulled her close. She pressed into him. He didn't care if anyone was watching. The beautiful woman, the combat, the relentless pace all combined to create desire within him.

"Let's live while others are dying, Ian. Be with me," she said.

"Where should I tell the pilots?"

"Samjiyon. Where you built our Manaslu facility . . . or what you might call your spy station."

Gorham pulled away and looked in her eyes. Who was this person? Dare he question her?

Instead, he went to that room in his mind that dealt with probabilities. "All the reports I'm getting on my iPad are that China is shooting down everything that flies in their airspace. Anything that even gets close."

"We can get into Russian airspace from here. Iran has Syria and then it's about a ten hour flight in your jet to the North Korean border without crossing into China. You can operate from there."

Gorham nodded.

He broke away, found Stasovich, and soon they were in the air, flying north over Damascus and airspace protected by the Russians.

Her idea was brilliant. He could ride out the remaining hours of the war and bide his time bunkered up with the beautiful Kal.

Whose name meant *knife.*

CHAPTER 17

MAHEGAN HUDDLED WITH GENERAL SAVAGE, OWENS, AND O'MALLEY in the Farah command and control facility, be that what it was. The Russian wolfhound lay quietly in the corner, a gauze bandage wrapped around its left rear leg. Mahegan had put some concentrated milk and water in a bowl. Apparently, the wolfhound thought the same of the milk as did the troops because she stopped lapping at it after a few lashes with her tongue. He dumped the milk and poured a bottle of water into the bowl, which she drank as one of the nurses took her time stitching the dog's wounds. The army nurse had affectionately rubbed her head and named her, "Ranger."

White boards and pin up maps hung from the walls in haphazard fashion. A digital map that O'Malley had transposed onto a 55-inch monitor showed the European and Asian continents. Red symbols reflected the progress of the North Korean Army about midway through the Korean Peninsula; the Russian Army's blitzkrieg through Belarus and into Poland; and the Iranian Army rapid advance into Jordan.

"As bad as all that is," Mahegan said, pointing at the monitor, "it gets much worse. But first, just so I'm clear with everyone, getting Cassie back is central to anything we do next. I'll go in by myself if I have to."

"No need, Jake. We all get that," Savage said.

The phone rang. He answered and said, "Roger that, sir." He

punched the SPEAKER button and placed the handset in the cradle. "Mister Secretary, you're live with me, Jake Mahegan, Sean O'Malley, and Patch Owens. We've got a missing soldier, Captain Cassandra Bagwell. She was captured in Iran. We have two prisoners and were just getting ready to debrief."

"Bart Bagwell's daughter?" Secretary of Defense Thad Trapp asked.

"Roger, that, sir," Savage said.

Cassie's parents had been kidnapped and killed by Syrian terrorists seeking revenge for a bombing mission that General Bagwell, the former Chairman of the Joint Chiefs of Staff, had approved.

"Need to get her back," Trapp said.

"Understand, sir."

Mahegan thought the defense secretary sounded as if he wanted to avoid the public relations nightmare of having to deal with Cassie's disappearance, which was nonsensical because the world was on fire and about to melt down.

"Why don't you proceed with your update. I'll listen and then tell you what we're doing. I've got about ten staffers in here listening and taking notes. I update the president in an hour. Things are . . . bad."

Savage nodded at Mahegan and said, "Jake."

Mahegan turned so that his voice could better be heard by the team listening in the Pentagon. "Sean, can you share our screen with the command center in the Pentagon?"

After a minute of typing and chatting with some anonymous JWICS operator in Washington, DC, O'Malley said, "Shared."

"We've got it," Trapp said.

"Good. Here's what we've got. There are three low earth orbit nanosatellite systems that support the three attacks. They move and geo-locate with the center of the convoys moving through South Korea, Jordan, and now Poland. These satellites can do everything that little briefcase did at the bar. Shut off power, cut digital links, disable Wi-Fi networks, and fry everything with directed energy. They are synchronized electronic, digital, and en-

ergetic warfare platforms that communicate with similarly optimized ground-based stations."

"Briefcase at the bar?" Trapp interrupted.

Mahegan paused, bit his tongue, and said, "Roger that. We had
a tip that a major operation was happening domestically in Detroit. We went there, disrupted that attack, captured one of our
prisoners, and have been following the intel ever since. That intel
took us to Iran, where all of the leaders met to enable a nuclear
strike on America." He deliberately left out the mention of the
original three RINK captives from the Detroit bar.

"Nuclear strike on America?" Trapp interrupted again.

"Sir, if you let me finish, I think we will all have a better understanding of exactly what is happening. I just interrogated our prisoners and we are piecing this together on the fly."

Despite some murmuring in the background of the Pentagon
command post, Mahegan continued. "Sir, I'd appreciate it if you'd
mute on your end unless someone there has something to add. We
think the prisoner called Spartak is of Russian descent, but we believe she was the chief financial officer for the tech company,
Manaslu. A woman named Nancy Langevin. She defected from
Manaslu knowing what Ian Gorham had in mind. She knows the
plan and says that Gorham has been able to infect our weapons
systems with viruses over the last couple of years, thus making our
smart bombs dumb, our radars misread, and our intelligence systems report inaccurate information. Everything we're shooting at
or receiving as information is a degree or two off. Most everything is missing."

The phone clicked and Trapp said, "First, we're sure about
Gorham? He's on the President's technology Blue Ribbon Com-
mission."

"Positive," Mahegan said.

"Okay, second, yes, your information confirms what all of our
field commanders are telling us. Everything is inaccurate," Trapp
said.

"Roger. That's because Gorham used a guy named Shayne to infiltrate the research and development and manufacturing facilities

of every major defense company in the West. He opened hack-able portals where Manaslu could either go in through the wires, so to speak, or do over the air penetrations. Then placed remote access Trojans that only activate when the weapon is fired. This combination of digital bomb, directed energy, electromagnetic pulse, and disabling our weapons and intelligence systems has led to major conventional success on behalf of the RINK alliance. The first task, Mister Secretary, is to have CyberCom find a quick patch for all of this so it can be deployed and we can be more ac-curate, fight back, and survive."

The phone clicked again. "Roger," Trapp said.

Mahegan continued when the phone went silent again. "The bad news is that all this conventional action—save what happened in Tokyo—is a prelude to planned nuclear annihilation of the United States. Gorham wants to destroy the United States so he can rebuild it in his Utopian image of a borderless land that has no rule of law, or whatever those pinheads believe."

"My God," Trapp said.

"The key is that we have to assume that what they have done to the conventional forces, they've also been able to do to the nu-clear arsenal."

The phone had not been muted and there was a rustling in the background until a voice said, "That's impossible! Mister . . . Mister Mohican, or whatever your name is. This is General Fred Turner with the United States Air Force Strategic Command. Our nuclear arsenal is pure. We are prepared to defend."

Mahegan looked at Savage, who rolled his eyes and waved his flat hand across his neck. He mouthed *Don't do it.*

"Do you hear me, mister!"

At that point, Savage shrugged.

Mahegan's eyes bored into the phone. "Mister Secretary, we've got very little time so if you have a pistol handy I recommend you shoot that guy. We just wasted a minute when we have less than forty-eight hours to solve this thing. We've got a missing soldier and three wars raging. We don't have time for egos or bullshit. I can punch the OFF button here or we can continue."

The phone went silent briefly then came back alive.

"Proceed," Trapp said.

Mahegan hoped the phone had been muted so that they would not hear the pistol shot.

He continued. "We need someone competent and humble to conduct a thorough inspection of our nuclear arsenal from our bombs, to our boomers, to our ICBMs. Everything. We have to assume that we have been neutered from a nuclear standpoint just as every commander in the conventional force has been."

"Roger," Trapp said.

"So, two key tasks and we may be able to turn this thing around. One, CyberCom patches the bugs that make us miss when we shoot. Two, inspect the nukes and when we find what they've done, fix them. Without the assurance of mutual assured destruction, we will be destroyed. With it, we can bargain. That's the task. Get our nukes back on line."

"Could take days, even months," Trapp balked.

O'Malley leaned over and whispered in Mahegan's ear.

Mahegan nodded and turned toward the speaker phone. "Just a second. Let's make this easy. You guys kill the satellites and ground stations and we'll find the biometric keys for the nukes. So, all you need to do is find three RIM-161 missiles that haven't been bugged—or debug three—and put them on airburst to destroy the low earth nanosats Gorham has in circulation. Those are the backup systems to the mobile command posts the RINK are using to advance so quickly. They have full electronic, network, and digital warfare comms suites. And then find the mobile command posts and destroy them with JDAM bombs. So that's six weapons. You can prioritize that and have Cyber Command working the over-the-air patch of the rest of our systems."

A RIM-161 was an ASAT, or antisatellite missile in the U.S. inventory. Typically used for ballistic intercept, it could also penetrate and destroy low earth-orbit satellites. Better at kinetic impact kills than airburst, the ASAT might be able to disable an array of satellites, not just one. It wasn't a sure thing by any measure. Gorham had built in redundancy and Mahegan believed that more than one satellite would be capable of continuing operations, if not all of them. Like a bowling ball, those ASATs needed to score perfect strikes on three different constellations of nanosats. The JDAMs needed to precisely target and disable the ground-based cyber platforms within the command centers that were commanding and controlling the forces. Mahegan and team needed to capture the biometric keys and unlock the newly impenetrable nuclear arsenal launch codes so that the arsenals could be hacked and shut down.

Three major problems. No good solutions. Everything took time.

"Okay, what about Ian Gorham? Why not bring him in?"

"Like I said, that's our mission. High value targets. As we're recovering Captain Bagwell, we will also snatch Gorham in the next twenty four hours. One prisoner tells me Gorham is the key to overriding the system and another tells me that Gorham's number two is the key. Of course, they both could be bullshitting. Either way, we've got Shayne and we also have a solid shot at capturing Gorham. He's starting to be careless."

Mahegan wasn't sure if he believed that Spartak/Langevin had the access she purported or if they could get her in the facility to do what needed to be done.

Savage interrupted the conversation. "Mister Secretary, as Jake said, there are three fixed facilities and three satellite constellations that need destruction. Jake's plan is a good one. More troubling is that there is one person per country that has the biometric identifiers to shut down what may have already been launched. In the event that we do not capture Ian Gorham, we need a backup plan executed right now to find the three biometric keys."

"Okay." The secretary paused and then said, "You're going to tell me that we have no idea who these people are."

"Exactly," Savage said. "I'd start with anyone who is in the doppelganger program for each of those countries. My guess is that the actual leadership may not have been scanned."

"Those are some pretty thin databases, General. Human intelligence isn't so hot in Iran and North Korea. Now, Russia's a different story, but even there, stuff's changing all the time," Trapp said.

"Work with what you've got. When we get positive identification, I'm sending in Patch Owens on the first one we identify, wherever that person may be. I'll need a Delta or SEAL team to go with him and so a few hours ago I ordered the SEALs from Coronado to head our way. It would be good to know what we've got going on conventionally."

After a long pause, a voice said, "This is General Tim Barrett, the Chairman of the Joint Chiefs of Staff. At the moment, we have every army and marine division preparing to deploy. Every aircraft carrier group is either remaining on station where they are, turning around to be where we need them to be, or deploying. There will be nothing left. All the boomers are doing the same. Every air force wing is repositioning to support the threat theaters of war. Rangers are on the way to secure airfields in Korea. As you know we've got two eighty second airborne brigades in Korea and now two in Estonia. They should be closing in on those combat zones pretty quickly. Plus they're securing multiple airfields throughout the region for follow on forces to deploy."

The Chairman paused and Secretary Trapp said, "Out of time."

Savage said, "Roger," and hung up.

Mahegan thought *If the United States pushed every soldier, sailor, airman, and Marine into combat, along with all their equipment, besides the Coast Guard, who would protect the homeland? Was this a possible ploy?* He thought not, but anything was possible right now. They needed to stay focused on capturing three random people, and getting them to the Manaslu facilities in those countries while the Pentagon focused on destroying the satellites and with it the conventional ComWar capabilities.

As Mahegan was thinking through the possibilities and visualizing the American military mobilizing and responding, his satellite phone buzzed. Only four people had that phone number, three of whom were in the room.

He retrieved the phone from his outer tactical vest and checked the screen.

Jake it's Cassie. The Jordanians rescued me. They captured Iran Key.

Mahegan: **What is tat on my right arm?**

Cassie: **Teammates ;) It's me**

Mahegan: **How do you know about Keys?**

Cassie: **Mossad working with Jordan. Mossad knows everything that Sean is tracking. Also have NoKo Key destination. Not there yet, but OTW.**

Mahegan: **Send it.**

Cassie typed in a latitude and longitude, which O'Malley immediately put into his satellite function. He turned the screen, which showed the earth image spinning and zeroing in on a location labeled SAMJIYON.

Cassie: **Got it?**

Mahegan: **Yes. Are you okay?** That question had been the first he wanted to ask.

She never answered. He lowered his head. His heart leapt. Unaccustomed to the emotions surging through him, he put his hand to his eyes. Pinched them. Took a deep breath. Blew it out, like steam escaping from a valve. Relief washed over him. She was safe, but still. Nothing was a sure thing. She was with Mossad, Israeli intelligence, and Jordanian Special Forces. They were some of the best. He sighed with relief.

Mahegan turned to see everyone looking at him.

This was what love did.

"You okay, bro?" Owens asked, putting a hand on his shoulder.

"I'm good. What do we have?" Mahegan asked. *Cassie was okay.* He regained his composure despite his heart and stomach doing flips. Steadfast normally, Mahegan wanted to shout.

"Cassie was rescued by the Jordians and some Mossad. She's saying that the North Korean Key is going to this airfield here. It's about seven miles from the Chinese border in the northern reaches of North Korea. The satellite shows that Manaslu recently built a factory there. There's an intel folder on this thing. Just reading it sounds like the deal was brokered by the Chinese and necessitated that it be built within a twelve-mile zone of China for trade and labor purposes. Chinese workers come through the border every day, evidently."

"What do you want to do, Jake?" Savage asked.

"We have two missions, right? One is to have Cyber Command fix whatever Gorham and Manaslu did to the weapons and systems that we and our allies use."

"Roger. Nothing we can do there except tell them what we're seeing," Owens said.

"Second, *our* mission has to be to prevent nuclear war everywhere, and most important against the United States. If we are naked right now, Russia could attack without fear of retaliation."

"Roger," Owens said again.

"What's going on in Russia? How do we deal with the fact that the Russian Key is dead?" Mahegan asked. "We can shut down a part of the nuclear option if Cassie and the Jordanians have the Iranian Key and we can get someone on top of the North Korean Key. But Shayne says the Russian key is dead."

"A lot of assumptions built into that assessment, but I agree," Savage said.

"Yes. We must keep the Iranian and North Korean keys alive and make them walk through whatever the device is—and wherever it is—and have all their biometrics checked out. I get that. But without them, we know we're screwed. So we have to find the key *and* a facility. The right person and the right facility. Regarding the Russian key, if Gorham in fact stole the biometric data, Spartak/Langevin says the Manaslu facility in Idaho is our best bet," Mahegan said.

O'Malley chimed in. "We have zero intel. I can do some research on where Manaslu did construction, but what it looks like happened is Gorham used Manaslu as an entrée into these countries so that he could subversively take over their command and control systems."

The room was silent for a moment, then Mahegan spoke. "Idaho is the only state not programmed for retaliation in a two thousand missile scenario."

"Two thousand missiles?" Owens asked.

"There are maps. WikiLeaks. Other sources," Mahegan said. "It's all out there and in here." He pointed at the classified JWICS terminal he was using to communicate with the Pentagon.

"Iran and North Korea are on countdown. Less than twenty-four hours there. We know this much from what Sean's shown us. Maybe because Russia is bigger, harder to coordinate, we've got a little more time there. But the bottom line is that we need the biometric keys to get in, confirm their identity, and then open access to the networks in the RINK countries."

"You get me into the system, I can shut them down," O'Malley said.

"Okay. Sean, you've got nukes. Spartak, Langevin, or whatever her real name is, I'm not sure I trust her, but she's out there in that container and can help. If she can shut down those conventional capabilities like she did those MiGs, she'll be useful. We don't have a lot of time to debate whether or not she's a spy or whatever. If she is, she could be just as useful being right here with us."

"How so?" Savage asked.

"Gorham has sensors everywhere. She seems to be at odds with him. Even if she's working for, say, the Russians, which is a possibility, she'll still try to keep tabs on Gorham. Keep him off our ass."

"It's a risk," O'Malley said.

"But not a gamble," Mahegan replied.

"I don't know. Could be a gamble," Savage said.

Mahegan and his team had always talked in terms of a risk being something from which they could recover and continue to mission success while a gamble was an action that could lead to catastrophic failure. Unrecoverable.

"You're in charge, General. I say we use her. We'd all be dead at the bottom of the Pacific if it weren't for her."

"Execute. You're killing time," Savage said.

Mahegan noted that the general never technically gave his approval for using Spartak/Langevin specifically. Regardless, he continued. "Okay, Patch, we go with what we know. You will take

Hobart and Van Dreeves and secure the North Korean Key, breach the Manaslu factory there, and find the biometric key reader. Walk this person through it and open the portal so that Sean can disable whatever nuclear capability North Korea has."

"Easy," Owens said.

Mahegan squinted at him, essentially saying *Quit being a smartass,* which was impossible for Owens.

Mahegan continued. "And to reiterate, Sean, we need you to stay here and be in a three-point stance ready to launch into those systems and disrupt their launch commands once we get the biometric key through the portal. This is a cyber war. And it's a race. The whole idea was to catch us flatfooted, which worked."

"But what about Russia?" O'Malley said.

"Shayne and Langevin both hinted that Gorham could be a Master Key. I think Langevin may even be a biometric override, but I wouldn't bank on it. Something is off about that woman. But Gorham, I can believe he would be able to override everything. We will put our money on him for use as the Russian Key. Unless we get more information in the next few hours, I'm going after Gorham. So we need intel collection to find Gorham," Mahegan said.

Savage nodded. His hair glistened in the bright fluorescent lights like bristles of cut steel. "We know you want revenge for Cassie being captured, Jake. Keep this on the level."

"Cassie's fine. She's a survivor and ends up getting herself into the right place at the right time. Because of her, we've got eyes on the Iranian Key operation right now, which Sean will be ready to shut down once the Jordanians get the Iranian Key into Yazd. I can promise you that. One less thing to worry about. We get on North Korea and Iran, shut them down, and then figure out Russia."

Without warning, computer screens began showing spinning rainbows and the lights in the command post were off. O'Malley yanked a flash drive from the MacBook.

"This is ComWar coming at us. EMP followed by digital bomb. Iranian tanks can't be far behind." Electromagnetic pulse. Not good. Turning to the army special forces commander in charge of the base at Farah, Mahegan asked, "What kind of Apache gunship support do we have?"

"Six Apaches," the colonel replied as he picked up his radio and directed his teams. "Launch the Apaches now. Get eyes on whatever is moving out there."

"Doubtful they'll be much use, but we can try," Mahegan said, remembering the F-35s that lost the dogfight with the North Korean MiGs. "If nothing else, they have guns."

"That are digitally controlled by the pilot's helmet," Owens said.

"Patch, we've got to get you ready for your mission. Sean, were you able to print out or store anything we got from Cassie?" Mahegan asked.

The bone-chilling sound of tank main gun rounds whistled overhead. A dozen soldiers were manning the operations center.

In the darkness, Mahegan ordered, "Everyone out! Now!" He swept Ranger the wolfhound into his arms and raced outside. He took a left toward the containers—and the enemy fire. Machine-gun rounds punched through the thin container walls. He ran through the door, tracers zipping past him at supersonic speeds with high pitched whining noises that ended with sickening thuds into metal, wood, and bodies. Two soldiers dropped to the ground, wounded, but Mahegan's focus was on his two prisoners. He kicked open the container door and saw Spartak/Langevin huddled in the corner.

"What the hell is going on?!"

"We're taking fire from the Iranians. Need to keep you alive."

"No shit."

He led Spartak/Langevin behind her ersatz prison cell, as the enemy fire intensified. "If you want to live, stay here until I return." He laid Ranger next to her, and she immediately pulled the animal close to her. "Lay down behind this container. Hold Ranger. Protect her. I'm grabbing Shayne."

Running into the hail of fire, he reached Shayne's container, which was riddled with bullet holes. Shrapnel flew into his face, cutting his chin. It was as if they were targeting these two containers. Did Shayne alert Gorham somehow? He didn't seem the type to die for any cause, though he did seem allegiant to the CEO. Had Gorham placed micro-chips on his people?

Mahegan lost that thought as a tank high explosive round plowed into the far end of the container, ripping it open. Iranian infantry was on the ground maybe a quarter mile away. At least the American M4 carbines and M240B machine guns would be effective against the ground soldiers.

Opening the door to Shayne's container, he saw the young man trying to crawl. He had been wounded. Mahegan flipped him onto his back and ran toward Spartak/Langevin, who was impatiently waiting.

"We stay here, we die," she said.

"Follow me," Mahegan said.

"Holy shit. You've really got Shayne. Keep him alive! He's the only one who can unscrew all of this."

Less than 300 meters away, the Green Berets were cutting down the infantry that had deployed from armored personnel carriers. Mahegan carried Shayne on his back like a harvested deer, felt the blood flowing down his back, and ushered Spartak/Langevin along, who was bitching about her handcuffs. He linked up with O'Malley, Owens, and Savage who were in a Gator all-terrain vehicle that somehow had survived the ComWar attack.

"Airfield, now," Mahegan directed. He nodded at the Green Beret colonel who was running toward the fight with his men.

"You've got some pull man. B-2 bomber is going to drop some dumb bombs on these guys and then land to pick you up. SEAL team is waiting for you at the airfield," the Green Beret said.

Just then Mahegan noticed the bat-winged aircraft slicing through the darkness less than a half mile above ground level. Normally the B-2 would drop smart bombs from 40,000 feet above ground level and it was almost in close air support mode. Its bomb bay doors opened and rained large bombs on the enemy formation. Some were direct hits, others were wide, short, or long, but they were effective. A few came near the camp, but it was danger close and Mahegan was okay with that.

The bombing run kicked up enough dust and debris that it made Mahegan think of the shamal they had jumped into just twenty-four hours earlier. With the sun nosing over the mountains, they would have to hustle. Less than forty hours now and all indicators were that Russia, Iran, and North Korea would conduct a major nuclear strike against every target they could range. Shoot their entire wad.

The B-2 made a wide, arcing turn, exposing its underbelly to the enemy tanks, but thankfully leveled out and managed to stay ahead of the barrage that came its way. It banked, lined up on the runway that Mahegan and team were approaching, and then popped its landing gear.

The B-2 skidded to a landing on the two-mile runway. Hobart and Van Dreeves linked up with Mahegan, did the combat shake and half hug.

Wasting no time, Mahegan said, "Patch is your man. He has all the intel. Bring him back alive after you get the North Korean Key into the chamber."

"Roger that, Jake," Van Dreeves said. He was a tall man, wearing dark clothes and a helmet with the earpieces cut out. A scraggly black beard hugged his chin and bounced as he spoke.

Mahegan turned to Owens. The two longtime friends and battle buddies stood on the tarmac of the Farah Airfield. The same XB-2 bomber from which Mahegan and Cassie had jumped into Iran was impatiently blowing hot jet wash along the runway.

"You've got the target folder in all of your comms, Patch. You'll be jumping into North Korea right on top of the facility. Even though Dear Supreme Leader is dead, this woman, Kal, is the Korean Key. She is supposedly on her way back from the Iranian meet up. You must take her alive and walk her through the chamber in Manaslu's Samjiyon facility. You've got Hobart and VD jumping with you at 35,000 feet. You'll be in the bomb bays of the B-2. They've got heaters and sleeping bags. You'll only be in the air for three, maybe four hours. Jump, snatch, breach, and shut down the Korean nuclear countdown."

"Then what?" Owens smiled.

"Smoke a cigar. We'll figure the rest out. Maybe bring you back to the states. Maybe send you to Moscow. Who knows. We're making shit up as we go," Mahegan said. "You ever seen anything like this?"

"Combat's the same wherever we go, isn't it? Good people doing the right thing for the right reasons. Like you say, 'Better to die a hero than grow old.'"

"Don't be a hero, dickhead. Just execute like we always do and find a way to contact me."

Owens smiled and nodded. "Roger that."

Mahegan and Owens clasped hand to forearm in the warrior's grip, cognizant of the fact that they may never see one another again.

Mahegan didn't have time to think about the downsides, only the upsides. "Seriously, get this done, Patch. We'll drink a beer in Wilmington when we get back."

"No worries, Jake. See you soon."

With that, Owens, Hobart, and Van Dreeves raced to the XB-2, where they were helped into their parachute harnesses, then into the bomb bays, given artic sleeping bags in which to stay warm. Once the bomb bay doors were closed, the XB-2 crawled, then sped, then raced into the sky.

Mahegan watched it climb across the desert to the east and found himself thinking it was odd that the safest place to fly right now was over Afghanistan. He turned to O'Malley and Savage, thinking his way through the next problem set. "How's Shayne?"

"Hanging, but critical, I'd say." O'Malley also doubled as the team medic. He had grabbed an aid bag from the medic station and was poking an IV into Shayne's arm.

"Okay, there's our ride," Mahegan said, pointing at the XC-17 that had ferried them to Kandahar and then landed behind the B-2, stopping short and turning onto the distant apron.

The commander in Afghanistan had ordered U.S. A-10s and Apache helicopters to join the fight. Some were effective, most were not. Missiles missed, rockets flew crazily into the sky, and cannon rounds punched harmlessly into the dirt.

"Where are we going?" Spartak/Langevin demanded.

"We will figure that out in the air," Mahegan said.

They jumped into the Gator and rode the quarter mile to the XC-17.

Mahegan linked up with the two pilots and said, "If you're fueled up, we need to at least get back to Kandahar."

"We're good to get back there, Jake. Also got two refuel tankers off the coast in the Indian Ocean. Thinking those might be a good idea. Diego Garcia is an option, too." Diego Garcia was an island in the Indian Ocean where the U.S. military maintained a power projection base.

"Let's just get in the air," Mahegan said. "We've got to keep this prisoner alive." He pointed at Shayne being lifted out of the Gator. "We've got it about ninety percent figured out, but that last ten percent is in his head."

They clambered aboard the XC-17 via its open cargo ramp, which quickly closed as soon as Mahegan, Savage, O'Malley, Spartak/Langevin, Ranger, and Shayne were inside. The loadmaster was wearing a space-age helmet and face shield. He motioned them to sit down and buckle up. Mahegan helped situate Ranger on one of the center console medical litters. The animal seemed to be hanging in there. Breathing was a bit labored, but her eyes looked clear. A good sign. She was going to be okay.

He had a long history and close connection with animals and was glad he was able to keep the beautiful canine alive. Next, he helped O'Malley position Shayne on a stretcher. He hung the IV bag above the prisoner and for the first time inspected the wounds.

Shayne had been hit in two places, the left shoulder and directly in the stomach. Being gut shot was never good. Too many organs could be damaged and internal bleeding was always an issue.

Mahegan leaned over the coder and looked into his milky eyes. Shayne was dying in the next five minutes.

"How do we solve the Russian Key issue?" Mahegan asked. He put his palm on Shayne's face and turned his head toward him. "You're dying. There's nothing we can do to save you. Make it right with your God. Tell me how we stop nuclear armageddon."

Shayne's head lolled around back onto the stretcher so that he was looking at the ceiling of the aircraft. His eyes were still open and registered a hint of recognition.

Spartak/Langevin had walked to the opposite side of Mahegan, her hands still bound.

"Shayne. Tell him," she said. "We need to know. Russia will launch two thousand nukes at the United States and allies."

"That's enough," Mahegan said. She could be giving him code words so that he didn't reveal the information. The airplane banked hard to the right and climbed. Threats were everywhere and no one was safe. Tank main gun rounds, antiaircraft missiles, and enemy drones were all distinct threats in the region. The plane engines revved to what sounded like max throttle as they hurtled through the sky.

"Deploying chaff!" the loadmaster shouted through the intercom.

Mahegan remained calm and still, staring at Shayne, watching him die. He glanced at Spartak/Langevin briefly, looked at Ranger's shallow breathing one litter over, and then refocused on Shayne, who was staring at him now.

"It is better to die having done the right thing than to grow old," Mahegan said, paraphrasing and bastardizing the Croatan saying he had learned from his mother.

"You're looking at the only one who can stop this," Shayne said. It was his last breath. The man died, his eyes frozen and fixated on the ceiling.

"No!" Spartak/Langevin shouted. "He was the last chance to stop everything."

"If we get Ian Gorham, we can override it all. That's what Shayne said earlier in the cell," Mahegan said.

"You don't know that. I don't know that. Just as the other country leaders aren't the keys, Gorham might not be the key or have the biometric data. I know for a fact that Shayne was and did. He was everything to Gorham. It was intentional. Like the person who carries the nuclear codes for the president. It's the same thing." She pointed at Shayne's lifeless body. "This! This was a sure thing!"

They spoke loudly above the din of the jet engines whining at full throttle with Shayne's dead body between them. Mahegan understood. There were military officers that carried "the football," a briefcase full of nuclear codes and instructions that the president of the United States would use in the event of needing to launch a nuclear strike somewhere in the world. These drills were rehearsed so that everyone up and down the chain understood their precise role in an operation that required flawless execution. Mahegan wondered about the wisdom of having human biometric keys as part of the chain. So much could go wrong, as had been proven.

It made a kind of simple sense to him. Today's world was highly digitized. Sometimes analog solutions provided the best security. Where just about everything could be mined and hacked on the Internet, going analog was an asymmetric form of protection. Mahegan had seen it in combat before. When the U.S. Army deployed high tech jammers to block wireless signals from triggering bombs, the enemy would counter by using pressure plates and a battery, or a clothes pin and two thumb tacks to provide the metal to metal contact necessary to carry the electric current. High tech was good at beating high tech, but sometimes not so great at beating low tech.

Manaslu had hacked the nuclear command and control centers of at least four countries, Mahegan guessed—America, Russia, North Korea, and Iran. America had 6,000 nukes. Russia 7,000. Maybe half of each of those stockpiles were operable. Intelligence reports showed North Korea with up to ten nukes and Iran with perhaps five. Mossad was estimating twice that in Iran's case, but there was little doubt that the money received by Iran in the nuclear deal went two places—funding terrorists like Hamas and Hezbollah, and rapidly developing nuclear weapons in concert with Russia and North Korea.

The nuclear component to this conflict had to include Russia attacking the United States. Iran attacking Israel. And North Korea wreaking havoc in the Pacific Rim. It was all underway.

Still, there had to be alternatives. Why would Gorham, the master of the Internet of Things, marketing, social media, and online shopping, not build redundancy into his scheme? It didn't make sense. The answer was that he wouldn't. There had to be another way to turn off the nuclear countdown. Mahegan looked at Shayne. He looked at Ranger. Stared at his team, each and every one of them. Then looked back at Spartak/Langevin. Thought about Patch Owens going to North Korea. Thought about Cassie in Iran.

Russia was the key. Cassie and Mossad and Jordan special ops would take care of Iran's nuclear missiles. Patch, Hobart, and Van Dreeves would take care of North Korea and whatever limited capability they had. It was up to Mahegan, Savage, and O'Malley to stop Russia.

Mahegan continued to think it through. His mind replayed the images from the attack on the tunnel complex in Yazd. The first car out. Then the next cars. Capturing Shayne. The dead North Korean general. Retrieving Ranger. Losing Cassie. It all seemed like a distant memory even though it was less than twenty four hours ago.

About the fifth time he played that movie reel in his mind, Mahegan thought he had figured it out.

CHAPTER 18

*C*ASSIE FINISHED THE TEXT EXCHANGE WITH MAHEGAN. SHE LOOKED up from the borrowed smartphone and watched her Jordanian and Israeli captors. They were all standing in the mouth of a cave above a narrow valley. Since she had been blindfolded and strapped to the floor, she had no idea where they were. She had counted in her head to about twenty minutes. If the helicopter was moving at a hundred knots, that would put them about thirty to forty miles from the Iranian front lines. Machine-gun fire chattered in the distance. Absently, she rubbed her wrists from where a member of the Jordanian and Israeli joint special forces team had flex-cuffed her wrists together. He had done it smoothly and she was impressed . . . and thankful.

"You are on Mount Nebo. The Dead Sea is over there." A Jordanian soldier pointed it out. "The Iranians are pushing against the fortifications of Amman. Our cyber team did facial recognition of you and we now know you to be U.S. Army Ranger Captain Cassandra Bagwell."

Cassie nodded. "That's me." More than anything, her ankle was killing her, but she ate the pain. She recognized the subdued Jordanian JSOC patch with its spread winged eagle, sabers clutched in talons, wreaths on either side and crown above the eagle head.

"Yes, we know. I am Captain Mohammed Hattab. I am commanding the king's JSOC team. We have other members that we shall not discuss."

Cassie saw the men in dark gray uniforms and knew they were Mossad. They stood in the recesses of the cave, Uzis at the ready. Each of the men had dark beards trimmed closely to their faces. The Jordanian JSOC team wore black fatigues and no helmets or head cover. Each wore an earbud connected to a personal mobile radio and spoke in a combination of Arabic and English to one another.

After a brief conversation with another soldier, Hattab turned to her. "We must right now conduct a mission to this location you say you just came from. Our intelligence says that Iran is prepared to launch a nuclear weapon in less than forty-eight hours."

"I can show you the cave they went into. I didn't get inside. The soldier I just spoke with on your phone did, but I didn't. They took my GPS and map. I've got nothing."

"It's okay. You can show us where it is on the satellite map. We know what to do when we get inside." He chinned in the direction of the captive who was sitting on the rock shelf with his back to the wall of the cave. "He is the Iranian Key that will unlock the system. He carries all of the biometric markers."

"You know this how?"

"We were monitoring the meeting in Yazd that you and Mahegan disrupted."

Cassie nodded. Felt her heart warm at the mention of Jake's name. The text conversation was as much to pass information as it was to connect with him.

"Okay. Like I said, I can point it out, either on a map or on location. Whichever you prefer."

Hattab smiled. "You wish to go on our mission?"

"I want to stop this war. I want to prevent nukes from hitting Jordan or Israel. So, yes, I'll do whatever you need me to do."

"We need the tunnel location."

"I can show you on a map, I think."

Hattab produced a tablet device and punched the button. "Over here." He led her to the darkened crevice just before the doorway, and pinched and spread his fingers on the tablet until she recognized the airfield and valley floor upon which she and Mahegan had jumped.

"There." She used her finger to hover above the screen, indicating the mountain and tunnel compound they had targeted.

The whooshing sound signaled an incoming rocket propelled grenade, or RPG, which exploded at the base of the overhang. Hattab immediately used his body to protect Cassie.

She said, "Not me, you moron. Protect the Key."

Two men had already covered the Iranian Key and were dragging him into the recess.

"The helicopter is two minutes out. Return fire!" Hattab shouted.

The trail to the landing zone above was now precarious. Machine-gun fire chewed beneath their feet and more RPGs smoked in their direction. The two men with the Key lifted him and began running up the goat trail to the top of the mountain. The other four members of the team used thermal scopes and long rifles to return fire. Cassie followed for no other reason than she didn't want to be the only one left in a bunker on the side of Mount Nebo, especially if the Iranians were advancing so quickly.

"Come. Yes," Hattab said over his shoulder.

They hustled up the mountain, the Blackhawk helicopter flared to a quick hover, and in seconds they lifted off to the south. Cassie knew that they couldn't reach Baghdad, much less Iran, on one Blackhawk tank of gas. They banked hard over the Dead Sea twinkling in the moonlight, and Cassie wondered whether the centuries of war raging through this valley had anything to do with the naming of the body of water or was it just the salt?

They landed at a remote airfield south of Tel Aviv, made obvious by the city lights shining brightly at four in the morning. After a seamless transition from the Blackhawk to an MC-130 Combat Talon special operations airplane, they were wheels up.

Headed to Iran, Cassie guessed. She saw the static-line parachutes stacked on a pallet strapped to the floor and thought *tough mission, Ranger.*

The Combat Talon aircraft seemed to bank ninety degrees at times, sliding through tight defiles. She hung on to the red webbing troop seat support that lined the interior of the fuselage. The oval porthole window gave her flashes of lights, then water, and then the gray morning sky. An F-35 buzzed past them and then pulled up and held steady off the wing. It had no markings, but she had the impression it was Israeli. The stealth fighter should be able to assist their entry into Iran, which was a good thing. They would be jumping in broad daylight by the time they got to the target area in Yazd, Iran.

The Jordanian special operations commander came and stood next to her, his large olive hands clutching the metal bar upon which the red webbing was supported. He pulled a combat ration and water bottle from his cargo pocket and handed them to her.

"Thanks," she said. As he spoke, she tore into the MRE and ate like a Ranger. *Like a snake eating a rat,* she would always say. Wolf it down and let it sit there in your stomach. She gulped the water.

"I guessed right," he said.

Wiping her mouth with her forearm, she said, "Thanks, again. Where are we?"

"Red Sea, then low across the desert in Saudi Arabia, the Persian Gulf, and then into the center of Iran. I'll jump with the biometric key strapped to my chest."

"He must weigh three hundred pounds. It's static line. Put him in his own parachute."

"What if he burns in? Knows how to undo the canopy release assemblies? Cuts his lines?"

"We're jumping at what? Five hundred feet AGL? He'll be under canopy for five ten seconds maybe. Tape his feet and knees together. Remember gait recognition is part of this thing. Can't have him breaking a leg. You jump him in and it will be a cluster."

"Some of the others were against you coming." He looked over his shoulder at a scattering of men resting, staring, and planning along the floor of the aircraft.

She shrugged, used to the sentiment. "Our intel shows that Iran got five nuclear weapons from its own program and two from Russia."

"Six of their own. Four from Russia. They are prepared to launch five of them to destroy Israel. Necessarily, Jordan will suffer as well if this happens." After a pause, he added. "I'm glad you came on this mission, sister." He reached out his hand. The large paw smothered her hand like a catcher's mitt holds a baseball.

"Thank you for bringing me on the team," she replied.

He was a handsome man, brown eyes, trimmed beard, olive complexion, rugged face, hook nose, pursed lips, good teeth. His black outer tactical vest held a knife, pistol, first aid kit, ammunition magazines, a snap link through which his M4 three-point sling was looped. The M4 hung by his side.

"I'm sorry about your parents."

Cassie looked away.

"Captain," Hattab said, looking at her distant stare. "I'm sorry. I know it's a sensitive subject."

Cassie snapped out of her reverie. "No. We have a mission to do. Let's execute. I'd rig the key, tape his legs together, and push him out first. No chance of entanglement."

"Okay. This is why I came to you. I like your idea."

"Is there a chance we can air land? There's a runway there," Cassie said.

"Always a chance. Doubtful but a possibility." He looked at her ankle and boot. "Are you okay to jump?"

She stared at the tight wrap and new walking boot the Jordanian medic had emplaced. Butterfly bandages covered shrapnel wounds on her neck and face. "I'm good. Better if we air land, but I can jump." She knew that was crazy. Her ankle was most likely broken. The pain was sharp and unforgiving. Sixty days of Ranger school and not a single injury or illness and on her first true combat jump she snapped an ankle. *Great job, Cassie.* "We have a base in Farah, Afghanistan. We can exfil there."

Hattab looked away then came back and met her eyes.

"What?" she asked.

"The Iranians have overrun that base."

She immediately thought of Jake and the other members of the team. They would have survived.

"Well, we can make it to Kandahar."

"Cassie, this is more of a suicide mission. You understand that? Look at all of these men. Their faces are set with distant stares because they know they are not coming back. They are brave Arab and Israeli warriors. We know the threat to our different, but collective peoples. Iran is a menace and we must defeat their nuclear capabilities."

Cassie nodded. She had understood that this mission, similar to the one she went on with Jake, was high risk. But she didn't consider anything irrecoverable. She refused to accept the term *suicide mission,* though she understood the odds.

"Always look for a solution, Hattab. Everything is possible."

He nodded. "I like your style."

She detected the slightest hint of flirtation, perhaps an overture. Most likely just a man wanting to connect with a woman before he died. It was natural; a fact of life. Though speeding along in a combat talon aircraft prior to a combat parachute jump wasn't exactly Club 21 in New York City. Plus, she loved Jake, something that she knew in her core. Nothing could shake that and she chose to believe that he was alive and well, executing some portion of the mission. His last communication with her had been *Are you okay?*

Hattab had snatched the phone from her when it had turned personal. True, she was a captive, but they had already begun vetting her and knew she was an American military intelligence officer.

"I'm getting some rest before the fight," she said. "When we know air land versus airdrop, let me know. I'm a paratrooper. Send out the biometric key all taped up and dispatch left door and right door jumpers directly after him. I'll bring up the rear. We've got what? Ten soldiers plus the Key?"

"Yes, nine. Plus you, plus the Key."

"Like I said. *Ten.* I'm a soldier."

With that, she turned away from Hattab and walked toward the aft of the aircraft. Men were huddled near the ramp, studying maps. Others sat and stared at the opposite side of the aircraft.

Cassie laid along the uncomfortable red nylon seats and thought about Jake and his words to her in Bald Head Island. He had been standing at the window, curtains fluttering in the ocean breeze.

Waves crashing beyond the dunes. He had mentioned the Croatan maxim, *It's better to die a hero than to grow old.*

She had said, "I'd kind of like to do both."

He had slid back into bed with her, pulled her close and said, "Me, too."

She believed that for the first time Jake Mahegan was in love. She was completely in love with him, too. And sometimes the hard reality of an uncomfortable combat airplane seat brought home the most important truths. Her father had been chairman of the Joint Chiefs of Staff. They'd had a very public dispute about her attendance at Ranger School and her being the first female graduate to not be recycled. Not completely estranged but not completely okay. Then Syrian terrorists had kidnapped her parents, held them in a cage in the Blue Ridge Mountains. Executed them. She had been on the hunt for them with Jake Mahegan, whom she'd met randomly at a gas station. Afterward, was when she and Jake had fallen in love on a short vacation on Bald Head Island at the mouth of the Cape Fear River.

But she was a soldier and she had her duty. Just as Jake had his. What were the priorities of each? Love or war?

She didn't know how long she had slept, but Hattab woke her, saying, "Twenty minutes. Time to rig up."

They were close! She would revisit Yazd and hope for a different result this time. Despite her overall optimism, part of her never believed they would make it that far. Cassie pushed off the red seat and saw the other members of the team buddy rigging their T-11 parachutes. They were the newer square parachute that carried more weight and allowed for softer landings. Cassie was going to need every inch of canopy she could get. She stepped into the harness and soon was fully rigged.

Hattab gave her an M4 rifle and a weapons case, which he hooked on to her parachute harness. "The Iranian Key is rigged just as you suggested. He's like a bundle we're dropping. Hope you're right."

"No time to second guess. No air land option?"

"We're jumping behind the target. There's a drop zone there. The airfield has infantry guarding it."

"Sounds like the same drop zone. It's rocky. The satellite imagery doesn't do it justice."

"Ten minutes!" the jumpmaster shouted.

"See you on the drop zone," Hattab said.

Cassie nodded. A ball of fear boiled in her stomach, which was normal. She'd made dozens of training jumps and was performing her second combat jump in two days. She hooked up her static line, shuffled forward, feeling the pain of her ankle, conscious not to cheat to the other ankle on her landing because two broken ankles were definitely worse than one.

The light turned green and the jumpmaster shouted, "Go!"

Hattab pushed the giant Iranian Key out of the door, his static line popping tight to deploy the parachute, and then followed him into the morning sky. The paratroopers filed out quickly and soon Cassie was dropping like a stone toward the ground. Her parachute deployed and she felt the groin synching tug of going from 140 miles per hour to 32 feet per second.

She checked canopy. All good. Observed her fellow jumpers. All good. A group of three were clustered around the Iranian Key, who was moving his hands frantically, trying to release his canopy. She hoped that Hattab had welded or taped those shut. Evidently, he knew that he was going to be taken into the bowels of the biometric chamber to lock down the Iranian nuclear arsenal.

She was shocked when she saw his parachute float free into the sky—disconnected from the big man—and he began dropping to the ground from one hundred feet above ground level.

Half a world away from Cassie Bagwell, Patch Owens stood in the bomb bay door above North Korea with two of his former teammates from Delta Force, Hobart and Van Dreeves. Their combat bona fides included every single combat operation the United States had undertaken in the last twenty years.

The light turned green and Patch dropped straight down from 40,000 feet above ground level. The height was no big deal. Others had jumped from three times as high. That altitude was a good, safe drop altitude as long as the airplane remained off radar and was not intercepted, which seemed to be the case.

Night was falling—good for their cover and concealment upon landing. The ride had been smooth. Each jumper had an oxygen mask tethered to the oxygen supply of the aircraft so that they looked like fighter pilots laying in the closed bomb bays. The modification of the XB-2 included the masks and heating vents that kept the jumpers warm, allowing them to survive the high-altitude jump.

It had been awhile since Owens had jumped with Hobart and Van Dreeves, but everything came back to him as they were delta diving through the air. Soon they were just three human missiles screaming toward the ground from seven miles above ground level.

"Airfield at two o'clock," Owens said.

"Roger," Van Dreeves replied.

"Got it," Hobart said.

"Manaslu facility at nine o'clock. Airplane inbound to airfield, time now," Owens said. He saw a large commercial airplane landing at the Samjiyon facility."

"Wasn't on the schedule. Nothing should be landing there," Van Dreeves said.

During the flight, they had passed around a digital tablet that had PDF files with target folders for the airfield and the Manaslu facility. They'd studied the interior passageways and found what they believed was the biometric chamber. Their mission was to capture the woman, Kal, the North Korean Key, and walk her through the chamber. The dossier on her included information that she was an assassin with one vulnerability.

Her father had saved her life during a house fire, having come home from work to find the entire home ablaze. He ran through the flames, plucked her from the closet in which she had been hiding, and carried her to safety. The next day the Korean Central News Agency ran a story that American special forces had infiltrated her home and killed her mother because she was an engineer with the North Korean nuclear agency. Her brother had died, also, hardening her soul, making her ripe for government wet work. The next year after the fire, she graduated from high school and joined the North Korean special forces, or "NickSof," as some called the elite troops.

The village of Rimyongsu had lionized her father and the larger city of Samjiyon a few miles away had honored him with a medal from the Great Leader, Kim Jong Il. Her father, though, had been humble and deferred to his daughter, placing her in the spotlight. It was customary for humble servants such as her father to save face, be humble, and deflect attention. That deflection had tipped off a North Korean special operations recruiter when he learned of her athletic skills. Young Kal was particularly adept at killing game for her family to eat. Often she would sit with her bow and arrow on the North Korean side of the Tumen River and pluck deer, fox, and the occasional wild boar. She provided well for her family as had her brother.

Her father was her responsibility today, and he was in an elderly care home in Samjiyon. Hobart had the mission to link up with the father. Van Dreeves and Owens would go into the Manaslu facility with Kal.

Owens and Van Dreeves landed in a rice field a mile from the Manaslu facility on the south side of Samjiyon. They removed their parachutes and oxygen gear, put their weapons into operation, and huddled tight.

"That airplane had to be Kal returning," Owens said.

"Roger. There might be another HVT on that thing, as well. Big as it is," Van Dreeves said. High Value Target was a euphemism for some type of principal that deserved capturing.

"Too far to get a tail number and doubt it would do us any good. Just have to assume she has a plus one," Owens said.

Hobart had landed near the ski slope on the opposite side of the city. His voice came through their respective ear pieces. "Target is at my ten o'clock. Moving now." Two sentences was a long conversation for him.

Owens knew the operator was in good shape. "Roger. Confirm when target secure."

"Wilco. Eyes on your bogey moving from airfield," Hobart said. It made sense that being on the ski slope he would have a view of the airfield and the solitary road five miles away.

"Roger, out," Owens said. To Van Dreeves, he said, "Let's go. Follow me."

Owens followed a patch of low ground through the woods. The terrain was steep and jagged, where glacial till had cut V-shaped wedges into the ground. Staying in the depression behind the first row of buildings in the city, Owens was able to lead them to an alley about a quarter mile from the Manaslu facility.

Leaving the protection of the forest, he picked his way through a dark alley. A stray dog loped along the right-hand side. On either side of the alley were the backs of businesses shuttered for the evening. He imagined they were basic goods types of stores. Hardware. Groceries. Nothing fancy.

The alley came to a T, and they were staring at the razor wire of the outer perimeter of the Manaslu grounds. The actual building was another 400 meters away across an open field. Their analysis had indicated that this spot would be the best location to breach, but Owens had another idea.

"The main road is a hundred meters through this wood line," he said to Van Dreeves.

"Roger. Want to ambush the car?"

"Seems like the best way in."

"I've got one tire shredder we can throw in the road."

Owens pressed his microphone and said, "Chase car with the vehicle leaving the airport?"

"Negative," Hobart said.

Turning to Van Dreeves, he said, "Let's move."

They hurried along the fence line through a small wooded area that was steep on their right-hand side. The terrain kept forcing them toward the fence and Owens kept pushing them sidehill to avoid any contact that would alert the motion detectors. They reached the end of the ridge and the road and he saw that their location was perfect for an ambush.

"Great spot," Van Dreeves said. He wedged his M4 carbine into the V of a low tree branch, placed the butt on the ground, and re-

moved his rucksack. He pulled a collapsible portable tire shredder kit from his ruck and opened it. The size of a small microwave
oven, the shredders would either cause the vehicle to stop or, less
preferably, puncture the tires and render them inoperable. The
teeth on the specialized gear were so long that they disabled Run
Flat tires, as well.

"I've got you. Toss it in the road," Owens said.

The headlights from the approaching vehicle were a speck in
the distance, maybe a mile away. Depending on the vehicle speed,
they could have a full minute. Van Dreeves spread the matting on
the side of the road, ensuring the long, razor sharp teeth were exposed upward.

Returning to his firing position, he said, "Should slow him
down. What next, boss?"

Owens wanted to say that he wasn't Van Dreeves' boss, but he
understood the need for clarity and mission focus at that precise
moment as the car approached from two hundred yards.

"Remember, we have to capture her alive. That's part of the
plan. Disable the car and we'll politely join them in the vehicle
and drive through undetected.

"I'd be happy with a one and done thing here, but I think this
is major, Patch," Van Dreeves said.

Just then, Hobart called. "Package secured," which meant that
he had kidnapped Kal's father from the nursing home where she
kept him. The dossier indicated the man may be wheelchair
bound, but Hobart did not seem to have run into complications
just yet.

"Roger. Twenty seconds from execution. Stand by. Be ready to
video chat," Owens said.

Hobart did not reply.

Owens low crawled across the street to the far side, found a low
spot behind some rocks and prepared for Van Dreeves to deploy
the twenty-five-foot Defender Stinger Spike System. This device
was employed by police departments across the United States to
protect routes or stop criminals. It consisted of accordion style
collapsible hinged metal bars with dozens of hollow spikes that
penetrated deeply into the tire, leaving the nail inside. The hol-

low core allowed for the fast escape of air and rapid flattening of the tire.

"Vehicle fifty meters," Van Dreeves said. He low crawled into position.

"Execute," Owens said.

Van Dreeves slung the Defender across the narrow road. Owens snatched the chain on the first toss and pulled it snug. The matting scraped and rattled, but otherwise was black and obscure. The same color of the black asphalt road that led to the Manaslu compound.

The car approached, slowed, and braked as its front tires crossed the Defender and immediately deflated. Backing up did little good except prevent the rear tires from being deflated also. The driver attempted a Y-turn, sensing that he was in some sort of ambush. Van Dreeves put two silenced rounds into the rear tires and Owens did the same on the passenger side of the vehicle. The car was still drivable, but with less speed. More troublesome for the driver was the ambush location—a narrow defile where any attempted turn would take multiple back and forth maneuvers.

Owens and Van Dreeves had worked out that whichever way the vehicle turned to conduct the Y-turn, the man on the opposite side would approach and breach the rear doors while the operator in front would take on the security and the driver. Assuming the windows were bulletproof, each man had a crowbar for prying open the doors.

Van Dreeves tossed a smoke grenade under the car and it boiled thick gray smoke around the car, obscuring the windows. Owens approached the passenger side and used a jimmy to open the door as he slid his pistol in and began firing. A Glock 17 tried to work its way out the door, but Owens' shots found some kind of target. He pulled the door open, keeping it between him and the driver, who he assumed was also armed. Good assumption. Pistol shots rang out from the driver side and were effectively blocked by the armored car's own protective windows and doors.

Owens slid around and double tapped the driver in the forehead.

Van Dreeves cautiously approached the rear, wary that security might be in the trunk. He used the crowbar on the trunk lid, saw the security guard lifting his pistol, and shot the man in the forehead. Owens covered him and watched the interior of the vehicle, seeing a privacy shield between the front and back seats. He felt time slipping away from him. He knew the biometric key might have instructions to kill herself. Or worse, there might be a guard designated to kill her. She was of no use to the North Korean government now. The arsenal was armed and not penetrable by hackers, according to the reports, albeit they were changing by the hour.

Owens received a text on his wearable technology chest mount. He flipped open the small device the size of a smart phone. It was from Mahegan.

North Korea scheduled to fire three more nukes at Japan and Philippines in two hours. Timeline is accelerated.

Owens typed **Roger.**

With a clock now ticking, he had no time to spare. In sync, he and Van Dreeves jimmied the rear doors, which pushed out at them. Probably part of the tactical plan the people in the rear had discussed in the less than fifteen seconds since the car had run over the Defender tire flattener.

Two throwing stars clinked off Owens' body armor and one whizzed past his head.

Kal.

According to her dossier, she was an expert at all things sharp and lethal. She bolted from the car on the rear passenger side and dashed into the woods. She was quick and agile, leaping over tree trunks and rocks with ease. Owens was reminded that this was her home turf. She would know every trail.

Van Dreeves stayed focused on the car. "Have another bogey in the car," he whispered into the microphone as Owens was in hot pursuit.

"Might need your help. This is more important. She's the reason we're here."

"You're giving the orders. I've got a dude just sitting here. Can make out his face through the smoke."

Kal stopped running and turned, spun a throwing star at Owens' face. He reacted quickly as it laced across his cheek like a buzz saw, drawing blood. He saw the fence behind her and knew that she was blocked. A seventy degree incline was to his right, her left. The perimeter fence hooked into the rocky crevice and rose a considerable distance into the sky above the rock formation. He imagined that she could scale the rock face with some effort, but knew that he would catch her with her backside to him.

He removed a Cap-Chur tranquilizer pistol from his holster as he aimed his M4 at her face from fifteen feet away. "We need to get you into your command post so you can stop this nuclear attack that has been automated. We understand that you are an unwitting accomplice."

"Don't pity me, Mister Owens," Kal said. Seeing the shock register on his face that she knew his name, she followed up with, "That's right. In the thirty seconds that you needed to stop us and kill innocent guards and drivers, I was able to review your top secret dossier hidden in the Pentagon. You're with Jake Mahegan and some of the other not-so-clandestine military operatives from the United States."

Patch stepped back. A bullet smacked into the rock to his right. She had led him into ambush. In his periphery, he noticed the slightest movement. Something primal kicked in. An instinct. Years of combat honed into one moment. Survival of the fittest. He'd seen too much to not have learned and lived.

"You know I have to live, right?" Kal said, obviously disappointed that shot had missed. But others were coming faster.

He was surprised the guards had been able to react so quickly. The bullets seemed to be drifting closer to Kal than to him.

"I need you to live," Owens said. "They need you to die." He chinned toward the guard tower two hundred meters away. "No hopes and dreams for a future?"

"None." She smiled.

"What about your father?" Owens held up a tablet with a live streaming image of Hobart pulling a garrote around her father's neck.

"No!"

The reaction was better than Owens expected. Her face pulled back into a tight knot. The rifle fire pinged closer and closer. She was oblivious to everything but her father's bulging eyes that showed on the tablet.

"You come with me, he lives," Owens said.

She spun and dove toward him, beneath the hail of bullets blasting the rock wall to his right. Prepared, he dodged her lunge and used a swift blow of his rifle's buttstock to knock her unconscious. The rifle fire started chasing him as he dragged her low along the trail back toward the road. Bark splintered above his head and he could see the faint outline of the car about fifty meters ahead. The thick trees shielded their movement and the shooter lost visual on them, but that didn't stop him from guessing. Some of his guesses were too good, too close. Others raked high into the leaves, spitting branches and bark into Owens' face as he carried the unconscious Kal as if he were doing the sidestroke in a pool.

Van Dreeves said, "I've got you. Car was empty. Was like a hologram in the back. Looked like that Internet guy we've been talking about. Gorham. But it was just a projection from the backseat."

"I've got Kal. She's alive but unconscious," Owens said.

"What do I do with this guy," Hobart said.

In the excitement of the moment, Owens had forgotten that Hobart was strangling Kal's father. "Stick with him. Keep him alive. See if you can't get to the airport and see whose airplane that was. We're going to need a way out."

"Roger. I'll see what I can do," Hobart said.

It was clear to Owens that Hobart wasn't optimistic about relocating four miles up the road toward the airport. And the likelihood was that the plane had already departed, though he hadn't heard anything take off or land.

Van Dreeves came around and helped Owens put Kal in the back seat of the car. Owens snapped a seat belt around her and then sat next to her and snapped one around his chest. With no element of surprise anymore, it was just a brute force attack. The timing of their drop and the airplane landing had led to this course of action. Now they had to adapt and overcome.

"I've cut through the security system and disengaged the override. It's still locked, but we should be able to get through with the weight of this car." Van Dreeves buzzed his window partially down and extended his M4 carbine through the gap. "Here we go," he growled.

The rear tires were smoking as he kept the brake and the accelerator to the floor, then released the brake and slammed into the gate. Thanks to cheap North Korean steel it buckled, but not without a fight. The car spun ninety degrees and Van Dreeves overcorrected twice, fishtailing until he leveled the car into a steady top end of one hundred miles per hour.

Their study of the facility had shown fives guards, one at each fence corner and one rover. Owens predicted they would collapse on the central facility. There wasn't much to guard other than Manaslu's technology, and the former North Korean leader didn't care much about that.

"Left access is looking good," Van Dreeves said. "What's the countdown?"

Owens looked at his tablet. "Twenty-seven minutes to nuclear launch. We've got to get her awake, in the chamber, pass the biometrics, and then confirm with Jake."

"Comms with Jake good?"

"Roger. I'm here. Staying out of your way. Keep up the progress. We're tracking. Sean is standing by to shut down the nukes once Kal confirms," Mahegan said.

Owens thought he heard the whine of jet engines in the background and imagined that the team was relocating to go after the Russian Key. "Roger, out," he said. It was good to hear his friend's voice. The mission was tough and tight on time. Reassurance was always a good thing.

The car began taking fire, which Owens returned with suppressive shots at muzzle flashes. He had night vision gear, but they were doing one hundred miles per hour and about to slam through a garage door.

"Hang on," Van Dreeves said.

The car barreled through the loading dock elevating door and screeched to a halt. The seat belts did their job. All three passengers stayed in the car despite the enormous forces propelling them forward. As the engine smoked and ticked, Van Dreeves and Owens exited, weapons up. One military police guard appeared on the dock and raised his rifle. Owens double tapped him in the chest. No body armor. They weren't expecting an attack. One down, four to go. Maybe more. Collapsing.

He lifted Kal over his shoulders like a sack of rice and began running with Van Dreeves in lead. Another guard popped out of the far left corner of the warehouse. It was the size of a small gymnasium. Van Dreeves fired three rounds. At least one caught the man and spun him to the ground. Two more shots sparked off the floor and skidded into his body. Van Dreeves was shooting low and using the ricochet effect. Up on the loading dock, Owens laid down Kal and placed C4 explosives on the door handle to the interior of the facility. They covered Kal, ducked, and waited for the explosion.

Pouring through the buckled door, Owens had Kal over his back again. Van Dreeves was in the lead again.

The hallway was dark and smoky from the blast.

"Left," Owens said. Then after a few seconds, "Right. Okay up ahead."

Van Dreeves turned the corner and fired five shots, took some backfire in return. He spun to the ground and slid, shooting as he flew under the high shots. Owens came around the corner with Kal in tow. Saw two dead guards.

Four down, one to go. Maybe. Maybe more. Maybe less. Collapsing to the middle. Defending the biometric chamber.

"Here." Van Dreeves used another block of C4, blew open the door and then opened a second door that led to a small command room with five rows of stadium seating. It looked like it could have been used for presentations or school plays, but Owens knew that on the stage was the biometric chamber.

"Hit the power at the rear of the curtain," Owens said.

"Roger." Van Dreeves flipped the master switch. The lights came on. The clear walkway buzzed with neon blue lights and red LED numbers flashing. Six red Xs were next to the words *Gait, Voice, Handprint, DNA, Eye scan, Facial features.*

"Smelling salts," Owens said.

Van Dreeves reached into his kit bag while still looking outward, eyeing for the last guard. He tossed Owens the smelling salts and a shot of B-12 adrenaline booster.

After a few waves of the salts, Kal was coughing and rubbing her head. Owens used that time to disarm her—three more throwing stars, a small knife on her ankle, and a pistol in the small of her back beneath her black coat. He stuffed those items into his own small rucksack.

"Hobart," he said.

"Roger."

"Video."

"On."

"Here's your chance to save your dad, Kal. Let's go. We've got less than fifteen minutes."

As she stood, she reached for a throwing star, but came up empty.

"You want to live and you want your father to live. So get this done."

She nodded. "What's the use?" Walking to the chamber, she reached out to steady herself, causing Owens to clutch her upper arm tightly.

"Don't do anything but walk normally and go through the process," he said.

"You can't walk in there with me," Kal said.

"No, but your father will be watching you." Owens pointed at Van Dreeves who was simultaneously holding the tablet displaying Hobart and Kal's father, and scanning for threats.

Owens stood at the entry to the glassed-in walkway, which was no more than twenty feet. He clutched her arm. Her eyes flicked to her father's image, his face all puffy and red. Hobart standing behind him, garrote tightening second by second. Owens wondered if the man would live. Hobart was something of a machine . . . a killing machine. He had little remorse and little patience. Kal seemed to sense that, as well.

"Tell him to let go. I will walk. I will do everything," Kal said.

"It's a race. The quicker you finish, the sooner he can breathe," Owens said.

"Let him go, damnit!"

"Walk."

Kal stiffened. "Very well."

She stepped onto the Plexiglas floor and walked straight for ten steps. The green box checked *Gait.* Standing before the biometric scanning device, a green check appeared next to *Eyes.*

The mechanical arm came out and stuck a Q-tip in her mouth. After returning it inside the gray metal machine, the green box checked next to *DNA.* She spoke her name. "Kal Song Kim." Another green check mark appeared.

She placed her hand on the outline of a hand on the face of the biometric scanner. After a few seconds, the green box checked *Handprint.*

Shots rang out. Pock marks appeared in the glass near Kal's body. She stood, despite being hit, like the Spartan boy holding the fox. She was stoic. The facial recognition wasn't complete.

Owens quickly returned fire, but it took him a moment to find the source. The final guard was back of the stage, behind the curtain, hiding in the dark like a forgotten actor. Kal remained standing. She was bleeding. Van Dreeves angled himself so that she could see Hobart squeezing the life out of her father.

"Stay strong, Kal!" Owens said.

The green check mark appeared. *Facial Recognition.*

All six check marks were lined up. Like a perfect score. 100%.

A mechanical female voice said, "Kal Song Kim. Approved."

"Got that, Jake?" Owens said.

"Roger. Working it now. Keep her in there. Not exactly sure how all this works." After a few seconds, Mahegan said, "Okay, Sean's in. He's overriding the launch."

Van Dreeves kept the father's image on the tablet at eye level for the dying Kal, who was still standing despite a bullet in her back. She had been strong for her father to the end. Owens stood at the mouth of the walkway, watching and scanning over his shoulder. "Time check?"

"Three minutes," Mahegan said.

"Is it working?"

"Sean's doing his thing," Mahegan replied. "Two minutes now."

Owens locked eyes with Van Dreeves. In less than two minutes five nuclear missiles would be fired at Japan and South Korea. Other cities would suffer devastation such as Tokyo already had. Pusan, Osaka, and Kyoto would all be demolished. Hundreds of thousands killed, maybe millions.

"One minute," Mahegan said.

"Come on, Sean," Owens whispered.

"He's got it. Saying he's shut it down. Tricky but he got it."

"Confirm," Owens asked.

"Roger. Confirmed. Nuclear arsenal overridden. We have control of the nuclear arsenal now."

Owens nodded at Van Dreeves, who said, "Okay. Cease work."

On the tablet, Kal's father lurched forward, grasping his neck. Hobart stood there watching him, his ruddy face expressionless.

"Hard man," Owens said.

"The best," Van Dreeves replied.

"You can die now, Kal. It's okay. You served a higher calling and saved your father, just as he saved you."

On cue, Kal turned. A trickle of dark blood ran from the corner of her mouth. Her eyes were milky. She whispered and took a step.

Owens didn't understand her. "Say again?"

"Hold me," she said.

Owens was hesitant. She was an assassin, not a daughter. Not a woman. Not a friend. She should die a cold, hard death. But still, there was something about her noble act of saving her father and by extension saving Japan and South Korea from nuclear devastation. She didn't want to die alone. She wanted to be held as she bled out. What could it hurt? Plus he had a question for her.

"Come to me," Owens said.

She stepped warily, her hands pushing out at the chamber walkway glass like a rock climber maintaining balance. "Hold me," she whispered.

"Two more steps, Kal."

She approached him. Her eyes were red, nearly bleeding. The blood streamed from her mouth. The sorrow on her face was evident. He was sure she had much for which to repent.

She wrapped her arms around his back and laid her head on his shoulder. Her hands were out of view of Van Dreeves, who was storing the tablet in his rucksack.

Owens detected her hands moving and pushed up on her strong arms, but she was resolute.

She had removed a ring, which straightened into a three inch needle, which was aimed at the base of his brain. "You bastard. How dare you use my father!"

She slumped forward.

Van Dreeves' rifle had delivered the bullet to her head.

"Gotta watch who ya' dance with, Patch," he said.

"Roger that. She had about a minute left in her."

"Enough to do you in. Now let's get on the road."

"Was going to ask her who was on the plane with her."

"I think it was Ian Gorham. Hobart is at the airport. He stole a car. He's got eyes on a triple seven airplane with the Manaslu symbol."

"We need wheels. We need to unass this AO," Owens said. Leaving the area of operations quickly was paramount. The sound of rotor blades chopped against the night sky. Friend or foe? 99 percent chance it was foe.

Owens tossed a thermite grenade in the biometric chamber and they dashed through the hallway, the explosion chasing them. "Let's move."

They retraced their path, found a Mercedes panel truck in the warehouse, loaded inside, and raced toward the airport.

"We have Ian Gorham on this airplane," Hobart said. "And we've got the Task Force helicopters coming off a ship. A hundred miles each way. Gotta move."

"On the way," Owens said.

Two North Korean MiG fighter jets screamed low over the Manaslu facility and dropped bombs, which exploded with deafening thunder.

They were sitting ducks on the road to the airport, but they had little choice as the MiGs flared, corkscrewed, spun around, and lined up for a murderous strafing run of the roadway.

CHAPTER 19

*F*ROM THE SOARING XC17 COMMAND AND CONTROL AIRCRAFT, MAHE-gan studied two satellite shots—the airfield at Samjiyon, North Korea, and the initial meeting tunnel complex at Yazd, Iran. He watched as Owens and Van Dreeves raced along the narrow road to the Samjiyon Airport. Saw the two MiGs flaring and directed, "Disable those, now."

Spartak/Langevin was typing as fast as she could. She had eagerly tackled her role to locally suppress enemy capabilities and patch friendly Trojans that may have disabled allied weapons systems. "Apache gunships should be able to shoot. Tell them they're cleared hot," she said, her voice precise in clipped tones.

"Roger." Mahegan typed out a text message to the Task Force 160th commander that had launched from the deck of the USS Eisenhower fourteen miles off the east coast of North Korea.

Inbound was the reply text.

Very few Apache pilots had practiced air-to-air Hellfire missile shots, but that was the requirement at the moment. Two Apache Longbow and two Blackhawk MH-60 special operations helicopters were streaking across the monitor above the two video displays Mahegan was watching. The Apache Longbow were optimal because they carried AGM-114L Hellfire II missiles, which were fire and forget, as opposed to the Hellfire I, which required constant guidance. Hellfire II's millimeter wave radar detection afforded it the capability to lock on immediately and seek out targets in all weather conditions.

"Six miles out," the pilot in command called in to Mahegan.

"Need target lock now. Two MiGs turning on friendly vehicle."

"Roger. Ten seconds. Moving at two hundred knots."

"Make it quicker," Mahegan urged.

Rarely would he interject in a tactical mission underway, but the MiGs were probably five seconds, if that, from destroying the Mercedes with Owens and Van Dreeves in it.

"What do you have Spartak?" Mahegan asked.

"MiG one disabled. Working on two. They still have machine guns, but missiles disabled on MiG one," she said.

"Lock," the pilot said.

Mahegan looked at Savage, who held his gaze. The tension was unbearable. They had operators on the ground in grave danger. They were doing all they could to support them. People Mahegan—and Savage, he supposed—loved and cared about. Cassie and Patch Owens. Even Van Dreeves and Hobart were legends in Delta Force. Though in a different squadron, he knew the men well. Cut from the same cloth. Always in the right spot at the right time.

"Launch," the pilot said.

The missile flew at Mach one with a range of five miles, which was why the pilot had needed a few seconds to get within range.

"Taking fire," Owens reported.

Mahegan interpreted that to mean machine-gun fire, which wasn't good, but was better than the alternative of rockets or missiles.

"Think I've got number two," Spartak/Langevin said.

Two seconds later both MiGs disappeared from the tracking radar.

"Jackpot," the pilot called.

"Roger. I've got six more coming from the Yang. They're ten minutes out," Mahegan said. *Pyongyang* had devolved in combat parlance to "The Yang" amongst Mahegan and his team.

"I don't have enough missiles for them," Apache Six said.

"Do what you can. I need you to pick up my three and get out of there. We're working it on my end."

"Roger."

"You working these six MiGs?" Mahegan asked Spartak/Langevin.

"Yeah, but it's like Whack-A-Mole. I can't find them that fast plus someone has found me in our own network."

"Gotta be Gorham," Mahegan said. "Work it." Then to General Savage, "Sir, where are we on destroying the nanosats over North Korea?"

"Sir? Shit, Jake you haven't called me sir in years. What's the special occasion?"

"My bad," Mahegan said.

"We've got a sub about to launch an ASAT," Savage said. "Ten seconds."

Mahegan switched his screen to global view where he could see the low earth orbit satellites hovering above the Korean Peninsula like a swarm of bees. The anti-satellite weapons were their only hope against the ComWar satellite constellations.

"Airburst?"

"That's what we requested."

"Cruise missiles on the command post?"

"Simultaneous."

"Nothing's ever simultaneous, General."

"That's more like it, Jake. Had me worried for a second."

The antisatellite missile launch and the Tomahawk cruise missile launch were minutes apart but were, for all practical purposes, simultaneous. The screen showed the trajectory of the ASAT, its replicated explosion as indicated by a fire burst, and the subsequent damage to the nanosatellites.

"What's our BDA?" Mahegan asked. Battle damage assessment was key in knowing whether he needed to attack the target again. They had limited missiles.

"Not sure," Spartak/Langevin said. "The ManaSats are back up. The ground control stations are primary. Only when we knock out the ManaSats will we know if we were effective. Ian will freak."

Mahegan stared at her. She was sitting with one leg tucked under the other on a padded chair in the command and control suite of the XC-17.

"What?" she asked.

"Ian? ManaSats? Never heard that before. Where does this come from?"

She paused, perhaps a moment too long. "Come on. We worked together. Makes sense, right?"

"None of this makes sense. But it is starting to be clear to me that you were involved with Gorham more than you are letting on. You're not just some simple CFO turned hacker. You know what's happening. You know how to stop it. You may even have designed some of this," Mahegan said.

"We've discussed this. I told you everything I know." Her eyes darted away from his gaze. Evasive.

"There's something you're not telling us."

"Jake, focus. We've got Cassie on the radio," Savage said.

Cassie.

"Iranian Key is still alive. He tried to burn in by releasing his canopy release assemblies, but one of the Jordanians had hooked a twenty foot lowering line to the apex of his parachute during descent. Ballsy move. Had a better landing than I did on the same drop zone," Cassie reported.

Mahegan focused the satellite shot on Cassie who was on one knee near the pass they had used to get to the tunnel complex. His heart was in his throat. From relative safety to danger to safety and back to danger. Emotions swirled through his mind like an Outer Banks riptide.

"What's Gorham's time on target for the strike on Tel-Aviv and Jerusalem?" Cassie asked.

"You've only got thirty minutes, Ranger."

"We're moving out quickly." She stowed her radio and Mahegan watched her limp down the defile, leading the Jordanian and Mossad special forces team along the base of the cliff from which she and Jake had just a day ago waged battle.

On his other monitor he saw the helicopters land and pick up Hobart, Van Dreeves, and Owens. The Apaches were providing cover fire, but the MiGs continued on to the airfield. The Boeing 777 was racing along the runway and lifting into the air, escorted, it seemed, by the MiGs as it climbed above North Korea, crossed into Russia and then headed north, using Russian airspace as a protected area.

"Has to be Gorham," Mahegan said.

The airplane disappeared from the radar.

"What happened?" Savage asked. Both were watching the radar screen once the airplane flew out of the satellite picture.

"Did it blow up? Shot down?" Mahegan asked. "Spartak? Can you find it?"

O'Malley was focused on the nuclear countdown. "Twenty minutes on Iran launch. I'm waiting outside the launch portal, ready to go in and shut it down. They've got to get the boxer in there."

Mahegan ran through his priorities. Owens and team were on the helicopters and headed to apparent safety off North Korea. Cassie was rushing headlong into a brute force attack against the tunnel complex where the Iranians kept their biometric chamber. Iran was fifteen minutes from a nuclear attack. Possibly, Ian Gorham's airplane had disappeared from the sky. Lots to digest and synthesize.

"Cruise missile attack against North Korean command post effective. Target destroyed," O'Malley reported.

"Spartak. Satellites. Status?"

"So far no backup capability. They haven't refreshed since the attack on the satellites."

"Okay. General, let's get the shots on Iranian and Russian nanosats and ComWar command posts."

"Executing," Savage said, holding a phone to his ear.

On the satellite shot over North Korea, Mahegan saw the two Apache helicopters and MH-60s flare and land on an aircraft carrier off the coast of North Korea. Six F-35 jets with newly enhanced and debugged weapon systems swarmed into the sky in a dog fight with North Korean MiGs, the North Korean pilots no doubt in shock.

"Okay, North Korea is stabilized, I think. Where are we on Iran?" Mahegan asked.

"Cassie's at the front door. They're taking fire, but nothing serious so far. Seems the military there relocated to the airfield. Only a light force at the tunnel," O'Malley said.

"Roger. Let's go, Cassie," Mahegan whispered.

"Going," she shot back.

For a moment he had forgotten he had his PUSH TO TALK switch turned on. "You can do this."

Team Owens safe return to the Eisenhower had given Mahegan a blossom of hope. The mission so far had been a dark, locked room where they were having to feel their way out. At least they had resolved one issue, partially. The conventional fight still raged on the Korean Peninsula, but the U.S. and South Korean forces were now able to use most of their full capabilities. They could hold the Pusan Perimeter, at least, Mahegan thought.

"RPG!" Cassie's voiced bellowed through his headset.

In Yazd, Iran, Cassie dove to the ground. The rocket propelled grenade whooshed overhead. Her ankle screamed at her to take better care. She rolled to her left as machine-gun rounds walked up the tunnel toward her at the opening. Behind her the Mossad fire team fired 40mm grenades from an M4 rail mounted launcher. The Jordanian army fire team laid down a base of fire with M249 Squad Automatic Weapons, spitting nearly one hundred rounds per minute at whatever lurked in the darkness.

Using her night vision googles, Cassie studied the tunnel, mostly obscured by haze. After their return fire, everything went silent save the distant echoes rolling through the mountains behind them.

"Team one, move," Cassie said. "Stay in the middle. About one hundred meters on left is the room. Carports on left and right, so watch for stragglers."

"Roger," Hattab said. He led the team down the center of the tunnel to avoid the funnel effect from ricochets that would hug and ride along the walls. He was tossing smoke grenades ahead at regular intervals.

Cassie pulled up behind the two Mossad agents who were dragging the Iranian Key on a poncho litter as if he were wounded.

After moving the distance required, Hattab slowed the single file train of soldiers until they could see the door. For good measure, he tossed several smoke grenades into the deep recesses of the cavern, beyond the door to the biometric chamber.

Cassie dashed forward and pulled open the door, which was unlocked. Given the chaos that they had created twenty-four hours earlier, she was not surprised. Beyond the door, the lights were bright and everything seemed to be in working order.

They saw four walkways leading to the center stage, one from each cardinal direction, it seemed.

"Which one is for the Iranian?" Hattab asked.

From an airplane flying somewhere far away, Mahegan whispered into Cassie's ear, "Seven minutes."

"Any ideas? There's four chambers," Cassie said.

"Gorham got away first, so he was probably the one closest to the tunnel," Mahegan said. "The North Korean general was last, so he was probably the one farthest from the tunnel. That narrows it down by fifty percent."

"Wasting time," Cassie said, though she eyed the walkway nearest them and thought *Gorham.* Then she looked across the stadium and saw the walkway leading to the center and thought *North Korean.* She looked left and right and saw two identical walkways. There was an anomaly in the seating area at the end of the walkway on the left.

"Shayne said the Russian president shot their Key. Is one of them occupied?" Mahegan asked.

"Precisely," Cassie said. Then to Hattab, she said, "This way." She sprinted as best she could to the right, counterclockwise, around the rim of the stadium. She found the portal open and ran to the base while remaining outside. She saw the biometric scanners had reset. Six big red Xs."

"Better be right," Hattab said. "Or Israel, Jordan, and Saudi Arabia go up in flames."

"Four minutes," Mahegan said into Cassie's ear.

"Four minutes, guys. Let's go."

One of the Mossad agents was waving a smelling salt under the nose of the Iranian Olympian, the biometric key. And the only way to stop a nuclear attack on three nations. One man was inserting a syringe into the Iranian's massive forearm.

"Sodium Pentothal," Hattab said.

"Truth serum?"

"The only chance," he said.

"The machine is ready," Mahegan said into Cassie's earpiece. "Sean says it is prepped. Three minutes."

The smelling salts woke the Olympian, who appeared dizzy. He muttered a few words in Farsi and his eyes darted between the men hovering over him. He stood.

·"Into the chamber," Hattab said.

"I shoot myself first," Persi said. "I am loyal Iranian. Persian."

"Running out of time," Cassie said.

They stood at the entry. They needed him to walk to the Biometric Scanning Station twenty meters down the ramp.

A man wearing an Iranian general's outfit rose from the stadium seating, lifted a rifle, and shot Cassie and Hattab. Both dropped to the floor.

"Quick!" the general said in Farsi. "With me." The man raced up the steps and hugged Persi. "What is your name?"

"Alexander Persi."

"What is your occupation?"

"Persian Olympic champion boxer."

"What else?"

"I am the key to the nuclear arsenal."

"The arsenal is in trouble. We need you to walk through the chamber and confirm your identity."

"But General—"

"Do as ordered, soldier!" the general admonished.

"Yes, sir."

"Into the chamber. Now!"

"One minute," Mahegan said into Cassie's ear.

Persi walked down the chamber. Cassie watched through barely open eyes. The green check mark appeared for *Gait*. He stood in front of the biometric scanner. The green check mark appeared. *Eyes*. Then *Facial*. Then *Handprint*. Then *DNA*. Persi didn't speak.

"Thirty seconds."

The general ran down to the platform and was outside of the chamber, shouting, "Say your name!"

Cassie felt the ground begin to rumble. Top Secret intelligence speculated that Yazd was the location of one of Iran's fully functional nuclear missiles. She visualized a hatch opening somewhere. A missile smoking in the ground, ready for take-off. The thirty second countdown being watched by someone, somewhere.

Persi turned his head and looked at the general.

Remembering the truth serum, Cassie whispered, "What is your name? Ask him, 'What is your name?'"

"What is your name?"

"Alexander Persi," he said.

The green check mark appeared. *Voice.*

"Alexander Persi. Approved."

Cassie heard Mahegan say to O'Malley, "Go."

By her count they had maybe twenty seconds to overwrite the launch code. The ground kept rumbling like a heavy earthquake. The building shook. The fluorescent lights high on the ceiling rattled in their casements.

"Got it," O'Malley said.

"Hear that?" Mahegan asked Cassie.

"Yes. You sure? This place feels like we're in a volcano."

"Sean says he got it."

The vibrations reached a peak, then suddenly tapered. She visualized the fire and smoke disappearing, being sucked through the ventilation shafts. Crisis averted, for now.

"Rubber bullets cause any damage?" Mahegan asked.

"Nothing Bald Head Island won't cure," Cassie said. That was her cue to him that she was fine. 100 percent there. Lucid. Normal. Nearly euphoric. Their acting scheme had worked. The Mossad agent who had been hiding in the background the entire time had done so purposefully to avoid being seen by the Iranian Key. He had packed a full Iranian general's uniform and donned it during the rush into the tunnel, during the darkness with all of the machine-gun fire dueling back and forth.

Cassie stood, reached out a hand to Hattab, who was too late to stop the Mossad agent from running into the biometric chamber.

"No!" Hattab said.

The ersatz Iranian general lifted an Uzi and fired as he ran down the walkway, striking the confused Iranian boxer in the head, killing him.

The Iranians wouldn't be able to launch their nuclear weapons anytime soon. Further, five tubes had opened. Five missiles had been smoking and burning. Five signatures had been picked up by American intelligence, which was being shared with Israeli intelligence, most certainly.

Cassie looked at the Mossad agent dressed as an Iranian general. She looked at Hattab and the rest of the team. She wondered what came next for them. Was there a way out? She'd come so far.

The door burst open and Iranian infantry soldiers began spilling through, firing at will.

CHAPTER 20

GORHAM SAT IN THE LEATHER RECLINING CHAIR IN THE OFFICE OF his Boeing 777 Extended Range aircraft and studied the maps and images of the wars. "Done," he said, tapping the RETURN button. He had disabled the jet's transponder and they were flying off radar. Military radars would track them when they came within range, but they were not registering with the standard civilian air traffic control radars.

Stasovich sat by his side looking like Frankenstein's monster as the big man dumped a bottle of antibiotics and painkillers on the mahogany table. He had a vertical line of stitches along his forehead where Captain Bagwell had cut him with a scalpel. His left arm was in a sling where she had lacerated his hand and forearm. He had bullet wounds that had been surgically repaired.

So much for cyber war, Gorham mused.

Using a bandaged hand, Stasovich picked up two Cipro tablets and two OxyContin tablets, tossed them into his mouth, chewed them like candy, swallowed and smiled a broken-toothed grin at Gorham. "Where we going, boss? The Korean Key is dead. The Iranian Key is dead. Chasing that North Korean tang almost got us killed. Two of our satellite systems are trashed. Two of our conventional ground command centers are destroyed. All we've got are the Russians and from the way you made it sound, you didn't really give them anything to be excited about with respect to you, if you know what I mean."

"I know what you mean," Gorham snapped. "Khilkov is a moron."

"But a smart moron," Stasovich said, somewhat counterintuitively. "A moron that has outsmarted you, in a way. He kills his Key and there's nothing left. His hackers have built the great wall of Russia inside the Internet, the Dark Web, the Deep Web, you name it. Anywhere you can type commands, you're going to be detected, shadowed, assessed, engaged, and destroyed."

"This is true. It still means we have one play with the Russians, right? They have 7,000 nukes and the U.S. for all intents and purposes is probably unable to respond with 98 percent of its arsenal, if not less. We are watching the U.S. as they try to patch the weapons, but it is a slow process. So, a few nukes are able to respond. Russia can handle that. What we need is the Russian nukes on top of the United States with the two thousand nuke scenario."

"My point," Stasovich clarified, "is that the Russians will do what they want to do. With the temporary setbacks in North Korea and Iran, will the Russians have confidence in our capabilities going forward?"

Gorham looked at Stasovich, but thought of Draganova. Where was she? He needed her to help him think his way through this problem set. The boxes in his mind were scattered all over the floor. Unpacked, open, sealed. All varieties. The therapy was only good as long as it moved him forward in his thinking. He needed to make two calls, one to Draganova and one to Russian President Khilkov.

Plugging his iPhone into the satellite relay of his airplane he dialed Draganova and got the same message, the same sultry voice, the same rejection. Where was she? Next he dialed Khilkov and the president answered on the first ring.

"Yes, Gorham?"

"What is your time line for launch?"

"I am independent actor on world stage. I don't follow your time lines."

"I reviewed the tapes of the ambush at the tunnel. When we

were leaving. Your car took a hit, a door flew off, Serena fell out, but you kept going."

Khilkov paused. "Why do you mention this?"

"Because I saw the big man, Mahegan, grab Serena and take her. They got on the helicopters and flew back to Afghanistan. Then he took her onto an airplane. Your dog is alive. I know where she is. I can get her back for you."

"She's just a dog," Khilkov said. "Insignificant in the larger scheme of things."

Gorham heard the hollow bluff for what it was. "It is sad to hear you say these things, Konstantin. Serena is a beautiful animal. Your best friend. Perhaps your only friend."

"Stop," Khilkov demanded.

"Okay. I'm sorry."

"Yes. Serena is like my child. I thought she was dead, was mourning her loss. You're sure she's alive?"

"Positive. The Iranians overran the basecamp in Farah, Afghanistan. Forensics teams there found the DNA of my chief operating officer, Shayne, and your Serena."

"Is your Shayne still alive?"

"I'm not sure," Gorham said. He was ambivalent. A trade was no longer possible because the American captain had escaped. Shayne had been important to him, but he seemed to be doing okay so far without him. He would miss him as a friend, but so be it. He could get a dog, too.

"What is your proposal for retrieving Serena unharmed?"

"They are on an American cargo plane headed for a refuel stop in Hawaii, right now." Gorham watched his radar screen. Manaslu app developers had created an app similar to Flight Aware, but which also included all military aircraft. He'd disabled the civilian aircraft function and was watching American military jets and planes buzz around the Pacific Rim. He watched the action unfold near the USS Eisenhower and assumed that was the team that had disabled the Manaslu facility in North Korea. He watched the C-17 command and control aircraft come in for a landing at Hickam Air Force Base, most likely to refuel.

"And your solution is what? Or shall I say, your bargain is what?"

"Execute your two thousand missile contingency plan within the next twelve hours. I know where the airplane is going. I will secure Serena for you."

"Where is the airplane going? Where are they taking her?"

"That's not something I'm prepared to share, Konstantin. You know this," Gorham said.

Static filled the silence. His 777 droned along through Russian airspace.

"I could have you shot down, you know?"

"But you won't. And you don't want to waste resources on tracking me when you've got the Americans off your coast ready to invade, right?"

"The Americans are not invading. They prefer the localized action of North Korea and Iran. They do not want to take on Russia."

"Well, let's make sure they don't then. Your two thousand missile scenario. The next twelve hours. You get Serena back. Seems like a fair trade."

"Serena is worth every missile I have," Khilkov muttered. An uncharacteristic removal of the mask of command. "I had planned launches on just the American ICBM locations and their major cities. The five hundred missile scenario. What are another fifteen hundred missiles if it means getting Serena back?" He chuckled.

"I agree," Gorham said. "Say, in the next twelve hours?"

"That was my plan. We are still making good progress in Europe. Almost through the northern part of Germany. Berlin has fallen. Everything, for us, is going according to plan. Though I understand it is different for the rest of the alliance."

"Yes, but they are not as critical as you and your country, Mr. President. We need Western Europe to fall to conventional attack. The Iranians are still locked in battle in Amman and the Golan Heights. The North Koreans are moving toward Pusan and focusing the American military there. We want all of this done by tomorrow, before the first American tank division can deploy anywhere. Now, I've got some coordination to do. Let me know when you have begun the launch sequence."

After a brief pause, Khilkov said, "I have started the launch sequence. Mark your watch. Twelve hours from now, Russia will fire two thousand missiles at programmed targets."

"Excellent. I will secure Serena and deliver her back to you," Gorham said.

"If you don't, well, I know where you live," Khilkov said. He laughed from deep in his belly, a bellowing chortle that continued until Gorham hung up the phone.

Does he know where I live? Gorham wondered. Because that was important information. A nuclear warhead in Idaho Falls was entirely different from a nuke on his house. Two completely different things. One would kill him, for sure; the other he would easily survive.

He flipped screens to ManaTrac, the military jet tracker app his developers had created. He saw the XC-17 airplane take off from Hawaii, heading east toward the United States. Had they figured it out? They had stopped the ComWar systems in Iran and North Korea by targeting the ManaSat constellations. Gorham figured that the U.S. was slow in getting its antisatellite missiles reconfigured to be accurate. The Trojans his team had emplaced on the military weapons were not exceptionally sophisticated, but they did take time to locate, diagnose, delete, and repair. Even a common cold took a couple of days to recover from. And if he still had Shayne by his side, they would be disrupting U.S. attempts at repairing the infected weapons systems. Still, the two-year remote access Trojan program had been successful. The American and Allied militaries were inaccurate, defenseless, and confused. The bureaucracy had stymied individual efforts to warn the U.S. DoD of the threat of cyber warfare. Most generals and admirals were too linear, analog in their thinking to conceptualize the cyber dimension of combat.

They still had AOL e-mail addresses from thirty years ago, Gorham mused. His Mmail system had become the new standard, overtaking Gmail and all other forms of e-mail. He had hundreds of millions of e-mail addresses he was monitoring, archiving, and exploiting. There was no system, secure or unsecure, that was not within his reach. Manaslu had won dozens of information technology architecture contracts with the DoD and the Manaslu Deep Web had secret back door networks to each of them.

He bounced his signal off the secure Bap-Bird satellite and pinged the secure phone inside the XC-17 that was a route to . . . Idaho Falls? The ManaTrac software was able to hack into the autopilot of the airplane and mine for the destination latitude and longitude.

"So, they know," Gorham said to himself.

"Who knows? And what do they know?" Stasovich asked.

Gorham had forgotten the big man was next to him. "General Savage and his merry band of JSOC geniuses are headed to our facility in Idaho Falls."

The phone rang. A man answered.

"Line unsecured," the man said.

Mahegan stood from his metal chair inside the command and control console. Noticeably absent were Cassie and Owens. Still alive, though, as far as he knew. His last image of Owens had been a quick debrief onboard the USS Eisenhower. Owens' first words had been, "How's Cassie?"

Mahegan had confirmed that they had stopped the Iranian launch and satellite constellation, but that the situation on the ground remained unclear. The Iranian Army had overrun the Farah airfield, but the Rangers had flown from Kandahar to Herat—north of Farah—and were planning an exfiltration mission.

Cassie had reported that they were in a hide position on the drop zone after successfully exfiltrating the tunnel complex. The Mossad and Jordanian agents were in defensive perimeter laying amongst the rocks, awaiting some type of miracle. Their sole communications pipeline was through Cassie back to Mahegan, who was communicating with the Jordanian and Israeli commands.

The plane had refueled at Hickham Air Force Base in Hawaii and was now headed toward the United States. Mahegan walked back to check on Ranger, the Russian wolfhound. Her eyes locked with Mahegan's. He rubbed her head and belly as she lay on the medical litter. She hobbled up to her front legs and laid her head on Mahegan's shoulder. He continued to soothe her, feeling her heart rate steady, imparting his energy to her. He closed his eyes and visualized Ranger healthy, running at breakneck speed, fur sweeping to the rear as she gave chase. She had a strong spirit and was improving. As he rubbed her neck and thought mostly about Cassie, he was reminded of unmitigated love. An animal loved wholly and completely, no questions asked. Mahegan continued to soothe Ranger, his thumb hitting a small hard spot in the back of her neck. He knew that many animal owners had chips inserted in their pets to keep track of them or have them returned in case they were lost. No doubt, Khilkov would want his wolfhound returned. His hand continued to circle her ears and chin and she was closing her eyes, resting her head on Mahegan's broad shoulder.

Thankfully, the nurse had joined them on the trip and was tending to other soldiers who had been wounded during the Iranian attack. They had kept Shayne's body on board in case they could use him in the biometric chamber to shut down the Russian launch.

The plane leveled out over the Pacific Ocean. Through the porthole, he saw the Big Island of Hawaii beneath them through scattered clouds, its black volcano prominent.

His phone buzzed.

"Line is unsecure," Mahegan said.

"I'm guessing Chayton Mahegan. Native American. Frisco, North Carolina. Former Delta Force. Gray listed. Possibly detain. Mother raped and murdered. Father murdered. You were investigated for murdering a detainee. Now you're trying to stop World War Three. Correct?"

"I'm guessing, Ian Gorham. Twenty-nine-year-old founder of Manaslu, Incorporated. Bringing Genius to the World is your motto. You see Dr. Draganova for deep psychotherapy counseling related to your inability to love and be loved. While you are the wealthiest man in the world, you feel empty and so you have to reshape society in your image, the image of Manaslu, which is a borderless Utopian empire where everybody likes photos and exists on thin air while they pay for your advertising."

Spartak/Langevin and O'Malley watched Mahegan.

"One in the same. Though the thing with Draganova is over. She's been missing in action. Perhaps she was in Tokyo two days ago. As they say, timing is everything."

"What do you need?"

"Well, it looks like we're headed to the same location and I was curious if you wanted to grab a latte? Starbucks? Idaho Falls?"

Mahegan paused. Of course, it made sense that the most invasive Internet company in the world would know where he was, how to contact him, and where he was going.

"Sure. What did you want to discuss?"

"The Russian president wants his dog back."

Again, no use in fighting the information. Gorham knew. Somehow he knew that Ranger was on board this airplane. Maybe it was one of the grasshopper looking drones or maybe he had watched video footage at Farah or Yazd.

"She's mine now. I don't trade animals, anyway."

"What if I told you he would not launch the five hundred nuclear warheads he's got poised to launch?"

"He knows that is a useless drill. He'll be destroyed."

"Come on now, Mr. Mahegan. You were doing so well. You know that all of your information is public now, right. I believe someone called it *publicy*, not privacy. And you of all people should know that the United States is defenseless to retaliate now. So, a simple dog to stop five hundred nuclear missiles in the United States? I think some may find you irresponsible," Gorham said.

"So, just make the trade at Starbucks? Seems pretty easy," Mahegan said.

"Okay. I'll see you there. Looks like we'll arrive at the same time. And if you shoot me out of the sky, there's no one left to walk through the chamber and shut them down. So, make a call for me, will ya, pal?" Gorham hung up.

Mahegan looked at O'Malley, who shook his head.

"What are the chances he's the override key?" Mahegan asked

"I don't think so," Spartak/Langevin said.

"Why Idaho Falls?" Mahegan asked.

"That's Manaslu headquarters. You made the call and why we're going there," O'Malley said.

"No. Why build the headquarters in Idaho Falls?" Mahegan asked.

"Why not? It's a great climate. Affordable housing. Lots of recreation. All the bullshit millennials love," O'Malley replied.

Mahegan pulled up a satellite image of the earth, spun it to Idaho Falls, then zeroed in on a building complex north of the city and across the Snake River from the Idaho Falls Regional Airport. Manaslu's facility was north of the airport near Osgood off I-15.

"See this?" Mahegan said. "This is Idaho National Laboratory. It is the think tank and research lab for all things nuclear. Every nonwarfare related discovery and application of nuclear power has been conceived of and constructed here. Every nuclear power plant. Every nuclear generator. Everything."

Savage said, "What are you thinking?"

"It makes no sense. If the Russians were shooting five nukes at us, this would be one of the top five targets, much less five hundred. Attacking energy supplies is a key maxim of nuclear warfare."

O'Malley pulled up a classified map that showed the probable targets of the 500 and 2,000 missile scenarios. "Idaho Falls isn't on either, Jake."

"If he knows where we are and that we have the Russian president's dog on our airplane, then he can change a map on the Internet," Mahegan said.

"Well this was from our JWICS, but you're right. He's way deeper than JWICS. Wouldn't be too hard for him to put his own map in there," O'Malley said.

The map showed black dots and open triangles. The black dots were for the 2,000 warhead plan and the red triangles were for the 500 warhead plan. There was virtually no place in the United

States uncovered. Every state had multiple black dots and red triangles on major cities, airports, ports, roadways, military facilities, and, of course, nuclear missile silos.

Mahegan picked up the phone, convinced that the threat was real enough. He nodded at Savage. "Make the call?"

"Make the call," Savage said.

The phone rang deep in the Pentagon somewhere. The Chairman of the Joint Chiefs picked up. No aide de camp. No executive officer. The general himself. "Talk to me."

"We're on a secure line. What is the status of our nuclear fleet?"

A long pause preceded the reply. "You were right. We are completely shut down. We have our best people working on it, but even they say it could be days."

"The Russians have been unlocked. The man who claims he can lock them back down is about to leave Russian airspace. He may be our only chance. Instead of shooting him down, we need to intercept him and escort him. My main concern is that the Russians will figure it out and knock him out of the sky. For some reason he feels safe there."

"So you're saying we should penetrate Russian airspace and have a dogfight just to keep this asshole alive?"

"Pretty much."

Ranger limped over to and sat next to Mahegan. He rubbed her ears as he talked to the chairman. She nuzzled up to his leg and rubbed her nose against his hand. Mahegan took his water bottle and gave her a sip, then took a drink himself and put it back on the table to his front. He scratched her under her chin and felt her panting lightly against his touch. She was a good dog. No way was he giving her back to the Russian.

"Okay. Orders sent. Anything else?"

"Update on the wars?"

"North Koreans have stalled about fifty miles north of Pusan. We're now being effective against their heavy armor for the first time. Iran has broken into Jerusalem, but the IDF has pushed back. There's hand-to-hand fighting going on in the streets between American and North Korean soldiers. The Russians, how-

ever are still going strong. We're having a problem getting the
ASAT up against that constellation, but we think we're about to.
As you know, nuke capabilities of North Korea and Iran have
been locked down for now. We've got full-time cyber capability
making sure it stays that way. Plus we're bombing the locations
that were smoking. B1s and B-2s dropping massive ordnance on
those locations."

"What about us?"

"Eighty-second Airborne is jumping into about five different
airfields in Europe so we can get the Third Infantry, Tenth Mountain, and 101st Airborne Divisions in there. Full up Eighteenth
Airborne Corps effort. I Corps heading to Korea into the airfields
the Rangers secured. III Corps heading to Israel and Saudi Arabia. Full mobilization of reserves and national guard. About fifty
enemy sleeper cells are attacking cities around the country. Shopping malls, roadways, everything. It's a shit storm. But nothing on
the magnitude of what they've got in Tokyo. Estimates are about
30,000 dead so far. Ten times that wounded and injured. But really
too early to tell what even an approximation might be."

While Mahegan knew the Tokyo blast had to be bad, he hadn't
fully processed the threat against the home front with all of the
activity happening overseas. They had done well to stop the primary threats against Israel and South Korea. Now they were focused on protecting the homeland against a nuclear strike. With
mutual assured destruction removed from the equation, and with
the conventional provocation, the threat was real that Russia
could play that card. If there were ever a moment in history to do
so, now was the time.

"Jesus," Savage said. "Look at Tokyo." He pointed at a satellite
feed on one of the monitors in the command pod. "I've talked
about this. Seen it. But never fully comprehended it. Now say that
happens just five hundred times in the U.S. They're attacking
everywhere."

Mahegan stared at the Tokyo images then at the nuclear option map with its 500 red triangles and 2000 black dots. Had a
thought. "Except here," he said, circling the state. "Idaho isn't
touched except for Boise."

"I think they plan to hit every state capital," O'Malley said.

"Gorham has to know about the national lab," Spartak/Langevin said.

Mahegan's mind spun with the rationale. He tried to get inside of Gorham's genius, figure it out, at least part of it. "He's a genius. We know that. So what is he thinking? What are his weak points? We've been too busy fighting the symptoms of this thing. What is his real genius? How can we get at him?"

Those were mostly rhetorical questions. Mahegan was doing something he didn't often do, but didn't feel he had the time to compartmentalize his thoughts. He needed the entire team—even Spartak/Langevin—thinking through the next moves. Four heads were better than one, kind of thing. She could be a spy and secretly communicating with Gorham or the Russians somehow, but Mahegan didn't allow himself to be bothered by those thoughts. He needed to find the thing that no one else had considered.

He had another thought. "Earlier, Gorham mentioned Draganova. What do we have on her?"

O'Malley hammered away at the keyboard. Spartak/Langevin looked away, thinking. Savage was on the phone with the chairman.

"Dr. Belina Draganova. Russian therapist who specializes in deep psychotherapy. Layers of the mind, kind of bullshit. Unpacking boxes and opening them," O'Malley said.

"That just means she charges more," Savage said after hanging up with the chairman. "All the same crap."

"Tell me something useful," Mahegan interrupted.

"She went off the grid about a month ago. Had been with Gorham for the last two years. One session, every week, usually via ManaChat, Manaslu's version of Skype or FaceTime. Sometimes in person. Different cities it looks like. A few trips to Portland."

Spartak/Langevin's head snapped up. She stared at the computer screen, frozen.

"What?" Mahegan asked.

Recovering, she said, "Something just occurred to me, that's all. About how we might shut down the weapons. But I need to think on it more."

Bullshit, Mahegan thought.

"So, two women missing from Gorham's circle? The CFO, Nancy Langevin, and his shrink, Belina Draganova?" Mahegan asked. His mind was on full throttle now, digesting the low probabilities of those disappearances being coincidences. He looked at Spartak/Langevin, who was still staring over O'Malley's head at the wall of the command console.

"Which one are you, really?" Mahegan asked.

CHAPTER 21

"*I* AM DRAGANOVA," SPARTAK/LANGEVIN SAID.

"You're Gorham's shrink?"

"We prefer a different term, but yes."

Mahegan's mind buzzed. Should he believe her? She had lied before. What would stop her now?

"A shrink that is an expert coder?"

"The other way around."

"You saw what he was doing a couple of years ago and worked your way into his life?"

"Like that."

"Sean, pull up a photo of Dr. Belina Draganova from a basic Google search," Mahegan directed.

After a few seconds, O'Malley tilted the monitor. "That's her. Harvard University."

Spartak/Langevin/Draganova removed two contact lenses. Her brown eyes were suddenly blue.

Mahegan could see it, also. The wide blue eyes. High cheekbones. Long black hair instead of shaved stubble. Harvard University medical degree in psychiatry.

"Is this real? Or Internet bullshit?" Mahegan asked.

Draganova confirmed. "That I was Langevin was Internet bullshit. I used my picture. I attended Harvard. I have a real medical degree. Dr. Belina Draganova is a graduate of Harvard Medical School." She smiled.

"Why the act? Why the cook in the restaurant?"

Draganova paused. "You thought I was Langevin. Why argue? It kept me alive."

"But why pretend to be Langevin?" Mahegan asked.

"I needed to be her to get into their system. She's a real person. I phished her identity."

Mahegan looked at O'Malley, who nodded. "Phishing is a real thing."

"Like that," Draganova said. "But still, they caught me in their system. Didn't know who I was, but they triangulated where I was and I had to run. You underestimate Manaslu's capabilities. You underestimate *Gorham.* Every camera at every airport, bus station, street corner, police station, television feed, convenience store, big box, little box, stop light cameras, everything. Even live streaming video is processed through their equivalent of Carnivore."

Carnivore was the U.S. government's e-mail and text scanning capability that could decipher trillions of e-mails and texts daily.

"Actually, Carnivore is antiquated compared to Manaslu," Draganova continued. "I was inside the mind of Ian Gorham as I mined through his Dark Web a few years ago. Then I was inside his actual mind, simultaneously. He grew to trust me implicitly. He told me his fears and weaknesses. In a way, I love him. In a way, I hate him. He is a genius, but I'm afraid he's so diabolical that his unpredictability makes him a psychopath."

"Hitler was a psychopath," Mahegan said.

"Like that," Draganova replied.

"I kept buying burner cell phones, but the Target or Walmart security cameras picked me up, recognized my face, zoomed in on the purchase, and Gorham was able to trace the phone back to its originator. His team had been chasing me for two days. Finally I set the trap. I saw that your man O'Malley was snooping around in Manaslu's Deep Web. I don't think he knew where he was, but he was there."

"That's fair," O'Malley said.

"I had eaten at the bar the night before. I was on the run. They had a HELP WANTED sign. I cued O'Malley, teased him with some information about a raid at the bar. I bought a new phone. Kept it on. Knew they would come to me. Just didn't know when. Thought that you would come also," Draganova said, pointing at O'Malley.

"We came."

"I know. And here we are."

"They were going to capture you. They were prepared to kill you."

"Ian would have stopped them," she said.

"Gorham wasn't in charge."

"He was there. I saw him through the pass through from the kitchen."

"Convince me you're Draganova," Mahegan said.

She paused. Savage and O'Malley had looked up from their computer monitors and were staring at them.

After a moment, she said, "Jake, your mother, Samantha, was your magnetic north. How does it feel now after so many years? Do you still have a true north? Are you living the life she sought for you?"

The engines whined. A light shudder of turbulence rattled the airplane. Ranger whined.

Mahegan said nothing.

"Tell me, Jake. You love Cassie. Is it commitment that scares you? Or losing her? Can you bear another loss of someone you love? Or is it the fear that keeps you from crossing that line? From planting roots and growing with another person? Is it easier to be a lone vigilante doing what's comfortable? What you know?"

Mahegan said nothing.

"Your father? Maqwa. Slaughtered by the man who raped and killed your mother. Did the revenge taste sweet when you killed Gunther? Put him down that hole?"

Mahegan said nothing.

"That's enough," Savage said. "Still doesn't prove anything. All that bullshit is on the Internet in some fashion or another. Easy enough to put two and two together, anyway." Savage would know. He was the one directing Mahegan.

"She wouldn't know about Cassie," Mahegan said.

"Bullshit. You guys have it written all over you. We just don't say anything," Savage said.

Mahegan looked at O'Malley, who simply shrugged in agreement with Savage. Draganova lifted her arms in a *what do you have to say about that?* gesture.

"Assuming you're Draganova, what do you know about Gorham?"

"Everything. He's told me everything, which is why I had to stop him."

"He's looking for the hacker . . . the cook. Does he know it's you he's looking for?"

"He may. I don't know. He's missing two women, remember? The CFO? But to get at your point, he was calling me several times a day before this all began. I'm assuming he has continued calling. He may draw a conclusion from that. At the very least, he suspects me. At the worst, he has been able to confirm it is me."

Mahegan turned to O'Malley. "Sean, what do we have on Draganova from NSA, other intel files. Russian spy? What?"

"Nothing. Been looking. Everything on her is clean."

"Someone who can go toe-to-toe with Gorham and Shayne on the Internet is good enough to clean up their Internet presence."

"That's an insult to Sean, Jake," Draganova said. "He's good. He would be able to find something on me, if it were to exist. Remember, I've seen him in action."

Whether it was the realization that she might be Draganova or his imagination, Mahegan began to detect more of the Eastern European lilt. He superimposed the picture O'Malley had shown him onto her face. It fit. The hair and makeup were different, but otherwise it was the woman in the picture.

"Okay, so what's his play?" Mahegan asked.

"That's what I was trying to figure out. He scared me enough to go rogue on him, though. And now this," Draganova said, pointing at the screens that showed the three separate theaters of operation.

Turning to O'Malley, Mahegan asked, "Where are we on Cassie and the Jordanians?"

The last check had shown them waiting for another Night Stalker and Army Ranger pickup. Every mission was a combat mission, Mahegan knew, and there would be nothing easy about getting a second sortie of helicopters into the Yazd beaten zone.

"Rangers just crossed the border into Iran. They took a different route. Cassie led the Jordanians about five miles north to a different pickup zone. She dropped a pin." O'Malley turned the monitor so that Mahegan could see it.

She had led them through the rocky landing zone they had originally used, over a ridge, and into a valley beyond a tall mountain peak. The satellite showed them huddled in a defensive perimeter, facing outward. Iranian jets and airplanes zipped through the sky in a methodical grid search pattern. Mahegan figured that Cassie and the Jordanians had maybe an hour before they were located. Two hours before infantry could reach them, less if they were moving by helicopter. In his estimation, they were well camouflaged. If Cassie had not dropped the pin locator and if O'Malley had not zoomed in on that exact spot, it was doubtful whether he could find them just scanning the terrain. But he had to assume the Iranians had thermal capability, which would make Cassie and the Jordanians stand out to an average intelligence analyst. Mahegan felt the worry begin to boil in his stomach. He suppressed it.

But still, the concern was there. *Two hours. Max.*

They had about two hours until landing at Idaho Falls as well. Everything was going to come to a head all at once.

"Jake?" Draganova repeated.

"Yeah. I'm listening."

"It's all about Gorham. He claims to want a new society. To burn down the United States and rebuild it in the Utopian vision he has. That's all bullshit. I think on some level he believes that, but mostly he's a narcissist who just wants to be loved."

"You asked me about my parents. I loved them. They're with me. I'm Croatan. I have unique beliefs about death and dying. You asked me about Cassie. I love her, too. That's a different deal. She knows the risks. Signed up for it. Can hold her own. My parents were slaughtered by the most vile and brutal people you could ever meet."

"I've analyzed serial killers," Draganova said.

"Gunther, who killed my father and raped my mother, would chew up, spit out, and then piss on whatever serial killer you think you talked to."

"But you killed Gunther," Draganova said.

"And delivered him to evil. Sent him straight to Hell without batting an eye. So don't tell me about psychobabble. Tell me about Gorham. What's his next move? What is he seeking? Does he want to destroy the world? Or is there an ulterior motive?" While Mahegan was a brute force actor, he also believed that the mind was an equally effective weapon. Knowing your enemy's strengths and weaknesses was fundamental.

"I would never underestimate Ian," she said. "He is a complicated man. Nothing is ever as it seems. No one predicted he would have the commercial success he's had. And now he's caught the entire world flatfooted."

"Hey, Jake. General," O'Malley said. His fingers were clicking away on the keyboard.

"What?" Mahegan asked. The boiling in his gut, his heart, renewed with ominous fervor.

"I just did a deep dive on one of the Russian nukes in Vladivostok. They've got massive firewalls at the system level, but I got fairly deep into one of the fringe missiles."

"Just lay it out, Sean," Mahegan said.

"This missile is on countdown. Four hours until launch."

Gorham was back in *spin cycle.* He needed Draganova, but she didn't answer his calls. She was ghosting on him. The pull. The allure. All of it was like a drug to him. He needed her voice like an alcoholic needs a drink. No twelve-step program for him. Gorham was decidedly *not* sober when it came to Draganova.

He tried some of his body scan meditation moves she had told him to use. The self-soothing of the body. Knuckles against the thighs. Eyes closed. Humming to himself. Hugging himself. Massaging his neck, his chest, his legs. None of it was working.

Instead he pulled up another video.

There she was. Dressed in a short black dress, showing ample thigh. Gorham licked his lips. The black hair, much longer, fell around her shoulder blades, swishing as she turned to reach for her notepad on the table. They were in an office building in Cincinnati. The Ohio River slipped by in the background. He listened to their dialogue.

"Do you know about Frederich Nietzsche's Beast with Red Cheeks?"

"I do. Am I a beast?"

"Do you need to be valued, recognized? Is that where you derive your self-worth?"

"Maybe another box we need to open," he said.

"You're doing all the opening, Ian. I'm just giving you the box cutter." Draganova led him down that primrose path of recognizing his own need for recognition.

"An apt metaphor. The box cutter."

"Perhaps. But back on topic, is that why you have become so successful, Ian?"

"Perhaps. It's not the money."

"Then what is it, Ian?" Her voice was a seductive melody.

"It must be the social change?"

"Do you really care about change? Why not just give away your money to every poor person in the country? You make more money than most countries."

"Because I have a vision."

"So it's about your vision?" Or is it about you?

"The vision. My vision."

"You're bringing genius to the world?"

"Exactly."

Draganova paused for a long time before saying, "You are talking about broad, sweeping change that cannot be done normally. There are no legislative solutions."

"No. It must be done through force," Gorham said.

"Force? Military force?"

"Every type of force. It is a revolution. You can already see it happening. Half the country wants it, already."

"And you can win over the other half through force?"

"My algorithms, my global social network penetration, my hackers. They all combine. I have a plan," he said.

"We are back to this being about . . . you?"

Gorham paused again. "You may be right, but it is my idea, my vision, my plan."

"Then just admit that you are the Beast with Red Cheeks, exactly as Nietzsche outlined. You require the fame, the attention."

Gorham watched himself flinch at her unusual directness.

"But I want to make the social change. That counts for something," Gorham said.

"It is a means to your own end. Recognition, adulation, adoration. You need those things, Ian. Why?"

Why? He snapped the tablet shut again and looked out the window, unable to see beyond the image in his mind. The box was open just like that. Stuff was scattered around on the floor of his brain. How did he get it back in? Could he function with such a cluttered workplace in his mind? The more clutter, the more difficult the functionality.

Spin cycle got everything flying around, made it harder to think, but so far, he'd been doing okay. Better than okay. The body scan meditation and self-soothing in the past had worked for him.

Military jets hung off the wings. He opened his tablet. The jets had picked him up over the Aleutians and escorted him over Mount McKinley, through Canada, and now The Grand Tetons loomed large out of the port window. The Manaslu Boeing 777 approached from the north. Two F-35s had swapped out multiple times as a KC-135 refuel aircraft had flown in serial with the six fighter jets, all taking turns with escort, rear security, and refuel operations. Landing, they looked like a military formation for a hero's homecoming.

Gorham would be a hero soon. That much he knew. He was in

the classic win-win position. Everything was recoverable and achievable. Building the Manaslu headquarters near Idaho National Labs was, of course, genius. Just bringing more genius to the world! That was all he was doing. Everything Manaslu could be wiped out with a single missile strike. He chuckled at the thought of military imaging experts looking at the purposefully leaked Russian 500/2000 target option maps. Idaho was wide open; only it wasn't.

The plane touched down. Gorham's black limo was waiting for him. He was thankful that none of the sleeper cells were in Idaho. He had seen enough combat for one lifetime. The point of the cells in the United States had been to wreak havoc, distract leaders, and create general chaos.

And they had.

A SWAT team motorcade was lined up behind his Tesla. Gorham smiled. He'd get his own O.J. Simpson slow speed chase. He thought about calling Mahegan, but decided against it. They had to treat him with kid gloves. He was the answer to their prayers, though they were praying to an empty altar. Gorham smiled as he deplaned. He lifted his hands to the sky, as if he were saying, "Shoot me!" A cool October wind from the Salmon Challis National Forest Mountains reddened his cheeks.

Stepping down from the airplane and stepping into the Tesla, Gorham said, "To the headquarters, of course."

Stasovich occupied the front seat with Gorham in the back right, where they each belonged. The car pulled away slowly and the SWAT team convoy followed. Snipers were secured to the roofs of the boxy vehicles. Rifles poked from the windows of the police cruisers. The drive from the airport to the factory north of Idaho National Labs was under thirty minutes.

Helicopters buzzed overhead. Fighter jets left donut holes in the sky as they circled. Ten Blackhawk helicopters flew in formation low and slow, five on either side of the convoy. Delta Force snipers trained rifles in all directions.

Gorham felt like the most protected man in America. And well he should. He had convinced the American military that he was the key to stopping a nuclear attack on a defenseless United States. In less than two hours, the Russians were launching 2,000 missiles into the United States. Mutual assured destruction was neutered and the United States would be no more. Two thousand nukes from Russia without any possibility of recourse. He had brought genius to the world. Dismantling mutually assured destruction was brilliant. Gorham could blackmail the two most powerful countries in the world, the United States and Russia, if he wanted. So far, his odds were looking good. Russia was poised to execute his plan. The United States was dealing with him. Had allowed him back into the country. Was escorting him to his facility with the full protection of the military and all law enforcement personnel available. The world was at war and he was commanding the attention of the entire United States.

So are you the beast with red cheeks, Ian? Is this all about you?

Of course, it was all about him. Anyone would be insane to think otherwise.

They passed the Idaho National Labs facility and continued north until they reached the main Manaslu headquarters. The Idaho Falls Chamber of Commerce loved Manaslu because while he employed very few locals, he brought great international and national attention to the region. He had also set up a test facility for different merchandise delivery techniques. Drones, parachutes, hyper-loop, and a variety of other experimental formats. Some were in prototype and others were in full production mode. The ManaPack was a drone that could fly along a street and deliver packages wrapped in high-tech bubble wrap. The drone would drop the package with a small parachute deploying to slow its ascent. Like in the old days when a kid on a bicycle would toss newspapers into the bushes, except the ManaPack was highly accurate.

The Tesla turned into the gated facility. Gorham looked over his shoulder and saw a giant anaconda of vehicles snaking along behind him. The parking lot would not be large enough to hold them. To his front, snipers were on the roof of his compound. One had wedged his long rifle in the V of the *M* on the Manaslu logo with its white capped mountain peaks.

In the distance, media helicopters hovered, filming, recording history in the making. They weren't sure what they were filming, but it had to be something newsworthy with the armada of military equipment escorting this lone car.

So, it's all about you, Ian?

Gorham pressed some buttons on the digital touchpad screen in front of him. CNN popped to life and was showing the slow speed "chase" of his vehicle.

One of the anchors was saying, "We believe this is Ian Gorham. We saw the Manaslu plane land at the Idaho Falls airport. We saw him step off and raise his arms. We presume he was glad to be back. Our sources are telling us that he had been trying to negotiate a cease fire with the Russian, Iranian, and North Korean leaders, but that an American military raid of the meeting location actually disrupted the discussions, resulted in multiple foreign leaders being killed, and ultimately put the United States at risk. Now, our sources are telling us that Ian Gorham is the man who can save America. That Russia has either begun, or will soon begin, a nuclear countdown of the five hundred target option, which includes us right here in New York City."

Of course, that's what their sources were telling them. The stories were being pushed out on ManaSuite, just like Hootsuite, in preprogrammed fashion. As part of the planning over the past two years, Shayne had created a Web page that would appear on the third day of the operation—this morning—until a confirmed news source viewed it and reposted it in some fashion on Mana-Book, Facebook, Twitter, or in the mainstream media. Shayne had programmed the post to then disappear, making the entire situation all that much more mysterious.

But the bottom line message of the news story, which fed into the revolution in the country was that Ian Gorham was the savior, not the bad guy; the American military was the bad guy, not the savior.

Perfect for his narrative.

Once the vehicle stopped in front of the floor to ceiling glass entrance, Gorham and Stasovich exited the vehicle. They had every type of weapon trained on them. Every type of sensor was recording their every move. The most protected man in America. He wondered what analysts reviewing the satellites and intelligence feeds were thinking of Stasovich. He was a beast, battered and worn. Scars raked across his face. His left eye was shut. Towering over Gorham, Stasovich projected the image of a savior, as well. He had saved the chosen one. The man who could save the United States from annihilation. They made the perfect picture for the 24/7 news cycle. The genius and his protector. Mystery cloaked their appearance and their purpose.

Gorham approached the front doors of his facility, ready for the end game.

Mahegan and team had taken a more direct route to Idaho Falls. That, coupled with his instructions to have the fighter jets warn the Manaslu pilots that they had to follow certain air speeds to allow for proper security, gave Mahegan about an hour head start on Gorham.

The team had rested, researched, and planned during the remainder of the flight. During the research, O'Malley had been relentless.

They landed, ushered the C-17 into a giant Air National Guard hangar at the far end of the airport. As they deplaned, Ranger had insisted on sticking by Mahegan's side. She limped and hobbled a bit, but he was impressed by her fortitude and welcomed her working through her wounds. She was a tough spirit. Standing in the hangar, Ranger sniffed the back of Mahegan's hand, which was the size of an infielder's glove. Cuts and scrapes were healing but still fresh. She licked his knuckles and nuzzled closer. He absently rubbed her ears and neck, glad to have the companionship as he thought through Gorham's next move.

"Plan?" O'Malley asked.

"Boss man is going to stay in the command suite here, monitoring the op to get Cassie. That's priority. You and Draganova here can push intel my way until I get Gorham to walk the plank. He's mine." *Walking the plank* was Mahegan's terminology for entering the biometric chamber.

"You know what we saw, right? This could all be bullshit," O'Malley said.

"Five hundred nukes. Two thousand nukes. Not much difference. The one key is that Gorham has an ace up his sleeve. Several really. He's got Stasovich. He's maybe got Draganova, here."

"I am not spy for Gorham," Draganova spat. "I risked my life to warn you and the U.S. If not for me, no one would know about this."

"Perhaps. Sean found you," Mahegan said. "You've lied multiple times."

"He found me because I wanted him to. That's my point. And I lied to survive."

"Perhaps you're still surviving?"

"I'm here. I'm helping. I'm contributing."

All true, but not a denial.

With no time to waste, Mahegan said, "Okay, I've got to get over to Manaslu HQ. Wish me luck."

"Never needed it before," O'Malley quipped.

Ranger whimpered with a squealing moan, sensing Mahegan was leaving.

He knelt down, rubbed her ears again, looked in her pouting eyes. "Sorry, girl. You've got to stay here and protect Sean."

She stared at him, leveled her gaze, locked it in place. Her eyes were golden, flecked with green. Her face was long and angular. She playfully snapped at him with her teeth. Mahegan clasped her lower jaw and ran his thumb across her bottom row of teeth. She lolled her tongue out and pressed her nose against his cheek. A sense of calm washed over Mahegan. He closed his eyes and listened to the rapid heartbeat of the animal. Taking a full minute to center himself, he thought about Cassie and Owens. Prayed they would be okay. That his mission would go well. The others had done what they had to do. War was raging, but the one real threat to the United States lay in a domain that was not his expertise, not his forte, the Internet of Things. Could he stop the Russian countdown? If Gorham was the universal biometric key, they stood a chance.

Ranger tilted her head at Mahegan, as if to ask *Whatcha thinking about?* Or maybe it was a simpler communication, such as *It will all be okay.* He ran his hand along the length of her back and she nuzzled sideways into him until her body was pressed into his chest. She was almost begging him to lift her and take her with him.

"See you in a bit, girl," Mahegan whispered. Ranger turned and pressed her nose against his face again, then ran her tongue along his chin. Mahegan smiled when he noticed her drool on his shirt sleeve. He rubbed her head and kissed the top of her brow between her eyes.

"Gotta go." Mahegan nodded. "Sean, keep her close."

"Roger that. Just waiting my turn with her," O'Malley said.

"Please, it's just a dog," Draganova scoffed.

"Most likely more valuable than your life, Doctor." Mahegan leveled a hardened stare at her, causing Draganova to take a step back. He handed Ranger's leash to O'Malley, who knelt and pulled her close.

"Mess with that animal and you mess with me. Understand?"

Draganova nodded cautiously.

Ranger whimpered again as Mahegan walked to the government SUV left for them in the hangar and exited away from the throng of military and law enforcement vehicles near the main tarmac nearly a mile away on the other side of the runway. He carried with him the peace of an innocent animal, unpolluted by the vagaries of the world. He followed Interstate 15 north until he hit State Route 33 East, traveled until he saw the giant *M* looking like a snowcapped, treacherous mountain. He kept driving and turned off to the north, parallel to Gorham's compound, dipping into low trenches called wadis. In the dry season the drainage areas made perfect infiltration routes. Mahegan kept the SUV in the low ground, bouncing and pitching over ruts and rocks. After another fifteen minutes, he figured he had cut back close enough to be able to walk to the fence.

The sun was low in the western sky. The air was warm with a slight zephyr. Mahegan stood in front of the SUV, listening to the engine ticking and cooling. He found a wadi that ran to the west, toward the river. In the rainy season, the water would be up to his waist, at least. He walked toward Gorham's compound, thinking, no fence was perfect, no technology flawless.

If you defend everywhere, you defend nowhere.

He had to find Gorham and convince the Internet mogul to walk through his own biometric chamber in order to unlock the Russian nuclear command system. Mahegan walked about a mile before sliding up to the lip of the ravine. He was less than two hundred yards from the back fence. The sun had dipped behind the mountains in the west, but he still had considerable daylight.

The large rectangular building looked as though it could have been a castle in a previous life if he hadn't known that Gorham designed and oversaw the construction from day one. What they had learned from studying the blueprints and construction documents—to the extent they were real or accurate—was that Gorham had constructed a test range running north, all the way to Spencer, some fifty-two miles to the north at the base of Signal Peak.

He and O'Malley had debated about what the test range could be, but the one thing they agreed upon was that there appeared to be an underground system that ran in a straight line. Thermal imaging radar showed an anomaly, like a tunnel, that was 100% linear from Manaslu HQ in Idaho Falls to this compound near Spencer.

Mahegan guessed that was Gorham's home. Accustomed to using cover and concealment, he admitted to himself that Gorham had made any approach difficult. The compound was one hundred meters inside a high razor wire fence with one hundred foot towers. The cameras atop the towers were up-fitted with slew to cue technology. If the sensors picked up movement, the cameras would turn and focus on the "cue." There was very little chance he could enter undetected. That was never his plan.

Plan A was to attempt an undetected breach, fully expecting to be discovered. Based upon Draganova's insight into Gorham's psyche, Mahegan was betting that Gorham wanted a showdown with him. Gorham needed to win and to be recognized for that win. He most likely knew that Mahegan was the one who had disrupted the raid in Detroit and the meeting in Yazd. Mahegan figured that Gorham could extrapolate from there that he had a role in stopping the ground attacks on the Korean Peninsula and into Israel.

"Jake, we've got an ASAT going up to the Russian minisat farm now," Savage said into his earpiece.

"Roger," Mahegan whispered. "Ground terminal?"

"Destroyed five minutes ago," Savage said.

"Cassie?"

"Rangers are experiencing some resistance. Still en route. We have eyes on," Savage said.

"Get her out of there, General," Mahegan said.

"We'll get her, Jake. Focus."

"Time on target?"

"Less than an hour. Ninety-seven minutes until a launch."

"Roger that. I'm focused." And he was.

He backed down into the ravine and walked another half mile until he saw animals gathered together at a single point. Some birds, a coyote, and some desert rats. As he approached, their heads turned and sized him up as a competitor or perhaps looking for a seat at the buffet. The food chain participants told Mahegan that this was some form of carrion, perhaps just an aged-out animal that had died and fallen right there.

Then he saw the light brown hair, the skeletal remains of a hand where a bird picked at flesh, and tattered remnants of blue cloth. He walked up to the remains of the human, the coyote being the last to leave. The blood around its mouth looked like a macabre lipstick as he sized up Mahegan then trotted away. The buzzards flapped away a short distance and repositioned, perhaps calculating that Mahegan could be next.

Kneeling in the sand at the base of the wadi, it was clear that it was a female. The shirt had been pecked away and the body was laid bare. Mahegan used his phone to snap a picture of the remnants of the face, but he thought he already knew who it was. Nancy Langevin, the Chief Financial Officer. Picking lightly through the remnants of clothing, he found no identification. Murdered and left for the animals.

Gorham? Shayne? Draganova?

What was left of her neck showed ligature remnants. Draganova's preferred method of killing. He uploaded the picture back to O'Malley then texted **Draganova killed Langevin. Lock her down.**

He continued to walk until he was directly between the mountain peak to his rear and the compound to his front. The best reception. The most visible.

As hoped, a dozen small drones buzzed past his head, forming an outer perimeter around him. These were the same grasshopper looking devices he had seen in Iran, more evidence that Gorham was the mastermind of everything taking place.

"Welcome, Captain Mahegan," a voice called out.

The drones served as speakers. In digital surround sound, they added a surreal quality to his detection, still a quarter mile away. Gorham was someplace he could control the drones.

When a small helicopter landed, the drones echoed, "Please board the aircraft."

Mahegan stepped onto the Manaslu helicopter. Saw a light quickly flash, like a copy machine. Dax Stasovich smiled at him. The teeth on the top row were broken and crooked. His face was badly scarred, with a long vertical slash barely healing. But he was still recognizable from the photos O'Malley had provided him and the action on the ground.

This was the man who had pulled Cassie off the helicopter and placed her in danger. Mahegan felt something tick in the back of his mind. The flywheel that governed his emotions was being put to the test. He needed to get inside Manaslu and shut down the nuclear strike, not succumb to simple revenge—yet.

Plus, Stasovich held a pistol in his face. "The pistol and the knife. I know you have those. Plus the radio and earpiece." Stasovich was looking at a radar scan result on a small monitor in the back of the helicopter. It was similar to what a TSA agent might be using at the airport security line.

Mahegan looked at the helicopter door and saw the runners for the scanning device. The light he had seen. He retrieved his Tribal and his Blackhawk knife and placed them on the seat between him and Stasovich. Reaching up, he removed his earpiece and pulled at the wire and radio secured to his rigger's belt. He laid his communications devices atop his pistol and weapon. Shoot, move, and communicate were the maxims drilled into him as a young army Ranger. Now all he could do was move. Yet, now was not the time to get fancy. Not the time for revenge. Five hundred nukes. Maybe two thousand. A different world. Cassie's survival depended on him successfully executing this mission.

On the quick flight, he noticed three rows of fencing with razor wire on top, followed by a moat with clear water circulating around the compound. The straight line underground anomaly was visible only because he was looking for it. He thought about what that might be and hoped that he and O'Malley were right. Everything could depend on that anomaly, or, of course, it could just be a water line, in which case, it was useless.

The best and quickest way for him to gain entry to the compound was to be captured.

The helicopter whined as its blades slowed. In each cardinal direction was a concrete walkway to a low tan brick building with a roof covered in solar panels and satellite dishes. From the inner courtyard, it appeared to Mahegan that the design was like the Pentagon.

Stasovich stepped outside of the helicopter on the starboard side, Mahegan, the port. The helicopter quickly lifted away and buzzed to the west, toward the mountains. The sun was setting. The night was cool. The noise of the helicopter, as always, was replaced by utter silence as Mahegan's mind zoomed into singular focus on his mission.

As he turned to get his bearings, Mahegan saw Stasovich standing on the tarmac on the opposite side. Two handguns, his knife, and his communications equipment were lying on the ground ten feet away from Stasovich. In his beefy paw, he held a bull whip, which he snapped in Mahegan's direction.

Stasovich held the whip in his right hand. His left arm seemed unnaturally positioned, as if he had injured it. Something to bear in mind. He looked at the pile of gear and thought, *shoot, move, communicate.*

All he could do was move.

The whip lashed out at him like a serpent's tongue, sparking off his left ear. Searing pain rocketed through his body. Stasovich was quick and Mahegan had no advantage at that distance. He rushed Stasovich as the hulking beast lashed again with the whip. The whip's popper reached over Mahegan's shoulder and stung his hamstring. He reached for the whip as he raced the ten yards across the helipad. Stasovich's strength and quickness proved too much, as the rope's thong and fall seared Mahegan's palm on the big man's retraction. Thinking Stasovich had too much upper body strength, Mahegan dove low. Stasovich's legs were powerful, though, and the big man pounded him in the back of the head with a heavy fist.

Mahegan's goal was to imbalance Stasovich and control the whip. He was successful in getting his hand on the whip's handle. Stasovich's powerful arm attempted to wrest the whip away, but Mahegan's vise grip matched his opponent's power. Mahegan rose from his wrestling move and came face-to-face with Stasovich, who was leering at Mahegan.

"Fun, no?" Stasovich said in a taunting East European voice.

Mahegan head butted Stasovich's left eye, bursting the seams on the healing scab and whatever sutures had been applied. Blood burst everywhere, spraying into Mahegan's face. Stasovich howled as if the precision of Mahegan's impact had struck ground zero of his injury. Mahegan wiped the blood from his eyes and grabbed Stasovich's right arm, pulled it forward, ducked beneath it, and executed a perfect Roman Greco near fall trip on him. He slid out of the way of Stasovich's bulk, allowing him to land with a thunderous thud onto the helipad.

Mahegan was channeling the rage of what Stasovich had done to Cassie, the predicament in which he had placed her, and the uncertain future she immediately faced. His forearm pummeled Stasovich's larynx until the man was choking and reaching for his neck. For good measure, Mahegan stood and planted a size-twelve boot toe in his ribs five times, grabbed the dormant whip, and looped it twice around Stasovich's neck. He spotted a U-bolt anchor on the helipad, most likely for tying down the aircraft when not in use. He tied a quick bowline knot through the U-bolt and then cinched the whip as hard as he could in the opposite direction. He had concocted an effective garrote around Stasovich's neck and was torqueing it down tighter and tighter. The large man's eyes were bulging out of his face. Mahegan created a quick bowline loop at the end with the popper, looped his hand through the new handle, and then turned his back toward Stasovich. He put the whip over his shoulder as if he were carrying something heavy or dragging a large object.

As he walked in the opposite direction, the rope tightened around Stasovich's neck and he figured it wouldn't be long before it snapped.

That was the precise moment Mahegan was shot in the head.

Like an emperor speculating as two gladiators tear each other apart, Gorham had been enjoying watching Stasovich and Mahegan fight. Once Mahegan swiftly turned the tide, Gorham became concerned. It was not a good idea to have a monster like Mahegan inside his compound unabated.

The nuclear weapons were less than thirty minutes from launch. Two thousand of them. Even one was targeting Idaho National Labs. That was a primary target and the main reason he had moved to the region. The nuke would destroy all evidence of Manaslu involvement. Everything else he could explain as being an emissary on behalf of the United States. A Dennis Rodman or Sean Penn negotiating in good faith where the pinhead bureaucrats couldn't.

Gorham leaned over from his perch, laid his binoculars down, and grabbed a nonlethal beanbag rifle that had been resting against the wall. He was like the safari guide checking to make sure the big game never got out of control. Aiming through the Armalite scope at less than one hundred meters was easy. Mahegan's motionless head was the size of a pumpkin. The man was leaning into the makeshift noose he'd looped around Stasovich's neck. Hopefully he hadn't killed Stasovich, yet. Gorham needed Mahegan. Oddly enough, Gorham wanted to face the beast. Draganova had called *him* the beast with red cheeks primarily because he wanted attention, but Mahegan was pure beast. The man was relentless and skilled. *He should have been a gladiator,* Gorham thought.

Pulling the trigger, Gorham watched the nonlethal munition strike Mahegan in the temple, a perfect shot. For good measure, he pumped another round into the man's rib cage. Target practice. He retrieved a Glock 19 pistol from the table by his bedroom window and walked across his expansive chambers, into the hallway, and down the steps. He checked his phone and saw that there were twenty seven minutes remaining before the nuclear launch.

Two thousand missiles. Hundreds of targets.

Including Idaho National Labs.

He stepped into the courtyard near the helipad, ready to check on Stasovich and get him to drag Mahegan into the dungeon below.

Mahegan felt the beanbag impact his head. It knocked him down flat, but not out. The second beanbag into his ribcage told him that Gorham, if he was the shooter, believed he was unconscious. Otherwise, Gorham would have given him another head shot.

But he was semiconscious. He had been too filled with rage to have his mind stop for any reason. He gave Gorham ten seconds to leave his sniper hide, wherever that might have been, then pushed up quickly. He looked at Stasovich, his eyes wide, mouth open, and blood trickling from the corner of his lips. Close to dead. Maybe dead.

Mahegan stood in the middle of the helipad. No reason to run or hide. Every camera and drone conceivable was covering him. Gorham knew the twitch of every muscle.

On cue, the Manaslu CEO came barreling through the door into the evening lit bright by spotlights shining on the helipad and swimming pool. He was bigger than Mahegan expected. Not much shorter than him, Gorham was also reasonably fit looking. Not soft, not toned, but somewhere closer to toned than soft. He was wearing a form fitting T-shirt and blue jeans with running shoes. Not exactly fighting clothes, but Mahegan figured Gorham didn't have to do much fighting and had expected Stasovich to subdue him.

The tech CEO was on plan B, something he most likely had not expected. How well would he adapt?

"We're wasting time, Gorham," Mahegan said.

"I've got all the time in the world, Jake," Gorham replied. "What's the rush?"

"You tell me. You're the one who has created this war for whatever purposes."

"I'm the CEO of Manaslu, Incorporated. I'm one of the wealthiest men in the world. Why in the hell would I want a war? Lose my fortune? Already the market has taken twenty-five percent of my market cap. Why would I do that?"

"I don't know, but you've ordered five hundred nukes to strike the United States," Mahegan said. As soon as he said it, the look in Gorham's eyes that told him he'd gotten the number wrong. Either high or low, but Mahegan was guessing he'd been low.

"Interesting." Gorham rubbed the faint whiskers dotting his chin. "I'm here in my home and you're accusing me of an international conspiracy. I've been running my business, worried to death about what has become of the world."

"How did your man Stasovich get all beat up?" Mahegan asked. "Some kind of home security issue? The big bad asses of Idaho Falls storm the fence lines of your compound? Stasovich dispatch them one by one? Or did Cassie Bagwell slice and dice him and then escape to foil your attempt to destroy Israel?"

Another hint of recognition. Gorham was playing it cool, for sure, but facial tics at the mention of Cassie were the tell in his lie.

"Yes, well, it seems Captain Bagwell is in a bit of trouble," Gorham said. "It's good that your man Patch Owens successfully returned to the aircraft carrier . . . provided that ship doesn't unfortunately sink in the ocean."

The night air was still save the buzz of dozens of drones clicking around the courtyard like mechanical beetles. Mahegan wondered, why Gorham would position himself close to a certain nuclear target and then collude with Russia to attack the United States? Draganova had called him the beast with red cheeks. Mahegan understood the concept. Gorham wanted fame. He wanted to be a savior. He wanted to be loved and idolized. He had a thought.

"If I can get the media involved here, can you shut down the attack? By my count we have less than twenty minutes until launch," Mahegan said.

Gorham was silent for a while. He studied the stars that beamed brilliantly in the sky above the curtain of artificial light in the courtyard. Eyes back on Mahegan, Gorham said, "I have relationships all over the world. If there's something I can do to help the country, then of course I'll help. I'm a proud American. I'll do my duty."

"For example, you'd walk through the biometric chamber and unlock the Russian system so that your team of hackers could stop the nuclear launch?"

"My team of hackers? I have industry IT professionals, Mr. Mahegan. We are but a simple business fighting every day for market share."

"And I'm your average soldier just eating three squares a day," Mahegan replied. "So we both can just try our best."

Gorham laughed. "I like your style, Mahegan. If Stasovich doesn't make it, I've got an opening."

"I serve the people, not myself," Mahegan said.

"Well, you'd be serving me, and by extension, the people. We have billions of users who rely daily on our retail operations for everything from medical supplies to fitness gear; our social media platform for critical communications about natural disasters, safety, and important family events; our search functions help people learn more rapidly. We are an impressive governing entity across many domains," Gorham said.

Mahegan listened carefully. He heard Gorham's tinny voice rattling off the fine attributes of his company, but his hidden message was something deeper. *Governing entity.*

Either way, he wanted to be in charge, wanted the fame, wanted the adoration. This was a win-win for him. The United States avoids destruction because he's able to pull off a last minute diplomatic save; he's the hero. The United States is destroyed, impacting a core piece of his business, but his global diversification would buoy him until he used his positional advantage to be the lead *governing entity*.

That had to be what the Iran meeting was all about, Mahegan figured. Face-to-face. Old school deals done right.

It all clicked into place. He thought about the ability to control the weapons, the remote access Trojans, the manipulation of offensive and defensive systems. Idaho National Labs would be one of the most protected hard sites in the United States' inventory. Gorham could have easily switched on the Terminal High Altitude Area Defense (THAAD) around Idaho Falls. Let the rest of the United States suffer nuclear defeat while his facility remained to command and control the country. Manaslu would be the first choice, the only choice for survivors to communicate and coordinate.

"Which do you prefer?" Mahegan asked.

"What do you mean?" Gorham looked at his ManaWatch. Shook his wrist. Nervous. Time was nigh. He had to make a decision.

"Do you want to be known as the savior of the free world, America? Or do you want to be the beacon in the night in a nuclear holocaust?"

After a long moment, eyes locked, Gorham smiled thinly. "Man, you really should come to work for me."

"Don't flatter yourself. Not everyone loves you or even admires you. Some people think you're a huge asshole."

Gorham's smile remained frozen on his face as if he'd received instant Botox injections and nothing was moving.

Draganova had been right. It was all about his ego, his likeability, his fame. Did he have it in him to cause nuclear war? He had certainly created large scale conventional havoc. There was a huge degree of difference, though, between that and the nuclear radiation that would persist for years. Some estimated one year, others up to ten years. Judging by the look on Gorham's face, 500 missiles was low and 2000 was the more likely scenario. A lot of radiation. Most of the country.

"Looks like you've been doing some research, Mahegan," Gorham said.

"I just know your type. Never enough. Never satisfied. Always climbing the next peak, so to speak."

His vague reference to Manaslu Peak was not lost on Gorham. "Did you know that some consider Manaslu the most difficult climb in the Himalayas?"

"I don't care. What I know is we have a few minutes to figure out your path to being a hero. You're all about the ends. I'm all about the means. I don't really care if you come out of this a hero. I just don't want a thousand nukes raining down on the United States."

"Are you worried that we are in the impact zone being so close to the national lab?" Gorham asked.

"No. The way I figure it, you've cleared the THAAD missiles around the lab to shoot down anything coming this way. But you need to understand that those things are a fifty-fifty shot. Might hit, might not. Plus, lots of missiles in the sky. How do we know the THAAD will hit the right one? Worst case, the Russians have the Tsar bomb with a burst radius of over thirty-five miles. No one is really sure because the tests all showed everything within thirty-five miles leveled. My odometer clocked fifty-two miles. Maybe safe, maybe not. Is that a risk you're willing to take? The nukes will be in the air shortly. Two thousand of them. At least one, maybe more, for Idaho Falls. Did you miscalculate? Is Manaslu machine learning so perfect that it will deduce immediately how many missiles are in the air and ensure the THAAD defenses protect you? Or is there a margin for error?"

"Enough, Mahegan. I don't know where you're getting your information, but we can't afford to waste any more time."

"I was just painting the picture for you. Let's go to your biometric chamber. I've got two of the best hackers standing by." Worry began to creep up Mahegan's neck. He had killed some of the clock, but he needed to show Gorham that the only real option was to unblock the Russian system and have O'Malley and Draganova hack to shut down the launch."

Mahegan leaned down and grabbed his radio and earpiece. "Going to need this." He left the pistol on the ground but did scoop up his knife, pressing it against his forearm like a magic trick.

"I'm watching," Gorham said, leveling the pistol.

"Just going to need to communicate."

Mahegan led the way into the compound and Gorham ushered him from behind with a series of lefts, rights, straight aheads, and pushed the elevator buttons. He was doing everything that Mahegan needed done, leading him to the biometric chamber. Mahegan had always believed the Croatan maxim *If victory is easy, you have not met the enemy.* Was Gorham the ultimate enemy? Was there someone pulling his strings?

Soon they were deep in the compound where Mahegan saw the entire command center. In the middle was an elevated circular structure with computers and monitors. Bullpen cubes in either direction fanned out as far as the eye could see. Long tubular fluorescent lights hung from tiny chains fixed into the concrete ceiling. Rows of generators were lined against the wall with exhaust outlets poking into the concrete walls. A large circular portal was behind him—what he figured was south—and he saw what he had hoped to see. If he and O'Malley were right about the straight line construction that had taken place two years ago, that opening would be the terminus, the connection to Manaslu headquarters. It was Mahegan's only chance if Gorham was overconfident about his status.

To his left, next to the command post, was a thirty meter walkway and biometric chamber.

"We have sixteen minutes before launch. I'm sure you've figured out that I'm the universal biometric key," Gorham said. "But first let's turn on some entertainment." He used a remote to switch on large television screens that showed a satellite image of the drop zone in Yazd, Iran.

The satellite zoomed and captured the raging fight that was

taking place. Rangers were leaping off helicopters. Iranian jets were rocketing low and bombing the infantry on the ground. American AH-64 gunships attempted to maneuver against the advancing Iranian infantry while steering clear of the enemy jets. Cassie was in the mix somewhere, Mahegan knew.

"Looks like quite the predicament, Jake. You're not the only one who reads dossiers." Gorham smirked and rubbed his chin. "Now what were you offering? Because I'm willing to trade. I can shut down those jets. I can stop that infantry. I can save your girl-friend."

"Not trading. We have fifteen minutes now. You have two options. Nuke America or save America."

"And you have two options. Save Cassie or let her die."

"Cassie is a better soldier than I ever hoped to be. She'll be just fine."

There was no play for Gorham. No trade that made sense. If he could shut down the Iranian attack, what was he getting in return?

"I see your mind spinning. You're wondering what my upsell is here. I'm a hero either way. Either world hero or an American hero."

"Sure, stop the attacks if you can," Mahegan challenged.

"Oh I can. But why should I? You killed Shayne. Shouldn't I go tit for tat?"

"The Iranians killed Shayne. Stop the attack."

"Got your attention, Mahegan?"

He did have his attention and Mahegan figured out why when he heard the elevator door open. Mahegan turned around.

Stasovich stepped forward looking like a zombie. Eyes bugged out. Deep purple bruises around his neck.

"Still think I'm the biometric key?" Gorham asked, diverting his attention. "I'm happy to walk in here." He was pointing at the chamber.

A hologram popped up to his right. Images of wispy figures firing weapons and dodging rocket propelled grenades as they sought cover behind rocks. He saw Cassie on one knee, her mouth forming the word *Medic!* Her hand was atop a soldier's chest, pressing down to stop the bleeding. Tracers whipped in every direction as if she were in the middle of a beehive.

"Walk? Stop the Iranians? I'm so confused, Jake. What shall I do?"

Two thousand nukes. Countdown probably started. O'Malley on standby. Cassie in the firefight of her life. Her short blond hair matted to her head. Blue eyes searching for her next target. Rifle at her shoulder, firing until she dropped a magazine and reloaded. Was one life for millions any different from Cassie's life for millions?

It was. He loved her. The life he wanted was with Cassie Bagwell, but she was half a world away.

"Walk," Mahegan said, gritting his teeth.

He whirled as he snatched his knife from his cargo pocket and flipped it into Stasovich's bruised neck. The monster kept walking toward him, but slowed with each stepped. Blood oozed around the knife blade and down his neck. Mahegan ran toward Stasovich, grabbed the knife handle, twisting it as he retrieved the blade. He turned around.

Gorham had gotten nervous. He was in the chamber, but nothing was coming up with green check marks. It was all red Xs. Zeros. Nothing. Freaking out, Gorham ran his hands through his hair.

Mahegan wondered. Had he always planned on being the savior? Like the kid who started a fire at his girlfriend's house so he could later save it and be loved by the family?

Seeing Gorham's failure as the biometric key, Mahegan ran into the chamber and dragged the sobbing entrepreneur away, preventing any further damage. Dragging him to the computer terminal, Mahegan held the knife to Gorham's throat and said, "Stop the Iranians."

Gorham stared at him. "You're right. It's only fifty-fifty on the THAAD. And there are probably five nukes alone headed here. Was hiding in plain sight. You know, Gorham lives here so how could he plan a nuclear attack on the country? That was the plan, but, still, we should be okay down here. But I *always* planned to pull us back from the brink. Be the hero Belina wanted me to be."

Belina Draganova. His partner? His shrink? Or, perhaps, more likely, a Russian spy working for Khilkov.

"Stop the Iranians," Mahegan emphasized.

Gorham shrugged. "Since this is the only thing keeping me alive for now, I think I'll wait. Besides, I need you to protect me from Khilkov."

Before, Gorham's status as supposed biometric key had been his saving grace. Now, Mahegan stood over him with a knife ready to kill him. Instead, he struck Gorham on the head hard enough to make him unconscious. He lifted Gorham's mass onto his shoulders and carried him toward the portal.

A clock on the wall chimed. Ten minutes. The nuclear launch countdown had begun. Cassie's fight in Yazd raged on the hologram. The only way to save her was to save the world. He was half a world away and the only thing he could do was his very best to stop the nuclear war.

Mahegan turned and lumbered toward the oval opening he had seen. He and O'Malley had studied the construction permit. While it had been cloaked in code words, it was clear enough that a tunnel had been built. Fifty miles of straight line tunnel. No deviation. Like the high speed railroads in Europe and Japan. Perfectly straight lines led to perfectly high speed rail. But still, fifty miles.

He stepped into a transport vehicle, carrying Gorham on his back. He had read about Elon Musk's idea of a hyperloop. It was advertised as traveling at 760 miles an hour. Twelve miles a second. By his count, he had to go about fifty miles. The system sat on magnets and was vacuum sealed like the old time bank check deposit tubes. The invention was intended to move cargo faster for quicker delivery. Enhanced speeds would equal greater sales volumes.

Mahegan's radio connected with the ManaWeb and he was communicating with O'Malley. "Sean, this is Jake. Copy?"

"Roger. Standing by."

"Gorham isn't the key. I'm in the hyperloop. Find the chamber and make sure Ranger is there. And I need you to hack into the Iranian conventional capability. Cassie's in the shit."

"Been listening in. Breaching their portal now. Draganova stepped out with Ranger before you warned. I didn't want to leave the terminal, but will now. Meanwhile, look at your phone. I'm sending you a video."

Mahegan removed his phone from his pocket and entered the code to open the screen. He opened the browser and watched the video O'Malley sent. Gorham was kissing Draganova. They were naked in a hotel bedroom. The curtains from the balcony fluttered inward. Draganova pushed him onto the bed, went down on him, then mounted him, riding him until she let out a plaintive cry.

"Draganova and Gorham are lovers?" Mahegan asked. He looked at Gorham's inert form on the floor of the transit vehicle.

"Roger. Explains everything except why she was in the restaurant," O'Malley said.

"Because she needed us. She knew you were in Manaslu. What better way to keep tabs on us than to join the team."

"Makes sense."

"It does now. She killed the CFO. I found her body behind Gorham's compound. They're either in this together or she has her own agenda. Find her, Sean. We've got less than eleven minutes. I'll be there in four."

"So it's a hyperloop?"

"I'm banking on it going as fast as advertised." Mahegan punched the button above the control panel inside the cockpit of the vessel.

It was built like a metro car, except the nose looked like the space shuttle. The sleek design was for enhanced aerodynamics at 1,000 mph. The doors shut. Something whirred beneath the vehicle, and Mahegan was suddenly moving beyond Mach 1, which was 767 mph. The speedometer showed 1,100 mph with the needle pegged into the right side of the speedometer. Lights in the tunnel whipped by. He felt like he was in outer space, zipping past stars at light speed. What he understood about the system was limited. He knew that it operated on magnets and a vaccum push and pull system. The rear end was sealed off while the gaining end was open and pulling air using high powered fans. The magnets eliminated friction, which made all things possible for the hyperloop.

After nearly four minutes, he had traveled almost fifty miles. The vessel glided to a stop, Mahegan barely feeling the momentum shift. O'Malley opened the door as Mahegan exited, leaving Gorham on the floor of the vessel. He stepped onto a small ledge and balanced his way to the main platform.

"We've got to go," Mahegan said. "Where's Ranger?" He was counting in his head. Less than nine minutes until two thousand nukes. Four minutes back to the chamber. The door to the stairwell opened. A shrill yelp followed the squeaking hinges.

"She got the drop on me, boss," O'Malley said. "I was focused on the computers."

"I always said the best way to kill was to strangle someone . . . or something," Draganova said. "But guns are necessary, too." She was in the dark recesses of the Manaslu facility aiming a pistol at O'Malley.

The ManaLoop portal ended in a small foyer with two elevator doors. A stairwell door and maintenance doors were on the opposite side. Draganova stood with her arms cinching a garrote around Ranger's neck. The wolfhound was hobbling on her two hind legs, neck fully exposed, forward legs pawing at air as if trying to swim. Draganova's arms were flexed upward, holding the opposing ends of the rope. Ranger's movements made the pistol jump wildly in Draganova's hand. The wolfhound yelped again, gasping for air.

"Konstantin wants his dog back." Draganova tightened the rope, the pistol angling to the side.

Mahegan felt for his knife, folded and tucked into his cargo pocket. Maybe a one second drill to retrieve, open and throw, but she could snap Ranger's neck in that amount of time. It had always been a risk to integrate Spartak/Draganova in the operation, but she had saved them from being shot out of the sky and had proved crucial on the conventional front, helping to stop progress in Iran and North Korea.

Russian spy made sense. Her goal was to advance Russia's purpose. She had passed the background check that O'Malley had performed, but that was a contrived database.

Mahegan looked over his shoulder at Gorham, still lying inert. It was unclear if she had seen Gorham's unconscious body on the floor. To what extent did she love him or was she just using him also? Was someone like her even capable of love?

That was Mahegan's only angle. "We've got less than six minutes. No time to waste. Put Ranger down. You're hurting her."

"I've watched you bond. I know your history with animals. The red wolves of your North Carolina. You want this dog. I want the missiles to destroy your country. You'll kill a man, but not a dog. This much I know. I'm going to keep her alive, barely, and when the launch has started, she can run to you. My mission will be complete. So we just wait, no? There is no way to stop anything now. The chamber is fifty miles away."

Did Draganova not know about the ManaLoop? Perhaps she figured Mahegan had driven back.

Mahegan considered his options. Go for the knife and get the money shot on Draganova. Rush her and stymie her decision-making through action. Or have O'Malley divert her.

Killing Ranger wasn't an option, but it certainly was a potential byproduct of what he was about to do.

O'Malley acted first, perhaps reading Mahegan's mind. "You're right. There's nothing we can do, Belina. Why don't we sit down and take the rope off Ranger's neck?"

Draganova cocked her head. "You love this dog, too?"

O'Malley shrugged. "Of course."

Mahegan continued. "I just don't want her hurt. And what's the point? As you said, the game is over. Your missiles are coming here. Gorham was supposed to activate the THAAD, but sadly he's incapacitated."

Draganova's countenance changed from confidence to confusion. "How can you know about Ian?"

"Because I just kicked his ass. He dies if we don't help him." Mahegan stepped aside, putting Gorham's body in plain view.

Draganova dropped Ranger and raced to Gorham's side, brushing past Mahegan.

She loved him.

Ranger limped toward Mahegan and nuzzled him. He ran his hand over Ranger's throat, massaging where the garrote had been then said, "Let's go."

They entered the ManaLoop vessel where Draganova had knelt next to Gorham and was brushing his hair.

"What did you do to him?" she snapped.

Mahegan powered up the ManaLoop vessel. The door closed. They hit Mach One. During transit, he used flex-cuffs to bind Draganova's hands and removed a small pistol from her body. "Where'd she get this?" he asked O'Malley.

"Must have been where she went when she disappeared for a couple of minutes," O'Malley said.

Draganova remained focused on Gorham, lightly stroking his face. "We are all going to die, anyway," she said. "There is nothing we can do to stop the attack."

The ManaLoop vessel slowed. Mahegan led them out of the tunnel into the command center, having just traveled fifty miles.

"Two minutes," O'Malley said, still carrying his MacBook. "Still connected to the Web. There's the chamber." He set up in one of the vacant cubes near the chamber as Draganova remained in the ManaLoop vessel with Gorham.

Mahegan walked to the glassed-in walkway and knelt next to Ranger, the Borzoi—Russian wolfhound. He knew the breed was trainable over time and assumed that Khilkov had done every-thing he needed to do to ensure Ranger could walk through the biometric chamber. Her eyes were focused, her breathing shallow and rapid. In addition to having been shot, she had nearly been strangled to death.

Mahegan continued rubbing her neck and stroking the full length of her back. "You know what to do, girl." He used one hand to find the chip and massaged that area directly behind her head.

Her eyes changed from confused to determined. She locked eyes with Mahegan then turned and looked at the biometric chamber. Recognizing the entrance, she moved in the direction of the opening.

"Be strong." Mahegan was most concerned about the gait recognition.

He heard the noise a fraction too late. He had been in the zone connecting with Ranger, preparing her to walk the chamber. His guess was that she was the biometric key and Khilkov had somehow spoofed the system. O'Malley was poised to take control of the Russian nuclear arsenal once the biometric key opened the portal, provided Mahegan was right about Ranger.

He heard the scrape of a pistol being lifted. Turning, he saw Draganova as she shouted, "Stop!"

She had stepped from the Loop portal and was standing just inside the command center. She must have found a pistol hidden on Stasovich's body.

She shifted the aim of the pistol from Mahegan to Ranger, who was poised in front of the mouth of the chamber, ten feet away from Mahegan. He saw the fury in Draganova's eyes and knew she was going to pull the trigger.

Already kneeling in a modified runners start as if he were in the starting blocks, Mahegan leapt to block the shot from Stasovich's pistol, which Draganova handled with expert precision. The pistol fired, the round snapped from the bore, and Mahegan's body caught the bullet.

Ranger stepped into the biometric chamber and began walking along the path toward the scanning platform. Mahegan returned fire with the Ruger he had secured from Draganova, firing six rounds at Draganova. Turned out that was five too many, as the first one caught her in the forehead, but that didn't stop O'Malley from firing almost in perfect tandem with Mahegan another six rounds.

Draganova was dead.

Ranger was going through the biometric process.

"One minute," O'Malley said.

Savage called from the airplane. "Status."

"Working it," Mahegan said.

"Work harder," Savage replied.

Mahegan knelt and checked his wound. Right pectoral. The bullet was still lodged inside him. He needed a doctor, but not before they completed the mission.

Ranger got the Q-tip swab. She barked. The eye scanner lowered for her and blinked across her eyes. She pressed her nose against the handprint scanner. Mahegan knew a dog's nose print was as unique as a person's handprint.

Green boxes with check marks appeared, until the computerized female voice said, "Serena. Approved."

"Okay, Sean. You're open. Get in there."

O'Malley's fingers clicked across the keyboard. "In," he said. "Working it." His brow was furrowed as he focused.

Two thousand nukes. Hundreds of targets. Less than thirty seconds.

"Not working," O'Malley said.

"You're in, man. What's different?"

"They're playing defense. I need some code word to get past the final layer. Every time I think I'm through, something is there blocking me, asking to authenticate."

Mahegan thought about Draganova, Gorham, and Khilkov. It was Khilkov's system.

"Fifteen seconds. Special intelligence is counting over eighteen hundred nukes. One thousand, eight hundred, and ten to be exact. All smoking in their silos," Savage reported from the command and control aircraft on the Idaho Falls runway.

"Try Serena," Mahegan said. He had not known Ranger's real name, but if Khilkov was in charge of the system, his beloved animal's name might be the code word O'Malley needed.

"Worked," O'Malley said, fingers still flying across the keyboard. "Shutting down by grid. Nine grids. Roughly two hundred nukes per grid. Grid one, down. Grid two, down. Three. Four. Five. Six. Seven. Eight."

And Mahegan knew they were out of time.

"We're showing launch from Vladivostok," Savage said. "Just ten nukes, but they're headed our way."

Just ten nukes. When did anyone decide that was a good result? Mahegan wondered.

"Anything you do can in flight? Like Draganova did to the MiG pilots? Got to be something, right?" Mahegan asked Sean.

"I'm trying. I'm in and can see the missiles in the system. They each have a manual override, but they know I'm in the Russian sensitive information network now. I can't find a way to control the nukes. Working it."

To Savage, Mahegan asked, "Where are we on our nukes? Anything? We need to work our own defenses. Shut down all but the last ten."

"The morons in STRATCOM say they need more time," Savage said.

"Well they've got about forty minutes, I guess," Mahegan said, referencing the flight time of a nuclear missile from eastern Russia to the United States. "Send a car for us so we can get to the airplane. Want to get back en route to Cassie. This thing is over except for those ten nukes and I think I know where they're going."

"Where's that?"

"Just send a car to the HQ."

Mahegan walked into the biometric chamber and nudged Ranger. Her wide eyes looked up at him for approval. "Yes, girl, you did exactly right. Time to go."

At Mahegan's "Go," Ranger began following him and O'Malley. Mahegan led them into the ManaLoop again. Gorham was still unconscious. Stasovich and Draganova were dead.

"What's the azimuth on those nukes?"

As O'Malley worked the keyboard, the ManaLoop shot them fifty miles back to the Manaslu headquarters in Idaho Falls. A Humvee with a nervous looking sergeant was waiting for them.

"How did you know?" O'Malley said as they headed to the airport.

"Gorham was never acting alone. He had Draganova working him. Shayne mentioned Baeppler was Gorham's mentor. Draganova had lots of travel between Portland and Idaho Falls and all the other places she and Gorham met. She seduced him. Khilkov probably realizes by now that Draganova was working more for Baeppler than Russia. The two places we don't want to be are Portland, Oregon and Idaho Falls. Five nukes each. Am I right?"

"No. Six here. Four Portland."

At the airfield, The XC-17 was blowing hot jet wash on them as they raced up the open ramp. Mahegan made sure Ranger was walking okay. She still had a limp, but was growing stronger.

Savage greeted them by saying, "I think we've got THAAD working along the west coast."

Sitting in the command pod as the XC-17 began taxiing, Mahegan's phone rang. "Line unsecured," he answered.

"I want my dog back," President Khilkov said.

"She's mine. And by the way, your spy, Draganova, took twelve bullets to the head."

"Overkill, don't you think?"

"A little like two thousand nukes?"

"Touché, Mr. Mahegan. Now what do I have to do to get Serena back?"

"There's no price on her, Mr. President. Besides, we just found the chip you put in Draganova. We're downloading it and I'm sure it will have all of her communications to you. UN Security Council should be interested in that."

"Will prove nothing."

"Shut down those missiles in flight and we'll make sure it doesn't."

Khilkov paused.

Mahegan had guessed the only way that Khilkov could have known what was happening at the moment was because the chip in Ranger's neck communicated back to Russia in a way similar to that of a nanoradio. He'd assumed—apparently correctly—that Draganova was similarly up-fitted.

Khilkov bit on Mahegan's bluff. "Take good care of Serena and don't hurt her when you remove the chip. Any man willing to fight for Serena is a man I trust to take care of her."

"Deal." Mahegan hung up and said to his team in the command pod, "Okay. Let's go to Iran." Turning to General Savage, he asked, "Status?"

"Well, the Fulda Gap finally happened. And we won. Our systems coming back online have stopped the Russians. Stalemate or progress in all three theaters. Not bad for three days and a cold start."

Mahegan said nothing. His focus was now completely on Cassie. Perhaps always had been.

"And good job, son," Savage said.

As they flew, night fell on the third day of World War III.

Perhaps over before anyone realized it happened, Mahegan thought. He stared out of the small oval window of the aircraft. Small lightning bursts appeared in the sky. He counted five. Maybe there was one on the other side of the plane. He hoped so. Those bursts were THAAD missile intercepts or Khilkov making good on his promise to destroy the nukes before reaching their targets.

"Got nine of ten," Savage said. "One got through onto Baeppler's compound about twenty miles outside of Portland. Direct hit, but his airplane took off five minutes before that, so I'm guessing the weasel escaped."

"Will give me something to do when we've got Cassie back."

O'Malley looked up at Mahegan, then looked away.

"What?" Mahegan growled.

"It's not looking good, Jake."

EPILOGUE

*T*HE XC-17 HAD LANDED IN JAPAN TO PICK UP OWENS, HOBART, AND Van Dreeves. China, which was still attempting to figure out its best play given all that had transpired, afforded Savage's transport plane safe passage over its territory and into Afghanistan where Mahegan and team spent a few minutes on the ground getting supplies such as parachutes and ammunition.

The airplane took off again and flew under the escort of F-35 stealth fighters that had been rekeyed. Their missiles were accurate and radar precise. A few explosions burst bright into the night sky as the pilots bore toward Yazd.

Leave no soldier behind.

With Ranger lying at his feet on the floor of the aircraft, Mahegan stared out of the window, caught in his conflict between war and peace. He thought of the uncertainty and danger of combat versus the stability and grounding of family. Peace was as elusive for the world as it was for him and he figured that as long as there were missions to be completed, he would be in the mix.

The air force loadmaster tapped Mahegan on the shoulder. "Ten minutes, sir."

Mahegan nodded.

For all the high-tech wizardry in the world, nothing could replace the human domain. Weapons could become more lethal and accurate and automated, but it was the human spirit that made everything worth fighting—and living—for.

The estimates were not good. The analysts were saying it was a total wipeout. Mahegan's team was expecting heavy combat when they jumped in. Mahegan had opted for a straight in mission instead of a fancy jump off the B-2 Bomber because it was going to take the air force a while to get them an aircraft. They had the XC-17 and they were less than ten minutes from the drop zone.

The plane rattled and dipped. *As it avoided enemy fire,* Mahegan presumed. Tracers arced past the windows in neon orange and green colors.

He hooked up his parachute with O'Malley, Owens, Hobart, and Van Dreeves behind him. The door opened. The green light flickered.

Mahegan shouted over his shoulder, "Follow me."

He jumped into the night, parachute harness pulling tight around his crotch. He immediately began scanning the ground. Enemy were everywhere, shooting up at them. The F-35s were doing their job. Bombs exploded. Machine guns spat. Fire billowed high in smoky plumes.

Mahegan landed, put his weapon into operation. Saw his teammates and linked up. With a fury he hadn't felt in a long time, he stepped into the fire that was raging.

His team fanned out in an inverted V as they moved, shot, and communicated their way across the landing zone where Cassie and the Jordanian special forces had last been seen. Across the drop zone were the burning hulks of two MH-64 helicopters.

Iranian infantry fired from protected positions, but every time they shot, either the F-35s were on top of them or one of Mahegan's teammates suppressed the fire. They gained a foothold on a ridge and had the high ground. From there, they systematically killed the enemy. By Mahegan's count it was a thirty man rifle platoon holding the drop zone until further Iranian reinforcements could arrive.

The fire had diminished sufficiently.

Mahegan said, "Let's move." He had a GPS coordinate based upon the last satellite shot that O'Malley had been able to take.

After twenty minutes of climbing and lowering through rocky

crevices, they came to the flat area where the Jordanians had chosen their pickup zone. Or perhaps Cassie had picked it because it was about five miles away from their original drop zone three days ago.

He saw Jordanians lying dead in their perimeter, some with eyes still open. They were positioned behind their rucksacks and had been defending, waiting for the Ranger rescue that had been caught in a hailstorm of bullets.

Mahegan flipped every soldier over, checking their faces. When he had searched the entire perimeter, he still hadn't found Cassie. He knelt in the rocks, staring at the cold, dead face of a bearded man wearing captain's rank. Perhaps the commander of the team.

So far he had only seen Jordanian soldiers and he knew that Mossad operatives had been on the mission as well.

A rock struck his boot. He lifted his pistol to the left and flipped down his night vision goggles. Two infrared blips appeared in his display.

He returned the signal. "Cave, nine o'clock. Activity," he said to his team.

"Roger," Owens replied.

The team closed ranks around Mahegan, facing outward as they protected one another. O'Malley walked side by side with Mahegan as they ducked into the cave.

Mahegan switched from infrared to flashlight as he lifted his night vision device.

Eyes were peering at him like animals caught in the headlights. *They've been through hell,* Mahegan thought as he counted four men. An inert form lay to their rear as if they had protected the person.

"I'm American," Mahegan said.

"We are with the Jordanian team," one man said. "We need ammo, food, and water."

Mahegan continued walking until he knelt next to the soldier in the prone. He saw her blond hair, matted with blood. Her skin was cold, but it was a cold night. The others were shivering.

He ran his hand across the cheek facing him. Her eyes were

closed. Placing his hand on her back he felt for wounds. He pressed his fingers against her neck, but got nothing in return. Perhaps it was a bad angle.

"We tried," one of the men said.

His comment set off a fuse in Mahegan's mind. Opened a gate that should never be opened. He felt the primal fury of anger and loss well inside him.

As he was about to scream, Cassie's hand clasped his and she muttered a dry throated, "Jake."

ACKNOWLEDGMENTS

First, thanks to the great team at Kensington Books: my editor, Gary Goldstein, publicist, Karen Auerbach, publisher, Lynn Cully, and president Steven Zacharius. They all worked hard to make *Dark Winter* a better book and I'm grateful for this team every day.

Likewise, Scott Miller and the team at Trident Media Group continue to prove they are the best in the business.

Thanks to Rick French of French/West/Vaughn, the national powerhouse in public relations. A huge shout out to Charles Upchurch, who continues to do a great job for Team Tata.

A special shout out to Kathie (and Roy) Bennett and Susan Zurenda of Magic Time Literary Agency. Quite simply, the best with whom I've had the privilege to work. They do indeed make magic happen, every day. Also, thanks to Nina Miolane, who walked me through the details of artificial intelligence and machine learning.

Thanks to Thad Trapp of Raleigh, NC, Nancy Langevin (via Mike McCarley) of Wilmington, NC, and Luiz Yamashita of Charleston, SC for making donations to the Wake County Heart Association, North Carolina Hero's Fund, and Charleston Literary Council, respectively, to be named as a character in the book. With each book, we raise thousands of dollars for charitable causes and I appreciate everyone's support. Hope you like your characters!

And finally, thanks to my beta reader and friend, Kaitlin Murphy, who makes me a better writer with every book. You're the best, Murphy.

As always, research continues to be a favorite aspect of my writing and I hope you enjoyed the story. I look forward to delivering the next Jake Mahegan novel to you.

AJT